2012

Accidental Ambition

A novel by

Rhett DeVane
and
Robert W. McKnight

Copyright © 2010 by Rhett DeVane & Robert W. McKnight

Cover photograph by Karen James
Rhett DeVane author photo by Lance Oliver
www.LanceOliverPhotography.com

The excerpt from "Redneck Rivera" was used with the expressed written permission of Dixie Hall.

Rhett DeVane's website: www.rhettdevane.com
Robert W. McKnight's website: www.goldenyearspoliticalcollection.com

ISBN 0-7414-6036-X

Printed in the United States of America

This is a work of fiction. Names, characters, places, and incidents either are the product of the authors' imaginations or are used fictitiously. Any resemblance to actual events or locales or persons, living or dead, is entirely coincidental.

Published July 2010

INFINITY PUBLISHING
1094 New DeHaven Street, Suite 100
West Conshohocken, PA 19428-2713
Toll-free (877) BUY BOOK
Local Phone (610) 941-9999
Fax (610) 941-9959
Info@buybooksontheweb.com
www.buybooksontheweb.com

Reviews

"Only the right combination of experience and talent could create a book such as *Accidental Ambition.* Former Florida State Senator Robert McKnight and southern fiction writer Rhett DeVane have teamed up to skillfully provide the necessary ingredients for this fast-paced novel that often reveals how the game of politics is actually played... the authors have come up with a unique blend of state, national, and even international political intrigue, along with strong doses of action and suspense that should keep readers hurrying to the next page to see what will happen now. The authors introduce us to a fascinating array of characters who come together to provide both a believable and unforgettable experience."

— Dr. James M. Denham and Dr. John Santosuosso,
Center for Florida History, Florida Southern College

"For readers fascinated by American political intrigue, *Accidental Ambition* blows the door wide open to its darkest nightmares. This absorbing work of fiction brims with profound insights into the schemes of politicians and their supporters to achieve and hold on to influence and power. Its themes remind us of much we have taken for granted in the political process and should not, and of the deception and falsehoods in campaigns we lack the will and the energy to try to ferret out from the truth.

This novel will stay on my bookshelf and be read again. It's that good!"

— Bill Gunter, Former U.S. Congressman, 1973-1975
Former Florida Insurance Commissioner and
State Treasurer, 1976-1988
Former Florida State Senator, 1966-1972

Dedication

Rhett DeVane

In honor of three of my favorite high school instructors who embody the best of role models:

Mrs. Sharon Lasseter—English and Creative Writing. You encouraged a budding author and told me you expected me to pursue my writing endeavors. I can never thank you enough for your friendship and support.

Mrs. Martha Jean Woodward—History and Civics. See? I did listen to you when you said national government could be interesting.

Mrs. Sarah Ruth McKeown—Math. I'm still not great with numbers, but I love you anyway. You put up with a lot.

Robert W. McKnight

I dedicate my role in this book to my parents, Joel Roy and Gwendolyn Krumm McKnight. They were the most loving and supporting parents, and a true inspiration for me in life.

I love them and miss them so much.

Acknowledgments

Rhett DeVane

I would like to acknowledge my covey of close friends. To Denise Fletcher for the many pep talks and support. Also, my boss Dr. William N. Cooke and my coworkers—who are also my friends. What would I do without all of you?

To my coauthor Robert McKnight—you are one dedicated and knowledgeable man. If you could help me understand the web of political meanderings, you could help anyone. I wish you would run for President so I could spearhead your campaign. Thanks to Susan McKnight for putting up with both of us during the creative process.

Robert W. McKnight

I would like to acknowledge the love and support of my soul mate of 40 years—my wife, Susan. She continues to prove, we ran the wrong candidate.

I would also like to acknowledge the wonderful support and cooperation of my co-author, Rhett DeVane. Rhett is an extraordinary writer, a patient mentor, and a true friend.

Characters

Brad Silver: Incumbent Republican U.S. senator from Florida.
Eleana Silver: Wife of Senator Silver.
Gwen Reynolds: Chief of Staff to Senator Silver.
Mark Cox: Political advisor to Senator Silver.
Mike Belan: Fraternity brother and fund-raiser for Senator Silver.

Joel Orr: Former Democratic state senator and assistant state attorney from Miami-Dade County.
Karen Orr Hernandez: Daughter of Joel Orr and Gwen Reynolds' friend.
Don Farrington: Co-Democratic political advisor to Joel Orr.
Ronnie Taylor: Co-Democratic political advisor to Joel Orr.

Russell Nathan: Former Democratic governor from Florida.
Buddy Benton: Former Democratic U.S. president.
Lawrence Collins: Incumbent Republican U.S. president.
Tad Myers: Incumbent Republican governor from Florida.

Ramiro: Limo driver for Mrs. Silver.
Sid Dillard: Photographer and paparazzi.
Louise Hampton: *Fort Myers News* press reporter.
J. R. King: wealthy Florida landowner. Democrat.
Brenda Gayle: owner of the Ironclad Alibi Bar.
Dorothy Claxton: wealthy mentor of Eleana Silver.

CHAPTER ONE

Washington, D.C.

Brad Silver—republican senator from the State of Florida—scanned the *Miami Herald*'s front page headline as he stood at the window of his national office.

"United Sugar Buyout Talks Continue," he read aloud.

He pitched the daily south Florida paper onto his desk. A familiar acidic burn radiated mid-chest. Anytime the sugar industry made the headlines, he felt the ripples. In the nation's capital, it wasn't so much who he was, but who loomed over his shoulder.

Privilege. Power. Tradeoffs. Everyone around him wanted a sliver. *A sliver of Silver*, he often remarked. Somewhere—between keeping all parties in a shaky stasis—Senator Brad Silver managed to fulfill a few of the promises he had made to constituents.

For a few moments, Brad admired the clear view of the Capitol from the third floor of the modern Philip Hart Senate Office Building. Part of him still marveled at how far he had come. Twelve assistants stood at his beck and call in Washington, with an extended staff of twenty in the district offices in Miami, Orlando, Jacksonville, and Tallahassee. And, as the ranking member of the Senate Intelligence Committee, he had an additional ten staffers who provided an on-going analysis of current issues related to the committee's concerns and afforded the minority Republican perspective.

The suite of rooms suited a man of his political stature. In the reception area, two assistants—both attractive young females, one black and one white—guarded the inner sanctum with courteous efficiency. An expansive wall mural of a space launch from Cape Kennedy filled one wall. In the middle of the rug, a large depiction of the Florida State seal. At his Chief of Staff Gwendolyn Reynolds' suggestion, a self-serve dispenser filled with Florida orange and grapefruit juice stood in one corner. Well-maintained tropical plants and several wind and surf paintings from renowned south Florida artists added to the Sunshine State theme.

Behind the double wooden doors, the senator's private office spread out, tastefully decorated with rich dark wood, a scattering of antiques, and light blue wallpaper highlighted by the white trim. A plush leather sofa and two upholstered high-back chairs surrounded a hand-carved, marble-topped coffee table. Centered on the table stood a breath-taking brass sculpture of a Seminole Indian in a canoe. On the walls, pictures of the senator with various dignitaries and celebrities attested to years in the limelight of national politics: enough to impress, yet not enough to convey an overblown ego.

A scrabble of voices broke his contemplation. The doors from the reception room swung open. Mike Belan strode inside with the two assistants caught in his slipstream.

"Sorry, Senator Silver," Ashleigh, the blond, said. "We tried—"

The second assistant, Twyla, stood with her hands on her hips.

"That's okay, ladies," Brad said. "I'm just finishing up here before going to session."

The assistants exchanged glances and left the room.

No use trying to shrug Mike Belan aside. The man was responsible for most of the senator's success since college, starting out with Brad's representation of big sugar thanks to a referral from Mike. From there, the budding politician moved on to make a living off his wife Eleana's family's lucrative sugar business and Mike Belan's connections. Because of his over-the-top support of *devil sugar*—root of all evil and nemesis of children's well-being—Silver constantly dodged the barbs of public health advocates. Brad Silver: public enemy number one.

Mike Belan clamped a meaty paw on Brad's shoulder. "Thought I'd drop by and take my old frat buddy to an early dinner."

Brad glanced at his watch. "No can do. I've got another committee meeting in a half-hour, then I'm speaking in session."

"Ah, yes. Latest in the line of schmooze-the-Senate speeches. Can't miss that, now can we?"

"Check my schedule with one of the assistants. I'm sure we can pencil in something for end of the week."

"Damn, Silver. You sound more and more important every time I see you. Don't forget what side your bread is buttered on."

As with most of Belan's humor, the comment held undertones. Mike Belan had changed little since their college fraternity days. Same boyish, football-jock good looks topped off with an air of roguish infallibility. Dead-on partier and past-midnight reveler. The kind of guy most parents hated. Then and now, Mike Belan might not throw a man under the bus, but he'd certainly hire someone to do it and watch from a safe distance.

Brad felt a certain camaraderie with his old fraternity brother, born of shared memories. Having him as a friend was not unlike keeping a wolf for a pet. No matter how tame, the wild beast lurked within. Best to be vigilant. Mike Belan had a bevy of hidden agendas. Always.

The lobbyist helped himself to a shot of bourbon from a crystal decanter purposely hidden in a discreet cabinet. "Join me? Surely you can't face that bunch stone cold sober."

"Later, maybe."

"Jesus, Silver. What's happened to you, son? You get any more milky-white, and we can petition you for sainthood." He took a sip of bourbon. "Where's your hot pit-bull

Chief of Staff? Usually, she's up your ass twenty-four seven."

Silver stuffed his irritation. "Gwen—Miss Reynolds—is in Miami visiting family for a few days."

Belan ran his tongue across his lips. "You really should be more watchful of how much late-night time you spend with her, my friend. Just add fuel to the rumor mill that you're sexing up your staff. Though why you'd do that with the likes of Eleana waiting in your bed in Miami, I couldn't say."

"What are you implying?"

Belan took a noisy swill of bourbon. "Just one too many intimate late dinners with you two huddled together in the low candlelight. This town has eyes that can see through walls."

"Over dinner is about the only time I can confer with Miss Reynolds for more than ten minutes at a time. The days are crammed full with committee meetings and Senate sessions. Most weekends, I fly out to Florida. You tell me. When am I supposed to find time?"

Mike shrugged. "I'm just saying…You have reelection coming up. No time to wag the weenie. You know what kind of trouble that got Buddy-boy into."

Silver shook his head over the crude reference to a former President—Buddy Benton—who had crossed the line.

"Maybe you should meet with her at that fancy Georgetown townhouse of yours."

"Right. Great idea, Mike. Having Miss Reynolds come to my private residence would be better than here or appearing in public?"

"Not like I give a damn if you're banging your staff. Hell, she wasn't such a ball-buster, I'd do her, myself."

"Gwen and I maintain professionalism at all times."

Belan huffed. "Right. Anyone caught between the hot glances you two exchange can attest to that."

"What are you now, my conscience? Like I should take ethics lessons from you?"

Belan shrugged off the question and moved on. "You know what keeps me up more than worrying about you and your Chief of Staff?"

"Besides waking up and reading that United Sugar has closed up shop in Florida?"

The lobbyist scowled. "Rumors. Rumors. Rumors. It will never happen. No. I was talking about terrorist attacks on the capital."

Brad stared at him. "Not to ever downplay that tragedy, but it's been awhile since nine-eleven, Mike."

Mike Belan took a big swig of alcohol and winced as it trickled down his throat. "Ah...but that's what they're counting on—that we let down our guard. There's not one person in this district doesn't still lose sleep over it. We're the number one target, my friend. You have to find a way to get me into Greenbrier."

Greenbrier—nestled in the hills of adjoining West Virginia—was favored by the elite. Few knew of the series of tunnels beneath the stately resort that served as the country's fall-out shelter if an enemy attack created a national emergency.

Belan jabbed a finger toward Brad. "I know that rabbit hole is just for selected senators and members of the House, but I am going to find a way to get a crack or crevice for myself when the commies come calling."

"Don't worry so much, Belan. I will make sure there's room for you."

"You better be on the level. It might not be an attack from Russia anymore, but no one can predict what the Muslim extremists will do. It doesn't help that you are so involved with international affairs, though most of your focus is on South America. Hell, they won't stop to consult a map when it comes to taking aim. Who am I kidding? Just being within a hundred miles of this place puts me at risk."

"Mike, you fret more than any old woman."

The intercom beeped.

"Yes?"

"Senator Silver, Mr. Cox is here."

"Please, send him in." Brad Silver felt the tension in his shoulders ease a little. In college, Mike Belan's dark humor and drama had been a kick. More and more, Brad found his old frat buddy's presence draining.

"Well, hell. Now it's a party for sure." Belan poured another shot of bourbon.

Mark Cox stepped into the room, acknowledged Belan with a curt nod, and settled onto the leather couch. Anyone seeing the man for the first time might shrug him aside. His slovenly appearance reminded Silver of the bumbling old television show detective character Columbo—rumpled overcoat, slight shadow of a dark, coarse beard, a paunch that hung over his frayed belt, and one of the worst comb-overs in Washington.

As with practically everything in the capital, appearances could be deceiving. Mark Cox—Silver's P.R. guy since his debut in the national political arena—was one of the most cunning cut-throat men Silver had ever known. Horrible to have as an adversary, heavenly to have as a proponent.

"Well, Cox. What say you about my buddy's upcoming campaign?" Belan flopped down into one of the upholstered chairs, slipped off his shoes, and propped his feet on the coffee table.

Disapproval flickered across the public relations man's features for a moment before he masked it with a bland expression. Silver had seen this talent many times in the past. And it still amazed him. No small wonder Cox played a mean hand of poker.

"The senator is positioned to win this thing, big." Cox's gaze shifted from Belan to Silver. "Rumor has it that Russell Nathan will run on the Democratic ticket."

Mike Belan laughed. "That used-car-salesman, good-ole-boy Dixie-crat?"

Cox tilted his head to one side. "Nathan's a popular ex-governor with a lot of low friends in high places. He has the

6

Bentons and a coven of loyal lobbyists in his corner. He can raise some serious campaign funds."

Belan leaned forward. "You seen him lately? He's put on the pounds, and he looks like he could keel over at any point. Russell Nathan is one Happy Meal away from a massive heart attack."

Cox nodded. "Granted, he won't win any beauty contests, but don't underestimate the man, all the same."

Silver grabbed a handful of papers and stacked them into a leather briefcase. "I put my fate in your hands, Mr. Cox."

"We are one run away, Senator. Just…N.M."

Mike Belan stared at Cox. "N.M.? What the hell's that supposed to mean?"

"No mistakes. We all have a role to play. So—no mistakes. That applies to all of us. Even you, Belan."

"The last mistake I made was in 1968, Mr. P.R. genius." Belan pretended his right hand was a sidearm, took careful aim at Cox, fired, then blew a quick puff of air over the make-believe barrel. "I never misfire. Not with women. And certainly never with politics."

"Not what I heard your wife say," Cox volleyed.

The senator smiled and glanced at his watch. "Enough, guys. I have to get to my committee meeting, and then the floor for my Castro six o'clock-news diatribe."

Mark Cox stood and motioned for Mike Belan to slip on his shoes. "Good point, Brad. Wouldn't want you to miss that golden opportunity. I assume Gwen has all the Florida media ready for it?"

"Done deal. She took care of that before she left the city, and she confirmed with me just this morning via cell phone." Silver grabbed the briefcase from the top of his desk. "You and Mike just make sure the money guys are making note. This speech is our meal ticket to the Chair of the Intelligence Committee. Remember guys: let's keep our eyes on the prize." Silver flashed an even white smile.

The intercom buzzed and the assistant's voice sounded. "Senator Silver, Senator Larson asks that you to stop by to walk with him as usual."

Silver, Cox, and Belan stopped by Senator Larson's suite. The eighty-four-year old, thirty-year Senate veteran from Mississippi greeted them just outside his office door. Silver and Larson shared little in common—other than kibitzing over a shot of bourbon on Friday afternoons in Silver's office—yet, Larson had been a mentor of sorts since Silver's arrival in Washington in 2002, two years after the great Florida vote debacle.

"Good to see you, gentlemen," Senator Larson said.

Silver nodded. Good thing the old man had his hearing aids in, for once. Whether he forgot them on purpose or not, conversations with the elderly legislator amounted to a lot of near shouting, with everyone within range overhearing every word. Silver often took the role of interpreter.

The four headed to the building elevators that led down to the transportation tunnel. Senators Silver and Larson got in the front seat of one of the underground cars, and Cox and Belan sat immediately behind them.

Senator Larson remarked to Silver, "How does the polling look, Brad?"

Cox leaned forward and said in a low voice. "Sir, as I mentioned to the senator in his office, the only thing to fear is fear itself...and the masked marvel from the South."

Senator Larson huffed. "Mark, are you getting completely paranoid about former President Buddy Benton? The Bentons might have a considerable amount of clout, still they have their own problems, you know."

Mike Belan's cell phone trilled. He recognized the song—a hot salsa number, one he associated with Miami and reserved for a man placed in a key position.

"Mike, how can you pick up a signal in this tunnel?" Brad asked.

"Just a damn good BlackBerry, Senator." Mike pressed a key to silence the musical alert.

Best not to answer, in present company. No one seemed to notice, or question, why he hadn't taken the call.

The underground train drew to a halt. The four rose and blended into the crowd of passengers, all headed to various committee meetings.

Miami, Florida

Karen Orr Hernandez watched the patrons of Gold's Gym preen and prance. One tanned and oiled young man flexed between machines and admired his reflection in the long line of mirrors. A couple of barely-legal females studied him, not bothering to appear discreet. Karen shook her head. How could they work out in those teeny-tiny little shorts with their butt cheeks hanging out?

Usually, she immersed herself in a smutty romance novel, a good way to pass the miles on the treadmill and ignore the singles' bar atmosphere and rampant hormone soup around her. No such luck this evening. She had finished the last paperback and the only reading material in her car was the latest sales-prep propaganda from Universal Bank and Trust.

She closed her eyes briefly, trying to push work from her mind. Ten years in the banking industry and she was burned out and used up. As the manager for one of the busiest branches in metro Miami, she had scratched her way to a good-paying career. Not that she meant to end up in banking. The meager wages of a teller had helped put her through the college she attended before she lost the desire to finish a business degree. Then, on to head teller supervisor, customer service advisor, operations manager, associate manager, and finally, branch manager. Good benefits: health insurance, 401(k) plan, retirement funds, and security.

It had all come down to security.

At first, she enjoyed the work. Loved to interact with the regular customers. A few were pains in the ass, but she knew how to deal with them, and they were accustomed to her.

The industry changed from one of service to one of sales. Amongst her coworkers the jokes flew about who would be assigned to be the lobby lizard of the week: the person who lurked just inside the double glass doors, ready to smile and pounce. *Welcome to Universal Bank and Trust. What can we do for you today?*

Karen smiled. People weren't stupid. At least, not all of them. Lately, she heard the same words: *I'm here to just cash my check. I don't need another checking account. I don't want to open another savings account. I don't want to hear about your CD rates.*

The managerial position with Universal Bank and Trust helped her meet people. One in particular—her ex-husband, Jesus Hernandez—she could have done without. Hispanic men attracted her like a cliff summoned lemmings. Something about their swarthy sensuality. So opposite from her ash blonde, fair-skinned, girl-next-door appearance.

Karen sighed. Why was it, when her mind wasn't occupied with some mindless fictional drama, it felt as if it had to slide through the litany of old wounds? God. She had to get a life.

Her muscles settled into a comfortable rhythm. She had that going for her. At twenty-nine, she had a fantastic set of legs. Not an ounce of fat on her. No cellulite. Five foot four, eyes of deep brown, few wrinkles, pert features, a splash of freckles across the bridge of her nose. She could pass for someone much younger and still got carded occasionally when she stopped by the liquor store for a bottle of merlot.

Karen pushed aside thoughts of her ex and moved on to pick at the next worrisome scab.

Her father.

How was Joel Orr doing lately? He wasn't dead yet. Someone would've contacted her, surely, since she was his only next-of-kin. Last time they had spoken—four, five months ago?—he was working as a paralegal in a small Ft. Lauderdale law firm. Quite a step down from the Florida State Senate and Assistant State Attorney. More like a screaming roller-coaster ride down. Or, a log flume ride, only the carrier was liquor instead of dirty theme-park water.

Her mother.

Jacqueline.

Karen touched the edges of her feelings. It had been three years since Jacqueline Orr's battle with breast cancer. Her death seemed the catalyst for a world of hurt. Soon after, Karen miscarried the only baby she had ever conceived, and her marriage went up in flames. Then, her father—at the time when she needed him most—vacated his position of parental authority and concern. Granted, her parents were divorced. Their marriage had been a casualty of Joel Orr's climb up, and then down, Florida's legal ladder. Still, he had loved Jacqueline. His tether disappeared when she left.

Karen lost her mother, then her father. One to disease. The other to the bottle.

The pressure of tears threatened. Karen shook her head and almost lost her balance.

"Shit!"

"You always cuss your way through a workout?" a silky female voice asked from behind her.

Karen glanced over one shoulder and smiled. "Gwen!"

She flipped the switch to slow the pace of the treadmill, grabbed the sweat towel, and stepped off. "Why didn't you call me? When'd you get into town?"

The tall black woman reached out and hugged her tight. "Just this afternoon. About an hour ago. And I did call. Your cell phone went straight to voicemail. I took a chance. Figured I'd find you here."

"I don't have a social life. Might as well work out and at least look good." Karen mopped salty moisture from her upper lip. Her mother had always insisted that ladies didn't sweat; they glowed. Not true for July in Miami, and not for her. Her sweat glands worked overtime no matter how unattractive and unfeminine she might appear.

"Don't stop on my account. I'll just pull up the treadmill next to yours."

11

Karen shrugged. "What's another couple of miles?" She mounted the machine and programmed the digital monitor. "What brings you to Florida? Figured you'd be mired down in Washington about now."

Gwendolyn Reynolds deposited a small leather duffle on the floor and stepped onto a treadmill. "Actually, it's a good time for a break. Senator Silver is getting ready to fire up his campaign for reelection. Pretty soon, I'll barely find a few moments to eat and sleep. Besides, I can use space from all of that." She waved one manicured hand through the air. "I need to spend some time with my father, and being back in south Florida helps me brush up on my Spanish. I get rusty."

"A couple of days here, and you'll be back in the grove. Some days, I speak more Spanish at the bank than I do English."

Gwen's long legs swung in easy rhythm. "How about you? How's the world of high finance?"

"Same old shit. Don't get me started."

Karen studied her friend's face. A few more worry lines around her lips and eyes. Otherwise, flawless skin the color of caffe latte. The woman could pass for Whitney Houston's double, or at least a cousin. All that, and brains. Gwen knew more about the underbelly of national politics than most government officials.

"Rough time in the political bull pen lately?"

Gwen smirked. "It shows?"

"In subtle ways. Not to everyone."

Gwen inhaled and released a long exhalation. "Washington is like being in a viper pit. No. More like a park with a nice pond. Only, the water is filled with piranhas ready to rip your skin to the bone if you misstep. And the lush green lawn is crawling with land mines."

Karen laughed. "Sounds like you've been tangling with lobbyists again."

"Lobbyist." Gwen held up one finger. "Mainly just one overblown pompous pain in my ass."

Gwen's gaze swept the room—a habit grown from necessity. In the nation's capital, even thin air had ears. She trusted a handful of people, and none with every detail. Anything she said—even in jest—could be screwed around and misquoted. It wasn't just her hard-scrabble reputation on the line, but her boss's, Senator Brad Silver.

"Mike Belan, Mr. Big United Sugar himself. He waltzed into the office yesterday like he owned the place, like he always does. Wouldn't even give me the time of day. He treats me like some window-dressing flunky most of the time, when he doesn't ignore me completely. I can't tell you how many times I've asked him not to hit on the two executive assistants in the reception area, or any of the other females who wander across his path. The man's a cretin. Senator Silver will just mumble something like *boys will be boys* and shrug it off. He and the senator are old frat buddies. Hoo-rah. All that crap."

"Now who's cussing her way through a workout?" Karen smiled.

Gwen reached over with one hand and gave Karen's shoulder a quick squeeze. "God. I miss talking to you."

"You can call me any time. You know that. Or email. It's not like you're on another planet."

Gwen huffed. "Might as well be. I wouldn't dare put anything down in writing, and I've gotten paranoid about even talking over the phone."

"Maybe you ought to get out of there. With your background, you could go most anywhere and practice law."

A few moments passed before Gwen answered. "Maybe I should. Only, I couldn't leave Brad…Senator Silver…to wade through it all alone."

The feel of Brad's name on her lips brought the familiar blend of pride and longing.

"He has his wife Eleana," Karen said.

Gwen stuffed the urge to roll her eyes. How many times in the past few years had the flashy Hispanic socialite graced the Capitol with her presence? Gwen couldn't pull an exact count, but was reasonably certain she could tick them off without running out of fingers. An important state dinner. Some flashy high-profile charity event. Anything with the assurance of national press coverage. Brad's wife offered a beautiful, compassionate façade to the world, but Gwen saw beneath.

When Eleana did leave south Florida, she treated Brad Silver's staff like her personal gofers, rarely made eye contact, and seldom remembered their correct names. From the little Gwen had witnessed, coupled with Brad's confidences, Gwen surmised Eleana's goals in life: her beloved motherland of Cuba, designer fashions and accessories, and the clutch of moneyed cronies at the Vizcaya Museum on Biscayne Bay.

Brad fit in, barely, as a political means to stick it to the Castro regime.

Gwen picked up her pace on the treadmill. "Right. He has Eleana."

Washington, D.C.

Senator Brad Silver looked around the august Senate chamber. A few of his colleagues were present, maybe a half-dozen. Not unusual; the important ones were watching the session on C-Span in their offices. Most significant: the big money dudes were present, lined up in the gallery overlooking the chamber. The players *inside the beltway* were well aware of his keynote speech today on Fidel Castro—the bearded wonder ninety miles off the coast of Brad's beloved Florida.

Brad loved being a senator. By most accounts, he was one of the most effective. He did not develop a private law practice after graduation, and really never had to. His professional start was launched in college through the Young Republicans. The introductions to Republican big-wigs— made for him by Eleana's wealthy family— catapulted him quickly from local representative to a national level. It was a bit of a fluke that he had made it all the way to join the top one hundred members of the country's most exclusive club: The U.S. Senate.

Brad noticed that the Majority leader was in the rostrum; unusual normally, but not today. The big-money talks brought out the big players. For a few minutes, Brad observed his colleagues on the floor as they debated points of the appropriations bill. His speech could be viewed as off-topic, and called to order as such. Cox and Silver had discussed the fact, supplementing his talk with just enough economic tie-ins to justify the interruption in the Senate proceedings.

The continuing resolutions were merely the Congress's method of keeping the government running while the Democrats and Republicans continued to argue about how to really allocate the country's precious resources.

"Will the senator yield the floor?" asked the portly senior senator from Missouri.

"I yield," said the North Dakota senator handling the spending bill for the Democrats.

"At what point does the distinguished senator from North Dakota envision that we can finally balance the people's budget?" The Missouri senator's voice held an edge of sarcasm.

"Senator, as you know, we have troops in harm's way, and I for one, will not leave them without the necessary resources to defend our great country," answered the frustrated bill manager. A non-written understanding dictated: senators did not ask questions that might become embarrassing. The senator from Missouri's badgering bordered on poor taste.

"Will the senator further yield?" said the growingly irritated Missouri senator.

"No, I will not yield the floor to a senator who obviously has a partisan motivation in this series of questions," declared the equally irate bill manager.

Brad watched with a twinge. This was seldom, if ever, done. Decorum dictated that one member graciously yield to another's comments. He felt as uncomfortable as his beloved colleague from Mississippi, Senator Larson, sitting across the aisle. At times, his colleagues reminded him of preschool children pitching clods of dirt at each other in a crowded sandbox.

The second presiding officer—a female senator from Oregon—pounded the gavel to restore order, almost never done in the stately Senate chamber.

"Order. The Senate will come to order! Does the senator from North Dakota wish to move this legislation to final reading?"

Brad was relieved. If the tension continued, it would easily carry forth, affecting other legislation, including his bill on funding for pet projects in South America.

The presiding officer looked at Silver as he stood.

"For what reason does the senator from Florida rise?" she asked.

Senator Silver fixed a microphone to his upper coat pocket. "I rise, Madam President, on a point of personal privilege."

Personal privilege: the highest order of senatorial recognition. Unlike the House of Representatives, no time limit applied to such an anticipated address.

"The senator is recognized."

Silver immediately set the stage for the heart of his address: his linkage to Cuba, his wife's family ties with the island, the millions of his constituents affected by the ruling dictatorship. And, oh yes, his intense ambition to become the next Chairman of the Senate Intelligence Committee.

As Mark Cox and Mike Belan looked on from the gallery, Cox thought, *Silver is really a streaky speaker. Sometimes he is on, and sometimes he is, well, awful.*

Cox hoped with all his might: this was the one that he hit dead on.

As Silver reached the mid-point of the nearly one-hour address, he described Eleana's heart-wrenching experiences under the Castro regime. The ruthless murder of her father. Being ripped away from her brothers. The harrowing boat lift that brought the young girl Eleana and her mother to Florida. Thoughts of his beautiful wife chased through his mind, even as he effortlessly colored the real-life drama.

Why can't my wife be here to witness the most important address of my career? He knew the answer.

Though Eleana probably cared enough about him and his career, her real interests centered on her society activities, especially the constant whirl of engagements at the Vizcaya Museum in Miami.

Brad reached a crescendo, paused, and looked directly into the C-Span cameras.

"The United States holds a grave responsibility to further global freedom wherever possible, even if it means supporting the removal of a dictator so close to our national shores."

Brad held his shoulders squared. Precise, balanced posture. His features settled into a practiced mask of gentle, yet determined, concern.

"If not us, Senators, then who?"

The final question hung in the air as Silver tipped his head toward the presiding officer. A round of unanimous applause broke out among the senators. The guests in the gallery joined in and stood with pride in recognition of a truly great speech.

"Madam President, thank you. I yield the floor."

Cox smiled and winked at Brad. Mike Belan—with financial and fraternal interests in Silver's success—clapped with vigor. In the press gallery, computers and BlackBerries buzzed. No doubt the senator's speech would be page one, above the fold in tomorrow's papers and centered with a digital picture for the online news editions. Bloggers and political commentators across the nation would paraphrase his remarks. The buzz could morph easily into a drone by election time. Perfect.

Brad took a seat and removed the microphone from his jacket.

His colleague from across the aisle, Mississippi's venerable Senator Larson, leaned over and shook his hand. "I sure wish I could vote for you in Florida, son. You are truly a great American."

Brad Silver smiled. He had slammed one out of the park.

When he walked from the chamber, the Capitol press corps surrounded him, firing off questions in quick succession. Through the maze, Brad spotted Louise Hampton of *The Fort Myers News Press*. Pretty, petite, fiery, and with the same determined expression he had seen in her byline pictures.

"Excuse me ladies, gentlemen. I will be available in my office in two hours. I'll be happy to answer your questions at that time."

The press corps broke up like petulant children denied the ice cream truck. Silver motioned to Louise.

"Ms. Hampton, I have to catch the train back to my office. Could you join me?"

Louise's mouth hung open for a second before she recovered composure. "Senator, why of course. But I didn't think the press was supposed to ride with senators."

"We can make an allowance. This time. Louise—I may call you by your first name—?"

"Y-yes. Please."

"Louise, I have noticed your tenacity and off the record, Southwest Florida has always been my political blind spot...let's discuss my speech."

Back in his office, the senator and reporter spent the next forty minutes sharing exclusive questions and answers about the speech. They moved on to discuss other pressing international issues. Louise Hampton landed the scoop of a lifetime: highly sensitive information about potential nuclear treaties with the Russians.

After the reporter left, Silver resisted the urge to pour a shot of bourbon, opting for a tall glass of iced water with a sprig of fresh mint. Soon the remainder of the press corps would gather. Even if he gave them everything they wanted, one whiff of alcohol on his breath might sour the soup. Sometimes, caulking every little chink in his armor grew tiresome.

Long after the troop of press reporters left, Brad walked through the silent rooms and into his Chief of Staff's private office. So like Gwen. Neat. Orderly. A few female touches: a rose-colored wireless mouse, an African violet filled with fuchsia blooms, a couple of tasteful watercolor prints.

He closed his eyes. The faint aroma of her perfume lingered in the room. Unlike his wife's signature cologne—a cloying musky floral that clung to everything in her orbit—Gwen Reynolds' scent reminded him of sun-dried linen and the fresh-scrubbed aftermath of a summer thunderstorm.

The senator smiled and shook his head. The way he felt, he might as well be a teenaged boy hot after the prom queen. He took one last look around the room and flipped off the light switch.

Brad sat at his desk, relishing the peace. The tie came off. He lowered the lights and leaned back in the leather executive chair. He sipped bourbon and allowed his thoughts to wander. Gwen Reynolds came to mind. He wished his Chief of Staff wasn't away. The private cell phone vibrated in his coat pocket. Brad glanced at the caller I.D. and answered.

Gwen's voice: "Congratulations, Senator. You made me proud today."

Brad smiled. "Figured you'd be too busy drinking mojitos and shopping to notice."

"You're kidding, right? Wouldn't have missed it. All of Miami is buzzing about you. Besides, I don't drink mojitos. Too sweet. And even after two glasses of merlot, you still sounded fantastic."

Brad threw back his head and laughed. Mirth. So easy with his Chief of Staff, unlike his wife. He couldn't recall the last time he and Eleana laughed together.

"Are you still at the office?" she asked.

"I am."

"I can just see you, now. You're relaxing with a shot of bourbon, aren't you? And, you finally managed to ditch Mark and Mike. Good for you."

Brad nodded. "If you were here, it would be complete. I could use some intelligent conversation about now."

He heard Gwen's low chuckle.

"Ah, c'mon. You're surrounded by people who can offer that."

"Maybe." *But none without transparent motives,* he thought.

Gwen's voice belied her excitement. "You did a smooth job of mixing your concerns about Castro with the ongoing appropriations debates. Brilliant. Tell me. Tell me. Everything! Did the press show?"

"You did well. I spoke with one personally,immediately afterward. The rest of the herd left about a half hour ago."

"Who was the lucky one?"

Brad took a sip of bourbon. "Louise Hampton. Fort Myers. The one with the weekly column you and I have read a few times lately. Keep an eye on Louise, Gwen. She's going to be a star."

CHAPTER TWO

Vizcaya Museum on Biscayne Bay—Miami, Florida

Dorothy Claxton—president of the Vizcayans, Miami's premier social networking organization—dabbed the corners of her lips with a linen napkin.

"Don't leave yet, Eleana dear. I have something I want to discuss with you, if you have a few moments."

The remaining members of the event planning committee nodded their farewells and milled away from the Café on the north side of the Vizcaya's main residence.

When Dorothy Claxton asked, women said *yes.* Especially if they wanted to hold a position of any importance in Miami's social scene. Besides the fact, Eleana truly liked the distinguished octogenarian. Only Dorothy's personal physician knew her real age of eighty-one. Most people assumed her to be mid-sixties, at best.

Eleana settled into a chair beside her friend and mentor. "I always love spending time with you."

Dorothy motioned for a refill of her iced tea. "Out of you, I believe that, Eleana. Most of the others…" She waved a hand. "They would gladly watch me pluck my eyebrows and pretend to care."

Eleana smiled. The waiter set two fresh glasses of minted tea in front of them.

"I haven't had one second to find out how you are faring after your terrible loss, Eleana. Your health, are you…okay?"

Eleana glanced away. "I am well. It was difficult."

"And after all you went through to conceive. The loss of a child is a woman's most unbearable agony."

Eleana's eyes watered. "At least you understand. Not everyone is so kind."

"No small matter that you lost your daughter before she was born. She was real to you. And the pain pierces to the center of your soul."

Eleana squared her shoulders. "I'm fine, Dorothy. Really."

Dorothy nodded. "It's times like this a woman needs the counsel of her mother. I can't take her place, but I am here for you if you need me."

Not trusting her voice, Eleana only nodded. Four years had passed since her mother died. The grief, so palpable at times she could taste the bitter aftermath.

"It was wonderful to see you and the senator at the Red, White, and Blue Celebration," Dorothy continued. "The party was such a success."

"My husband wouldn't miss one of our events."

"No matter how they fancy themselves up there in the nation's capital, nothing can rival an evening by Biscayne Bay. It was positively beautiful this year. I can't imagine a better way to celebrate Independence Day. I watched the fireworks aboard a patron's yacht. Spectacular!"

Eleana agreed. No place in Miami felt as much a part of her as the Vizcaya Museum. The first time she visited the mansion and gardens, her reaction was visceral. She stood in the grand entrance hall, immediately transported to her childhood and the vast estate of her family in Cuba. The images flitted through her memory, wisps of a long-forgotten dream.

Constructed during the Gilded Age—a time when America's most wealthy created lavish homes inspired by the palaces of Europe—Vizcaya originally served as the winter residence of American Industrialist James Deering. Now a Miami-Dade County facility, the home and grounds provided a diplomatic seat, hosting some of the world's most renowned dignitaries and international events. Vizcaya housed some of the most important occasions in Miami: weddings, commitment ceremonies, and *quinceañeras*—the rite of passage celebration marking a Hispanic girl's fifteenth birthday. The elite charitable events funding the museum provided a bridge between Anglos and Hispanics in Miami.

Eleana loved Vizcaya—from its orchidarium to the unrivaled view of Biscayne Bay. She adored being an integral part of the organization in charge of raising funds to promote its maintenance, support, and success. Seeing pictures of herself and her handsome senator husband in the *Miami Herald* as they kibitzed with the patrons of Vizcaya added to the enchantment.

Dorothy's voice called Eleana to attention.

"Sweetheart, you know I think of you as I would my own daughter."

"Of course, Dorothy. I feel as close to you," said Eleana.

Dorothy's gaze roamed the near-empty room. Only a handful of the lunch catering staff remained in one corner.

"I don't know how to bring this up or even if I should...it just tears at me, sweetie."

"What is it? We go so far back and have shared so much over the years..."

Dorothy pursed her lips. She studied Eleana's face for a moment.

"During a chance meeting with one of our members last week, I heard a rumor that Brad and his aide—what is her name? Gwen something? — might be more than, shall we say, professionally acquainted." The older woman reached over and rested one hand over Eleana's. "I just don't know if I should even discuss this with you. I just care so much for you. I struggled over whether to keep this to myself."

"Dorothy, thanks. I know it's hard to bring up things like this, and I appreciate you coming to me. I have heard it before." Eleana forced a tight smile. "It bothers me. But I have no proof, and frankly, really don't want to spend the time trying to find out if it's true."

Dorothy nodded. For a moment, the two sat in compatible silence.

"Men will be men. No matter how they try, they're all just little boys at heart. They don't have the innate sense of propriety a woman has to have." Eleana's mentor fixed her with a steady gaze. "How are you and your husband getting along...really?"

Eleana forced her expression to remain neutral. No need to share—even with her best friend—the growing resentment she felt toward her husband. Even when he came home to Miami on weekends, Brad Silver's attention stayed on Washington. No matter how she tried, she couldn't compete.

"Brad and I have an understanding, and that includes just enough intimacy to keep my marriage. Then, there are the Vizcayans. As you know, you and this organization are my soul."

"Neither of us—me or this mausoleum of a building—will keep you warm at night."

Eleana felt a flush color her cheeks. "I'm not sure..."

Dorothy winked. "Why do you think young buff personal trainers are all the rage among our kind? A woman has certain *needs*."

"Dorothy!"

"All I'm saying, my dear, is that what's fair for one is fair for the other. As long as one shows the proper amount of care and discretion."

Eleana's thoughts flipped to the Silvers' handsome Hispanic driver. Even now Ramiro awaited her summons. The fine hairs at the base of her neck stood erect.

"Don't worry." Dorothy picked up her glass and tipped it in a mock toast. "Our conversation is just between you and me."

Destin Beach, Florida

"Governor, some man named Benton is on the phone for you."

The barely legal—Russell Nathan was pretty sure she was over age—topless young woman stepped onto the back deck of his Destin beach house and waved the phone.

"Sugar, if I've told you once, I've told you a million times—at least put on a shirt when you step outside."

The tanned young woman shrugged. Was her name Julia? Juliana? Jolene? Joanne? Russell couldn't recall. Best to call her *sugar*. Names just got in the way.

"Damn girl," he muttered. "Doesn't even know who the former President of the U.S. of A. is."

One problem with the young girls: no sense of history. She should have recognized Wallace "Buddy" Benton's name, unless she had been reared in a cave by wolves. The man was a popular president during her lifetime—though she would have been in late childhood during his two-term tenure. Still, her parents would have talked about him.

The former governor of Florida took a long look down the pristine beach—mostly deserted at this time of the morning. Other than one lone jogger, the white sands stretched for miles in either direction without interruption. God, how he loved north Florida's coastline! They could have the rest of the state from about Gainesville on down, as far as he was concerned. South Florida was nothing but a bunch of transplanted Yankees, Cubans, and ill-dressed tourists running around in mouse hats. The beaches down there were too crowded and polluted to boot. Give him this stretch of the *Redneck Riviera* any day.

"Good Mornin', Mr. President. How did you find me down here?"

"Rolodex, Russ. Forget Google and Yahoo—this thing is worth millions." Buddy Benton chuckled.

"Man, it is hotter than a three-peckered Billy-goat down here, Buddy. But I would surely love to have you join me and my... friend."

"I'd love to take you up on that some time, Russ. What I need now is for you to get focused on Silver's situation."

"Well, if you insist. Silver can come, too. Reckon I can round up another one for him. No. Cancel that. He's got a wife who's the full package. I ain't getting him shit."

Benton laughed. "C'mon, Russ. Work with me. I called to talk business this morning."

Russell waved for the young woman to bring him a cup of coffee. "Well, hell. All right. If you insist. You mean his reelection, or do you guys have something else on him?"

"His reelection. The man's like black ice. Nothing sticks to him."

Russ smiled. "You know what I'm looking at right this moment?"

"Can't say I do, Russ."

"I'm looking at the three million-dollar beach house next to mine, here on Destin Beach. And you know what?"

"What's that, Russ?"

"Fine as that house is…it still has stink-pipes sticking out the roof."

His comment was met with silence on the former President's end.

"Oh, c'mon. You're from the Deep South. You know what a stink-pipe is! That's the exhaust pipe that vents the methane away from the toilet for God's sake."

"Okay…"

"You been hanging around the Yankees too long, Buddy." Russell Nathan took a noisy swill of coffee. He took a moment to admire the hot pink thong underwear his consort wore before continuing. "My point—even someone who might appear squeaky clean has some dirt somewhere. We might just have to take a closer look."

"Ah…," Benton said. "Now, back to what I was saying…I don't know if you've seen the papers or if your local panhandle stations carry congressional news, but Silver made a powerful speech on the floor yesterday. The press has dubbed it his meal ticket to the chairmanship of the Senate Intelligence Committee. Russ, we can't let that happen. Silver is an empty suit that is only there by the grace of God and his wife's family fortune in Cuba."

"Uh-huh."

"You are probably the most popular former governor—at least among those who have not been indicted—in the last fifty years." The former President laughed. "Just joking, Russ. But seriously, I can help raise the money, and if we can land a punch on this guy, we can take his seat. What do you say?"

"Buddy, give me a second."

Russell held his palm over the phone to muffle his words.

"Honey, go put on a shirt. You're distracting me." He pinched her tight tanned bottom as she passed by on her way back inside the house.

Then, to Benton, "God, Buddy. These young babes are enough to drive you nuts, you know what I mean? Now what was your question...oh yeah, would I run against Silver? I never really liked the guy. He pretends to be a conservative, but up here in North Florida, we can smell a phony a mile away. Brad Silver is a blue-blooded phony."

Russell Nathan paused, considering the offer.

"If you will really help me, I'll do it. I'm counting on you, Buddy. If I commit to this thing, you got to come through. Mr. President, I'm calling them all in on this one."

"You can put it in the bank, Governor."

"Them words are sweet to my ears, Mr. President."

"Watch yourself down there, Russ. You are still a former Governor, and the press would love nothing more that getting a picture of you with a...uhh...lady...I guess."

"I understand, Mr. President, but boy it sure does keep a man young. Keeps the old blood pumping. A little *strange* every now and again helps a man tolerate the ordinary. You know what I mean?"

Buddy Benton chuckled. "And how is your sweet wife Miz Sarah?"

"She's off on some kind of church mission trip."

"Be sure to give her my regards when you see her."
Russell huffed. "I'll do that. And you tell Mrs. President
I said howdy, too."

The Ironclad Alibi Bar—Miami, Florida

Bar owner Brenda Gayle folded her arms across her
ample breasts and leaned back. The barkeep had to be at
least—what?—mid-fifties or more? Hard to tell beneath the
layers of make-up and dim lighting. After a few scotches,
every woman looked like she was beneath thirty and
something a man might be able to *talk home* with him.

Brenda Gayle could cold-cock the Devil himself. Joel
Orr and the team of regulars had witnessed it. Just short of
instigating a full-scale riot, she loved to toss out a few well-
placed comments, add liquor, stir, and watch the fireworks.
Sometimes, she could remark on religion and get a reaction
from the patrons. When former State Senator Joel Orr leaned
over the counter nursing his fourth or fifth scotch, Brenda
Gayle had known exactly which subject to broach.

Life could be downright dull if she didn't whisk the pot
from time to time. To think that she had fired the starting gun
on the free-for-all tonight with just one word: *Silver.*

Joel Orr held court with a small gathering of The Alibi's
usual patrons.

"Son of a bitch! You would think the guy could at least
support the damn Brady bill, after all his worshiping of
Ronald Reagan."

Joel knew his politics. Until he took on the National
Rifle Association, he had been an up and coming star in the
Democratic Party. Joel had voted against one of their pro-
gun bills in 1989 and paid the price for it. The NRA stuck in
his craw and festered.

Downing a double scotch, Orr bellowed, "That piece of
crap Silver doesn't have the balls to stand up to those NRA
pigs."

Brenda Gayle held her breath for a beat. Any talk slamming a man's right to tote a gun proved dangerous, especially in a bar frequented by rednecks galore. She glanced around the smoke-fogged room. Other than the four seated in front, the remaining customers were too immersed in drinking and pre-sex to find the discussion interesting.

A lone beer-drinker at the opposite end of the cigarette-burn-pocked bar glared in Joel's direction. Not one of the regulars. He'd be one to watch. She had pegged the man using her special brand of nomenclature as soon as he stepped up to the bar—an *I and B*. Itchy and Bitchy. Aggravated at the world and spoiling for someone to take it out on. Brenda Gayle glanced down. Her two enforcers rested within easy reach: a Louisville Slugger and a Glock 9 mm.

"What you think you can do about it, Joel?" she asked.

Joel Orr was no fool. Maybe, the others didn't know his identity. Brenda Gayle did. She made it a point to know the regulars. No matter what else the man was, he was smart with a keen sense of justice. Too bad more men weren't like him.

Don Farringdon took a sip of beer and grinned. Joel Orr had some good points. Senator Silver was a renowned Reagan loyalist, and the Reagan supporters in Florida had helped elect Silver as attorney general and U.S. senator. Even after Reagan took a near-fatal bullet, Silver still didn't support what proponents called a very watered-down bill requiring a twenty-four hour cooling-off period for handgun purchases. If that wasn't enough, the bill was named after Reagan's own press secretary, Jim Brady, a man critically wounded by the same would-be assassin.

"For two cents, I would run against that guy myself." Orr kicked his head back and downed the remainder of his drink in one easy gulp.

"Maybe you should. I'd vote for you," Brenda Gayle said.

The man at the end of the bar shoved his empty beer bottle across the bar toward Orr. It bounced once and crashed to shards on the floor at Brenda Gayle's feet.

Brenda Gayle glared at the man "Okay. Enough, buddy! You're out of here!" She reached for one of the enforcers.

The stranger stood. Easily, he could take on any of them. For a frozen couple of seconds, conversation in the bar calmed. Everyone watched to see how far the drama would unfold.

The man gathered a fat wad of spit and hawked it onto the floor. Without a word, he sauntered to the door and left.

"Glad he's gone. I was about to ask him to step outside. Teach him some manners," Joel said. His words slurred together.

Brenda Gayle's grip relaxed on the Glock. "Some folks just can't abide an intelligent discussion without taking it personally."

A few minutes later, Farringdon watched Orr stagger from the bar stool. What a long slide downhill Joel Orr had made from the man Don remembered. Someone Don had looked up to when he was just a youngster running campaign material on the streets of Miami. A man who stood up for dead-end causes against horrible odds while he was in the Florida legislature. In all the years Farringdon had followed state and national politics, he had witnessed similar metamorphoses. Good men. Smart men. Men who were too idealistic. Beaten down. Used up.

Joel Orr was out of shape, obviously downtrodden since he had to borrow money for his drinks, and surely in no condition to defend loose remarks about a popular U.S. senator.

"You okay to get home, Joel?" Brenda Gayle asked. She used a small broom to rake the broken beer bottle glass onto a dustpan. "I can call you a cab."

"Nah. I'm good." Orr rummaged in his pants pocket and threw a set of keys onto the bar. "Hang onto these. I'll pick up my car tomorrow."

They watched Joel's unsteady gait as he lurched from the bar.

Farringdon frowned. "Maybe I should give the guy a ride home."

Brenda Gayle shook her head and wiped the drink sweat-rings from the bar's top with an off-white rag. "Might as well stay and finish up that beer. He wouldn't take it. He'll be all right. He only lives a few blocks from here."

The sucker punch came from nowhere. Joel staggered once and went down. Something hot and wet filled his left ear. He moaned. Tried to focus.

"You god-damned faggot communist!" A voice growled.

Joel tried to stand. The attacker delivered four savage kicks to his midsection. Joel curled into a ball, trying in vain to protect his stomach.

"You and your bunch of commie friends ain't taking my god-damned guns away from me. Fucking socialist pigs!"

Joel blinked through a stream of blood. "Wha...wait..."

The kicks came again. This time, to his head and shoulders. A roar sounded in Joel's ears. He tried to speak, but the words came out in a series of staccato moans.

The blows finally stopped. Joel heard the ragged breathing of his attacker. The salty brine of fresh blood filled Joel's mouth. The man muttered a series of unintelligible curses.

In the dim light, the man loped away. For a few minutes, Joel focused on taking small, ragged breaths.

The last thing Joel Orr remembered before everything went dark was the face of Don Farringdon.

CHAPTER THREE

Miami, Florida

"Do people just get crazier by the day or is it just me?" Karen Orr Hernandez asked her assistant manager.

"It's South Florida. We live for crazy."

"I'm in the middle of the weekly sales productivity report. Do you really need me down there at this moment?"

"The customer insists on speaking with the head person in charge."

Karen closed her eyes and sighed. "I'll be right down."

When Karen entered the bank lobby, she spotted the woman in question standing at the entrance to the safety deposit box area, her hands planted on her hips. Bright white frizzy hair, pouched-out lips, earthy sandals, a long gauzy skirt and so many bangle bracelets, Karen could hear her chime from several feet away.

"Ma'am?" Karen pasted on her best *how-may-I-help-you* smile.

"You the manager?"

"Yes, Ma'am. Is there a prob—?"

"Someone has been inside my bank box! Come right in here and I will show you!"

No way, José. "Ma'am, I'm not allowed in the back room with you. Bank regulations. If you bring your safety deposit box in here to the table, I'll be happy to hear your concerns."

Karen glanced at the overhead security cameras. Anything between the two would be captured by the digital monitor.

Earth-woman retrieved the metal box and slammed it down on a small table in front of Karen. "Someone has been in here since last time I checked it. I know exactly how I arrange things, and they aren't in the right place!"

"Mrs...,"

"Eloise Watson."

"Mrs. Watson, the bank doesn't have access to your private box. You were issued two keys—the only keys to your box. I have the bank guard key that allows me or a bank associate to unlock it, but we can't do it without *your* key. If we have to go into a box—because a customer has deserted it, or whatever—we have a company who comes in and actually drills into the box."

"I don't care what you say. Someone has been in here! Look. My purple inventory tablet is on the bottom. I never leave the purple inventory tablet on the bottom! The purple inventory tablet is always on the top! I know perfectly well where the purple inventory tablet is supposed to be."

If I hear the word **purple** *one more time,* Karen thought, *someone is going to get hurt.*

Karen glanced at the small pile of papers fanned out on the table. Unless she misunderstood something vital, how could the woman know if anything was amiss? Karen saw no writing of any kind on any of the papers. Even the purple inventory pad—flipped open to the first page—held only a list of numbers.

Karen took an even breath. "Perhaps last time you visited your box, you slipped it in there first by mistake."

"No. No. No. The purple inventory tablet always goes at the top. I'm telling you; someone has been in my box! I would think that Universal Bank and Trust would have a better vault."

"I've been here for a number of years, Mrs. Watson. This vault is quite secure. Actually, it is better than many of the ones at our newer facilities, and they're top of the line, too. It made it through Hurricane Andrew."

Earth-woman didn't cave. "I pay good money for secu-rity!"

"Excuse me just a moment, please."

Karen left, returning shortly with a clipboard. "Every time you enter this area and take your safety deposit box out, you must sign this log. Is this your signature?" She pointed to a scribbled name.

"Yes."

"The last date is in December."

"Yes."

"Each time this particular box is opened, the correspond-ing record must be signed. This shows no other dates or signatures for this box. This is regulation. Carefully audited. We do it this way each…and…every…time."

Earth-woman scowled. "I don't care what you say. My privacy has been invaded! I want to close out my security box. I want my money refunded to my account! I just paid for six months, and I want every last dime back."

"No problem, Mrs. Watson. I'll get the appropriate pa-perwork."

A few minutes later, the woman headed out the double front doors, a cloth hobo-style bag of her precious blank papers slung over one shoulder. Karen heard her ranting and raving until the doors closed in her wake. It took every ounce of professionalism she could muster not to yell, *Peace out! Don't let the back door hit you where the Good Lord split you!*

Sharon, the assistant manager, stepped up beside her. "You think she'll come back in and close all of her ac-counts?"

"If we're lucky. It's got to be the heat. It's making eve-ryone a little more nuts than usual." Karen shook her head.

"You amaze me, Karen. The way you can defuse people. You really should be in public relations, or maybe politics."

"Oh, God. Hardly."

Karen's thoughts rushed to her father—at one time, the ultimate statesman. Had she inherited his gift for pandering?

"I'm going back upstairs, finish the reports, and then I'm going home, taking a big dose of aspirin, an *Ambien*, and going to bed in a room so cold, you could hang meat in it." She glanced at her watch. "I've been here since six-thirty, and my head is splitting in two. I was supposed to be out of here by three today. It's now ten 'till five. First early day I've scheduled off in as long as I can recall, and I still can't manage to leave."

The assistant manager gave her a gentle push on one shoulder. "Go, hon. Go. This place will be right here when you come back tomorrow."

Karen mumbled under her breath as she walked to the stairs. "That's comforting."

At two a.m., the bedside phone rang. Karen clawed her way up from a deep, dreamless sleep and groped for the handset.

"Karen Hernandez?" a deep voice asked.

Karen dragged one hand through her hair and squinted at the illuminated digital clock. "Yes?"

"This is Miami General. A Mr. Joel Orr has been involved in an accident. Your number was listed as his emergency contact."

"Accident? What?"

"I'm sorry, Ma'am. I can not offer any details over the phone."

Karen kicked the sheets from her legs. "I'm on the way."

Senator Silver's Office—Washington, D.C.

Brad Silver left the Senate floor after casting a critical vote on the bloated, out-of-control federal budget. When Brad reached his office around three p.m., Mark Cox and Gwen Reynolds awaited.

As Silver entered, Cox blurted out, "Did you vote to balance it, Senator?"

Silver slid his briefcase onto his desk, shucked his jacket, and reached for a glass of iced water. No matter if he dashed from one air-conditioned cubicle to the next, late July in the nation's capital sucked the life from him.

"You know I couldn't do that, Mark. I will never leave the troops without funds to fight the war, even if it means not voting for a balanced budget." Silver grimaced. "I find it particularly distasteful to have to vote for a budget with such an astronomical deficit. I'm not the only one who feels betrayed by the Administration on the presence of Weapons of Mass Destruction in Iraq." He shrugged. "Oh, well. What else could I do?"

Cox glanced at Gwen and thought, *I hope Russell Nathan doesn't zero in on this issue, or we could have trouble in November.*

Silver waved a dismissive hand. "Let's move on to our meeting."

The three settled into the seating area. Brad slipped off his shoes and loosened his tie.

"Senator, why don't you start off by bringing us up to speed on your trip home?" Cox prompted.

"All in all, a fruitful trip. The constituents and the local media interviews went well. Mike Belan has arranged for us to pick up some sizable campaign contribution checks. Icing on the cake, for this pass."

Silver paused, stared directly into the eyes of Gwen and then Cox. "Folks, let me tell you. For the first time during this trip home, I became aware of a serious threat to our reelection. Belan had mentioned something to me in passing a few weeks back, but I just marked it up as the usual Washington sniping. Apparently, I need to pay closer attention."

Cox sat up straight. "What is it?"

"Eleana confided in me that there are rumors—perhaps only whispers at this point—that Gwen and I are having an affair up here."

"Oh my God!" Gwen blurted. "What—?"

"I don't know where they got started or who is behind them, but I think at least one source is in Eleana's pet Vizcaya group."

Cox frowned. "Those people have ties to every major campaign contributor in the state. Senator, if we don't hammer this thing shut—I mean tight—we can kiss this thing goodbye."

"I know, Mark. Not only the election, but the real prize of the Chairmanship of the Senate Intelligence Committee."

Cox shot a loaded look at Gwen.

Silver held up his hands. "Now listen. Let's not over-react, but recognize that we now have a new dynamic out there. Any other time, and this would just blow off like chaff. But not now. Not with elections pending. Not that it's necessary for me to drive this point home with either of you; you both know how it is. Anything and everything becomes fair game—true, or not. I'll need both of you more than ever to help me on this...a fail-proof plan.

"Now, Gwen—outside of this office—we are not going to be seen together without others present, unless it is absolutely necessary. We can use phones, faxes, e-mails, but they absolutely must be secure. Mark, I want you to work the press to see if you pick anything of this up, and if you do, bury it at any cost. Am I making myself clear?"

Mark nodded. "Yes, of course...but do we have any reason to be worried about this...I mean, is there any truth to the rumor, Senator?"

Color rose in Brad's cheeks. "Mark, Gwen and I are adults, and this kind of subject is between her and me. End of story. Get it?"

"Yes, sir. Son of a bitch! You bust your ass for over a year to get yourself in position to knock one out of the park, and something like this comes up. Shit."

"Enough, Mark." Silver turned to his Chief of Staff. "Gwen, do you have anything to add?"

"No, sir."

"All right then, let's discuss our original subject for this meeting: a fact-finding trip to Brazil for the next Chairman of the Senate Intelligence Committee." The senator smiled. "Mark?"

"Whew, okay, here's the deal. The minority leader will join Brad after the committee meeting on Tuesday at three p.m. to announce our trip. We time the announcement so we get the prime evening news segment, and it still leaves time for Brad to get on *Hard Ball, Olbermann,* or *Larry King* to discuss the trip. We've used our back channel sources to arrange a visit with the Monsignor from Brazil to add to the profile of the trip. The purpose is to position Brad Silver as the most influential political figure in the region, bar none. Senator, we will have briefed the press that will be present, providing them our talking points, suggested questions, and of course, our answers."

Brad nodded. "This must make the cover of *Newsweek, Time,* or *US News and World Report,* Mark, or I am going to have your ass."

The P.R. man smiled and nodded. "I think it will still be mine afterwards, Senator."

Gwen pushed the sting of the senator's previous comments aside. She added, "The timing is perfect. I am told there is continuing unrest among the uncommitted countries in the region, mainly Brazil, Argentina, and Chile. And your visit—if presented with fanfare and credibility—will be received like manna from heaven."

Mark Cox agreed. "As long as you meet with both the government officials and leaders of the dissidents, it will be perceived as it always is. The United States as the watch dog, guardian angel of South America. You are anticipated as a major player in international affairs. Your timely visit will be seen as a clear message of your commitment to Latin countries to the south of Florida. That you are not only focused on Cuba."

Brad nodded. "I'll be sure to hit on economic concerns and fair trade. Also, funding for the poor children in the underserved remote mountainous regions."

Gwen added, "I see nothing but good coming from this—for the countries involved, and most important, for you."

"I hope you're right, Gwen. I'm counting on both of you to deliver on this one, like none other before. I meet with the President on Friday, and will brief him on the trip so he can include it in his Saturday televised address to the Country."

Silver stood. "Okay, guys. That's the deal. We now have a new concern that I trust we have laid out an ironclad plan to address...and we have a chance of a lifetime event. I am betting the farm on this one. For me. But you, also. Let's meet again next week on this."

Mark Cox gathered a handful of papers. "I'm out of here." He nodded to Brad, then Gwen. "Senator. Miss Reynolds."

Gwen stood and turned to leave.

"Gwen, a moment, please?"

She sat down. "Yes, sir?"

"I'm sorry to have hit you with that without any kind of prior warning. I hope you didn't perceive that as a personal attack."

Silver noted the sheen of moisture gathering in her eyes.

"Senator, you know I would never do anything to jeopardize your career."

"It's not just mine, Gwen. You have a reputation to uphold, too. One you have worked very hard for."

"Maybe...maybe it would be best if I stepped aside."

Brad shook his head. "No. No way. You are one of the most gifted political minds in Washington. I can't imagine being here without you standing behind me."

Gwen's gaze fell to her hands clasped in her lap. "Your opinion of me means a great deal, Brad."

"*You're* not going anywhere. *We're* not going anywhere."

"Eleana, she must feel…"

"I can handle my wife."

Gwen nodded. "If I am not being too forward in asking…How are things? I mean, I know she must still be grieving the loss of your child."

"I wouldn't know. She and I barely talk about anything of any consequence. Her big concern, currently, is designing our costumes for the Vizcaya Halloween Sundowner Event." He chuffed. "Maybe I should go as Fidel Castro with a noose around my neck. That might make my wife happy."

Gwen offered a slight smile. "Considering he could be deceased by that time, perhaps not such a good idea."

"All the better. Eleana would be ecstatic. Maybe, she might even lighten up a little on me. The tension at my house was so thick…" He raked a hand through his hair.

"I'm sorry."

Silver shrugged. "It's as if, on some level, she blames me for the miscarriage. If I hadn't been up here in Washington when it happened, the baby might be alive and well."

"How?"

Brad took a deep breath and exhaled. "I am at a loss, Gwen. Even before we were married—when we lived together right after my divorce—she never mentioned wanting to have children. I had my two, though she never really spent much quality time with them. So, she didn't feel as if she needed to carry on the family line. She's always been so busy with trying to glean information on her family in Cuba, and in the social soup that is her life in Miami."

He shook his head. "I know she looks like she's in her mid-thirties, at best, but Eleana is forty-six. All that time she never wanted to be a mother. Thought of any excuse in the world not to be around when my children were with me on infrequent holiday visits. She barely knows them. Until she passed forty, then she suddenly became obsessed with the idea of motherhood."

"I suppose the idea of not being able to have children after a certain age…"

Gwen stretched to empathize with the senator's beautiful wife. More likely that Eleana Silver had latched onto the idea of a baby as a fashion accessory or extension of herself—like a handbag or pair of designer pumps.

"The money we spent on those fertility shots! We could have adopted ten times over. Once she learned she was pregnant, she immersed herself in it."

"Never underestimate the power of impending motherhood."

"It could be—the aftereffects of the hormones. I've heard they make a woman more...unsettled. The normal ones with pregnancy, plus the added impact of the injections prior. Perhaps, it will pass soon."

Gwen rested a hand on her flat stomach. What would it feel like, to know the son or daughter of Brad Silver rested inside of her body? Warmth rose in her cheeks.

"I'd rather hike barefoot through the Middle East than figure this out. Women are a mystery to me." Silver smiled. "Present company excepted."

"Glad I stand out." Gwen rose. "Now, if you'll excuse me, I have several different pots to stir for you."

Silver stood in front of her and rested his hands on her shoulders. "I don't say it enough, Gwen. But thank you. I don't know what I would do without you, or your...friendship."

Brad brushed the side of her face with one finger. She closed her eyes. He leaned down and kissed her cheek. The air seemed to crackle around them. Gwen held her breath for a moment. His lips hovered over hers, then lightly touched.

They both jerked back at the same instant.

"Gwen...I..."

"Brad. Don't. We...can't."

Gwen stepped back, dipped her head, and walked to her private office.

CHAPTER FOUR

Miami General Hospital

Karen Orr Hernandez pushed past a swirling mass of infirm humanity to reach the reception desk in Miami General's emergency room. Saturday before even the hint of daylight, not a good time to visit any of the hospitals in the city. Especially Miami General, a facility that took the majority of the non-insured.

"Excuse me, please."

The harried woman—Triage Specialist, according to her name tag—glanced up from a computer monitor. "Sign in and take a registration form."

"I'm not here for treatment. I was called in. My father—Joel Orr—is here somewhere. Some kind of accident?"

"I'll need to see identification."

Karen dug in her purse and handed over her driver's license. Since the Federal HIPAA privacy regulations, security had become a primary focus for any kind of health facility.

The receptionist shoved the license back toward Karen and tapped the keyboard. "He's in room four." She handed over a laminated clip-on visitor's badge. "I'll buzz you back." She waved toward a set of doors to her left. "Check with the charge nurse at the circular desk on the right after you go down the hall. If he's not in the room, he could be in Radiology."

"Thank you."

As she turned, an imposing, tall white man stepped into her path.

"Karen? Karen Orr?"

"Do I know you?" Karen frowned.

"No. But I know your father. I was with him when they brought him in." He offered a large meaty hand. "Don Farringdon."

The aura of cigarette smoke and stale beer lingered around the man. "So, you're one of his drinking buddies?"

"Not exactly. Your father has been a hero of mine for some time."

"Well, Mr. Farringdon. That makes one of us. Now, if you'll excuse me."

Don held up one hand. "I'm really not trying to impose myself on you or your family. I found your father after he was assaulted, and..."

"Assaulted? They told me he was involved in some kind of accident. I figured he had probably crashed his car into something, or someone. It was only a matter of time, with him."

"No. First of all, from what I know of your father, he'd never drive after a couple of drinks. As a matter of fact, he left his keys at the bar last night...actually, this morning."

"Look, Don." Karen stepped aside so that Don Farringdon didn't block her path. "This is all extremely fascinating, but I need to get back there."

"Of course. I'll be out here. I'd appreciate it if you would take a moment to let me know how he is. Or, if there is anything I can do for you."

"Sure. Whatever." Karen nodded toward the receptionist and a buzzer sounded as the lock released. "It might be awhile."

A long hallway punctuated by glaring overhead fluorescent lights led to the heart of the emergency unit. The round desk was deserted. Karen managed to stop one of the nurses as he whizzed past. "Joel Orr? He's supposed to be in room four?"

The young man pointed at a series of rooms. "Over there. But he's not in the room. He's having an MRI now."

43

"Where is that?"

"Second floor, only you can't go there. I'd suggest just waiting in the room. They'll bring him back here when they're done."

"What then?"

"Depends. They may admit him. Either way, the doctor will be in after they get the test results."

Room four was barren, except for a couple of monitors and a molded orange plastic chair with spindly metal legs. The gurney was with her father somewhere in the labyrinth of Radiology.

Too bad. Given a bed and some low lighting, she might crawl up and sleep while she waited. Her eyelids felt as if they held half of Miami Beach.

Forty-five minutes later, the curtains parted. Karen jerked awake and watched as the nursing assistant wheeled the gurney into the cramped room.

Karen stood at the side of the bed. Joel's face was colored a sickly ashen gray. Dried blood still crusted around his left ear; the ghostly track of one trickle painted down his neck. An IV fed into one arm, and a series of wires led to the digital monitor.

She had seen him passed out more times than she cared to count. The sickly sweet scent of metabolizing alcohol oozed from his body. So many times, his daughter had seen him just the other side of consciousness. But never so…dead.

"Daddy?"

Her father's breathing: deep and even. His eyelids flickered, but didn't open. Karen sank into the molded plastic chair beside the gurney. She hated hospitals. The harsh overhead lighting. The blended scent of cleaning chemicals and human animal odors. Too many hours spent confined in four drab-painted walls with anxiety gnawing a hole in her stomach. No small wonder she didn't support a bleeding ulcer the size of Miami. First, her mother. Now, her derelict father. Metastasized breast cancer versus drinking yourself into disaster. No comparison.

For a few minutes, the two pushed past the strain of time and managed the first real discussion in as long as either could recall.

The door opened and the shift charge nurse walked in. "Well, well. Isn't this wonderful! Your father is awake! I'll contact your doctor, Mr. Orr. And I'll make sure you're down for a meal. I'm sure he'll want to start you off slow. We've got to get your strength back up. Get you back on your feet. Get you out of here and back home to your family."

She bustled around the room for a few minutes, checking Joel's vital signs and the IV's before leaving.

"She's my nurse, I assume."

Karen nodded. "One of many. They've been great here."

Don Farringdon knocked twice before entering. He smiled when he saw Joel holding his daughter's hand. "Karen, I'll stay with your father if you'd like to get some lunch. I know you didn't have breakfast. They've got a pretty good-looking salad bar up and running."

She brushed tears from her cheeks and stood. "Probably a good idea. I'm starting to feel a little light-headed."

After his daughter left, Joel said, "My daughter tells me I have you to thank."

"No need. I just happened to be there. Wish I could've prevented this. Maybe if I'd left a few minutes earlier…"

"No clue as to who that guy was?"

Don shook his head. "We assume it was the man who took offense over the discussion about Brad Silver and the gun issue. The police have asked around. I don't think there's much of a chance of finding him. He wasn't a regular and Brenda Gayle had no clue as to his identity. She sends her best, by the way."

When Joel nodded, his head felt as if it was filled with concrete.

"My late wife always maintained that things happen for a reason." Joel shifted to relieve his back. He studied Don

She sat for the next forty-three minutes until the doctor walked in.

Is this guy even old enough to shave? Karen thought.

Either she was getting older, or doctors were getting younger. Lately, it seemed as if every one she met looked like a teenager.

"I'm Dr. Johansson." He used a notebook computer to access patient information.

"Karen Orr Hernandez. I'm his daughter."

"Your father has suffered a head injury, Mrs. Hernandez. Thus far, he has not regained consciousness. His vitals are within normal range, for the most part. Blood pressure and temperature slightly elevated. The MRI reveals internal bleeding. I am going to admit him into the Neuro ICU."

"How long before he…?"

"With a head trauma, it could be a few hours, or a couple of days. Depends on the swelling, the amount of trauma to the brain. We've done preliminary treatment of his wound, but he'll need a few stitches."

"So…"

The doctor looked at the compact computer monitor and entered information.

"Someone from admissions will be in shortly to speak with you. Now, do you know of any allergies, or anything else about your father's health history?"

Karen hesitated. "Um…he can't take penicillin. I really don't know about anything recent. We've been…out of touch for awhile."

"Family physician?"

"He and Mom used to use Dr. John Crane. He could've changed doctors since then."

"Do you know what, if any, medications he is currently taking?"

Besides bourbon? "I'm sorry. I don't. My father never has been big on going to doctors. I doubt he is on much of anything."

The emergency room physician nodded and tapped the keyboard on the computer. "We can do a more thorough follow-up when he can speak for himself." He nodded. "Shouldn't be too much longer. They're checking on a bed in Neuro Intensive Care. As soon as the admissions people come by, he should go right on up to the third floor."

Don Farringdon stood at the window of Room 416. Beyond the rows of air conditioner units and vents on the roof of one of Miami General's lower wings, he could see a snatch of blue sky between the twin towers. Good thing most people weren't too interested in the view. Behind him, Karen slept in a stiff recliner. Poor woman. In the two days since Joel Orr had been moved from intensive care to a regular floor, she hadn't left the hospital, and he had to practically force her to walk to the cafeteria for meals.

Don could tell a lot about people by the way they handled crisis. Judging from Karen's vigilance, she was quality.

Don heard the first words Joel Orr had uttered in three days.

"Bug? Is that you, Bug?"

Karen jerked awake and rushed to stand beside the bed. "Daddy? Daddy?"

Joel Orr moaned. He lifted one hand to touch the bandage covering a third of his scalp. "What…?"

"It's okay, Daddy. It's going to be okay. I'm here."

Joel Orr shifted. He noticed Don's presence. "You…you were…where have I seen you?"

"Don Farringdon, sir. We met at the Alibi."

Joel winced when he moved his head. "Feels like I was hit by a truck."

"Close, sir. If it was who we think it was, the fellow was pretty big."

Joel squinted at the wall clock. "How long…?"

"Four days, Daddy."

"Damn." He fixed his gaze on Don. "We were talking about politics. Something about…" He frowned.

"Don't worry about anything right now, Daddy. The important thing is that you're going to be okay."

Don smiled. "I'm going to go grab a quick cup of coffee. Give you two a little time alone."

"Will you please tell his nurse that he's awake on your way by the desk? They'll want to know."

Don nodded. "Will do."

The door closed. Karen turned to her father. The bruises on his face had turned from red to purple. One of his eyes was still swelled shut. "You scared me."

Joel reached over and grasped his daughter's hand. "I'm sorry, Bug. I'm sorry…for so many things."

"What was so important that someone came after you, Daddy? Don told me a little. The police have no clue about the man who hit you. No one seems to know who he was, or anything about him. Just some stranger in a bar."

"It's a bit fuzzy. We were talking politics. All I remember is saying I should run for the senatorial race against that clown Silver. Next thing I know, I'm outside, face down on the pavement."

Karen pulled up a chair and sat down next to the bed. "When is it going to stop, Daddy? The drinking. When?"

Joel sighed. "I know, Bug. I know."

Karen felt the familiar anger bubbling inside. "You want to end up like Uncle Clancy? Hmm? In prison for killing some family while you're under the influence? Hey, maybe you and your brother could share a cell? A family affair. Two brothers: one incarcerated for robbery, the other for vehicular homicide."

"I have done a lot of things. Driving under the influence is not one of them."

"Ah. Well. Sign you up for the good behavior club. Like you could actually run for office. Get real. Who would vote for you, Daddy? Honestly. You've managed to throw everything you've worked for away…and for what? So you can end up like this?"

with his one operational eye. "I know I've seen you somewhere else besides the Alibi."

Don sat down. "I've been involved in South Florida politics—though, way in the background—since I was a kid. It's kind of a hobby, or, if you listen to my ex-wife, an addiction of mine."

"It's coming to me, now. Aren't you tight with the Reverend Louis Jones? Seems to me, I recall you being in good with the black churches...you're a fund-raising, public relations-type."

"I tend to stay behind the scenes—me, and my buddy Ronnie Taylor, best research and numbers guy around. But, yes, that's me."

Joel smiled, then winced at the dull pain the gesture elicited. "Then perhaps we all need to become better acquainted."

"Sir?"

"Because, Don, I'm going to run against one of the most popular senators in Washington. And I'm going to need your help."

CHAPTER FIVE

Miami, Florida

Three weeks later, Don Farringdon and Ronnie Taylor walked into the Cup O' Joe, a small coffee shop one block west of the no-frills store front building on 36th Street that housed the official campaign headquarters of *Joel Orr for Senate*.

"Great news, Joel. Tiger Bay has scheduled your announcement for the Silver seat." Don grabbed a cup of self-serve coffee and sat down.

Orr added three packets of sugar to the already-sweetened coffee. One thing he had noted about his trial of abstinence: he craved sugar like it was crack cocaine. No guarantees he wouldn't ever pick up another drink. Who could say? In the time since he had left Miami General, he had only slipped once.

"Good job, Don. It will be good to be back in front of those folks. Frankly, I'm surprised they'd schedule me. Guess Brad and Cox don't have the lock on them I expected."

"That means we should get all the major feeds...CNN, the big three, and FOX at a minimum," said Ronnie Taylor, Farringdon's politico sidekick.

Don Farringdon added artificial sweetener to his cup of black coffee and stirred. "You're right, Ronnie, but we still have to stoke the fire, especially with the Hispanic outlets. *Diario* is a must, and that one outlet will be your responsibility."

Ronnie and Joel nodded agreement. The venerable *Diario Las Americas* was the Spanish daily that all Cuban politicos read before anything else in Miami.

Ronnie frowned. "We have to watch out for Mike Belan, too. He's up to his eyeballs in Silver's camp. I've run up against him in the past. He typically plays both ends against the middle."

"Good point," Don agreed. "Belan reminds me of an iceberg. Most of his clout is below the surface."

Farringdon stared at the quarter-pound banana nut muffins on Joel's plate and smiled. "All right. Let's get to work on the speech. Even though we know the twenty-four-hour cooling-off vote is the real reason you decided to take Silver to task, we're going to have to look more substantive if we hope to make the prime news."

"Still can't believe the guy couldn't pull the trigger on that one," inserted Orr.

Don pinched off a small piece of muffin and popped it into his mouth. The way things were going, he'd have to add a few hours at the gym to overcome all the junk he was bound to eat, hanging around his candidate of choice.

"Yeah, well, he didn't," Don said. "Whatever it took to get you into this race was worth it."

DuPont Plaza Hotel, Biscayne Bay—Miami, Florida

DuPont Plaza occupied prime real estate in the heart of the city, on the banks of the Miami River adjacent to Biscayne Bay. Not elegant by some standards, yet tested over time. At one time, the DuPont had been home to the politically powerful Standard Club.

The location for the monthly meetings of the Tiger Bay Political Club—reigning supreme back to the leadership of Steve Ross and Hal Bergida—the complex housed a blend of hotel and offices, with a few retail stores. Former presidents, U.S. senators and representatives, cabinet members, and foreign dignitaries had addressed the club over the years. For

Joel Orr and others seeking to achieve the pinnacle of Florida politics, accepted protocol required all major announcements to be made at the Tiger Bay Club at the DuPont Plaza downtown.

Don Farringdon surveyed the meeting room on the mezzanine floor. At total capacity, the room held two hundred. Today, it was packed to the gills. As usual, the film media dominated the room. Don spotted a few club regulars who had arrived early to snatch the best seats. He smiled. So much like Hollywood, with bright lights and cameras readied for action. So much like Hollywood, with the prime actor in place—his man Orr ready to make his comeback speech. The only thing missing—Don wished he had thought of it—was Orr jogging up several flights of stairs, sweaty and determined, dressed as the movie prizefighter Rocky Balboa. Don hummed *Eye of the Tiger*.

It really was going to be a fight. Someone would get knocked out in the final round. No doubt, the gloves would come off.

Joel Orr felt a trickle of perspiration between his shoulders. His mouth felt as dry as the morning after a bucket of bourbon. He felt—what did he feel? A mixture of flat-out fear, doom, and exhilaration. For the first time in as long as he could recall, Joel Orr felt energized. Somewhere in the dusty confines of memory, cogs sealed with years of rust turned.

The Tiger Bay president called for order. After a few announcements, he turned to the corner where Orr and Farringdon stood. Ronnie Taylor looked on from the back of the room, his gaze taking in the scene.

Joel stood at the podium. He inhaled. Made it a point to glance from one side of the room to the other, nodding to a few of the media old-timers he recognized.

"Good afternoon." Joel's voice cracked. He glanced at Don Farringdon and forced himself to take an even breath to calm his nerves.

"Some people may call me crazy. I am. I admit it. Crazy like a fox. Folks, there are bigger issues than just Castro to Floridians. The War in Iraq is draining critical resources, the economy is in shambles, crime is out of control, and the criminal justice system is buckling at the seams."

As Joel settled into the bulk of the speech, the slight hesitation at the beginning of each statement gave way to a tone of deep understanding. Don studied the faces of the media grunts. Several eyebrows lifted. Surprised glances flipped back and forth across the crowded room like volleyed tennis balls.

"Now, I've said my part. You all know why I'm here. I'm open for your questions."

Don held his breath. *This is the crucial part, Orr. Keep it simple.*

"Senator, you have not been in politics for some time, and you were defeated soundly in your last election. Why do you think Floridians will support you now?" asked the AP reporter.

"That was then, this is now."

Digital cameras whirred. Strobe lights popped.

The CNN reporter won the next spot. "Other than gun control, what is the major issue affecting the citizens?"

"The economy," responded Orr.

And so it went, question after question. Orr answered directly, but with rather terse responses. Farringdon smiled. His man rolled out the plan: no bullshit, just straight answers. Whether they had the good sense to put it into words or not, the public was ready for this.

Even if they weren't, the strategy was about all they had to go on with Joel's candidacy. The man wouldn't get by on his looks. He was at the bottom of the pit looking up. Don would use every bit of clawing and scratching and straight-talking to help Joel Orr drag himself up.

Don Farringdon culled through a stack of papers. Words like *short, empty, missing details, detached, lacking* and *huh?* peppered the pages. The evening news had held much the same.

"They tore him up, eh?" Ronnie shook his head.

"I had hoped for a different response. Really, at least it isn't totally critical." He grinned, thinking of the political jargon from the first President Bush. "As Bush-41 always said, 'all we need is a little mo for momentum'."

Washington, D.C.

Senator Brad Silver read the newspaper clips on the ride in. One headline stood out: *Crazy like a fox? Joel Orr makes bid for Senate Seat.*

"Why is Orr doing this? Wouldn't it be better for him to try and get his life back together and try to practice law again?"

No one was listening, but the question probably echoed through Florida and the Capitol.

Universal Bank and Trust—Miami, Florida

The interoffice line blinked in Karen's office.

"Karen? Sorry to bother you. A customer insists on speaking with you. It's Mrs. Watson's daughter."

"Who?"

The assistant manager lowered her voice. "Earth-woman from a few days ago. Remember? Security box? Purple binder? Nut job?"

"Oh, good Lord. First, the audit team was here bright and early. Now this." Karen pinched the bridge of her nose, a useless habit she had whenever she felt a headache brewing. Between the relentless heat, lack of sleep, and stress, the daily headaches had become a steady distraction.

"Would you mind showing her up to my office, please, Sharon?"

A couple of minutes passed before the assistant manager ushered a middle-aged woman into the room.

"Karen, this is Mrs. VanLandingham." The assistant manager said before turning and scurrying back to the downstairs lobby.

Karen stood, offered a hand, and motioned toward one of two upholstered chairs. She purposely eschewed her normal position behind the large wooden desk and took a seat in the second chair. Sometimes the removal of the appearance of authority eased intimidation, enough to defuse most situations.

The woman sighed. "I've come to offer you an apology."

Karen tilted her head to one side.

"You're the one, I assume, whom my mother blasted a few days back."

"Yes. That was me."

Mrs. VanLandingham's eyes watered. "I am truly sorry, Mrs..." she read Karen's nametag. "...Hernandez. My mother is not herself."

Karen settled back. One skill she had learned over years of dealing with customers: the art of listening. Most problems worked themselves out if they were allowed to flow naturally with a minimum of interference on her part.

The woman continued, "You wouldn't know it to see her now, but my mother is—was—a brilliant scholar. Professor Emeritus. About a year ago, my husband and I moved her down here. She was showing some signs of memory loss. Little things. My father passed away. After that, she just went downhill. Actually, from what we can piece together, Dad was covering for her. When he died, we were able to detect the changes in her behavior."

The woman sniffed. Dug in her purse for a tissue.

"She used to be so...tidy. Professional. Now...well, you saw her. She looks like some Woodstock reject. Like she belongs on a commune instead of the campus of an Ivy League College." She paused, looked directly at Karen. "Are your parents still alive?"

Karen usually avoided overt familiarity to mix with business. The woman's question caught her off guard. "My mother is deceased. My father...still alive." *At least, for now.*

"You hold your parents in high regard. Like they'll always be there. Like they'll always be strong and vibrant...and perfect."

The words stung. Karen stuffed her emotions down. "It must be very hard on you and your siblings."

"There's only me. And my husband." She paused. "I need your help. That's another reason I'm here today."

"What can I do for you?"

Another deep sigh. The woman didn't seem as if she could get enough air. Karen identified with the feeling.

"My husband insisted on having paperwork updated when Mom moved in with us. I have power of attorney. We put our names on her checking and savings accounts. At the time, it seemed a bit premature and extreme. Now, I'm glad he had the foresight."

Though she knew the answer, Karen asked, "Does your mother have accounts with us? Other than the security box. She closed that out when she was here."

Mrs. VanLandingham nodded. "Both accounts are with your bank. My husband and I have conducted all of our personal banking here for several years."

"And the problem...?"

"Mom somehow got hold of the mutual checking account book a few weeks back. I keep it stored away. I didn't notice until I went to write out one of her bills. She's written checks to...God, we don't really know. She might have just stuffed the checks away somewhere. The way she's been lately."

Karen stood and walked around her desk to the computer. "Do you know how many checks are missing?"

"Four. I've been online to see. So far, none have come in. But who knows?"

"The best thing for us to do is close out the checking account. Immediately. We can open a new account today before you leave and issue a few temporary checks for you to use until the order comes in."

"Just that easy?"

"Your name is on the account. You are just as much the owner as your mother. Also, you are just as liable. We should treat this as if the checks in question were stolen."

The woman's features relaxed. "Oh, thank you, thank you. I've been worried sick."

Worried sick. Good choice of words. Karen saved them for the next time she was called to some emergency room in the wee hours. Sure, Joel Orr seemed to be on a new path, but for how long? She knew the pattern. Had seen it before. The dance was so old; she couldn't whip up the enthusiasm to hope for a partner who could lead without stumbling into the punchbowl.

Karen snapped back to the present and the customer in front of her.

"Next time you have concerns, please come as soon as you suspect a problem. The earlier, the better. Now..." Karen smiled. "Unless you have the account number, I'll need your full name, address, and social security number. We'll pull up your account and have this taken care of in no time at all."

A few minutes later, Karen ushered Mrs. VanLandingham—her new best friend, Alisa—to another office off the lobby where a customer service representative waited with the necessary paperwork.

The exchange caused a mixture of guilt and intense longing for the protective essence of childhood. Soon, Karen vowed, she would call Joel Orr and try once more to have some semblance of a relationship. Since his release from the hospital, she hadn't heard from Joel. No surprise there. Why should she expect otherwise?

The assistant manager pulled Karen aside. "Was her daughter as nutty as she was?"

"No, and I feel like a big schmuck for jumping to conclusions. That's what I get for being judgmental."

As they walked across the lobby, Karen noted the television monitor and stopped in mid-stride. "Hey, John. Could you turn up the volume, please?" She called out to a young man behind the counter.

The teller aimed a remote toward the monitor. CNN news blared.

"Sounds like another one who has cast a bid for senator," Sharon commented. "Elections are like Christmas anymore. We seem to have one every other month."

"Uh huh."

"Who is that guy, anyway? God, I know so little about politics."

"Joel Orr." Karen stared at the monitor. "My father."

Destin Beach, Florida

Former Florida Governor Russell Nathan watched the Good Morning America show. When the state cut-away came on, he sat forward, watching the taped replay of Joel Orr's Tiger Bay presentation, bemused fascination painted across his features.

"Know what that man just did for me, sugar?"

"Whut?" The latest in the long line of jail-bait beach beauties grabbed a Diet Coke from his stocked refrigerator.

"That's the miserable has-been, Joel Orr. He's just got himself a bad case of *accidental ambition*. And he's just what your Big Daddy needs to run up some big numbers in the primary, come September."

The redhead shrugged. "I've never seen him." She chewed on the eraser end of a pencil, frowning down at the *USA Today* crossword puzzle.

"He was washed up when you were in kindergarten, sugar. Still, we'll use him like a baby uses a diaper. He's going to make me look real appealin' up next to Silver."

The young woman toyed with the chain around her neck. "I like gold better than silver. Silver's nice, but gold goes better with my coloring. Everybody tells me that."

Shit for brains, Russell thought. No matter. He didn't have her around to engage in mindful conversation.

"Honey, that man on TV...we're going to clean his miserable clock. Mark my words on that."

CHAPTER SIX

Vizcaya on Biscayne Bay—Miami, Florida

Eleana Silver watched her Goddaughter emerge from beneath a flower-bedecked canopy, a bouquet of white roses in hand. In the white *quinceañera* gown, Victoria seemed to float effortlessly through the parted crowd. One of Eleana's favorite Hispanic ceremonies unfolded—the celebration of a young girl's fifteenth birthday—combined with her favorite sanctuary, the gardens of Vizcaya. Surrounded by the elite of Miami. The finest food and drink. Perfect weather—80° with a gentle, steady evening breeze off Biscayne Bay.

The only thing missing: her husband. Too busy playing national politician to be where he was really needed. Too busy with the black slut Chief of Staff. Eleana's anger rose in her chest. She stuffed it down and focused on the occasion at hand.

To Eleana, each part of the pageantry marking a young girl's coming of age was delicious. The special thanks-giving mass—*misa de acción de gracis*— where Victoria entered in a processional with her court, carrying her last doll to leave at the altar as a symbol of her emerging womanhood. The priest's blessing of her rosary and Bible.

Then, the outside reception. The entrance of the court of attendants: seven boys—*chambelanes*, seven girls—*damas*. Her Goddaughter entering, dressed as a virginal bride in an exclusive designer gown, her hair swept up in an elegant chignon.

Photographers milled throughout the party, videotaping and snapping digital pictures of the court, food tables, and guests. Victoria's father knelt to replace his daughter's flat shoes with a pair of heels, symbolizing the change from girl to woman. He escorted her to the center of the dance floor where they performed a waltz.

"I'm so glad to see your godchild chose a waltz," Dorothy Claxton whispered into Eleana's ear. "So many are drifting away from tradition. I actually attended one last year where the young woman performed a belly dance, of all things."

"Victoria has always had a keen sense of taste," Eleana said. "Even as a small child."

As the young woman's Godparent, Eleana would soon present Victoria with a scepter to replace the bouquet. The Silvers' gifts: a designer clutch filled with money, and a delicate diamond and emerald necklace. She felt a brief flicker of anger toward Brad. As the young woman's Godfather and *padrino*, her husband should have been in attendance. How could anything in Washington be more important? Months ago! She had reminded him about Victoria's *quinceañera* months ago!

The first dance ended. Victoria's father handed his daughter over to her escort, and the remainder of the court joined them on the dance floor. Eleana watched the eight couples sweep in wide circles as the waltz continued. Later, the girls would trade the long, cumbersome gowns for shorter dresses, and the music would change as the salsa and more modern dance styles took over. But, for a few moments, the celebration—steeped in history—echoed the past.

Eleana thought of her own *quinceañera*. Not quite as elaborate. No father for the first waltz. Instead, her aloof uncle. On his arm, she had felt insignificant, frightened of making an incorrect move and receiving his instant disdain. No brothers waited in the court. Her mother's expression: proud, yet tinged with sadness. She felt the familiar sting of anger when she thought about her family still in Cuba. How many cousins, nieces, and nephews would she never know? The fires of Hell weren't hot enough for Fidel Castro and his brother Raul. The promise of hot tears stung her eyes. She took a deep breath.

Dorothy leaned over. "You look as if you are miles away, dear."

"Ninety miles." She glanced out across the water.

"Ah." Dorothy nodded. "It always brings you down, doesn't it? Remembering…"

Eleana recalled her studies of the times before Castro, during the Batista administration. It had been no better politically. More corruption, not less. But there had been class—recognition of success and privilege. Certainly, her family had inherited their wealth and protected it, but at least it was theirs to keep and enjoy. Not so under Castro's iron rule.

"I don't even know my family, Dorothy. I barely remember my brothers. To know they are so close, yet…I can't even send them food or money." Eleana's hands formed into fists. "Oh, how I hope Brad will win and lead a campaign to overthrow Castro and his thugs!"

Dorothy reached over and held Eleana's hand.

Eleana continued, "Yes, America has faults. I feel discrimination, even today in Miami. But, compared to my family's in exile, I have a wonderful life. So many will be born, live, and die without any knowledge of the glorious freedoms I have. I'm lucky that my mother could bring me here, to survive in a new land and find my way into the proper social level."

"Your husband deserves some credit, Eleana."

Brad Silver did merit praise, yet her resentment managed to overwrite any good feelings.

"Brad has been my ticket to success. Now, I can really survive on my own."

As Eleana said the words, the fine hairs at the base of her neck prickled.

Behind her, the party continued. Salsa music filled the tropical air. Had Brad been there, the two would have danced until the wee hours, possibly following the gathering as they vacated Vizcaya for the small clubs dotting the city. Eleana paused by the Mercedes. The radiant heat lifting from the asphalt battled with the night sea air. She wobbled.

"*Señora Silver¿Estás enferma?*" Ramiro asked.

"No, No. Thank you, Ramiro. I'm fine. Just...take me home, please."

As Ramiro navigated Miami traffic to the Silvers' home in Coral Gables near the Riviera Country Club, he checked Eleana's reflection in the rearview mirror. Even in the low light, he could discern the creamy shade of her skin. Her lips, full and moist. A long, graceful neck beneath thick curls of ebony hair. The rest of her would be as perfect.

So beautiful. So beautiful. Such a woman did not deserve to be alone.

A bougainvillea vine twined around four trellises that supported a shaded poolside cabana. In the middle, behind sheer curtains, Eleana rested facedown while her massage therapist worked.

The tension in Eleana's shoulders eased, and the slight headache that had become her constant companion since the night of the *quinceañera* faded. She cried, as she often did during her weekly massage. The release of emotion had frightened off several therapists, but this latest one seemed to take it in stride. The middle-aged man—blind from birth—sensed her sadness, yet continued to work. Eleana felt at ease with him. For once, the perfection of her body caused no jealousy. She simply became a person who required and received the trained touch of a healer.

After over an hour of work, the therapist covered her back with a soft sheet and rocked her back and forth; one hand rested on her head, the other at the base of her spine. Even after he slowed and lifted his hands, she could still feel the warmth of his touch. She heard him release a soft breath, gather his belongings, and leave. Someone—one of the staff—would help him into the house and contact a cab, leaving Eleana to rest for as long as she wished.

She sensed a presence.

Warm hands, different hands—rested on her shoulders. The scent of a man's cologne teased her nose.

When Eleana started to lift her head, a familiar voice said, "*está segura conmigo. Yo quisiera hacerte feliz.*" You are safe with me. I wish to make you happy.

Eleana's breath caught. She considered. With a word, she could send him away. Forever.

His hands lingered, waiting. When she didn't respond, they continued down her back in long, slow strokes. Back up again.

Eleana moaned.

Ramiro's fingertips teased the length of her spine. Touched the sensitive skin behind her knees. Danced upward, along the inside of her thighs.

Images flashed in her mind's eye. Lush, tropical foliage. The scent of exotic flowers. A slow Latino heat building. A hint of mingled flavors—recalled from some distant past—on her tongue.

How long since a man had touched her body with such reverence? The hands continued up and down her back with a warm, even pressure.

Eleana cried. For Brad.

She cried for Cuba. For her father—murdered. For her brothers. Still alive, somewhere? Perhaps. She cried for her mother. So sad and defeated. Now deceased.

Emotions bubbled to the surface and popped. Eleana wept. The warm hands caressed and soothed. She sighed. The tears slowed and stopped.

The touch changed. Morphed from one of compassion to building passion. Need. Down her back in long strokes. Lingering over the tender skin at the base of her spine. Moving from her ankles, over the calves, to her upper thighs. Kneading. Teasing. Light, then hard.

She spread her legs slightly. Fingers danced up her inner thighs. Stopped short. Lingered.

Eleana took a deep breath and turned onto her back. She kept her eyes closed as the hands and fingers continued their tender exploration.

Men took. Always. This man would be the same. She expected his need to dictate the next move. To her surprise, the fingertips circled and coaxed, accompanied only by his whispered endearments in her native tongue; the musical language feeding a deep part of her soul.

The fingers circled her breasts, then slid down her flat stomach to probe deeper.

Eleana breathed and gave herself over to the miasma of sensations.

CHAPTER SEVEN

Downtown Miami, Florida

The Grace Abyssinian Church in Overtown held at full capacity three hundred stomping soul-savers. The members recognized Don Farringdon seated in the front pew, almost always the only white man in the assembly. When Brother Don attended or initiated a special service, the elders took note. Though he might have an agenda, they could often align theirs with his, to everyone's advantage.

A white-washed cinderblock foursquare building, the church dated back to the late '30s. Movements had come and gone, a host of men of the cloth had sweated behind the pulpit, and countless human dramas had played out. If the black community of Miami had a true center, then Grace Church—as it was called by its members—stood at its heart.

Don Farringdon's gaze roamed the milling crowd. He nodded recognition to a reporter from the black-owned *Miami Times*. The men wore suits, even in the south Florida heat, and the women matched their styles in dresses and coordinating hats. The air—barely cooled by an aging unit struggling against the humidity—held a carnival-like feeling. From the looks of things, the attendance would exceed normal Sunday morning service capacity. Don noticed two young black men snapping open folding metal chairs, fitting them into any available space next to the walls and back of the sanctuary.

Everyone who was anyone had come to hear Brother Don's Man.

The Reverend Louis Jones swept down the center aisle. He stopped to shake outreached hands as he made his way to the front. By the time he placed his worn black Bible on the wooden pulpit, the room had settled into an expectant hush.

"Good morning!"

The crowd echoed his words.

"And what a glor-i-ous morning the Lord has given us, today!"

Amens and *Praise-be's.*

"Brother Don Farringdon has brought to us here at Grace Church, a special guest, this fine Sunday morning." The preacher smiled. "Now, I know some of you might be saddened, as I will not be delivering the normal service. You can hear me this evenin', at the six o'clock." He shoved a finger into the air. "But, I bee-lieve the Good Lord intends for us to turn our ears in the direction of righteousness."

Amens. God be the glory!

Don nodded. The man knew how to work a group to a fever pitch. He could not have picked a better place for the critical campaign launch in the black community.

"Now, I'm going to take my place and listen carefully to what Brother Don's Man has to say." He turned to the chair behind and to the left of the pulpit. "Give our guest, Brother Joel Orr, a nice Grace Church welcome!"

The congregation stood. Some clapped. Others raised their hands toward the heavens.

Joel stepped up to the pulpit and settled the handful of speech notes into place. He took a moment to close his eyes and breathe. Then, he gazed out across the gathering, deliberately pausing at each set of rows before continuing to the next section. The only sound was of the gentle swish of handheld fans.

"I am Joel Orr. I come to you—first and foremost, above all others—to take the first steps in my long journey to Washington as your senator. You don't know me. But my deepest wish is that you do—at least, a little more—by the time I step down from this podium today."

Joel stepped to one side of the pulpit and spread his arms wide. "Brothers and Sisters, our time has come."

A sprinkling of *amens.*

"We live in perilous times. The current leadership—Brad Silver and his cohorts—have put us in a horrible, non-winnable war. I can look out over this sea of gentle faces, and I know some of you have lost your sons and daughters."

He paused for a moment to allow silence.

"Our leaders up in Washington have run gas prices through the roof! We've lost who knows how many jobs to overseas! Jobs that have taken food off all of our tables!"

Amens.

Joel lowered his voice. "Most important: nothing—nothing has been done for civil rights."

Um-huh. I heard that! I know that's right!

"Who is this white man standing before us, you might be asking yourselves. And why should we care? What's he going to do for us? How can he possibly know what our lives are like?"

Joel walked to the other side of the pulpit. "I'll tell you who I am. I am nobody. I'm not even on those big politicians' radar screens. I live in a diverse neighborhood much like this one. I work every day for a living wage. I struggle to pay bills, buy gas, and make ends meet."

Keep it honest, Orr. Farringdon thought. *These folks can smell phony a mile away.*

"Oh, I've been where they are. Yes, I have. A few years back, I was right in the middle of their high-class world. I drove a fancy car. Lived in a fine house. Ate my fill of fancy food. I rubbed elbows with money so old…"

Joel bowed his head. He stopped speaking just long enough for the group to wonder if he was overcome.

"Life has a way of beating you down. I lost sight of the important things. Real people. Real issues. My daughter. My wife…" Joel shook his head. "I fell. And when I fell, I landed at the bottom."

He lifted his face toward the ceiling. "Then, one day not too long ago, I had a revelation!"

Amen. Praise be!

Joel raised his arms. "I can make a difference! I can rise up from the flames!"

Lawd oh-mighty! Praise God!

Joel pointed out across the congregation. "My friends, it's time to stop the slaughter of our children on the streets of Miami! Those people in Washington who follow the NRA around like whipped puppies need to go. We've got to get guns out of the hands of criminals who keep us prisoners in our own homes. We will purge—" He swept an arm in an arc across the heads of the group. "—our government from them. Make our streets safe again!"

Several people stood in place, arms extended upward. Don Farringdon felt the small flicker of hope grow. Maybe the old senator still had it in him. Perhaps not in front of the Coral Gables crowd, but here where the rubber met the road.

"Will you help me?" Joel's voice carried across the commotion. "Will you?"

Yes! Yes! Amen! Good God!

"With your help, we can rise up!"

Don Farringdon stood and clapped.

They had no money, no name recognition. Their first opponent—even before taking aim at the incumbent—was a former Florida governor with the backing of a former President.

But, Farringdon thought, we do have a candidate. A living, breathing candidate who might actually stand for something. With this kind of potential support in the black community, with some kind of hook on Silver, and with a little luck on Russell Nathan, we might just surprise some folks. But, *gawd!* It was going to be a lot of work.

Almost a half-hour later, Orr finished his remarks and took a seat on the dais. The audience still rocked and sang, the old words echoing through the historic sanctuary: *We shall overcome. We shall overcome.*

King's Ranch near Monticello—panhandle of Florida

The King Ranch ten miles south of Monticello, Florida, ranged across three hundred acres of prime hardwood forests and natural spring-fed streams. Deer and wild turkey roamed the woods, prize bass and bream stocked the ponds, and some of the biggest Southern diamondback rattlesnakes in the country hid in deep cool holes with gopher turtles for roommates.

The only cleared land: the twenty fenced acres surrounding the massive country-styled ranch house and its seven outbuildings. One barn enclosure housed J. R. King's famous farm tool and machinery museum, an ever-expanding exhibit visited by locals and tourists, especially following glowing articles in a handful of travel and leisure magazines, most notably *Southern Living*. Other than a few thoroughbred horses, goats, a donkey, several peacocks, and a clutch of Rhode Island Red chickens, the property fell far short of the traditional ranch model. The fact didn't stop John R. from wearing full western regalia: snakeskin boots, a tailored pearl-buttoned shirt, dark blue Levi's, a silver and turquoise bolo tie, and a ten-gallon hat.

The spread's owner—John R. King, *J.R.* to his friends—owned a piece of just about every money-making enterprise in Jefferson County, with interests in neighboring Leon, Madison, and Taylor counties, and parts of south Georgia. Locals loved John R. King. His ranch sponsored the annual 4th of July cookout and fireworks—free to the public. His two-thousand-square-foot party house had been host to a score of prestigious weddings, golden anniversary celebrations, charity and political fund-raisers, and the occasional wake.

"It's good to be King," Russell Nathan said. He slapped John R. on the back.

"Ain't it, though?"

Russell looked out over the elaborate setting: Tables lined up ten deep beneath red and white striped tents. Three massive barbeque grills belching hickory-scented smoke. A side tent dedicated to an open bar with every kind of libation favored by the attendees. Rows of metal folding chairs lined up in front of a flatbed truck that would serve as the speaking platform—a nice, homey touch suggested by John R. Everywhere he looked, Russell saw red, white, and blue balloons, streamers, ribbons, and banners.

"Looks like some giant puked up patriotic," John R. commented. "I told the staff to kick it up a notch, but..." He shook his head. "I hope it's not too over the top."

Russell smiled. "It's perfect. And I certainly appreciate all you're doing for me, J. R. I won't forget you once I'm in Washington."

"I'm counting on that, Russ. I just wish you could've stayed on in the Governor's mansion for a few more years. Term limits are a piece of crap, far as I'm concerned."

By noontime, the crowd and the heat had built. Massive misting fans created a cool breeze. Guests arrived in a steady stream, parked in the field adjacent to the house by J.R.'s staff. No expense had been spared when it related to security. J.R.'s people—in dark blue pants and light blue chambray shirts with the official gilded crown insignia—milled through the gathering. Off-duty county police officers hired for the event stood around the edges, their mirrored shades glinting in the midday sun. Men in dark suits—the Feds—stuck out like sore thumbs. The others—the ones an untrained eye didn't see—sipped on punch, dressed in plain clothes as if they were there for the party. Short of Uzi-toting guerillas, the campaign kick-off party had more security than most third-world dictators.

"I don't see our mutual friend yet, J.R." Russell's gaze roamed the crowd. "I sure hope he gets here on time."

"Oh, he'll be here. I've had Secret Service crawling all over this place for the past three weeks. Besides, I've never known him to turn down good southern cooking. You just go on about your business and let me take care of the details."

John R. King stepped up onto the flatbed and grabbed a microphone. "Howdy, folks."

Conversations ebbed. Those of the nearly-four-hundred-strong crowd not already seated wandered to the folding chairs.

"I'm so glad you could all join us today." He flashed a white smile. "The folks from Levon's Barbeque over in Madison are cooking up some good grub for us. Those of you from around here know; Levon makes some of the best pulled pork and baked beans this side of the Mason/Dixon line. Let's take a moment and give those fine cooks a hand, shall we?"

He waited until the applause died. "Now, we all came here today to help one of our fellow southerners—a fine, upstanding gentleman from our part of the state. He's running for Senate. And we are all going to be *here,* helping him to get *there!*"

J.R.'s people in the audience initiated a round of hearty applause.

"Help me, now, in giving our next senator a good solid North Florida welcome. My friend and yours, Russell Nathan!"

Russell stepped up, shook John R.'s hand, and positioned himself behind the microphone. "Thank you, J.R.! Well, hello to all of you. I see a number of faces I know out there. I appreciate you coming out on this warm summer day to hear what I have to say. And you know, J.R....I do believe I spotted Mrs. Maize's coconut cake over on the dessert table. You know where I'll be heading after dinner."

As the speech unwound, sweat trickled down Russell's florid face and dripped off the tip of his nose.

"My friends, this is a grave time in our country. Folks from other shores are taking over our jobs. Taking the food right off our children's plates. They are changing our way of life. Making a travesty of our freedoms." He paused. "Some of them come over by themselves. Some of them marry in. It's a foreign invasion, in every sense of the word.

"One man—because of his wife's family—has special interests in another Communist country. I don't have to say the name of that little Podunk of a country. All of us in Florida know exactly where it is! You could near'bout fire a shotgun from Key West and hit it!" He laughed. "Maybe, someone should."

A wash of laughter rippled over the group. Some were educated landowners. The others, not so much. If they could load up the backs of pick-up trucks and drive to Cuba, they would take care of any threat—real or imagined— from the southernmost tip of the United States. For a politician, the mix provided the ideal blend of money and biased ignorance. No use directing any comments at Joel Orr. That would be too much like flicking an annoying fly. Best to fire salvos at the incumbent, Brad Silver.

"Where I come from, up here in North Florida, we like one of our own to represent us. Not one of those city-slickers from Miami." He lowered his voice a notch. "Who, I understand, was a thespian back in school."

Russell Nathan paused to assess the effects of the statement: frowns, head shaking, and pursed lips. Using unfamiliar terms scattered in the speech had been his friend Benton's idea, a notion dredged up from the legendary race between Claude Pepper and George Smathers in the '50s. It had worked then, and based upon the crowd's response, it had worked again. Most associated the word *thespian* with something other than acting.

"If you will elect me to the Senate, I will send Silver and his Cuban backers back to Castro!"

The crowd clapped. A few gave rebel yells: *Yee-haw!*

As if choreographed to punctuate the speech, a long line of black vehicles sped down the long driveway, kicking a wake of dust into curling clouds. Flanked by police officers on motorcycles, the middle vehicle—a black stretch limousine—rolled to within a few feet of the flatbed. Men in black poured from the S.U.V.'s and formed a perimeter. From out of nowhere, two helicopters appeared, their propellers beating a staccato chop as they pulled circles above the cleared land.

The crowd waited. Russell Nathan glanced at John R. King and smiled.

Former President Buddy Benton emerged from the back of the limo. Ushered by Secret Service, he made his way to the flatbed, climbed aboard, and gave Russell Nathan a friendly slap on the back.

An aura of fanfare and rumors surrounded the former President, a charismatic career politician whose good looks, luck, and charm had provided his ticket to the White House. He was very clever—a mastermind at both managing and conducting campaigns. Buddy Benton's opponents—conservative Republicans frustrated because they could never pin any of his personal foibles on him—called him the second *Teflon President*. Reagan being the first. Elected Governor and President at young ages, Buddy Benton was still a powerful mover and shaker with pent-up creative juices. If the spotlight could not be directly aimed in his direction, he could at least share it with Russell Nathan.

"Well, look who's here!" Russell called out for the benefit of the audience,as if the former President of the United States had just happened to be in the neighborhood and decided to stop by for a barbequed pork sandwich.

Wild cheers flew. One woman—overcome by the heat, or the spectacle, or both—swooned, and a couple of friends helped her into the shade of one of the tents.

"Good day!" Buddy Benton stepped up to the mic and flashed one of his famous smiles. "I'm so happy I could make it here today. You know, Russ and J.R., I wouldn't miss one of your cookouts for anything. I just wish Helena could be with me."

Office of the Governor—Tallahassee, Florida

Tad Myers, the popular republican Governor of Florida, stood behind the desk in his Capitol building office, having what his most trusted aide referred to as the *daily eleven-o'clock worry session.*

Watching him, thought Kemp Johnson, was not unlike trying to keep track of a hamster with Attention Deficit Hyperactivity Disorder—one who scurried from the exercise wheel to the water bowl, to the wheel, to the food bowl, and back, paying each task demonic attention before making the split-second decision to move to the next order of rodent business. The Governor's aide had developed a coping mechanism: stand back with a clipboard in hand, scribble notes, nod in appropriate places, speak only when addressed, and never allow his attention to wander. He wasn't the top aide for nothing.

Tad Myers prided himself on *compartmentalized worry*, as if life was divided into neat folders. He could pull out one of any number under *State of Florida* and review the contents before moving down the list. Fortunately, Florida offered a rich variety: issues of the massive senior citizen population, off-shore drilling vs. the environmentalists, migrant farm workers, illegal aliens, and an overloaded health care system. During the season from June to November, a special red-lined folder rose from the deck, and the Governor turned a fraction of his worry time to keeping emergency personnel ready in case another Class V hurricane mowed across the Atlantic Ocean or Gulf of Mexico with the Sunshine State in its crosshairs.

"Did you catch CNN last night?" The Governor asked.

"Yes, Sir," Kemp said.

How could he not? Of seven televisions at Kemp Johnson's house, five stayed permanently tuned to a news channel. The other two, to the Weather Channel and Nickelodeon. Only in a high emergency would his wife allow his daughter's television to fall under Kemp's control.

Tad Myers frowned. "Could the run for the Senate seat get any more absurd?"

"No, Sir."

"We have that womanizer Russell Nathan buzzing around North Florida, chatting up every Democrat with a trust fund…" He stabbed the air for emphasis. "…not to mention, Benton and his group driving the fund-raising engine for him."

The Governor paced. Kemp walked a couple of steps behind. Sometimes, his boss mumbled and close proximity was best.

"Nathan was a pretty popular governor. He knew how to wheel and deal. People liked him. That whole good-ole-boy-next-door persona." Tad stopped so abruptly, Kemp almost collided with his backside. "I positively flinch to imagine what his campaign will be! No doubt, he'll pull out his Lawton Chiles manual. Hell, he might even put on a worn pair of shoes and walk all over the state. I will lose my mind if he starts calling himself a *he-coon*! Lawton was a fine man, a good governor, and a gentleman…to have the likes of Russell Nathan mimic his down-home tactics. It makes me ill to think about it."

Kemp raised an eyebrow and tilted his head.

"Kemp, you know I have great plans."

Ah, here we go. The real issue. Kemp nodded. "Yes, Sir."

"I know deep in my soul; I will make an excellent President. And I plan to be in the running, next time around. To that means, this election is pivotal! We simply must not allow a Democrat to fill that seat. The balance in Congress is at stake. My interests are at stake! I must have a unified front behind me when I run. Clear?"

"Yes, Sir."

"Brad Silver isn't perfect, but at least he's our guy. Matter of fact, the man has stepped on my last nerve more times than I care to count." The Governor mumbled so low, Kemp had to lean in to hear. "God forbid, if anything ever happened to Silver. What would I do? I couldn't appoint one of our Congressional members to take his place. I don't trust any of those bozos, especially the two Hispanics from districts fifteen and sixteen—Little Havana and Westchester. If one of those pushy, crazy Cubans got in, I might as well kiss my presidential plans goodbye."

The Governor walked back to the desk. "One thing's for certain. We don't have to worry about Joel Orr. He's so broken down, he will be lucky to even make it to the primary. Nathan—no matter his faults—will leave him eating dust. We just have to make sure Silver stays on top. There is no other option."

"Excuse me, Sir." Kemp checked his watch. "You have an 11:30 lunch meeting at the Governor's Plaza."

Tad Myers gave a quick nod. "Nothing really to worry about. Right, Kemp? Brad is in excellent health, and boy, what a bunch of clowns he has for opponents. I wish I had those guys running against me."

Kemp Johnson wasn't a particularly superstitious type, but as he trailed Florida's Governor from the executive office, he hoped his boss hadn't just pulled on Superman's cape.

CHAPTER EIGHT

Orr Headquarters—Downtown Miami, Florida

Karen pulled her Honda Civic into a narrow parking slot off 36th Street. Not the best neighborhood, mostly industrial and only vaguely remembered by most Miamians for the ancient Jai Alai fronton.

"Do I really want to do this?" she asked herself for about the tenth time since she left the bank for the day.

Sometimes, events conspired to prod her in the direction she had to move. Karen flashed back to the morning hours, when Alisa VanLandingham had accompanied her mother into the lobby for a routine banking transaction. Karen watched as the woman helped her memory-impaired mother write and cash a check—a minor issue for most people, yet a major feat for the ex-professor.

How telling of the daughter's character. Her gentle nature. The way she hung back and allowed her mother to conduct business to the extent of her capability. How Alisa offered respectful assistance without being overbearing or resorting to making her once-brilliant, but still proud, parent appear deficient.

The two ladies had only been in the bank for a short time. The entire transaction had taken five minutes. They asked for Karen by name, and she had gladly set aside the monthly reports to play teller and friend. For the first time in weeks, Karen felt a sense of job satisfaction.

Karen shut off the engine, grabbed her purse, and made darn sure she locked the doors before she entered the building. God willing; the car would be there when she returned. Time was, when she didn't concern herself with the theft of the inexpensive compact vehicle. With fuel prices escalating more each week, an efficient automobile caught more thieves' attention.

A one-by-two-foot sign aside the barred glass door— *Orr for Senate*—gave the only indication of the office's purpose. Karen shielded her ears against the overhead roar of jet engines.

"Miami International. Nice."

Karen pushed inside and stood for a moment to allow her vision to adapt to the low lighting.

"Hi," A young black woman said. Her head bobbed in time with whatever filtered from the iPod clipped to her shirt.

"This is the Orr Campaign Headquarters?"

"Yes."

Karen took a deep breath. Rousing conversationalist, this one wasn't. "I'm Karen. Is Mr. Orr in…or, maybe Mr. Farringdon?"

"Farringdon's in the back room." She waved over her shoulder in the general direction of the room's only dividing wall.

"Thank you."

"No problem."

Since when did the irritating *no problem* replace a simple *you're welcome* in common vernacular? Karen wondered.

She noted three workers in the front cramped room. Two were on cell phones, their heads bent over rosters of potential voters. The third banged away on a relic IBM Selectric Two typewriter. Karen forced herself to keep moving forward. Noticing the ancient piece of office equipment made her long to walk over and touch it, just to see if it was real.

She paused and gave the door a light rap. Two voices responded. Neither, her father's.

"Well, hello!" Don Farringdon stood. "Karen. A nice surprise."

A skinny little man glanced up from a laptop computer. Everything about him screamed *nerd*.

"Ronnie, meet Karen Hernandez. Joel's daughter."

Ronnie Taylor nodded once and returned his attention to the computer screen.

"So, you found us. Here, let me get you a seat." Don dumped a stack of papers onto the floor and slid the molded plastic chair toward her. "How about something to drink? We have..." He opened a scratched fake-wooden-finish compact refrigerator and peered inside. "Coke. Diet Coke, and some gosh-awful kind of jazzed-up energy drink Ronnie swills."

"A Diet Coke will do nicely. Thank you."

Don handed over the cold drink. "Sorry I can't offer you a glass. As you might be able to tell, we don't waste a lot of our campaign donations on creature comforts."

"Unless the creature is a cockroach. We have plenty of those, and they seem to be pretty comfortable," the bean-counter quipped.

Don smirked. "Ignore my friend Ronnie. No people skills. He spends way too much time online."

"Better be glad I do, buddy-boy. The video clip we shot of the Grace Church speech has already had over six hundred hits on YouTube." Ronnie's gaze slid to Karen. "You didn't happen to see it, did you?"

Karen shook her head. "No. I don't spend a lot of time on the Internet. I stare at a screen all day at the bank. It's the last thing I want to do once I get home." She paused. "I did hear most of the speech though."

Don nodded. "I thought I caught sight of you after the service."

"Hard to miss me. I'm sure I blended." She motioned to her light hair and complexion.

Don smiled. "Why didn't you stick around?"

Karen lifted one shoulder and let it fall. "I don't know. I arrived kind of late and had to stand in the foyer. I was curious about what he might have to say. But it was his deal. I didn't want to cause any disruption."

Ronnie sighed. "It could've been the perfect ending to the YouTube piece. You and Joel together, jumpstarting the campaign."

"You'll have to forgive Ronnie, Karen. When he's on a roll, everything becomes a means to an end," Don said. "The Internet—what a wonder. Free marketing at our fingertips." He nodded toward Ronnie. "He's already created a MySpace page with a blog and visits several online political forums."

"Might as well use every tool at our disposal," his long-time political junkie friend said. "Not like we're raking in the cash."

"A grassroots campaign?" Karen asked.

"More like bare bones," Don answered. "The heart and soul of our cutting edge technology—other than Ronnie's wired laptop—consists of three inexpensive Nokia cell phones, which came with virtually no bells and whistles. On a good day, we can operate for a couple of hours before losing a charge. Most important, they came with free long distance and without the installation charges of land lines. What I wouldn't give for even twenty minutes of Senator Silver's cash flow."

"Looks like you have a few worker bees out there." Karen motioned to the front room.

Don Farringdon nodded. "We have the Grace Church to thank for that. Their members have come out in substantial numbers, taking turns to cover the hours. A good number are from the Young Democrats for Change."

"I think some might come from the homeless community that lives beneath the underpass," Ronnie Taylor commented. "They come in, hoping for something free. Most of them don't seem to last long, since there are no perks here."

"Still, the ones who show are pulling out the stops. A real, targeted campaign solicitation right underneath Russell Nathan and Brad Silver's noses." Farringdon grinned.

"Cox—that's Silver's head bulldog—couldn't even find us down here if he had a GPS and a search-and-rescue bloodhound. We are literally saturating our people with calls. Just wait until the *get out the vote* push starts. We may not win, but they will know they've been in the fight."

"Let's rock and roll!" Taylor said.

Karen glanced from Taylor to Farringdon. The two politicos conveyed an electric energy.

"One thing's for certain. You two will blind them with enthusiasm. What about the huge Hispanic contingency? Can you capture any of those votes?"

"Not likely," Ronnie Taylor said without glancing up from his computer. "The Cubans in Miami don't historically vote Democrat. They haven't since Kennedy betrayed them in the Bay of Pigs fiasco in the '60s. Cubans don't forget easily."

Ronnie stared at the monitor. "Damn it, Don! There is no way we can catch Silver, especially with Nathan in the way." He reviewed recent polling numbers on Silver vs. Orr. "Add to that a two-million-dollar war chest that is overflowing with incoming contributions just when we are trying to get five figures into our next report to the Secretary of State."

Don clamped a hand on his friend's shoulder. "Faith, my friend, faith. My people will pull through."

The bean-counter's eyes lit up. "Look at this! Silver took a walk on more than half a dozen votes on the Everglades Bill."

Don Farringdon explained, "If a senator is not present for a vote, but is in town, the political jargon to describe that no-no is that he *took a walk*, and therefore was not present to vote. Missing repeated votes on legislation related to the restoration of the Everglades—especially for a senator from Florida—could potentially be a political kiss of death."

"You kidding? This will work for us," Ronnie Taylor muttered. "Every little chink in his wall..."

"Where do you get all this information?" Karen asked.

"Public record," Don said. "Available to anyone who wants to, or takes the time to, look. We can track votes and voting trends on the national Thomas web site—*Thomas* stands for Thomas Jefferson. We find all kinds of information there: data on Congress, legislation, and disposition of legislation. My buddy here considers it, and the public records of Congress, as his own personal Holy Grail."

Karen nodded. "It looks as if you two know a great deal. I always wondered how someone got into all of this."

The two men exchanged glances.

Don answered, "We're both from this area. I went to Miami Edison, while Ronnie went to rival Miami High. We didn't meet and become friends until Miami Dade Community College. From there, we got wrapped up with the Young Democrats at Florida Atlantic University in Boca Raton. We both naturally gravitated toward the underbelly of the political scene. I like the people end and Ronnie lives for the number crunching and data projections part of the business."

Ronnie Taylor spoke without looking up. "It's like crack cocaine. Once you get into it and feel the rush, you can't get away."

Don smirked. "Like you'd know how crack feels. Your drug of choice is caffeine." Then, to Karen, "The day Ronnie Taylor touches anything stronger than a beer, the world will grind to a stop."

Don flipped his laptop computer to stand-by mode. "You just missed your father. He walked down to pick up some fresh coffee and cinnamon buns."

Her mouth gaped open. "Walked? My Dad?"

The large man nodded. "It's only a block down. Plus, the cinnamon buns are homemade and worth walking halfway to Jacksonville for."

"Sugar fix," Ronnie offered. "Happens sometimes when a person stops imbibing alcohol. The sugar cravings kick in."

Before Karen could respond or ask any questions about her father's drinking patterns of late, the front door opened and shut. Joel Orr hurried to the back office with a bulging white bag of pastries and several tall to-go cups. He stopped in mid-stride when he spotted his daughter.

"Bug?" Joel shoved the bag and coffees onto the desk and grabbed her for a hug. "It's good, really good, to see you."

In contrast to the depleted man she had seen in the hospital, the person standing in front of her emanated energy. The gray skin tone had been replaced with a light pink glow, more the flush of health than sallow, drained flesh.

"You, too, Daddy."

"Glad you stopped in." He whipped an arm through the air. "What do you think? Pretty high-rent, eh?"

Karen offered a thin smile. "Not exactly the same as when you ran for state senator."

Joel shrugged and opened one of the coffees. Karen watched as he emptied five packets of white sugar into the steaming cup.

"We will make up for it, Bug."

Karen nodded. "Looks like you will."

"So, you just decided to stop in and see what your old man was up to?" Joel dug into the paper bag and pulled out the largest cinnamon roll Karen had ever seen. "Glad you did. A little out of the way of your neighborhood."

"Actually, I want to volunteer."

Joel and Don stared. Ronnie stopped tapping keys on the laptop and glanced up.

When no one responded, she added. "I mean…you can use the help, right? I can't come during bank hours, but I can make calls in the evenings or on weekends. Plus, I'm fluent in Spanish."

Joel grinned. Crusty flecks of powdered sugar glaze circled his mouth. "You kidding me? Bug, I…we…would love to have you here. For whatever amount of time you can spare."

Ronnie jumped. "Hey! I have a great idea! We could start *The Candidate's Daughter Speaks*! Your very own blog. Let you go online and post every couple of days. Tell what it's like to be in the midst of your father's campaign. How you feel about the issues and how you see him addressing them. Throw in some cheesy father-daughter pictures. It will be fantastic."

Karen glanced toward Joel. "I figured you'd have me folding flyers or going door-to-door. But, fine. Whatever."

"Good." Ronnie grinned. "I'll set it up. Give you my email addy. You can rough up whatever you want to say and I'll post it. You won't even have to be here to do that."

Joel bit into a second roll. "Why don't you sit down, and we can review our plan of attack? Ronnie here can show you the website he's developing."

Don Farringdon looked on with a growing sense of satisfaction. Anyone in campaign management knew one basic truth: a candidate with strong family support could go far.

As the battle for votes grew and the warriors tired, moments of disheartenment loomed. A boost from the people who knew Joel Orr best—warts and all—could mean the difference between wallowing in defeat or throwing the wild victory punch.

The Silvers' Mansion—Coral Gables, Florida

The intense summer sun bored into Brad's skin. He should reapply sunscreen, or go inside. But the warmth felt so good. Like the deep, penetrating touch of a healer. Rivulets of sweat drained down his bare chest, snaking between thatches of silver-tipped hair to his tanned stomach.

So, so good. To be home for a few hours reprieve. Not to have to watch his every move, monitor the expressions on his features, worry that one smile might be misinterpreted as inappropriate.

He glanced over at Eleana. Beautiful. Long, lean tanned legs. Even at forty-six, a body amazingly devoid of the effects of aging. She rested on a chaise lounge several feet from his, her back arched slightly. A small smile played across her moistened lips. Brad felt the slow burn of arousal.

"Penny for your thoughts."

Eleana frowned, turned her head slightly. "What do you mean by that?"

"It's just an expression, Eleana. For God's sake."

Why was it lately, that each exchange between them seemed loaded?

"Oh." She sat up and gathered the filmy cover-up. "I'm going inside. You want anything?"

Brad reached out and brushed her leg as she walked by. "Matter of fact, I do."

"Brad...I..."

"You know, Eleana. I haven't been home for almost three weeks. We haven't said more than a handful of words since I landed."

"What do you want from me, Brad?"

He sat up. "I'd like my wife back. Is that too much to ask?"

"Why don't you ask your Chief of Staff to take care of you?"

"What the hell is that supposed to mean?"

Eleana kept her voice calm and low. "I hear, Brad. You might think you can get away with anything, so far from Miami. I find out. Do you think I wouldn't?"

"I don't like what you are implying, Eleana. Miss Reynolds and I..."

Eleana huffed. "Gwen. Call her by her first name, Brad. Might as well, since you are fu—"

"Don't. Don't, Eleana." Brad started to rise. "I'm sure if you'll just take a few minutes to listen."

"I have to go shower. I have a committee meeting at..."

"Don't tell me. Vizcaya. For the love of God, Eleana. You might as well just move in there. Can't you miss one lousy meeting? I thought we might take a drive, catch a nice meal somewhere. Take time to talk. Wherever you want."

"I can't just drop my responsibilities because you decide to fly in from Washington, Brad."

"I leave next week for Brazil. I would hope you would spend a little of your time here, at *our* home, with *your* husband."

Behind the dark sunglasses, her expression was impossible to read.

"Maybe tomorrow. I really can't back out at the last minute."

"Fine. Fine." He snatched the towel up and draped it around his neck. "Guess I'll call up Belan. He's home this weekend, too. Maybe we can play a few holes."

"If that is what you want to do." Eleana turned to walk away.

"I can't figure you, Eleana."

She paused and tilted her head in his direction.

"You're all about me winning this election. I'm doing everything in my power to make that happen. This trip will put me in a much better position to help your precious Cuba. Everything I do, every plan I make, is for you. Yet, all I get is your hostility. Am I missing something here? Because I sure would like someone, anyone, to give me a clue."

Eleana took a deep breath and exhaled. "I know you are trying, Brad." She looked away. "I'm sorry. I'm so sorry. I don't know how I feel…"

He stood and brushed past her. "Well, when you do, call my office, because they'll know where to find me."

Washington, D.C.

Mark Cox and Mike Belan stood side-by-side in the Senate Intelligence Committee meeting. Anyone seeing the two without inside knowledge might think them the best of friends. Belan: perfectly natty. Cox: perfectly nappy.

"Looks like someone sent out a mandatory attendance memo," the lobbyist commented. "It's not often I've seen this room as packed."

"There's the reason." Cox tipped his head toward one of the long tables. "The senators just completed a meeting with the Secretary of State behind closed doors. No press present because the Chairman declared—as is his prerogative—that the country's national interest was at stake."

Cox continued in a low voice, "The closed-door meeting was a non-partisan, non-debatable decision by the Chairman, a choice always supported by the ranking member of the committee."

Mike Belan smirked. "So much parliamentary clap-trap. The secrecy. The drama."

Cox glanced at his companion. "Seems to me you'd be used to it by now, Belan. Not like you're a blushing political virgin."

Cox looked across the crowded room to where Senator Silver stood. "All the posturing aside—what matters today is Brad's segment. Gwen prepared some excellent talking points for him to aim at the Secretary of State. No way can the Secretary answer without at least flinching a little. Senator Silver has a good shot at making the nightly news."

"I really don't think of Brad as a *gotcha* kind of guy. Do you?" responded Belan.

"You have to do what you have to do. You know that. And he will. Brad has a shot at prime time. No one really cares what the questions are, much less the Secretary's answers. The only important issue is P.T. Get that prime time."

Belan agreed. Cox knew of what he spoke. So many happenings in the capital were staged for effect. Just fluff. The real pros could see through the smoke screens and palaver.

The Chairman recognized Brad for the preset fifteen-minute segment. He tapped the electronic red-and-green-light timer in front of him to avoid any bipartisan intention or provide one side an advantage. If the Chairman wished, he could use another set of established rules, thus allowing Brad Silver's allotted time to continue.

Brad knew: It paid for a senator to know the rules—to memorize the rules. The Senate provided the battleground, but the rules supplied the senator's weapon. Lacking detailed knowledge, any senator would be foolish to venture into the waters.

Brad had spent several hours the night before reviewing the appropriate motions and procedures. Prime Time glinted like fool's gold in the late summer sun. A senator running for reelection could not afford to be wrong. Cox and Belan knew it. Brad knew it. So did the Chairman.

"The senator from Florida is recognized for fifteen minutes, and the Chair will acknowledge the distinguished senator's upcoming trip to South America representing this Committee."

The timer clicked off minutes of precious time.

"Thank you, Mr. Chairman. Thank you, Mr. Secretary, for joining us today. I recall when we last met, you mentioned to me..."

Senator Silver settled into the prepared questions with the ease of a seasoned statesman. As the volley continued, Brad felt a deep appreciation for his Chief of Staff.

Her questions were perfectly constructed.

Gwen Reynolds: No window dressing. No flash in the pan. Just a solid, beautiful, intelligent woman who knew more about the machinations of government than most of the men and women in the room.

Senator Silver's Office—Washington, D.C.

"So..." Gwen Reynolds lifted one eyebrow. "You're telling me you went all the way to Miami to spend one last weekend with your beautiful wife before leaving today for your trip, and you ended up with Mike Belan?"

Brad smiled. "When you put it like that..." He sat down and sipped from a tall glass of cold orange juice. Might as well support the state he represented.

Gwen held up her hands like a balance scale. "Mike Belan in plaid golf shorts. Eleana Silver in a thong bikini. Hmm...I can see where you might have been torn."

He laughed. The tension in his chest eased. "I had good intentions."

"Which have paved several thousand miles along the road to Hell, if you believe the saying."

"I don't know, Gwen." He sighed. "Eleana and I...We used to fill the time talking about everything and nothing. Now every word is a potential mine field. And I don't even have a good enough handle on the problem to figure a solution."

"Whatever you do, don't mention anything to Cox. You know what he'll say."

"A divorce at this juncture wouldn't be good for your campaign, Senator." Brad mimicked the surly P.R. guy.

The word *divorce* hung in the air between them. Despite her attempts to stay neutral, to provide a steady source of support for her boss, Gwen Reynolds' spirit trilled at the thought of Brad Silver free of marital encumbrance.

Gwen sat down opposite her boss. "Has it really gotten that bad?"

"Beats me. You might ask her friends at Vizcaya. They probably know more about my wife's inner workings than I do."

"Okay. You played golf with Belan. Then...?"

"God, you're nosey." He grinned. "We all went out to dinner. Had a few drinks. When I came home, Eleana was still out. I slept in the study, got up the next morning, and came back to Washington."

"You didn't even say goodbye to her?"

"I tried. She mumbled something about having one of her famous marathon migraines. I grabbed a muffin on the way to the airport."

Gwen stared at him with no comment.

"Actually, it wasn't wasted time. Belan called up a couple of his Big Daddy Sugar cronies. By the time we reached the eighth green, he had secured two sizable campaign contributions."

"For a price, no doubt—to be named at some point in the future. You know those guys always come with empty dance cards and loaded agendas."

"I haven't been at this for a mere month, Gwen. I know the stakes."

She nodded. "Back to your wife. What do you plan to do?"

"I thought some kind of mini-vacation might be in order. Something to get me away from here, and Eleana away from Miami. Give us a chance to reconnect, if we can. When I return, it will only get busier. Not so much until after the primaries, but when I have to fend off Russell Nathan and his compatriots. You know how much I'll be on the road, then."

Gwen's spirit sank. So like Brad Silver to play peacemaker. Part of her wanted to scream and gather him in her arms. Tell him how little Eleana Silver merited his love and attention. She screwed up her professional ethics and stuffed her emotions.

"What did you have in mind? Something tropical? British Virgin Islands? Aruba?"

He shook his head. "Too much like south Florida. I was thinking something nearer to this area. I could fly Eleana up on some pretense and sweep her away for a spa retreat. She loves that crap."

"How about Cape Cod area? Nantucket? Or somewhere rural in upstate New York?"

"Any would be fine. Something near water. And quiet. Secluded. No press."

"That would be an oasis on Mars." Gwen jotted on a notepad. "I'll do some research while you're away. Give you a short list when you return from Brazil."

"That would be great. Call it a trade-off. Your time and feminine expertise in return for...?"

"I need to go check on my father. A couple of days would be nice—of course, not during peak time. I could go and be back before you miss me."

"Is he unwell?"

Gwen's features softened. "I don't know. He's so reserved when it comes to admitting any weakness. Comes from being a single parent, I suppose." Her gaze fell to the notepad in her hands. "More, I sense something is bothering him. I need to see for myself."

"We have a deal, then. You find me a wonderful spot Eleana will love. Then, you have my blessing to take off to take care of your family." The senator glanced around the spacious office. "It's easy to think this place is the entire world."

"Public servants have no life," Gwen commented.

"High time we do," Brad said. "I haven't even talked to my own children face to face since Christmas."

"How are Ryan and Bailey?"

He smiled. "Busy living their lives. Ryan is moving up the food chain in the insurance business. Smart boy. And, Bailey has plans to open a series of boutiques. She always has had a keen eye for fashion and trends. Everything she touches seems to blossom. Did I tell you she is working with a designer on a line of clothing for elderly women?"

Gwen shook her head.

"Bailey spends a lot of time with her volunteer work. Takes her golden retrievers for some kind of special visits to area assisted living facilities and nursing homes in Seattle. She was all juiced up last time we spoke about how older citizens have special needs—arthritis making their fingers useless with buttons and clasps, that sort of thing. Anyway, she's addressing that issue."

"You have two great kids, Brad. I know you're so proud of them—though, at twenty-six and twenty-one, I suppose they're not really kids anymore. Altruistic, just like their father."

"Probably much better people than I ever shall ever aspire to be. Besides, I can't take much credit for how they turned out. They have their mother to thank for that. I didn't spend a lot of time with them when they were growing up.

Not nearly enough time." Brad's expression grew wistful for a moment. "Now, because I hold you in highest regard, I'm giving you fair warning. Belan and Cox are stopping by in a few minutes before I leave for the airport. If you high-tail it out of here, you might miss both of them."

Gwen Reynolds laughed and stood. "I really owe you now, Senator."

The mirth drained from her features. "Be careful down there, Brad."

"I'll be fine, and back before you know it. You better enjoy the time. It will be crazy when I return."

"I worry."

Brad stood. "I take that as high praise, that you are concerned." He reached over and brushed her arm. "Watch over things for me, Gwen. I depend on your integrity."

"Always."

She turned to leave before he could notice the tears forming in her eyes.

Brad Silver heard Mike Belan even before he pushed through the inner office door. Belan anywhere around a pretty woman—and especially more than one—reminded Brad of a weasel in a hen house. No matter how quickly he passed by, there always seemed to be an inordinate amount of unsettled cackling on the part of the ruffled females.

"Buddy boy!" Belan called out. "Ready for the big trip?"

Brad watched Mike help himself to a scotch and sprawl on one of the chairs.

"Ready as I'll ever be. I have to leave in a few minutes."

Cox tapped twice before walking in. "Afternoon, gentlemen." He headed over to a side table and poured a tall cup of coffee. "Might as well drug up. I have a long night ahead of me."

"Hot date, Marky, my boy?" Belan asked.

The muscles at Cox's temples pulsed as he clenched his teeth. At the rate he was going, he'd have nothing left except stubs by the time the election was over, especially since it involved frequent cameos with Mike Belan.

"Just with top supporters with deep pockets. I'm happily married."

Belan shrugged. "Too bad. You should get out more. You're starting to look a little pale. You need something to get the old juices pouring."

Cox walked over to where Belan sat. "Speaking of raging juices, I think you and I need to have a little talk."

"Really, fella. You're pretty smart-looking in your outdated, wrinkled suit and all, but you're not my type."

Brad bit his lower lip to avoid laughing. The Odd Couple was at it again.

Cox said, "With all seriousness, Belan. I think you should consider getting off the reservation for awhile."

"What the hell you mean by that?" the lobbyist asked.

"Right now, everything we do is closely scrutinized. We have been successful in getting the buzz about Gwen and Brad stopped. The lifespan of any rumor around here is a nanosecond, before the next one takes over." Cox glanced at Brad, then back to Belan. "You might be seen as a bit too chummy with our candidate and his staff, especially with your ties to United Sugar."

Mike Belan's face colored. "I think you need to take a moment to consider this, Mr. Cox. United Sugar money put Brad in this office to start with, and they are pouring in support as we speak."

Belan shot a look at Brad. "Not to mention, I got you your first break with them. If it wasn't for Sugar and me, you'd probably still be some low-life public defender living in a duplex and driving a beat-up sedan. You sure as hell wouldn't be a pretty boy in Washington."

Cox took an even breath and purposely toned down his voice. "Look, Belan. We all know how much you have meant to the senator. We're all on the same team here. I have to keep my nose clean, too. We all do. You know how it is, Belan. The watchers circle like vultures over road kill, just waiting for one sign of weakness and humanity." He glanced at Brad Silver. "Brad needs us more than ever, now."

Belan huffed. "Suppose I'll lie low for awhile, at least until you start campaigning in Florida. Then, you can count on me to be smack dab in the middle of the action. You'll not deny me that. You know I can raise money."

Brad walked over and rested a hand on Belan's shoulder. "When you do stop in, you'll stop mongering my staff?"

Mike rolled his eyes. "People have lost their sense of humor. I swear. Yeah, I'll tone it down."

Brad grabbed his briefcase and a small rolling leather duffle. "Any last words of wisdom, gentlemen?"

"Just remember your objectives, Senator. The Chair of the Senate Intelligence Committee, then..." Cox pointed to the leather chair behind Brad's desk. "...that one."

Mike Belan stood and clapped his fraternity brother on the back. "Pretty women down there in Brazil...oh, hell...just make it a point to come back."

As Belan walked from the senator's office a few minutes later, his BlackBerry trilled with the salsa tune. He ducked into the men's room. Fortunately, empty.

"You goddamn moronic Cuban. I've told you never to call me. I call *you*."

The bathroom door opened and a young male page entered.

"Yes, and please remember to pick up my dry cleaning this afternoon," Belan blurted into the cell phone. "Got to go. Call you later."

Mike Belan washed and dried his hands and left the restroom.

Airstrip in Brazil

Brad Silver assembled his briefing papers in the back seat of a battered Jeep. Since leaving the main airport in São Paulo, the trip had smacked of a jungle-tour adventure. A private airstrip, deep in the Brazilian jungle, had taken an hour to reach over a barely passable dirt road. So much for the concept of easy connecting flights leaving from one location. The spot was as close to middle-of-nowhere Brad had ever been.

The government screened private contract air services, particularly for flights by U.S. dignitaries. Undoubtedly the pilot had passed a series of security clearances. He would have checked the plane thoroughly.

"What kind of a plane do we have here?" Brad asked.

Fortunately, his pilot—a native Brazilian—spoke perfect, if accented, English. "Senator Silver, it is a King Air. One of their six-seaters. I have flown them all: navy jets, Hueys, commercial liners. But this little turbo-prop is my favorite." He patted the metal skin of the small aircraft as if it was a loyal pet.

Silver made no move to board. "I normally like to fly on larger governmental planes when I'm on official business."

"This type of plane is particularly good in Brazilian jungle terrain, Sir. And, I have checked her over myself."

The maintenance man had inspected the craft carefully, too. Though he didn't know him, the pilot felt sure he would have picked up any problems his visual inspection failed to note.

"If air sickness is a problem, you have nothing to worry about. You won't feel a thing. Her ride is smooth as a mother's milk." The pilot studied the skies. "Storms are coming in, but we should be well ahead of any problems."

Brad nodded. "That makes me feel better. I guess it does have the advantage of getting us there and back quickly."

The pilot stored the senator's bag behind one of the seats. "This type of plane is much better for the short landing strips we are going to encounter. Really, Senator. I would stake my life on your safety in this King Air."

Good thing the man wasn't a politician. Anytime Brad heard that particular promise, he knew big lies waited beneath the surface.

Senator Brad Silver stepped aboard, sat down, crossed himself, and fastened the clasp on the safety belt.

At six p.m., mists hung in the dense vegetation. The torrential rains and gusty winds had calmed, leaving the jungle washed clean.

The two young boys who had heard the great noise in the afternoon cut their way through the vines and thick foliage. From their earlier vantage point, the plume of smoke indicated the possible source. With the sunrise, the telltale signal was weak, but still a sufficient beacon.

They stopped when they spotted the wreckage.

"Do you think anyone is alive?" one asked.

They moved cautiously forward. No fire. One boy peeked into a shattered window. Two men. Strapped in. A pilot and another man.

"Dead?"

The older of the two used the tip of his machete to prod both of the occupants.

CHAPTER NINE

Miami, Florida

Sid Dillard idled by the curb across from Senator Silvers' gated mansion, inconspicuous in a late-model, dark, 4-door Crown Victoria sedan. In his normal ride—a beat-up Dodge van, one he also lived in—he would stick out in the high-end neighborhood. Not so in the Crown Vic, the vehicle of choice for the Feds. Anyone passing by might notice, but brush it off. Surveillance in Miami was as common as crime. Anyone watching would assume someone residing on the street was either tied in with organized crime or tagged by Homeland Security.

Sid played with the dials on the pawn-shop digital camera he had purchased, complete with a telephoto lens and tripod: all he needed as a budding paparazzi. With no money—thanks to the car rental fee—Sid wasn't in luck for spying on local celebrities. He had no AP card, no contacts, and no idea of what he was doing, exactly. Everyone of any substantive notoriety in Miami had been staked out. Hives of videographers swarmed their every move. Sid looked around for the bottom tier—the relatives of fame—and spotted Eleana Silver. In an election year, a few good flicks of her doing something off-color—showing up with her hair askew or slumming in the wrong side of town—might yield a little extra cash. Enough for a steak. Enough to put gas in the van. Enough, even, to rent a cheap hotel room for the night. Since Sid's landlord had kicked him to the curb, clean bathrooms—much less a good shower—were hard to find.

Sid sighed and ate the last of a bag of Jalapeno pork rind chips. A swig from a bottle of warm root beer did little to ease the burn. He slopped the remaining crumbs from the bag and dusted his hands on his shorts. The Silvers' automatic iron gate swung open. Probably just Eleana leaving for another of her endless social affairs, or shopping. All the woman seemed to do was spend money and attend events.

A black and chrome Harley with two riders rolled onto the street. Probably the help leaving for the day. Both wore dark wind suits. In the waning late-day heat, the outfits had to be uncomfortable. Something about the way the rider on the back moved caused Sid to sit up and take closer note. The long legs. The tilt of the head. Even with the dark coverage, sun glasses, and helmet, Sid recognized Eleana Silver.

"Who knew little Mrs. Queen Bee would ride a Hog?" Sid said aloud.

He waited until the Harley passed by to start the engine and pull a U-turn. Sid followed at a safe distance, careful not to seem too anxious. The whole thing had to be a waste of gas and time. His eyes were playing tricks. No way was Eleana Silver a motorcycle mama. Even if she did ride, who was the driver? One of her high-class Vizcaya buddies?

Sid laughed. "Sure as shit. They don't even drive their own cars, most of them. Much less, hop on a Harley. Or, God forbid, risk helmet hair."

He was bored. Nothing better to do. He followed.

"This is kind of a kick," he commented. "No wonder people go into private investigation. I could do this for a living."

The Harley took a sharp turn. Sid cursed, accelerated, turned. He caught sight of the motorcycle in the distance before it made yet another turn. For the next half hour, the Harley and the Crown Vic played a strange game of cat and mouse, steadily moving toward the coastline bordering Biscayne Bay.

"Got to be her. This chick has some serious attachment to the Bay." Sid flipped a used toothpick from his breast pocket and gnawed on the flayed end. Chewing the wooden pick and saying *chick* made the whole thing seem so Philip Marlow *noir*.

Sid recognized the area as soon as the Harley made the last slow turn. Virginia Key Beach. Once a segregated beach, the area had morphed in the time since integration. Sid recalled a recent incarnation as a spot favored by gay couples.

A perfect place for a bit of privacy. Hardly anyone walked its shore in the early evening. Those who did were either brave or stupid. Definitely, not a hot tourist destination complete with a Tiki bar and Salsa band. Sid pulled the Crown Vic onto the dried vegetation of a vacant lot and watched from a distance.

The Harley parked. The rider in the rear dismounted. The helmet came off. A long mane of raven hair shook free. She shucked the jacket. The driver leaned the bike over on the stand and flipped his leg across the seat. Sid strained to see the identity of both in the gloaming light.

"Sid, you shit for brains. Use the telephoto!"

He pulled the camera from its case and snapped the long-distance lens into place. With the benefit of magnification, the identity of the smaller rider was unmistakable. And, God, was she hot in the tight black pants and white camisole top.

"Son of a bitch! It *is* her! Whoa baby!"

Sid snapped several photos of Eleana and shifted slightly to focus on the driver, a tall Hispanic male in his late forties to early fifties with ripped muscles and shoulder-length hair pulled back into a ponytail. Sid frowned. Who was the guy? He looked familiar. The realization hit him hard. The limo driver! The guy who shuffled Eleana to social functions, lunch dates, tennis, appointments, and shopping.

A ripple of excitement wrapped around his heart and squeezed.

The man reached into one of two saddlebags and pulled out some kind of rolled-up cloth, a small bag, and what appeared to be a bottle. The couple laughed and walked together toward the narrow beach.

As soon as the two disappeared from view, Sid slid from the Crown Vic and made his way to the shore, careful to keep a line of vegetation between him and the spot where the couple had vanished. His heart beat like a wild thing on good drugs.

Sid stopped and dropped to a crouch. The couple stood at the edge of the water, hand in hand. Using the blazing scarlet of the fading sun as a backdrop, he snapped a series of pictures. Eleana turned to the man. They embraced. They kissed.

"I can't believe this," Sid whispered.

When they finally turned away from the water, Sid flattened his body to the sand. If they spotted him now, he'd be dead meat. The man was three times his size and built. No sound: a good sign. Sid inched up to a crouch again. The couple was seated on the blanket. A wine bottle stood open beside two stemmed glasses. Sid took a few more frames. Good thing he had invested in a high-bit digital memory card.

As the dim purples of early evening pushed aside the fading sun's orange tints, Sid switched the camera to the night time setting and hoped he would have enough ambient light without using a flash.

He strained to see through the lens. The action had moved from romantic to passionate. Soon, Sid noted an unmistakable thrusting rhythm.

Since Eleana and her paramour were heavily engaged, and the light had disappeared from the evening sky, Sid took the opportunity to scurry back to the car. No use tempting fate any more than he already had.

Plenty of people would no doubt pay huge money to have the pictures, given that they were clear enough for identity. Surely, the senator's people would be interested.

But wait! How about that other guy—Governor somebody? Sid's skin prickled. The possibilities were limitless. He could move into a real apartment. Buy a car that didn't belch smoke and break down once a week. He could eat steak and potatoes every night.

"This is going to change my life forever!"

Washington, D.C.

At just past three a.m., the phone rang in the home of Senate Minority Leader Mickey Long. After six rings, he managed to grope in the darkness to locate the cordless headset.

"Ah...hello?"

"Mr. Leader, this is the President."

Senator Long sat upright and snapped on the bedside light. His wife shifted and moaned. "Mr. President, Sir?"

"I'm so sorry to call you at such an early hour. Mickey, I have terrible news. My people tell me that the plane Brad Silver was on down in Brazil has crashed. And, oh Mickey...it's confirmed. I am so sorry. Brad is dead."

Mickey Long ran a hand through his thinning hair. The times he, Brad, and Lawrence Collins—the current President of the United States—had served together in the Senate flashed through his sleep-dulled mind. The three had always hung together in the Republican Caucus. The three musketeers—*one for all and all for the one party*, they had often quipped. Long wasn't sure if he was in the midst of a bad dream, or if he had heard the President correctly.

"Mr. President, did you say *dead?* Oh, my God. Not Brad! Couldn't be. He had such a long life ahead..."

The senator's wife opened her eyes. "Honey...what?"

He held up one hand and shook his head.

"I know, Mickey. I am just as stunned. I don't have all the particulars yet. Apparently, there was no chance of any survivors. I have our people on the way down to aid the Brazilian authorities in the investigation."

Mickey waited for the President—his longtime friend—to continue.

"You recall; he was down there on that high profile fact-finding mission to seal his chairmanship."

"I know, Larry. I spoke with him briefly before he left. He was grateful that you included his trip in your national radio address last week. I've heard a number of folks mention your support of Brad. You are...you *were*..." He swallowed around the lump in his throat. "...a good friend to him."

Senator Long waited for a few seconds before he broke the silence. "Does Eleana know?"

"No. We haven't been able to reach her. You know she and Brad aren't together much, these days."

Mickey Long blew out a long breath. "I know. But this will devastate her. And all of his family. His kids...someone should..."

"I will speak to them personally, soon."

Senator Long's mind raced ahead. "Larry—Mr. President—I'm not thinking too straight right now, but have you given any thought as to who we will ask Myers to appoint? At this juncture, it's too late for another Republican candidate to declare a bid to run."

He heard the President sigh.

"No, of course not, Mickey. But I have to. The government must go forward, regardless... We really need to think this one through. Benton is really pouring on the help for Nathan, and we absolutely have no room for error now. Brad had this seat solidly locked in our red column."

"This changes everything. Unless we can sit down and map this out with Tad Myers—and, as you know, he probably has future plans of his own." Senator Long took a deep breath. His eyes burned with the threat of tears. "Listen to me, will you? Brad is dead, and all I can talk about is who to put in his place. For the love of God. I feel sick."

"Senator, we're all in this thing. What you say is between us," the President said. "The good Lord gives and the good Lord takes away. Let's both say a prayer or two tonight, and get to work tomorrow."

"I'll pick up the details from here first thing in the morning. I'll call Mark Cox. He can brief Brad's staff bright and early. And, oh, Mr. President, I will take care of getting the Miami-Dade County Sheriff out to the Silver residence to tell Mrs. Silver in person. I don't want her to hear it on the news."

"Thanks, Mickey. I'd wish you a good night, but I think this one's pretty much shot for both of us."

Mark Cox assembled Brad Silver's staff in the meeting room. Gwen Reynolds was the last to appear. She started to ask a question, then noted the stricken expression on the P.R. man's face, and took a seat.

"God, I don't know how to say this..." Mark Cox's voice cracked. He cleared his throat.

Gwen and the two executive assistants exchanged puzzled glances. The rest of the staff: quiet. No rustling papers. No murmured talk.

"We have received confirmation that Senator Silver's plane crashed in the Brazilian jungle yesterday, sometime in the late afternoon."

"Mark? Is he...is Brad?" Gwen leaned forward.

Mark Cox's reply was barely audible. "There were no survivors."

Gwen felt the room fall away.

Destin Beach, Florida

Russell Nathan dreamed of a tropical beach. Nubian women, half-naked, served drinks with little paper umbrellas. Music from a nearby marimba band filtered through the balmy sea breeze. A man in white shirt and shorts fanned him with a palm frond. The man's face looked familiar. Ah...Brad Silver. So fitting for him to be in a position of servitude. The only thing interrupting the perfection: a jarring buzzing beside his ear.

He opened one eye long enough to check the bedside clock. Five o'clock in the freakin' morning. Who would be calling at such an ungodly hour? Russell patted the sheets beside him. Empty. His muddled brain reminded him; your wife is due home today from some godforsaken third-world country. The babes had to clear out in the wee hours.

He picked up the headset. "This better be good."

"Russ?"

"Buddy? What the hell do you mean calling me at this time of day? For that matter, what are you doing awake?"

"I'm afraid I have some rather sad news, Russ. Brad Silver is dead."

Russell Nathan came fully awake. "If this is one of your sick jokes, Benton..."

"Now, Russ. You know me better than that. I wouldn't joke about something like this."

"Someone plug him? What, did he finally piss off the Cubans enough? Or maybe the Mafia? Or maybe the NRA found a *no* vote somewhere on him?"

"His plane went down somewhere in the mountains near São Paulo, Brazil. Just him and one pilot. Neither survived. Luckily, the staffers with him had taken an earlier flight."

Russell's mouth went dry. "Son of a bitch."

"I think it's appropriate that we send the proper condolences to his family...schedule a press release to say how the country has lost a great statesman."

"Of course. I'll make it sound like I lost my best friend."

"Between you and me, Russ. You know what this means, don't you?"

"It's our turn, Mr. President. And nobody is going to stand in our way now."

Miami, Florida

Farringdon slowed down and searched the parking lot of the Ironclad Alibi Bar.

"Bingo."

He parked and went inside. In a dark corner, he spotted Joel Orr. To his surprise, a coffee cup sat in front of him.

"Thought I might find you here, Joel." Farringdon pulled up a chair and waved toward Brenda Gayle. "One for me, please Ma'am."

The barkeep ambled over with a clean mug and a coffee carafe. "Anything for a man with manners enough to call me Ma'am." She poured and sat two creamers down. "Let me know when you two need refills. Today, it's on the house."

"Has she gotten less surly, or is it just my imagination?" Don asked after she walked back to the bar.

Joel offered a thin smile. "Brenda Gayle decides when and *if* she likes a person. I guess you're in."

Don poured both creams into the mug and stirred. Unlike Orr, he didn't require a pound of sweetener. A good amount of the time, he drank his coffee black.

Joel's gaze roamed around the room. Other than a handful of the regulars, the place wasn't hopping at two in the afternoon.

"I'm not drinking, if that's what you came to find out."

"I didn't assume you were, Joel."

Orr pushed back in his chair. "This place has been like a second home for me for three years. Granted, most times I stumbled out of here. But still, something about it...I just feel life lifting off my shoulders when I walk in."

Farringdon regarded the darkened room. "It does have a certain working-man's ambience."

Joel motioned to the television suspended over one end of the bar. "It's all over the news, about Silver."

Don nodded. "It's very sad."

"I know I slammed the man on a regular basis, but I still admired him on some level. He stood up for what he believed in…though, I think the special interest groups pulled the strings some of the time. Washington has seen much, much worse."

"I think we should offer our condolences to his family."

"I've already ordered flowers for the funeral," Joel said. "From what I understand, his wife is not going to take the President up on the offer of the forty-eight-hour repose in the rotunda of the Capitol."

"Eleana has never had a love for Washington. It doesn't surprise me." Don sipped his coffee, strong and rich. "You going to be okay, Joel?"

Orr nodded. "I just don't know, Don. What's it all for? Brad Silver spent his life in politics, and to what end?"

"To make some little bit of difference?"

"Maybe." Joel sighed. "I wonder what will happen now."

"It changes things. No doubt. This will give Russell Nathan a huge advantage."

"I'm sure the Republicans won't allow him—or us—to run unopposed in November."

Farringdon shook his head. "That call will be up to Governor Myers. No matter who he appoints for interim, or who he plugs into Brad's slot for November, he can't possibly stand up to Russell Nathan and the backing of Benton's machine."

Joel nodded.

"This isn't over, Joel. We just have to pull out every stop. We absolutely must win in September. This means we could really be in play, if we work hard."

Joel Orr motioned for Brenda Gayle to refill his cup. "I surely picked a bad time to give up drinking."

Office of the Governor—Tallahassee, Florida

Aide Kemp Johnson had never seen the Governor in such a state: ADHD hamster-mode times three. The morning worry session had stretched well past lunch into the early afternoon. From all indications, his boss wouldn't stop bouncing off the walls until dark. If then.

"I have big decisions to make, Kemp. Big decisions. It's all on my shoulders. I've got President Collins breathing down my neck, and every notable Republican this side of the moon has called this morning."

"Yes, Sir."

"Have you found out about the funeral plans yet? Mrs. Myers and I will have to attend."

"No, Sir. But I will. I have heard a few rumors. The service will probably be held at the Silvers' church. Beyond that…"

"See to the details, Kemp. I have too much on my plate right now. Those damned south Florida Cuban congressmen are sniffing around, sure I will pick one of their own to run in Brad's slot. Jesus, what a mess."

Thinking back to the service, Gwen marveled at how the men could offer the heart-felt eulogies. Had she been asked to speak, her voice would have betrayed her. Every time she spoke Brad's name aloud, the words caught in her throat. As a rule, she was one to hold strong emotions deep inside: tight, controlled. Brad had always touched a deep part of her soul. She had cried so much, she felt numb.

Everywhere, the press swarmed like annoying biting flies. Gwen and the others dodged microphones at every turn. No comment. No comment. No comment. The reporters all speculated—between sappy stories from everyone from the senator's old college soccer teammates to his former golf caddies—about what would happen next. Who would take his place? What would the Republicans do about the upcoming election? Not that she could blame them; they were doing their jobs. Couldn't they wait at least a few days to allow for a smattering of sadness?

Mike Belan stepped up beside her. "Pretty morning."

"Yes. It is."

"Our buddy Cox is a little green around the gills. You know he gets motion sickness. Good thing the seas are calm and they're doing this in the early morning before the wind and surf pick up."

For three people who had shared an at-best lukewarm fellowship with Brad Silver as the glue, they had migrated to each other since news of his death.

"He would've loved this." She looked out across the calm bay. The first streaks of sunrise reflected in gentle pink across the glassine surface. The air, clean and scrubbed by the retreating storm.

Mike's gaze followed hers. "I keep remembering all the times we came out here. Some of the boats back in college were barely seaworthy. This yacht would make four of them, easy. It's amazing we survived."

A wash of agony spread across Belan's features. Gwen reached over and rested one arm across his shoulders. "But you did. You were his best friend, Mike. No one can ever take that from you."

Belan sniffed. "What'll we do now? You, me…Cox?"

"I don't know, Mike. Carry on. There are a lot of loose ends in Washington. Who knows what the next few weeks will bring?"

"Have you talked with Eleana at all?" Mike asked.

"Other than to offer my condolences? Not really. Oh, she spoke to me, once. Briefly. Just to say she will be happy for one thing out of all of this—never to see me again."

"That's harsh."

"Not really. She thinks I was sleeping with her husband."

"Were you?"

Gwen stared across the water for a moment before facing Mike Belan. "That is really none of your business." She willed herself not to cry. "Does it matter now?"

Mike allowed the question to hang. He looked across the water to the lead yacht, the *Sugar Daddy*. "Eleana's uncle. What do you think of him?"

"Just another wealthy, powerful man. Abrupt. Rude. Accustomed to everyone around him scrambling when he barks. You know him better than I do, I assume. He *is* United Sugar. Why ask me?"

"Just curious." *Because he's just another person riding my ass at the moment*, he wanted to add. Gwen seemed the type to honor confidences. Mike stopped short.

"We've met before. One occasion when he visited the Capitol. Actually, it makes me feel sorry for Eleana. If he was her father figure, there's no small wonder she turned out so self-involved." Gwen shook her head. "Listen to me. I shouldn't be talking about the woman like that. She just lost her husband."

A few moments passed. Mike Belan pointed to the second boat's name, written in script across a throw-ring buoy suspended from a rope attached to the railing. "You notice the name of this boat Eleana's Vizcaya friends so graciously lent us for the occasion?"

Gwen glanced from the frothy wake of the *Sugar Daddy* to the buoy and read aloud, *"The Red-headed Stepchild."*

"Brad would've seen the irony in that, don't you think?"

As soon as Gwen stepped onto the dock, she turned on her cell phone. The voicemail indicator trilled.

"Hey, Gwen!" Mike called behind her. "Cox and I are going to go find some breakfast. See if we can get the old boy's stomach calmed down. Where're you off to in such a hurry?"

"My dad. Something's up with my dad. I had a message from Miami General." She headed for the rental car. "Can you two catch a ride back to the hotel?"

"Sure. No problem," he called back. "Hey, ring my cell later when you can. Let me know, will you?"

The Silvers' Mansion—Coral Gables, Florida

The black stretch limousine pulled to the curb just shy of the Silver residence. Tad Myers spoke to the driver. "Let's hold here, please."

Mark Cox shifted in his seat. The soft scrambled eggs and wheat toast he had barely managed to get down after the ceremonial boat outing rolled in his stomach.

"What did Eleana say, exactly, when you approached her?" Governor Tad Myers asked.

"She was angry to start with, Governor. Understandably so, I might add. I don't think this is really the time..."

Tad Myers brushed the P.R. man's opinion aside. "President Collins spoke with me personally about this matter, Mr. Cox. Time is essential."

"With all due respect, Sir. Why Mrs. Silver? The poor woman has just lost her husband. Not to mention, she's never been overly fond of either Washington or politics. I can count on one hand the number of times she's actually been up there. How can she be expected to overcome Russell Nathan and the Benton juggernaut?"

The Governor turned on his hundred-watt smile. "I have faith in you, Mr. Cox. If anyone can get Eleana Silver elected, it is you."

"I appreciate your confidence in my abilities, Governor Myers. I do. The fact still stands. Eleana told me unequivocally no. How did she put it?" Cox paused. "Oh, yes... *I can't imagine why I would want the hassle of being one of the two senators for the State of Florida. I'd have to actually leave Miami. Why would I do that, Mr. Cox?*"

Tad straightened his tie. "She might sing a different tune when the Governor of the Great State of Florida appeals to her civic nature."

The Governor smiled. "Besides, Eleana Silver won't have to be in the capital for long. A few weeks as appointed interim in her husband's spot until the election. Then, as soon as she *is* elected, she will resign. At which time, I will appoint an experienced politico we can both control. My plans, Mr. Cox—and I take you into utmost confidence with this—are to use her to secure the seat to solidify my base in Florida. I plan to make a run for President. You are welcome to be at my side if the idea suits you."

Tad Myers took Cox's silence for agreement. "We capitalize on her husband's tragic, unexpected death, the lack of public knowledge of Eleana, play on their focus on her beauty and poise—not to mention name recognition because of her husband. I've seen you work. You could get Attila the Hun elected. With our help, Eleana can, and will, win. Then, give me a little more time, and I will provide you with someone you can really get behind—all the way to the White House." He pointed to himself.

Cox took a deep breath. Any minute, and his stomach would mutiny. "Aren't you concerned that word will leak out that Eleana's campaign is just a Trojan Horse?"

"Now, Mr. Cox—Mark, I may call you Mark?—the only ones who know that small detail are sitting right here in this car. Would it serve either of us to let that out?"

Mark Cox considered. "Do you want me to go in with you, Sir?"

"More the merrier."

Tad Myers spoke to the driver and the limo pulled from the curb, stopped long enough to gain security clearance through the Silvers' gate, then parked in the wide circular drive at the mansion's front entrance.

CHAPTER ELEVEN

Miami General Hospital—Miami, Florida

Gwen Reynolds chewed a piece of baked chicken that refused to yield to mastication. She spit it discretely into a napkin.

"Bad?" Mike Belan asked.

"What was your first clue?"

Though she disliked the man on a visceral level, Gwen felt grateful for his company.

"Try to eat a little of the mashed potatoes. It's hard to screw them up, even for a hospital kitchen." He took a sip of coffee and winced. "I'd steer clear of this sludge. It's lethal."

She pushed the divided plastic tray aside. "I really should get back upstairs."

Mike held up a hand. "He's having a scan. All you'll do is wait in an empty room for God knows how long. You might as well take a break and enjoy my golden company."

What? Was Mike Belan her new best friend? The fact he had shown up at Miami General still amazed her.

"Where did you leave Mr. Cox?" She asked.

Mike shrugged. "He got some mysterious phone call and told me he'd see me later, back at the hotel. Who knows? I got one of Eleana's people to bring me here. I can catch a cab back to the hotel later."

"Why a hotel? You live down here."

"A good hour's drive with traffic. I wanted to be close-by during the ceremonies."

"I see."

"What about your father? Do they know anything yet?"

"The doctor's pretty sure he's had a stroke. His speech was slurred when he came in, and one side of his face was sagging. I'm just glad his lady friend got him here quickly."

Belan smiled. "Lady friend...haven't heard that term in years."

"That's what he calls Julia. They've been keeping company for the past couple of years, yet he won't admit to me they're a couple. He's pretty old-fashioned about things."

"Stroke. Isn't that some kind of blood pressure thing?"

Gwen sighed. "In his case, who knows? He has diabetes, high blood pressure, and some heart issues. Of course, he doesn't tell me everything."

"Still his little girl."

Gwen felt a fresh wash of tears form at the corners of her eyes. "Here I go again. I can't seem to stop crying. This is *so* not me."

He slipped a white handkerchief from his coat pocket and handed it over. The gesture, so chivalrous. Gwen cried harder.

"It's okay, Gwen. God, we've all been through the ringer the past few days."

She took a shaky breath. "My Auntie Shirley—that's my father's late older sister—used to say, *bad comes at you fast. Good takes its sweet time.*"

Mike smiled. "That ought to be on a plaque. Don't you miss the folks in that generation? I do. They seemed to have answers to just about anything. Of course, our questions weren't so damned complicated at that point, either."

Gwen studied him for a moment. "You surprise me, Belan. I always thought you were such a ..."

"Arrogant asshole?" he offered. "I am. Complete and utter. Pride myself at it. Majored in it in college." He sipped his coffee in spite of the bitter taste. "Nice guys don't get very far in my business, Gwen."

"Too bad. This person sitting in front of me, I could grow to actually like. Or at least tolerate."

Belan smirked. "Tolerate—not love, admire, or re-spect—but I can live with it."

Gwen switched the conversation to something less per-sonal. "I'm sure you know this. There have been rumors circulating that United Sugar may sell out to the State of Florida, with the land going toward restoration of the Everglades."

His features betrayed no reaction. "Change is always good, Gwen. And always a possibility when one is dealing with big business."

"What then, Belan?"

He grinned. "Oh c'mon, Gwen. What happens when one of those little chameleon lizards jumps from a leaf to a rock? It changes color to suit the new digs."

"Just like that?"

He shrugged. "Money doesn't factor in. I could easily kick back and play golf twenty-four/seven. I can't imagine throwing away my pass to the big party. Like you, I'll land on my feet."

Gwen chuffed. "I hardly think you and I compare."

His eyebrows lifted. "Ah, but we do. Both of us lost our meal ticket when Brad's plane went down—not to mention, a friend, or in your case…much more."

Gwen's eyes narrowed. "Belan…"

He held up a hand. "I'm just saying…with Senator Sil-ver gone, you might just find yourself cooling your heels in the unemployment line." He leaned over and smiled. "Especially if Eleana Sliver has anything to do with it. Correct me if I'm wrong. I don't think you're on her *let's do lunch* list."

Gwen stared at Mike Belan. When she didn't comment, he continued, "Don't you worry your pretty little head. With your inside knowledge, I'm sure there will be plenty of suitors at your door begging for a date for the dance."

"Anyone ever tell you what a delightful compassionate manner you have?"

Mike shook his head. His lips pouched into a pout. "Even when you try for sarcastic bitch you fall far short, Miss Reynolds."

Gwen stood and grabbed her plate and cup. "I need to get back upstairs."

Mike Belan trailed her to the refuse container, then walked beside her to the elevators.

"Really, Gwen. I meant no offense. You have me to fall back on. I can always find a place for someone of your caliber."

She stopped in front of the elevators and regarded him. "As a lobbyist?"

He held out his hands, palms up. "All I'm saying…"

"I know what you're *saying*, Mr. Belan. I'd rather sleep on the street than become a lap-dog conduit for big business."

"Sometimes, woman, you sound like a closet Democrat." Mike threw up his hands. "Your call. Your virtue is admirable. But it won't get you past the gates."

She jabbed the elevator call button and the doors slid open.

His expression changed to one of concern. "Business aside, you call me if you need me. I'll be heading back to Washington tomorrow afternoon. You have my number."

As the elevator doors closed, Mike Belan flashed one last toothy white smile for her benefit.

"Yes, Mr. Belan," she said to the empty elevator compartment. "I *do* have your number."

Miami Vizcaya on Biscayne Bay—Miami, Florida

Dorothy Claxton waved Eleana to her table in the Café. The older woman noticed the dark smudges beneath her protégé's eyes.

"My dear, you look as if you haven't slept at all." She motioned for the server to bring coffee. "Of course you haven't. You should speak with your physician for something to help you."

"I have medication. It works for a few hours." She brushed a hank of dark hair from her eyes. "I never imagined how much…paperwork, details."

"The only one death is easy for is the deceased," Dorothy said.

The server delivered two cups, a carafe of coffee, creamer, and a basket of hot scones with cream and preserves. "I took the liberty. I know the last thing you want to do is eat, but please, do try. Scones have been a comfort food for me for as long as I can recall."

Eleana spread mango preserves and butter on a scone and took a small bite.

"We should plan a little vacation for you, dear. Maybe, Greece? No…the south of France."

"I don't want to leave Miami just yet."

"That will change, Eleana. You are young, rich, and beautiful. Your life is far from over, though it might feel that way right now."

Eleana pushed the half-eaten scone aside. "I had a visit from the Governor."

"How nice of him to call on you."

"He had Mark Cox with him."

Dorothy's eyebrow lifted. "That's odd. I never quite thought of the two of them as…close."

"It was more than a polite call. They came with an agenda."

"One you might share with an old friend?"

Eleana offered a weak smile. "Friend, yes. Old, never."

"Good answer. I have taught you well. Now…?"

"Tad Myers has asked me to step into Brad's senate position."

Dorothy's face echoed her surprise.

Eleana continued, "And that's not all. The Governor wishes to appoint me as the Republican candidate for the upcoming election."

"Truly?" Dorothy pursed her lips. "Whatever is behind this, do you suppose?"

"Governor Myers said he and Mr. Cox would do whatever it takes to help me win."

Dorothy leaned over and patted Eleana's hand. "I think you should do it, dear."

She shook her head. "Why? I despise politics, and Washington is so…"

"Full of politicians. Someone needs to exterminate. Don't you think?"

Eleana laughed. "Oh, Dottie. You are so good for me."

"Hmm…yes, me and that handsome young man in your employ."

Eleana's face colored.

"Oh, honey. Don't you worry. I won't breathe a word. I can spot a woman in lust a mile away. Besides, you need the support and distraction right now more than ever."

Eleana's gaze dropped to the table. "I am ashamed. Here, with Brad…"

"Just because you do what you need to survive, does not take away from your feelings for your husband, Eleana. You were a good wife to him. You would have been more, if he had allowed."

Eleana nodded. "What would you do, Dorothy?"

The older woman offered a coy wink. "About the hunk or about the Senate seat?"

"The Senate seat. I know what you'd do about the other." She glanced around to make sure no one was within hearing distance.

Dorothy's expression grew serious. "Do it, Eleana. I'll support you, and I'll get all of our friends to do likewise. You get in there and do what you can for your Cuban family, once you're in a position to do so. As to Tad Myers and the Republican minions—screw them! They think they can use you. You use *them*."

A slow smile spread across Eleana's face.

Dorothy Claxton picked up a brunch menu. "Now, I say we order a huge meal. You have to keep up your strength for Washington." Her blue eyes sparkled. "And as for me...I have a new personal trainer coming for a working interview this afternoon."

Miami General Rehab Unit—Miami, Florida

When Gwen stepped into the hallway of the Rehabilitation Unit, a miasma of scents accosted her nose: bleach, urine, and flatulent air overlaid with a strong green-apple-scented disinfectant spray cleaner. So different from the hospital room where he had rested for the previous four days. Her stomach lurched. For her father's sake, she hoped his therapy would proceed swiftly.

She tapped on the door of room 216 and stepped inside. Her father's roommate—a seventy-five-year-old man with a newly-replaced hip—normally greeted her. His bed was tidy. Her heart sank for a moment until she spotted his toiletries lined up on the bureau beside the bed. Fred was such a nice man—ex-military—with a cheerful outlook. Gwen liked the idea of his presence for the times family couldn't be around. Though she and Julia had taken turns staying with her father, neither was allowed past nine p.m.

Julia smiled and rose. In the bed, her father rested. His lady friend motioned for Gwen to step into the hall.

"How is he today?" Gwen asked.

"His physical therapy went well. They have him standing up in front of the wheelchair now. Paul, his main PT, says he will proceed to a walker next, then hopefully to a cane within a couple of weeks. It's mostly a balance issue on the right side."

"How about his spirits? He's been so down."

"He wants desperately to communicate. The words just won't form yet. He motions over and over for a pad of paper and a pencil, but he's right-handed and can do little with his left. He gets frustrated."

"His doctor says he will improve," Gwen said.

Julia smiled. "And he will. Your father is the most determined man I have ever known."

"I'm here now. I brought my laptop along so I can catch up on some work. Why don't you go and get some rest?"

Julia nodded. "Believe I will." She reached over and grasped Gwen's hand and gave it a squeeze. "You know how to reach me."

Gwen settled into the one extra chair in the room and opened her laptop. Though she talked with the Washington staff twice a day, she couldn't help the lingering feeling of urgency. So many loose ends to tie up. And especially now, with Eleana Silver getting ready to descend on the capital. Cox had called, explained the Governor's interim appointment. A little odd, but it was only for a few weeks until the elections. No doubt, Tad Myers had plans on a good, solid person to put on the ticket. Gwen would be there, providing a sense of continuity and stability at a time when the staff would need it most.

A sound from her father caused her to glance up from the email screen.

"Hey, Daddy." She smiled and set the laptop on the wheeled bedside table. "Julia told me you're doing fantastic with your therapy. You keep it up, and you'll be breaking out of this joint in no time."

Albert Reynolds lifted his left hand and gestured toward the computer.

"I know. I'm sorry. I brought it along to work on some business. Now that you're awake, I'll put it back in the car. I can help you up and into the wheelchair. We can take a walk out into the atrium garden."

He jabbed his hand repeatedly in the direction of the laptop. A line of spittle formed at the corner of his lips where the muscles sagged.

"What do you want? I don't understand." She followed his frantic motions. "My computer?"

He closed his eyes, released a long breath, and nodded.

The realization hit her. Of course! She wheeled the table over and raised the head of his bed.

"I'm a little slow on the uptake, Daddy."

Gwen switched to a word processing program. A blank page screen appeared.

One side of Albert's mouth twitched in a smile. He lifted his left hand and typed.

"I love you, Girlie."

Gwen grinned. "Been a long time since you called me that."

"I need."

Gwen nodded. "Take your time, Daddy. Type it out. What do you need? I will do it right away."

"Joel Orr."

"Joel Orr?"

Albert's hand made slow movements across the keyboard.

"Saved me from prison. You would have been alone."

Gwen frowned. "Daddy, what do you mean? You've never been in any kind of trouble."

"Once. Did some dumb things. Joel Orr understood. He has daughter. He knew I had to be there for you."

Gwen sat on the edge of the bed. "Do you mean Joel Orr...the man who is running for office? That Joel Orr?"

Her father nodded.

"I owe him. Go to him. Tell him thank you for me. For us. Promise."

"I will, Daddy. I just don't..."

Albert Reynolds raised his left hand and touched her cheek, then lowered it once again to the keyboard.

"Help him in any way you can. Good man. Promise me you will."

Office of the Governor—Tallahassee, Florida

Aide Kemp Johnson watched Tad Myers' latest incarnation: happy-pill ADHD hamster. Happy, Happy! Joy, Joy!

Since Eleana Silver's call, his boss had been intensely focused: get the forces behind his plans for the senate seat.

Thirty minutes on the same issue. Had to be a record.

"We're in for a full-on brawl, Kemp my boy!"

The Governor clapped him on the shoulder for the tenth time in less than an hour. Would Workers' Compensation cover a dislocated joint? Kemp wondered.

Tad Myers flipped from one telephone conversation to the next, stroking and cajoling all of the movers and shakers of the state's Republican guard. Kemp recalled a scene from *The Wizard of Oz*, where the great and powerful Oz behind the curtain pushed buttons, yanked cords, and spun wheels to create the smoke and mirrors illusion of immense, irrefutable power.

CHAPTER TWELVE

Orr for Senate Headquarters—Miami, Florida

"Sweet Jesus wept; it's hot in here!" Don Farringdon used a wet bandana to mop the moisture from his brow and neck. "I don't believe the A.C. is working at all."

Ronnie Taylor glanced up from the laptop. "Suck it up, Don. Running these computers will make it a little warm, and we need them up and going. For every degree we crank the thermostat back, the bill goes up another ten percent."

"Isn't going to do us much good if the candidate dies of a heat stroke before the primary." Farringdon motioned to Joel Orr.

Joel glanced down at the growing circles of perspiration drawing salt-rimmed circles beneath his armpits and around his collar. "I'm fine. We're getting a little more cash flow in, guys. Maybe we can turn it back a notch or two."

Taylor—rail-thin, obviously more comfortable—rolled his eyes behind the black-rimmed glasses. "If you two would lay off the coffee. Get Jennifer to make it iced."

Joel smiled. Sweet bosomy Jennifer, owner of Cup O' Joe and architect of the biggest cinnamon rolls this side of Texas. She not only knew them each by first name, but by how they took their coffee. In a crunch, Jennifer would lock her front door and personally walk their orders down. When Joel thought about it for a moment, he marveled; now the woman who knew how he took his drink was a barista instead of a barkeep. Though Jennifer couldn't displace Brenda Gayle in his affections, she was running a close second.

Farringdon rummaged in the small refrigerator and pulled out a cola. He held the cold can to his forehead before popping the tab. "Ronnie, what kind of lit drop do we have for Jacksonville?"

"The usual: black churches, the Jaycees up there, and hopefully the Young Democrats." Ronnie Taylor stuck up a finger. "One more reason to practice conservation of our precious monetary resources. We don't have an unlimited supply to put towards materials, and you know, Don, the distribution of campaign literature is as important a function to our success as anything."

"Don't preach to me, Taylor. I was running campaign propaganda on Miami streets when you were still in diapers."

Ronnie smirked. "Highly unlikely, unless you did this in a previous incarnation. I am only one year, three months, five days, and..." he glanced at his watch, "twenty-six minutes your junior."

Joel laughed. "Any way you cut it, Don, you should know by now; never argue math with a numbers guy."

Ronnie nodded to Joel. "Thank you."

Don snorted. "Point taken. As to the literature—the pictures are everything. If we are in a predominantly black community, it is critical that Joel is pictured with black activists from that part of Jacksonville. The same for the Hispanic and Anglo communities up there in the part of our great state known as *The First Coast*."

Joel agreed. "It isn't rocket science. Put yourself in their position. If you live in a deteriorating neighborhood, and you are of...say...African-American descent, you want someone who understands your situation representing you."

Farringdon nodded. "That's why you're striking a chord, Joel. You come across as sincerely concerned about the types of issues they face on a daily basis."

"I am sincere. I don't have to fake it."

"And that's why Ronnie and I are behind you. You can be all of that and more, but the medium is the message. It is to no avail if we don't get it into the hands of the voters."

Ronnie flipped the computer to a spreadsheet file where he kept a running tab of current research figures. "Jacksonville is fertile ground for our campaign. Some pockets of sophistication, and with all those insurance folks. But, also pockets of active and engaged African-American communities, as well."

"Good job, Ronnie," Don said.

Taylor continued, "The way is laid out for us, and it's pretty simple. Tab A goes into Tab B. Not the other way around."

Joel glanced from Taylor to Farringdon. "Do you know what the hell he is talking about nine times out of ten? Or, is it just me?"

Don shook his head. "His analogies leave a bit to be desired. Good thing he's so darned cute."

Taylor fired both men the stink eye. "Can we be serious about this?"

Joel and Don wiped the smiles from their faces like two delinquent kids called in front of the principal.

Ronnie Taylor nodded. "Better. Now, the big question for the campaign in Jacksonville is whether we have enough support to get the literature into the hands of the voters. Is Joel's message resonating?"

Farringdon took a long drink of cola, then said, "I'll call in every favor owed me. I can rally the Black churches. From there, we work our way out."

Joel sat back, watching the volley between his two campaign gurus. Ronnie Taylor and Don Farringdon were bright, engaged, and committed to his campaign. He hoped Russell Nathan didn't have the equivalent on his team.

Farringdon frowned. "I hope what we're doing on this grassroots level will be enough to overcome the opponent's television buys. And maybe the biggest issue, what kind of phone banks do the Republicans and Nathan have to counter our lit drop?"

Joel said, "We can't worry about Eleana Silver just yet. We have to get past Russell Nathan and his Dixie-*rat* steamrollers, first. Then, we can really play in the big sandbox."

Farringdon smirked. "I still can't believe Tad Myers put her in. I can see the whole sentimental clap-trap—nice gesture to the widow to place her as interim. But, to actually put her on the ticket for November? It's like Mondale said in '84, *where's the beef?*"

Ronnie Taylor said, "Don't underestimate them. Big mistake. Myers is counting on that same sympathy and name recognition, no doubt. I've studied the man. He has a reason for every move he makes."

Farringdon grabbed one of the charged cell phones. "I'm going to find a quiet corner in the main room and make some calls."

Ronnie Taylor motioned to the small fan that strained to churn air in one corner of the office. "Take that with you. I can deal. If you wet down your face and neck and point it right at you, it might help you cool off."

Joel stood. "I'll go bug Jennifer for three iced coffees."

Ronnie Taylor didn't look up from the computer screen. "Don't forget the cinnamon rolls."

As Joel walked the block down to the coffee shop, he mulled over his dream from the previous night. Dreaming in itself was a recent happening. For several years, alcohol had robbed his sleep of nocturnal images.

In the dream, he treaded water in an expanse of green ocean. No land for miles. The ocean spread as far as he could see. Overhead, a lone seagull. His spirits lifted. Land had to be close-by. His legs and arms felt heavy and deathly cold. His heartbeat drummed a slow, strained throb.

He was dying. He knew it.

A lifeboat—fully inflated—fell from the sky: big, Day-Glo orange, and full of supplies. He managed to pull his body aboard. A porpoise appeared on either side of the boat. One was larger than the other. The smaller one wore nerdy black-rimmed glasses. They eyed him, cackled like Flipper-gone-wild, and started to nudge the raft forward.

The whole episode seemed perfectly plausible.

Joel smiled as he opened the door of the Cup O' Joe. It didn't take a dial-up psychic to interpret the dream.

The Silvers' Mansion—Coral Gables, Florida

Ramiro trailed the tips of his fingers down Eleana's inner thigh. She moaned and turned toward him. He had loved many women, but none her equal.

"Must I wake up?" Eleana opened her eyes, offered the lazy smile of a satisfied woman.

He brushed the hair from her brow. "If it was up to me, we would never leave this room." He kissed the soft skin beneath one ear and continued down her neck to the top of her shoulder.

"What am I to do, Ramiro?"

"Just lie back and let me love you again."

She pushed on his chest. "Later. I promise."

Ramiro propped his head on one hand. "What is worrying you?"

"I leave for Washington soon." She closed her eyes and took a deep breath. "What was I thinking when I told the Governor I would go? I must be crazy. It's not like here."

He leaned over and kissed her forehead. "No place is like Miami."

"You don't know how it is. Those people. They smile to your face and hate you the moment you walk away. No one is as they seem."

"You are stronger than they are, Eleana."

"And our place—Brad's place—in Georgetown. It's so...full of him. How can I possibly bear to stay even one moment there?"

"You miss him terribly."

Eleana thought for a moment. "I do. Yes, on some level. I don't mean to sound hard. I loved him. He was my husband. But once Washington sucked him in, there was little left for me. For us."

"You deserve so much more."

Her eyes glistened. "I don't know how I would be alive without you. You...you breathe me."

A slow smile played at the corners of his lips.

Eleana brushed the covers aside and sat up. "What do I know about anything? I know nothing about Brad's world. I don't care."

"What was it your friend told you?" He paused. "This is your opportunity."

"To help my family. Yes, I know."

Ramiro continued, "You are a rich woman, Eleana. You have the means to make your life anything you wish. The house—send your decorators up there in advance. They know what you love. You can walk into that place and make it yours."

Eleana considered.

"The same with the office. You get in, you make it yours. Who is going to stop you?"

"You are absolutely right."

He outlined the curve of her lips with the tip of one finger.

"Oh, God, Ramiro. How can I live without you? I could be gone for days...weeks!"

Ramiro laid back and Eleana curled into his arms.

"You've made it bearable. I can't do it alone."

"Shh..." he breathed into her hair. "You don't have to. I will go with you."

She lifted her head to study his face. "To Washington? You will?"

"Nothing holds me here. I will be wherever you are, Eleana."

"We'll have to be secretive, Ramiro. It's not like here, where we might slip away and be together. I will be in their harsh light. Even with my husband, we were always so aware of everything we did, everything we said..."

"You will require a driver, *Si?*" He grinned.

Eleana laughed. "I can't imagine driving myself— especially up there."

"I am at your service, Senator Silver."

She ran her hand down to his belly. "And the other...service?"

Ramiro's voice came out deep and throaty. "Graciously. And for free."

When he heard the shower running a few minutes later, Ramiro flipped open his cell phone. On the other end, the salsa music announced his call.

"Eleana is on board," he said.

Ramiro listened to the terse reply from the other end. "Yes. I will make sure she doesn't have second thoughts, *Señor.*"

CHAPTER THIRTEEN

Orr for Senate Headquarters—Miami, Florida

Gwen Reynolds pulled the rental car into a tight parking space on 36th Street. Few people moved about in the radiant heat of the afternoon. She glanced around. Good thing it was hot. Maybe most of the transients would be too lethargic to cause any problem. Not that she was a stranger to questionable areas. Washington had more than a handful, and her father's Miami Springs neighborhood had certainly taken a downturn in the past few years. She gathered her purse and slid from the car, mindful to hit the automatic lock button.

An older black woman with wispy white hair greeted her as soon as she pushed through the front door of the campaign headquarters. Gwen checked out the room. Joel Orr wasn't trying to impress anyone.

"Are you here to volunteer?" The woman asked. "We can use volunteers."

"No, Ma'am."

"You should. You're pretty, and polite besides. Someone like you would come in handy."

Gwen smiled. "Is Mr. Orr in, please?"

"He stepped out for refreshments. Should be back at any moment. Mr. Farringdon and Mr. Taylor are in the back room. You could pull up a chair and help me stuff envelopes while you're waiting." The woman's white-tipped eyebrows formed question marks.

That would be rich. The Chief of Staff for Senator Silver's office helping out at the Orr campaign's front desk. The tabloids would eat that for lunch and order seconds.

Gwen shook her head. "I'll just go back to the office and wait, if you don't mind."

"Suit yourself."

Gwen walked past four young people huddled around a printer, obviously arguing about who would kick it first. When she reached the office threshold, she stopped and rapped lightly on the door jamb. Two men—one of slight build and one who could have easily been a linebacker—glanced up. For a moment, neither said a word.

"Excuse me, gentlemen. My name is…"

The linebacker guy stood up so quickly, he nearly tipped a laptop computer onto the floor. "Gwen Reynolds." He stepped out from behind the long table that served as a desk and shoved a meaty hand in her direction.

"Don Farringdon." His hand swallowed hers.

"Pleased."

"This is Ronnie Taylor." He motioned to the skinny fellow, who offered his hand for a sweaty, dead-fish kind of shake.

"What do we owe the pleasure, Miss Reynolds? Oh…by the way, may I…we…offer our heartfelt condolences on the loss of Senator Brad Silver."

"Thank you." Gwen steadied herself. At some point, she would stop feeling as if she wanted to cry or bolt from the room when someone said Brad's name. "I'm here to speak with Mr. Orr."

The two men exchanged glances.

"It's personal," she added.

Don recovered. "Excuse our lack of manners, Miss Reynolds. Please, sit down. Joel only went to the coffee shop not far from here. He should be returning shortly…"

The front door opened and closed. Joel Orr delivered two carry-bags to the front staff before continuing toward the back office.

"Iced coffees!" Joel called out. He stopped when he spotted Gwen sitting next to Farringdon.

"Joel! Good, you're back," Don said. "Miss Reynolds just dropped by to see you."

Joel slid the bags onto the table. "I know you, of course. I haven't seen you since you were quite a bit younger. We have all watched you on television with the senator, but we haven't formally met." He stuck out his hand. "Joel Orr."

Gwen instantly warmed to his demeanor. Where she had expected the typical baby-kissing, back-slapping southern politician, Joel came across as neither. Her first impression: guarded, yet favorable.

"Are you checking up on the competition?" Joel smiled. "As you can see, we have quite the posh Political Palace here. Don't let looks deceive. This ..." he patted the metal-legged Formica table and chuckled. "Solid oak. We went with a renewable wood source."

Gwen smiled. "It's lovely."

Joel pulled out four iced coffees. "You're in luck. I brought an extra. Don't know why. Just did. I do things like that sometimes."

Don Farringdon decided to step in before Joel could ramble. "Miss Reynolds is here to see *you*, Joel."

"Oh, okay." He sat an iced coffee in front of her.

"It's personal, so..." Gwen glanced at Farringdon and Taylor.

Don grabbed Ronnie by the arm, and they left with two cups of the coffee. The door shut behind them.

"You have my full attention," Joel said. "Not to mention, my staff are probably all huddled by the door. Excuse me." He stood and opened the door. Farringdon and Taylor scampered away like sprayed cockroaches. "Now." He closed the door and sat down. "I offer you some modicum of privacy. But first, before you tell me what you've come by for, please accept my condolences."

Gwen's gaze fell to her lap.

Joel said, "I know the senator and I are...were...polar opposites on the political scale. Still, I admired him. Other than my differences on his gun control stance, I had no problems with Senator Silver. He was one of the few Republicans I thought worthy of the job."

"Thank you, Mr. Orr. I know his family appreciated the flowers you sent."

"Good. Now…?"

"I'm here on behalf of my father, Albert Reynolds."

"Albert Reynolds." He nodded.

"He sent me to thank you. I don't know the details, but you helped him somehow many years ago. Kept him out of prison? I don't understand, Mr. Orr. What did you do for my father, exactly?"

Joel took a sip of iced coffee to give him a moment to form an answer. "As Assistant State Attorney, I had some latitude on which cases to pursue. After reviewing your father's file and talking to him in detail, it was apparent that he was an honorable man who had hit on difficult times. The specifics don't matter now—time erases the need for such disclosure." Joel leaned back in his chair. "I remember saying to myself, *there, but for the grace of God, go I.* I reviewed the statute of limitations, which provided some latitude for the prosecutor, and applied it leniently in his case."

"If not for you, my father would have have been, what…bankrupt? Imprisoned?"

Joel nodded. "Yes, and you would have been at the mercy of the state's child welfare system. Don't make a huge deal about it, Miss Reynolds. You, or he, would have probably done the same for me if the tables were turned. I am not one to judge, as I have been on the brink of the same calamity."

"Mr. Orr. By your action alone, I was able to attend college and law school. Without my father…" She paused. The implications raced through her mind. "I had no idea."

"There aren't a lot of positive things going on in the world today, Gwen…I may call you by your first name?"

"Yes. Please."

"Gwen, maybe assisting your family in a time of need was my small way of lending a hand to good people." He smiled. "If karma is the rule, perhaps it will help me end up in at least a cooler layer of Hell."

Gwen said, "You have made such a difference in my life, and I never knew..."

"Your father and I are similar in many ways. We don't wear *giving back* on our sleeves. Believe me, I had no idea that my small effort on Albert's behalf would have resulted in the success of the brains behind a U.S. senator. I've kept up with you a little over the last few years. I am proud of your accomplishments."

"Thank you, Mr. Orr."

"I would be pleased if you would call me Joel."

She nodded. "I will always feel a sense of obligation to thank you for my father, but, now, for me. What can I do to ever repay you?"

"Just to know of your success as Brad Silver's Chief of Staff and your contributions to our state and country...those are repayment in full. For whatever I might have done, you and your father are most welcome. How is your father?"

"He has not been well, Joel. I hope for his improvement."

"You've had a heavy load, then. With the senator, and this...?"

She nodded. "Yes."

"Bad things often come in clusters. From my experience, it does improve."

Gwen offered a weak smile.

"Are you going back to the capital soon, then?" Joel asked.

"Tomorrow. My father is insistent that I get back to normal."

Joel huffed. "*Normal* is seldom a word I associate with Washington. I do hope things work out for you, Gwen. You'll always have friends down here. Hey, you can always work for us." He grinned.

"I'll remember that." Gwen stood. "I should be going."

"Please give your father my regards. Thank you for coming to find me. I know it wasn't on your way to anything."

Gwen found herself smiling again. Something about Joel Orr reminded her of Brad Silver. The way he made direct eye contact when he spoke. The way she felt as if she had his undivided attention. Too bad he was a Democrat.

When Gwen reached the rental car, a familiar voice sounded behind her.

"Gwen? Is that you?"

Karen Orr Hernandez rushed over and gave Gwen a hug.

Gwen smiled. "Hey, girl! I'm so glad I bumped into you. I was going to try to catch up and maybe meet you at the gym before I left town, but—"

"No need to explain. I thought about calling you up, but I was afraid you'd be mired down in everything. I am so, so sorry about the senator. You must be devastated."

"It has been a very intense few days, yes."

Karen glanced around. "What are you doing down here?"

"I had some business with Joel Orr. How about you? What, you volunteering for his campaign?"

Karen laughed. "Hey, remember? We made a pact long ago not to talk politics. A Republican and a Democrat can be friends. Some of my best friends *are* Republicans."

Gwen smirked. "I won't tell. So, are you?"

Karen nodded. "In answer, yes. I am working for Joel Orr's campaign."

"Always a hero for the underdog."

"You could say that." Karen shrugged. "Besides, Joel Orr is my father."

Miami Airport Radisson—Miami, Florida

Don Farringdon's gaze scanned the conference room of the Miami Airport Radisson. The members of the Council of

Jewish Women filtered in, dressed to impress. Two tables sat at the back of the room: one filled with finger foods and one with an assortment of fruit juice, tea, coffee, and water—no alcohol due to the lunch hour meeting time. Ladies being ladies, many walked away with over-loaded plates. Why not make a lunch meal out of the event? Don Farringdon smiled. With this bunch, the real skewer was usually the speaker, especially if he or she was foolish enough to come unprepared. Not a problem with Joel. For the past few days, he and Farringdon had brainstormed every conceivable issue from several angles. Joel had the answers, or Farringdon hoped he did.

All of the major south Florida media covered CJW events, a fact Don counted on. This wasn't Russell Nathan or Eleana Silver, just the long-shot opponent Joel Orr. Farringdon would take the press coverage where he could find it. And this was at the right price: free.

The prepared speech offered no cause for concern, but both Farringdon and Taylor stressed about the question and answer portion of the meeting. The CJW members—bright and determined—knew exactly how to cut through the bullshit. Joel would be on his A-game as it related to criminal justice issues, but what if they took it to a more personal level?

A bevy of niggling questions raced through Don's mind as he watched the well-appointed group mingle. What really happened in your reelection years ago, Mr. Orr? What say you to the rumors of your drinking? Are you still an attorney, or a Para-legal? Are you in good standing with the Florida Bar?

Farringdon's stomach rolled. God help them if they broached the subject of Joel's wife's cancer. Every time he and Taylor mentioned anything related to his deceased ex-wife, Joel slammed shut. Discussion over.

He bit the inside of his cheek, an old trick he learned to help stave off panic attacks. Joel could, and would, handle these intellectuals. Damn it! He had done the job of a good P.R. guy—prepare, prepare, prepare.

The CJW met once a month on the second Tuesday at the Miami Airport Radisson, a location central to South Florida and convenient for members traveling from as far as Broward and Palm Beach Counties. A rough head count confirmed the popularity of the meeting. Ten long rows of thirty seats stretched across the hall. In a few minutes, all were full and many of the fashionably late stood along the back wall. Several Radisson employees scurried to locate extra chairs.

Ronnie Taylor stood beside him. "I count three-fifty-one, and four more are in the ladies room."

"Not bad." Don leaned over and said in a low voice, "Amazing, isn't it? Even though they are Jewish, they sit in their seats as if they were in a Pentecostal Baptist Church. All the big hitters are in the back."

Ronnie smiled. "The more things change; the more they remain the same."

"Hope it's not to put more distance between themselves and Joel when they fire the rotten tomatoes."

Ronnie shook his head. "Mangos."

"Right."

Carol Rosen, President of the Miami branch of the CJW, called the meeting to order. She covered a few announcements before introducing the speaker. Taylor and Farringdon exchanged nervous glances as Joel stepped behind the podium.

Joel looked out across the room and took a deep breath. Game on.

"Ladies, it is so good to be with you again. I can remember when I was in the State Senate. CJW was the only true-blue organization to support me, even when the NRA finally took me out." He smiled.

A tittering of knowing laughter filtered around the room.

"Good. He's going for the humble approach," Don whispered.

"Most of you know I have long stood for a twenty-four-hour cooling-off period. No matter what the NRA throws at me, I shall not waiver from that important issue."

For the next forty-five minutes, Don and Ronnie listened to their candidate roll out his plans: economic stimulus, health care, the rising cost of homeowners insurance, with a special emphasis on proposed criminal justice legislation. The CJW had a long-standing interest in criminal justice, particularly as it related to juveniles. Joel spent a good amount of time covering his position on gun control: from registration, to support for the police on the beat, to judicial reform. In the time allotted, Joel Orr managed to touch many of the concerns of not only Floridians, but Americans.

"I've just gone on and on, Ladies. I open the floor to questions."

Judith Krieberg—one of the most recognized and respected members of the CJW—rose to her feet. "Senator Orr, I hate to be personal, but you are running for a seat in the United States Senate, and I think you will agree that the subject of your wife's health is fair game...?"

"Oh, shit," Don mumbled.

"Yes. I do agree," Joel said. "What is your question?"

"Tell us, Senator. What really happened to your wife?"

Joel paused and looked down at his notes. Nothing provided by Farringdon, Taylor, or even Karen could help him. He was on his own. In a split second, he decided to make his reply direct and honest. These particular women would flay him if not.

"My late wife, Jacqueline." His voice cracked, and he took a moment to clear his throat. "My late ex-wife..."

The crowded room fell silent.

"I don't know how to say this, really. So, I will just come out with it. She and I had just gone through a divorce. It was an amicable one, though it hurt each of us badly."

Joel looked out over the sea of female faces. "I'm afraid I fell into the trap that many men make. I worked long hours. I stayed in Tallahassee when I should have come south."

Too much information, Joel. Too much! Don watched for the audience's reaction. Guarded expressions. Some sympathetic.

"In the period immediately following our divorce, we failed—no, I failed—to make sure our health insurance issues were taken care of. Because of my commitment to my position, I failed her in this respect. The insurance policy through my office no longer covered my ex-wife."

Joel closed his eyes. Just when Don thought he might not continue, Joel said, "She found a lump in her right breast. Tests confirmed it was cancer, one of the most aggressive types. She had no insurance coverage—couldn't get any at that point— and refused to take any monetary help from me, or our daughter Karen.

"She had a double mastectomy. Then, she spent every dime she owned to have radiation and chemotherapy. To no avail. She died almost six months to the day of her diagnosis."

"Jesus," Ronnie Taylor said.

Joel's eyes watered. Even from the back of the room, Don could feel the raw emotion rolling from him in waves.

"I will carry the burden of her death for the rest of my life. That is why I assure you; money and support for breast cancer prevention, awareness, and treatment shall be at the top of my list when I get to Washington. That, and affordable health care coverage for everyone."

One woman sat near the door, a smirk on her face. When she leaned over to the group of women in her clutch, Don overheard her comment.

"Listen to him. He's playing on his poor ex-wife's death. Pandering of the first class. Just as I expected. This guy is phony baloney. Damned politicians! Just saying whatever they can to get the women's votes. That's why I'm a Russell Nathan supporter. He would never stoop to such."

Don's spirits sank as he studied the expressions of the women within the immediate area. Worse yet, a coven of reporters overheard the woman's tirade.

Another woman stood. "Question, Senator Orr."

"Yes, please..."

"What about your brother? I read somewhere that he is in prison."

Don Farringdon groaned. "From worse to hellish."

Joel cleared his throat. "Yes, my brother was tried and convicted of armed robbery a number of years ago. This is a matter of public record. While I love my brother, I do not condone his crime and I support the sentence bestowed upon him. He received a fair trial. He is serving his time. As it should be. It is my hope that he will be able to move forward and live the rest of his life as an improved, changed man."

Ronnie nodded. "Good, direct answer."

"We knew that had to come out at some point. Better early on," Don said.

For a few moments, Joel didn't make eye contact as he gathered his papers. Then, he answered a scattering of questions—none as loaded as the first—and seemed to collect himself enough to get back on track.

"In closing, I appreciate your time and consideration. Thank you, Ladies."

Don spoke barely above a whisper to Taylor, though the noise level in the room had risen. "Plan a speech for weeks on the issues, and these ladies come up with a personal question that requires a delicate answer. No matter how Joel answered that one about his wife, he was backed into a corner and bagged."

Farringdon recalled the Barack Obama bombshell when one reverend lost his marbles in a church sermon and almost derailed Obama's campaign. The prize was different—U.S. President as opposed to U.S. senator—but the stakes were similar. A heartfelt, emotional confidence about a subject as sensitive as breast cancer, and in front of a legion of women, could be twisted and misconstrued by the press.

As the last few members filtered from the hall, Joel stayed behind to shake hands and greet a few members personally. Don made it a point to hover close-by, listening to any references to the radioactive questions. None came. Maybe they had dodged the bullet.

As she exited, President Carol Rosen said to several women in her group, "I am not sure if he really has the chutzpah to pull this election off, but it feels good to know we have at least one candidate who is solid on criminal justice."

Joel Orr for Senate Headquarters—Miami, Florida

Karen Orr Hernandez walked around the table and pulled up a chair beside her father. "Sorry I couldn't make the speech today, Daddy. I'm trying to save my time off for later in your campaign. I really want to do a little traveling with you."

"If there is a later time, Bug. At this rate, I may not have a ghost of a chance past the primary."

Don Farringdon spoke, "I think we all agree, Joel. You did a great job. I was at the back of the room when the breast cancer question came up. I heard the lady question your motives. Worse, some of the press hounds did, too. My experience with this stuff is; it can be dangerous politically."

"I don't get it, Don," Karen said. "From what you told me, Daddy's response seemed reasonable, at least it did to me. He was brutally honest about what happened with Mom. I can't believe anyone would attack him for that."

Farringdon shrugged. "There's always so much more to any issue than what meets the eye. The barracudas in the press can twist things. Joel could be painted as uncaring for not being there for his family—even an ex-wife." He pitched the pencil in his hand onto the table. "Damn it! Joel works so hard—all of us do—and then something like this."

Ronnie Taylor glanced up from his laptop. "Look, if his answer is interpreted in a certain way, as if Joel was pandering for votes, and the press picks it up, and if Nathan hears about it, then we have a problem. We're down eight to ten points. And with little time left before the primary to gain any."

Don sighed. "It could be a real problem. Look, I'm not the message, just the messenger. We could have a game-changer here."

Joel pushed back in his chair. "Don, I appreciate your candor. If we have a problem, it's my fault. I've been over my response, and I don't know how else I could have framed the answer. It was the absolute worst time for me, and my family. Even had I tried, I couldn't have put a Pollyanna spin on it. We will know soon enough if Russell Nathan tries to exploit it. Frankly, I don't think he's bright enough to pick it up."

Don frowned. "Ah, but Joel. You aren't taking one person into account. If Benton's people run with it, you're toast."

Ronnie bent over the laptop. "I'll work on a rebuttal for the website. Hopefully, it won't draw undue attention, but being proactive never hurts."

"You think we should run interference with the papers?" Joel asked.

Ronnie shook his head. "Old school, Joel. Print media is a dinosaur. The best medium to turn a game-saver on a dime is a website."

Karen asked, "What if I put a rebuttal on my blog? Coming from me, the background story might not seem so...politically contrived. Besides, I think people need to know who my father really is..." She glanced over to Joel, "then, and now."

Joel nodded. "It amazes me, all this technology. Back in the day..."

Ronnie rolled his eyes. "There he goes again. Somebody slap him into this century, will you?"

Don Farringdon chuckled. The political game made the most unlikely people into instant comrades. In the back of his mind, he couldn't help but worry. He felt as if someone had left a lit candle burning in the house with no one to blow it out.

CHAPTER FOURTEEN

Old Omni Hotel Ballroom, Biscayne Bay— Miami, Florida

Russell Nathan sat at the dais awaiting an introduction to a room filled with over two hundred members of the most politically powerful female organization in the state of Florida, The League of Women Voters. When his people chose the location, the old Omni Hotel Ballroom stood out— on Biscayne Bay directly across the street from the *Miami Herald*. If he managed to woo The League with a few good points, maybe the karma would ooze toward the newspaper.

Nathan glanced around the audience, nodding to first one, then another. He spotted Marilyn Evans—a past president of The League—sitting in the first row. The woman was a true ball-buster, a skeptic who had raked him over the coals over an obscure environmental issue during his gubernatorial reign. He worried briefly about her proximity to his home in the panhandle. Blountstown was just a stone's throw from where he had grown up in Milton, and closer still to Destin Beach where he played. God forbid, if she had any cute nieces who liked to party. He might have slept with one or two—What if she was underage? The booze? The drugs? Disclosure of that sort would sink the campaign instantly. Russell shuddered.

He dismissed the notion. The woman had the face of an inbred pit bull and the demeanor of a water moccasin. No way would any female who came from her gene pool catch his attention. Besides, he generously provided food, drinks, and any kind of party supplements a young woman could want. Who in her right mind would upset such an apple cart by ratting him out to a dried-up relative?

His mind skipped to other concerns. Benton's recent comment still stung, though said in jest. *"Russ, you have the reputation of being a chandelier with a couple of empty bulbs. Your people need to line up an important, high-visibility address."*

The League of Women Voters—not exactly a coup. The League routinely requested to meet with candidates to hear their positions on the issues. No doubt, Joel Orr could get his say, too. If he chose. Instead, the poor misguided miscreant had picked the Council of Jewish Women: a hot-bed of liberals.

Nathan tilted his head toward the podium and painted a rapt expression on his face, though he barely heard the League president's brief biographical introduction. The applause died as he stepped forward, and he paused before speaking to allow the last- minute conversations and coughs to quiet.

"Good afternoon, Ladies. I am honored to be here with you." He offered a slight smile. Then, his expression grew serious. "Anyone can promise high-browed, costly solutions to fight things like crime, but it takes a real man to step up and balance a budget."

Russell Nathan—short on details, but long on rhetoric—took a few moments to preen and fluff about the record of his past administration. The Florida Constitution required a balanced budget, so the accomplishments during his reign were really less than stellar. It didn't stop him from taking credit.

Next, he pointed out how he had supported the League's positions, and struggled to pinpoint any major initiatives. Nathan claimed to be the champion of school funding. Once again, an area directed by the Florida Constitution.

Women exchanged glances. He was losing them. Time to flash the big guns.

"Many of you know my sweet wife Sarah. She has a star in her crown, putting up with me as a husband."

A titter of laughter rippled around the room.

"You know how it is, Ladies. We men are all alike. We leave our socks and shoes in the middle of the floor. We mark up the kitchen table with coffee rings. We forget important dates, snore like fog-horns, and often try to leave the house in clothes that don't quite match."

More laughter, nodding.

"Yet, you stand by us. You stand behind us. And we are who we are because of you."

A couple of women in the middle of the gathering initiated a round of applause.

"Sarah Nathan is like a rose surrounded by my thorns. Right now, as we sit here in this wonderful old hotel in air-conditioned comfort, my Sarah is toiling in Haiti, bringing her wealth of hope, compassion, and faith to people who have so little."

Silence. Point to Russell Nathan, thanks to his philanthropic wife.

"While we are on the subject of women, I would like to comment on an answer my opponent Joel Orr made to a question at a recent meeting of the Council of Jewish Women. About a subject very sensitive to us all—breast cancer. I'll be quite frank. I didn't totally understand my opponent's reference, but I am told, critics might say it amounted to pandering."

By the shocked expressions on the ladies' faces, Nathan knew he had hit a chord. Many had lost best friends, mothers, and daughters to the disease. Energized, he continued the diatribe on Orr's reported remark.

"I don't mind sharing with you; I'm a little troubled by his closest family member—his brother Clancy. I don't know if you ladies know this, but Joel Orr's only sibling is serving time for armed robbery."

With Sarah's glowing mission work and the timely insertion of his opponent's recent issues, sprinkled with a liberal dusting of brotherly-guilt-by-association, Russell Nathan mounted an offensive with the all-important women's vote. His mother would have been proud.

Destin Beach, Florida

"Life couldn't possibly get better," Russell Nathan said.

The phone—set to speaker—echoed with Buddy Benton's smooth southern drawl. "The speech you gave to the League of Women Voters went well; my people tell me. Good move—mentioning your wife's mission work."

Nathan settled down with an ice-cold beer and propped his feet on a rattan ottoman. "Buddy, I wish you could've been there. Should've seen the looks on their faces. A few stories about Sarah feeding and ministering to those poor, starving children, and I had those League of Women Voters ball-busters eating from my hands. After that, I could've called John the Baptist a queer and they would've rallied to have him erased from the Holy Bible."

Laughter sounded from the speaker. "You keep it up, Russ, and we can high-five each other in the Rotunda, come November."

"That's a date, Buddy-boy. I'll bring the libations if you round us up a couple of willing aides."

"Careful, Russ. You never know who's listening."

Nathan snorted. "Now, Buddy. You know I'm just pulling your leg. I'm completely and utterly devoted to my Sarah."

He heard Benton chuckle.

"You best be, son. Sarah's always struck me as a formidable woman. Trust me on this one, Russ. Only a fool crosses a formidable woman."

Nathan kicked up the heat on the Jacuzzi to a hundred and two degrees. His lower back felt like a marauding herd of Republicans had stomped all over it. The grueling miles of travel were extracting a toll, a factor he had dismissed from memory of previous campaigns when he was a much younger man. Too bad a candidate couldn't send a few emails and videotaped speeches and call it a day. A goodly amount of personal pandering and baby-kissing were still requirements.

Not only was his back complaining, but his digestive system as well. Fast food. Catered, southern-style banquets. Curdled, cold-eggs and hard-biscuit breakfasts. Barbeque. Pizza. Greasy burgers and home fries. Hot wings.

He was either dashing to the nearest toilet or popping laxatives to get things moving through the pipes.

Aging was pure hell. Every night, he bumbled to the bathroom three or four times to whiz, compliments of an enlarged prostrate. Without his bifocals, he couldn't read shit. More of his hair cluttered the drain after a shower. Viagra was his new drug of choice, second only to over-the-counter pain medications.

The weekend stretched out before him, a green valley glittering in the aftermath of a mild summer shower. Sarah had packed off once again for Haiti the previous morning, a publicity opportunity Nathan didn't miss. The photograph of him handing over his wife's duffle at the gate in Tallahassee Regional Airport hit the website immediately. *Loving husband bids farewell to wife*, the headline read. The major newspapers would follow suit.

Russell Nathan smiled and slipped, naked, into the bubbling hot water.

"Dip-shit Joel Orr pisses off the broads, and they can't get enough of me."

So what if Sarah Nathan carried a good eighty pounds over what she had in her twenties? With two chins and a behind that looked like two pigs fighting in a croker sack, she wasn't anyone's trophy wife. Still, her missionary leanings landed in her husband's win column.

"I'd put Sarah and her butt up against Eleana Silver's tight little ass, come September. Just as soon as I finish brushing Joel Orr aside like the annoying blowfly he is."

Washington, D.C.

Mark Cox noted the familiar number on his cell phone's caller I.D.

"Cox?"

"Good morning, Governor Myers."

"Where are you?"

Cox loosened his tie and settled onto a chair. "Senator Silver's office, Sir."

"You alone?"

Cox glanced over to the counter holding a coffee carafe and an assortment of fresh pastries.

"No, Governor. Mike Belan is here."

"Eleana?"

"The senator should be here at any moment. We're meeting about her opening speech."

"Good. I need your full attention on this. If she comes in before we finish, just hang up."

Cox shot a loaded look to Mike Belan.

"Do you wish for me to put you on speaker, Sir?"

"Not on your life. Matter of fact, I've changed my mind. I want you and Belan to leave there and call me back. Go to some coffee shop. Somewhere secure. I will await your call."

Cox hung up and frowned. "Follow me."

Mike Belan started to question him, then shrugged. He took a quick bite from a cheese Danish and washed it down with a swig of coffee. The two men left the Senate building and walked to a small bistro.

"What's with all the clandestine crap, Cox?" Belan asked.

"Governor Myers wishes to converse with some modicum of security. Who knows?"

Belan shook his head. "The man is a paranoid freak."

"Perhaps. But a powerful one. Be aware of him, Belan. He could just be our president one day. He has something to say, we listen."

"Like a cell phone is secure in this city. Give me a break."

They ordered two coffees and chose a corner booth far in the back of the establishment. Cox pressed the now-familiar number to Tad Myers' private cell phone.

"Belan with you?" The Governor asked.

"As you wished, Sir."

"Good. Don't put me on speaker, just listen and tell him what I've said."

"Yes."

Tad Myers said, "I know you've been paying attention to what's going on down here."

"Of course."

"It's only weeks until the primary, and Russell Nathan has got it in the bag."

"Yes, Sir."

"He's gaining some very powerful supporters, Cox. Several prominent members of The League of Women Voters have come out in favor of him. Why, I don't know. The man's the biggest womanizer this side of France."

Mark Cox heard a horn blast in the background. He pictured the Governor of Florida crouched in a parking lot or standing on Adams Street behind the Capitol building. The man had to drive his security staff insane.

"Listen, Cox. We have to nip this. Right now. Against Brad, Russell Nathan stood no chance in hell of winning. But, against Eleana...I can't say I'm comfortable. I don't like to feel uncomfortable, Mr. Cox."

"The most recent polls do favor Nathan."

"My point. You find a way, Cox. You *find* a way. I want Eleana running next to Orr in November. Benton and that group of his have too much influence. If we are to slow them down, our best bet is now, before Nathan can win the Democratic primary."

"Governor, I..."

Tad Myers' voice rose to carry over the noise of traffic. "See to it!"

"Yes, Governor Myers." Cox snapped the cell phone off and frowned. "What does he expect me to do, shoot him?" He offered a synopsis of the conversation to Mark Belan.

"The way I see it, Cox, old friend, we play on Russell Nathan's vulnerability."

When Mike Belan smiled, the hair on Cox's neck bristled.

"You leave it up to me, buddy," Belan said. "You take care of prepping the Ice Princess for her little debut speech to the Senate, and I'll see to Russell Nathan."

"Keep it...clean."

Mike Belan fished in his coat pocket for his cell phone. "*Clean* is my middle name. Don't worry. Nothing will come back to trip us up. Nathan will be his own worst enemy." He grinned. "With a little nudge. You go on back and wait for Eleana. I'll be right behind you."

As soon as Cox left, Mike Belan searched the address book for a familiar number and hit the talk button.

"Hey, Kitten. How's my favorite niece? Good. Look, I know you always need a little extra shopping cash and your uncle needs a little favor, so I have a proposition for you. It involves your two favorite things—plotting and pay-offs."

He laughed. "You think so much like your old uncle, I know you're from the family gene pool." More laughter. "I'll call you later with details."

Destin Beach, Florida

The view from the safari-themed bar at the *Red Rhino* looked out over a white stretch of beaches the developers referred to as *The Emerald Coast*—a portion of shoreline on the Gulf of Mexico, roughly bounded by Pensacola on the west and Port St. Joe on the east. Balladeer Tom T. Hall once sang lyrics, written by his wife Dixie Hall, about the area in the song *Redneck Riviera*.

Gulf Shores up through Apalachicola
They got beaches of the whitest sand
Nobody cares if Gramma's got a tattoo
Or Bubba's got a hot wing in his hand.

The water—on some days as crystal blue-green as any Caribbean sea—stretched to the horizon with whitecaps. The late summer heat built to the sweltering high-nineties by mid-afternoon. Off-shore storms ran small crafts to port and kicked up an occasional waterspout. Oblivious to danger, tourists flocked to the weather-induced waves with surf and boogie boards. The rip tides sucked in one or two nearly each week. The smart ones swam parallel to shore and waited for the undertow to release its hold. The stupid ones panicked, floundered, and made it to shore eventually, though not usually breathing.

Russell Nathan chewed on a handful of beer nuts and nursed a Long Island Iced Tea. Too bad it wasn't spring break, when drunk and easily-impressed young women flooded the bars and beaches. The serious students had fled inland for the fall semester. The few who remained were budding career barflies.

A feminine voice tore his concentration from the beer nuts. "You remind me of someone."

Russell glanced up, half expecting to see one of the many war-painted regulars who combed the bar scene. An unlined, youthful face greeted him.

"Movie star?" He winked.

She slid onto the padded stool beside him. "I think so. Kurt Russell, maybe. The little dimple in your chin."

"I've heard that before. Though, I'm surprised you know who he is." He motioned to the bartender. "Whatever the young lady would like."

"Martini. Very dry," she said. Her deep green eyes studied him. "Thank you…"

"Russ."

"Thank you, Russ."

"And, to whom do I have the pleasure?"

"Kiz." She glanced around the bar. Other than a scattering of late-season tourists, they had the room to themselves. "I hate this time of the summer. Don't you?"

"I don't know. At least, the service is good. No waiting lines."

She shrugged bare sun-kissed shoulders. Her mid-backlength brunette hair held red highlights. Not an ounce of fat marred any part of the skin Russell could see. He'd bet the unclothed view was just as good, if not better.

"What's with you, Kiz? Not back to college or whatever? I don't see many people in Destin Beach after Labor Day."

"I'm sitting the next semester out." She accepted the dry martini from the bartender and popped the olive into her mouth. "Tired of all that. Need a change. Life just gets so...predictable...sometimes."

"You from around here?"

"Now, Russ. Do I sound as if I am? If I do, let me just go shoot myself in the head."

Russell Nathan laughed. How refreshing. Body and brains. Not to mention, over the legal age. Benton would be proud.

She licked the moisture from her deep red lips. "What about you?"

"I am all over the state," he said. Not exactly a lie. "I own a beach house near here. I like the panhandle beaches better than the ones in South Florida. More private."

The young woman tilted her head. A slow smile played on her lips.

"Privacy. Don't find that much, anymore. Myself, I crave privacy." She picked up the martini and downed the remainder in one long draw.

Russell Nathan threw a handful of bills onto the bar. "You're in luck, Kiz. I have the perfect place for a little privacy."

Russell fumbled with the keys. The brunette was all over him. He pushed open the beach house's door. She grabbed his collar and drew him inside.

"What do you have to drink?" Kiz asked. She slipped her arms around Russell's thick waist and pressed against him.

"I got it all, sugar. Scotch, beer, wine. Help yourself to the bar."

The brunette kissed him hard. Her tongue flicked across his lips.

Russell felt tightness in his chest. This one was going to be a hot little number. "Jesus, sugar. You're gonna give your big daddy a heart attack."

Kiz reached down with one hand and gave his crotch a seductive squeeze. "Wouldn't want that."

"You fix us a couple of drinks. Scotch neat for me. I got to take a piss."

The former Governor left the room. Kiz searched a mirrored cabinet behind the lighted mahogany bar for two crystal rocks glasses. She poured two fingers of Tullamore Dew into each. To one, she added the contents of a small waxed paper pouch—a crushed Rohypnol. The drug—tasteless, odorless, and colorless—would leave no trace after seventy-two hours of ingestion and would not be found in any routine toxicology screen or blood test. Perfect.

"You will be the life of this little party, Governor."

Russell Nathan would act without inhibition, though Kiz doubted he had little to start with. Most important, he wouldn't be able to think clearly or retain a clear memory of his role in the evening's happenings.

Russell reappeared, wearing a pair of Bermuda shorts. His hairy, distended belly lapped over the elasticized waistband. Kiz bit her lower lip to avoid laughing. Good thing she didn't actually have to have sex with the man. The thought made her shiver.

"You cold, sugar?" Russell wrapped his arms around her. "I can help you out with that."

She pushed against his chest and handed him the tainted scotch. "I know you can. I can tell. Let's take this slow so we can savor it."

"I'm going to like you." Russell took a swig.

Kiz took his hand and led him to the couch. "I want to hear all about you. I am just fascinated by politics."

"Aw, c'mon, sugar. Let's not waste time on all of that."

She raised her glass. "I like to know my men. *Really* know them." She took a delicate sip.

Russell slugged the scotch. The room appeared slightly askew. "Whew. Reckon I should've ate something. This is going straight to my head." He winked. "Or, it could be just you."

Kiz grabbed her clutch. "Where's your bathroom?"

"Second door on the left down that hallway."

Kiz leaned over and flicked her tongue across his parted lips. "Don't miss me too much. I'll be right back. I just need to…freshen up a little."

Russell watched her walk away. The back view was as good as the front.

Kiz sat on the toilet and sent a quick text message: *Party is on. Spread the word.*

Some time later—hours?—Russell tried to focus through half-opened eyelids. Where did all the people come from? A strange, sweet scent filled the room. Music with a deep resonate bass thumped. He heard the sound of some kind of explosions outside. Was it the Fourth of July? Couldn't be.

Someone was throwing a hell of a party.

CHAPTER FIFTEEN

Homestead, Florida

Sid Dillard peeled three scratch-off lottery tickets from a roll and pushed them across the scarred counter to an elderly Hispanic woman. In the few weeks since he had started the cashier position at the Stop'n'Shop—referred to by locals as the Stop'n'Shoot—the same woman had regularly purchased three tickets every couple of days. She was skinny as one of the stray dogs that hung out around the dumpster behind the store, and her clothing was worn to wisps, yet she plunked down whatever change and bills she had to buy a piece of a dream.

Poor thing.

Sid Dillard knew better than to waste money on the lotto. Monkeys would fly from his butt before he won; the odds were too fantastic.

Besides, he possessed the ultimate in future security in the form of a handful of racy digital photographs: Eleana Silver and her Latino paramour. Sid smiled. Lady Luck had finally smiled on him. More than just smiled; she had beamed down, painted a halo over his head, and paved the road to the Emerald City.

Timing. Timing was everything.

The mindless job gave Sid ample time to think, to plan. Once he revealed his hand, he would be playing poker with the big dogs. What seemed to be such a simple transaction—memory card and photographs for cash—could end up poorly. This was beyond some passing flick of a drunken celebrity punching out a nightclub bouncer. Sid read the newspapers. He knew the Washington herd played with a loaded deck. People who crossed them often woke up dead.

He might live in the back of a van and work in a convenience store. He wasn't stupid.

Sid watched a teenager cruise the beer cooler. The kid barely looked old enough to shave. The flotsam of south Florida low society ebbed and flowed around him. He smiled, made polite conversation, and tried not to get shot.

The story of his stint as a poor man would make good chit-chat on Letterman.

Sid's heart rate accelerated. Just a few more weeks, and he would make his move. Just at the right time.

Washington, D.C.

Mike Belan glanced at his watch for the fifth time in less than fifteen minutes. "Where in the hell is she?"

"Her cell phone went straight to voicemail. I spoke to the housekeeper. She said they had left the townhouse," Gwen said.

Mark Cox straightened his tie. Gwen couldn't help but smile. No matter how hard the public relations man tried, he always managed to appear as if he had slept for several nights in his clothes. By the time they briefed Eleana—when she did arrive—the tie would be askew.

"We have to nip this, folks," Cox said. "It might be acceptable to arrive fashionably late in South Florida, but not here. Not with the press waiting in the wings. And certainly not for her first impression on the Senate."

The door flew open and Eleana Silver breezed in. Designer dress, shoes, and purse.

The senator's gaze rested on Gwen Reynolds. Cold. Accusing.

"Good morning, Senator Silver." Mark Cox nodded. "We were beginning to become concerned..."

Eleana cast her Coach purse on the desk. The metal embellishments clanged against the polished wood. Gwen flinched.

"Traffic is brutal in this place." She waved a hand dismissively. No need to tell them the real reason she was late. Sex in the back of a limo was something Brad Silver would never have condoned. Ramiro lived for the chance to touch her. Any place. Any time she wished.

"I'm here. What do I do now, besides give this speech? Pass some laws? Meet with the President?"

For a beat, Mark Cox had no words. Gwen glanced his way. Amazing. In all the time she had known him, she had never seen him speechless.

"Nice outfit, honey." Mike Belan spoke. "Not right for Washington, but hot all the same. You will make more than one of those stuffy coots in the Senate chamber sit up and take notice."

"Did you have a chance to read over the prepared speech, Senator?" Cox asked. His voice was a little strained.

Eleana smiled. "Mark...I have charmed the elite of Miami. I can handle Washington. Sure, I read it. Easy. I just get up and make an impassioned statement. My dear, departed husband, my love for this country, my dedication to the government and the great state of Florida. My issues with poor, premature babies. Blah, blah, blah."

"There is the matter of your attire," Cox said.

Eleana glanced down, then stared at him. "I paid more for this suit and shoes than you make in a month."

Cox's face colored. "I wasn't implying otherwise, Senator. Still, it is a little...provocative...for today's purposes."

The corners of her lipstick-wet mouth turned up. "If I can get you to think that, I can certainly wow the press."

Gwen came to the P.R. man's rescue. "I think what Mr. Cox is trying to say—if you please—is...your attire might be best if it's more in keeping with the conservative values of the Republican Party."

Eleana rolled her eyes. "It never changes, does it? It's all such a game up here. Brad loved to play. I don't. Nor, do I plan to."

Gwen Reynolds' spirits sank, the same way they had when she realized Eleana Silver wouldn't be just a passing irritation. How Mark Cox could back Governor Tad Myers' choice of candidates amazed her. Belan practically glowed. No surprise there. He was already in bed with United Sugar. Now, he would be rubbing shoulders with one of the ruling family's members.

Mike Belan stepped up to bat. "Listen, Eleana. We all know you're sexy. Hell, anyone with eyes knows it. But Gwen and Cox are right-on with this one. If you want to stay in the Senate seat come November, you have to play down the hooters a little."

The senator looked from one to the other. "What am I supposed to do? I can't run home and change."

Cox glanced at Gwen Reynolds. "You look to be about the same size as the senator. Change shirts with her. That will tone it down. We can spend some time adjusting for future appearances later on."

Eleana's perfect eyebrows arched. "Me? Wear her clothes?"

Gwen forced her breathing to calm. Several snippy replies battled for first place."I don't mind, Senator. We can switch back as soon as you return to the office."

Eleana considered. Sighed. "All right. But, you two leave."

Mike Belan grinned. "Oh, shucks. I thought we might get to stay for the show."

After Cox and Belan shut the door, Gwen slipped from her jacket and unbuttoned her tailored gray blouse.

"Let's get this straight, right off," Eleana said. She threw her silk shirt onto the floor and snatched the blouse proffered by the Chief of Staff. "You were Brad's friend—if that's what you call what you were to him—not mine. You best stay the hell out of my way."

Eleana felt a tingle. The twenty-foot twin oak doors with opaque glass provided her entry into the floor of the United States Senate. Would her father have been proud of her?

The familiar ache started deep inside. Eleana couldn't recall details about the man's face. Only in flashes within dreams did she see her father. A man of small stature. Of tight bear hugs. Unlike her aloof Uncle Sanchez, with his intolerance of little girls. His money had provided shelter, a good education, position in society. Little affection.

She remembered Brad telling her of his first impression of the most important forum for debate, perhaps in the world. He was right. It was beyond description. Earlier in the week, she had taken a tour of the Chamber by the Senate Clerk and been ushered to the location of her desk in the rear of room.

It was different now. Then, empty with little illumination. Now, senators moved across the aisles, overhead fixtures sprayed light, and the gallery was filled with visitors and the ubiquitous press. Before she made her way to her seat, Senator Eleana Silver paused a moment to admire her new home: the floor of the United States Senate.

"The presiding officer will cover a few housekeeping matters before he recognizes you," Mark Cox had instructed in a low voice before leaving her at the door. "Everything is planned and pre-arranged in the Senate. Usually, the surprises occur in the House."

In a few minutes, Cox nodded to Eleana from his seat in the gallery. She took a deep breath and stood.

"For what reason does the junior senator from Florida rise?"

Eleana fiddled with the lavaliere microphone pinned to her collar.

"Mr. President—to present my remarks and opinions on the inadequate funding of neo-natal intensive care for newborns in our country. I request for my remarks to be spread upon the pages of the Journal of the Senate, and that I may revise and amend the remarks as my time may consume." As she spoke, she stretched to recall the correct parliamentary jargon, but had to look down to her desk at the crib sheet Gwen Reynolds had prepared. Eleana hoped she had gotten it right.

She glanced up to the gallery and took note of the press corps. Cox had assured her; the members from the Florida print and electronic outlets would be in attendance. Louise Hampton of the *Fort Myers News Press* occupied a coveted front row seat.

Eleana had rehearsed the speech for three days straight; several times, standing naked at the foot of the bed with Ramiro as her admiring audience. She looked great. Now she had to sound great. She attempted to follow her notes as she had when she practiced with the dual TelePrompTer in her office with Gwen, Cox, and Belan watching.

"Remember to look up, and to the right and left," Cox had coached. "It's easy to remember to look at the television cameras because there is always a red light on a camera when it's recording."

Her desk was at the rear of the expansive room. The location of desks in the very front of the Chamber reflected seniority. Good for the ego. Mandatory when running for reelection. Senators coming in and out of the members-only entrance passed in front of her as she spoke. Even with the unsettling interruptions, she managed to stay on message.

The questions-and-answers element of a parliamentary address was normally reserved for the Committees in the Senate. Occasional exchanges did take place. Cox had warned that the Democrats might try to embarrass her by interrupting her speech. Each time a member entered the Chamber, Eleana watched out of the corners of her eyes to see if it looked as if he or she planned to ask questions.

"I hope the damned Democrats give her a break," Mike Belan said from his seat in the gallery. "She is like porcelain as it is."

"Lower your voice, Belan," responded Cox. "Don't give any of them ideas."

Eleana's speech was planned for thirty minutes. Her nervousness accelerated the delivery. She didn't realize it, but observers did. She did not pause for emphasis. She failed to look up as coached in her office. Her beauty and charm were lost on those watching her first speech. She was too mechanical. Too intense.

Considering all the pressures, the novelty of the experience, and the looming threat of embarrassment from Democrats pelting her with questions, the inexperienced senator pushed forward and did reasonably well.

One of her colleagues across the aisle rose to acknowledge the sincerity of Eleana's speech. "Mr. President, I rise to congratulate the junior senator from Florida. We all admired her husband, and we know he is looking down proudly to see his wife carry on their great family legacy, here in the Senate."

"The slime ball would probably like to get in her pants," mumbled Belan.

"Shh! Damn it," said Cox.

Eleana felt a rush of relief. She looked up into the gallery where the audience stood to applaud her address. Maybe they were just being nice.

Eleana removed the mic from her collar and sat down. Her heartbeat echoed in her ears. Perspiration dripped from beneath her breasts and armpits into the waist of her skirt. The presiding officer moved on to the next item on the calendar. Eleana barely heard his words.

Eleana Silver smiled. Dorothy Claxton was right. She could, and would, do this. She was going to be a player in this Senate. It might be dominated by men, but now they had one more woman. If she could help it, she would stay.

CHAPTER SIXTEEN

Destin Beach, Florida

Russell Nathan's head pounded. One hell of a hangover. When he had awakened in a jail cell in the wee hours, he figured he must've had more fun than ten New Year's Eve parties combined. Only, he couldn't recall a single detail much past meeting a pretty brunette in a beach bar.

Odd. He wasn't one for blackouts. No matter how knee-walking, stinking drunk Russell Nathan became, he always remembered every detail. Who needed humble apologies. Whether the latest female had been a true blonde. What kinds of liquor he had swilled.

The night before was a blank. He strained to recall the arrest and his one phone call. Now, he sat in campaign headquarters, wrapped in the Former President's wrath, with a roomful of workers shooting him disbelieving, disgusted looks.

"For the love of God, Russ. What the hell is your problem?" Buddy Benton paced back and forth.

"Calm down, Buddy." Russell tried to focus on the Former President. It was like watching a tennis match and the movement made him dizzy and slightly nauseated.

Buddy Benton stood still. "Calm down? Calm down! I get a call that my candidate is in jail. That he was found in a closet—a closet!—passed out, naked. And you want me to calm the fuck down?"

Former President Buddy Benton looked Governor Nathan directly in the eyes, "Russell, how could you have done this...with all we had lined up for you?"

"I don't know, Buddy...I guess a little partying just got out of hand..."

"Out of hand? Russ, a little indiscretion here and there, we probably could have finessed. But underage drinking, drugs, and who knows what else with those kids? The arresting officer told me there were over a hundred kids at your place. Someone was shooting off fireworks from your deck. Kids were higher than a Georgia pine and having sex in every room. They found pot and cocaine. Everyone was having a big old time. One of them was the daughter of a prominent local preacher! Not to mention, you were caught in the act with three minor females doing God knows what. Couldn't you have put a lid on that thing?"

"I guess that is what happens when Sarah is away. I just can't handle the temptation," responded Nathan. "It started out with just this one young lady. I swear, she was over twenty-one. Pretty little thing with long brown hair. Real class. She was around for awhile. Then, not. Before I knew it, a few more showed up. Then, more. I guess I was having such a ball, I didn't really notice how many were there. I was a little drunk."

"A little drunk? A little drunk! What you have done, Governor, is left us without a campaign and handed the nomination to that has-been, Joel Orr. Shit."

"Maybe we can find something to bail us out of this thing, Buddy. You're a lawyer, what about the statute of limitations?"

"Russell, you moron. The offense just occurred. The statute of limitations has not even started running."

"What about someone who can attest to my high nature and standing in the community? Maybe we can come up with something there? Or we could approach the witnesses at the party?"

Buddy Benton frowned. "Russell, I understand why you are not making any sense...I don't know if it is your alcohol-soaked brain or the stress of the situation, but messing with witnesses is the same as jury tampering. We are talking prison for a long time, and I want nothing to do with that."

"My God, O.J. Simpson got off a murder charge that everyone on this planet figured he committed, so surely there is another Johnnie Cochrane somewhere we can use."

"That is the only thing you have said tonight that makes sense. Maybe we can look at some world class trial lawyers to see if they can come up with something. Someone like Cochrane..."

Benton knew the trial lawyer industry well. They had bankrolled all of his campaigns. Through Benton, the trial bar had mega bucks already invested in the Nathan operation. The key to finding any kind of potential *technical out* for the campaign was probably through trial experts and consultants. They had experience at exploiting loopholes in legal cases. Even if their strategies didn't hold water, they were often persuasive with juries.

That's it! Former President Benton thought.

The incident had occurred in North Florida, which was as good as Mississippi or Alabama in a trial. Maybe there was hope they could beat the anticipated charges of providing liquor and drugs to minors. Not to mention DNA evidence from any of the probable hanky-panky going on with the kids.

The clock was running. If they could not find a technicality to lean on in the next few hours, the press would have picked up on the incident. With the tie-in to a race for the U.S. Senate, the sordid details would be splashed across the front page of newspapers and online magazines within minutes. They had to act. Fast.

Benton yelled, "Move now, people! Find the best trial lawyers in Florida. Call 'em at home, on vacation, get 'em out of bed, for chrissakes...whatever it takes."

The campaign team—mostly Democratic party participants—didn't really understand the reasoning, but started tapping on their BlackBerries.

Russell put his head in his hands and mumbled, "Why...why...we had it all...just because I can't control my pecker..."

"Shut up, Russ." Buddy Benton's face mirrored his disgust.

No one wanted to jump in with a show of sympathy. Most knew this was not Russell Nathan's first experience with rampant temptation. If he could just get the law enforcement folks to sit on the charges until his team could come up with something to buy time. Time to shuck the wave of negative press. Or, give him a face-saving way to pull out of the race.

Buddy Benton pondered the worst case scenario. "Is there any way we could somehow get someone else into the race in place of Russell?"

The top aides shot confused expressions at each other. Clearly, Russell Nathan wasn't the only one not thinking. Campaign qualifications were over. If their candidate had to duck and cover, no time remained to put another puppet into place.

The President paced. "Come on folks, the clock is running on this one."

Russell Nathan's head pounded. "What am I going to tell the League of Woman Voters? They actually believed all that load of crap I told them about Sarah, and about Orr's pandering."

The people who made the laws were expected to also uphold them.

One of the campaign volunteers turned pale. He stared at his laptop monitor. "President Benton? Governor Nathan? You'd better see this."

A crowd congealed around the volunteer. In the YouTube video clip—one of several—a nearly naked Russell Nathan danced around with a pair of lacy women's bikini underwear draped across his head. Two notably underage women—scantily clad—ran their hands along his bare chest. Someone passed him a lit joint. Nathan took a deep drag and fondled the breasts of one of the girls. His arousal, noticeably apparent.

Buddy Benton spoke. "We. Are. Seriously. Screwed."

Washington, D.C.

Mike Belan's cell phone vibrated. He checked the caller ID and smiled.

"Hello, Kitten. Yes, I've seen the YouTube videos. Beautiful. Absolutely over-the-top."

He listened for a second, then said, "You sure you don't just want the money? You could take a nice little trip on your fall break."

Mike Belan laughed. "Go to the Mercedes dealership and order it. Have the rep call me."

Mike Belan grinned and shook his head. His niece was a chip off the old block. If she chose, she could have a brilliant future in Washington.

Eleana Silver—accustomed to being catered to and for—made a rapid adjustment to the trappings of being a United States senator. This was pampering at an altogether different level.

"Gwen, I want to join the mark-up meeting on that continuing resolution," Eleana said to her Chief of Staff.

A mark-up meeting served for the routine amending of the appropriations legislation. In this case, the funds in question were earmarked for The Arts across the country.

"As I have said before, a senator can participate in any Senate proceeding, whether on the floor, in committee, or even in caucus," said Gwen.

Eleana avoided eye contact or any hint of civility. "I really would like to sit in on this one. Because of Vizcaya. You know they get a nice slug of federal dollars, I am told."

Gwen hesitated before answering. Surely, Eleana Silver understood the principle of *conflict of interest*. Or did she?

"Senator, it might be best if you waited until Mr. Cox and I can brief you on the proper protocol."

Eleana brushed her aside. "What meeting room are they in? Is it still at three p.m.?"

"It is over in the Dirksen Building. And, yes, three is correct."

The Dirksen Senate Office Building—the second office building constructed for members of the United States Senate—was named in 1972 after the late Minority Leader Everett Dirksen from Illinois. The seven-story building faced in white marble stood across First Street from the Old Senate Office Building, diagonally across the Capitol grounds from the Senate wing of the Capitol. More streamlined and less ornate, the newer building harmonized with its older neighbors. Bronze spandrels between the third and fourth-floor windows depicted scenes from American industry: shipping, farming, manufacturing, mining and lumbering. Below the building's west pediment, the inscription read: *The Senate is the Living Symbol of Our Union of States.*

How many visitors just passed it by without really appreciating its history and significance? Brad Silver had been an expert on the finite details of the city where he served.

Gwen doubted Eleana would care about anything of significant historic value in Washington. "I will call the Chairman's staff and let them know you are attending."

She shot Gwen a dark look. "No need to tell them what my interest is."

Gwen left for her private office. The scenario was a political embarrassment for a new senator. About to happen. Part of her wanted to stop it. A larger part urged her to allow Eleana Silver to make her own mistakes, no matter how huge. Having Brad's wife in Washington on a temporary basis seemed bearable. Once she realized the long-range plans, Gwen's spirit slipped into darkness. How long she could hold out working for *this* Senator Silver—or, if she would want to—was anyone's guess.

When Eleana arrived at the Dirksen Building for the mark-up shortly after it started, she announced, "I am Senator Silver from Florida. Where is the mark-up on The Arts?"

The members, staff, and on-lookers exchanged glances. How could it be that the senator—even a brand new one— would not know where to sit in the mark-up process?

Chairman Kawaski of Hawaii, sitting at the head of the table, said, "Senator, we are in the middle of the mark-up, but we will stop what we are on so you may join us."

Interrupting an important appropriations meeting, not good for a green senator who had not even taken the time to learn the mark-up process.

The Chairman asked Eleana after she was seated, "Senator, what would be your area of interest?"

"A little charitable group in Florida known as the Vizcayans, Mr. Chairman. I...they...are highly supportive of The Arts. We have worked for years to add to the preservation of culture in South Florida."

Bells and sirens clanged. Surely the new senator knew her personal interest in federal funding of a project would either be, or appear to be, a blatant conflict of interest?

"We covered that issue in the last meeting, Senator. As a courtesy to you, we will stop where we are now, and revert back to that area of the bill."

Everyone expected Eleana to decline the Chairman's generous and polite offer.

"Thank you, Mr. Chairman. That would be very helpful, because I have some personal business to attend to this afternoon. I won't be able to stay for the duration."

The Chairman, members, and all present in the meeting were aghast. What senator—albeit a brand new one—would come uninvited to a meeting of the Appropriations Subcommittee funding all of the arts in the country and insist her personal pet interest be bumped to the top of the agenda?

A reporter watching the entire spectacle, Louise Hampton of the *Fort Myers News Press,* scribbled notes at a feverish pace. The scene was unheard of in Washington, and there were very few other reporters in the room. This could be major news, certainly with the ethics watchdogs like *Common Cause*.

"I am not sure how this process works, but I really think the Vizcayan's project needs to increase its funding over previous allocations," insisted Eleana.

"Mr. Chairman, I respect the junior senator from Florida, but would like to be recognized for a motion," said a stunned senior Subcommittee member from Montana.

The Chairman said: "State the nature of your motion, Senator."

"If the Chairman recognizes the junior senator from Florida's request as a motion—in whatever form she intended—I would like to be recognized to lay the senator's motion on the table."

A barely audible gasp echoed in the hushed committee room. The senator from Montana had exercised a most extraordinary parliamentary procedure, one meant to send the junior senator from Florida a very clear message—don't barge in here and demand an appropriation out of order. And especially if it is for something for which the said senator has a real or perceived conflict of interest.

The Chairman nodded. Hopefully, the senator from Montana would not further embarrass Eleana by suggesting that her conduct be referred to the Committee on Ethics.

Louise Hampton wrote so fast, she broke her pencil tip. How could a U.S. senator know so little about the process of law-making and appropriating public funds? Conflict of interest aside, the Vizcayans in Miami were not the highest priority for the Federal government with the Iraq war and funding deficit spending.

Could this be something that might come up in the future during Eleana's first run for office? The potential for damage was huge.

CHAPTER SEVENTEEN

Orr for Senate Headquarters—Miami, Florida

After circling the block once and finding no available parking spots, Karen pulled into a loading zone and slammed the brake to the floor. She ran to the front door of the Orr Campaign Headquarters on 36th Street, flew past two bewildered volunteers, and threw open the door to the back office. Joel and Don sat at the table listening to Ronnie Taylor's flip-chart presentation on the latest available poll numbers from Bendixen and Associates, a multi-lingual opinion survey group in Coral Gables, Florida. Sergio Bendixen—the renowned Hispanic pollster—provided the latest information on Latinos in Miami/Dade County.

"Daddy! Have you heard?"

Joel checked his watch and glanced up. "You're here early. Shouldn't you be at work? What's up, Bug?"

Karen jiggled in place. Her father smiled. How many times had he seen the little happy dance when she was a tow-headed little girl?

"I was just listening to WIOD and they said Russell Nathan has scheduled a press conference for this afternoon. I had to come tell you! I tried and tried the cell numbers. They all went straight to voicemail," Karen said. "What's up with that?"

Don pointed to the cell phone on the desk. "Dead as a doornail. Had to charge it. The others are in use."

"Oh." Karen jiggled some more. "The rumor is that he is dropping out of the race and…"

Don Farringdon interrupted "What? You gotta be kidding, Karen."

"No, I'm not. I am as shocked as anyone. I came as soon as I heard." Karen glanced around the room. "I thought one of you was bringing in a television. I'm sure it's already on CNN."

Taylor spoke: "One problem. No cable. Up to now, it has been an expense we've passed on." He looked to Don and Joel. "We really do have to get on that. If...when...we make it past the primary, it would be nice to watch what the media is up to. I can find live-feeds on the Internet. Sure. I still think it's a justified expenditure."

Joel waved a hand dismissively. "We'll get cable. We'll get cable. Now, where can we go to check this out?"

Ronnie Taylor jumped up. "I know a couple of guys who are interns over there. That will be faster than looking online. I'll grab one of the cells from the volunteers."

Farringdon hooted. "My God! You know what this means? We win the primary." His brow wrinkled. "Oh...but what about the ballots?"

"That's what I wondered as soon as I heard it. I was thinking about it so hard, I almost side-swiped a kid on a bicycle," said Karen.

Don's question was significant. Because qualifying was over, the State Elections Division had printed the primary ballots with enough time to distribute the absentee ballots. With less than two weeks until the primary, the ballots were already in the hands of a percentage of the registered voters. It really didn't matter what Russell Nathan announced. His name would be on the ballot.

"Damn it. This could potentially be another Florida ballot screw-up. If we weren't the laughing stock of the country in 2000 with Bush-Gore, we sure the hell are going to be now."

Ronnie called one associate in the Nathan Campaign from a corner of the front office, careful to keep his voice low to protect his contact.

Ronnie Taylor walked into the office and stared blankly at the team. "Unreal. He is dropping out. For sure. My guy won't say exactly, but it sounds like something really embarrassing."

"That means it's like a stick of dynamite," Don said. "Listen folks. No one says a word to anyone until we hear it officially and discuss it as a team. Okay by you, Joel?"

"You bet. Damn. And I was just getting that buffoon lined up in my sights." Joel paused. "My God. Instead of warming up on Nathan, I have to go straight to campaigning against the gorgeous widow of a beloved dead senator. Shit, this thing just went from hard to impossible."

"It's worse than that, Joel," said Ronnie Taylor. "This ballot issue—in reality, we have won. But we still have to run against someone who will not serve, and what if Nathan wins?"

Don Farringdon pulled at his hair. "Agghh! My worst nightmare. What if we win by a sliver? No one will give us a dime."

Joel held up both hands."Now, slow down. Let me get this straight. After Nathan's announcement that he is withdrawing from the race, his name stays on the ballot, right?"

"Yeah," answered Taylor.

"We then have an election. If I win, fine; but what happens if I lose?"

"I suppose the courts will have to decide that one, Joel," said Don. "It is all moot if we win. It's possible that this announcement today might be reversed. For the love of God. My head is splitting. Does anyone have any Tylenol—the big ones?"

Karen dug in her purse and handed Don Farringdon two extra-strength tablets. He popped them into his mouth and took a huge swig of bottled water.

Ronnie Taylor picked at the tape wrapped around the bridge of his glasses. "The numbers really scare me. Not only do we have to win; we have to win big. This kind of reminds me of the *Seinfeld* episode...the one about producing a show about nothing—a show within a show. Ours could be about a primary campaign about nothing. No opponent. Nothing except the humiliation if we lose."

"Maybe I should have kept working instead of screaming over to tell you guys," joked Karen.

"Subject to thinking this thing through—especially after Nathan's press conference—I say we keep going as fast as we can," Joel said. "Ironic. We can win and still lose. Why do things like this happen to me? Anyone like to join me at the Alibi? I could use a drink."

Karen shook her head and hugged her father. "Daddy. We are going to overcome this, too. We have all come too far."

Don Farringdon balled up his fists and struck a he-man pose. "Let's strap 'em on and go after the little princess from Coral Gables."

"Take no hostages!" yelled Taylor.

The three stared at the normally-sedate numbers man.

"Ronnie, you give me hope, dude," Don said. "I don't think I've seen this kind of emotion from you...ever."

Taylor tapped Russell Nathan's name into the Google Search Bar. A few more clicks. He laughed. "Unreal. Get a load of this!" He pushed the laptop around for the group to view.

Russell Nathan gyrated across the screen with what appeared to be a pair of hot pink underpants on his head. His naked, hairy belly bounced in time. Young girls twirled at his side.

Karen shook her head. "I thought I had seen just about everything. This seals it." She pinched her eyes shut. "That image will be forever burned in my mind."

"Whatever this was...looks like it was one heck of a party. Way to go, Russ!" Ronnie Taylor grinned. Then his lips drew into a thin line. "Got to feel sorry for the guy, though."

"Why?" Don asked.

"His wife is a religious-nut, ball-buster, from what I've heard. She'll hit the roof. Probably take the guy down all the way to below zero. That could be way worse than what the media is going to do to him."

"Don't be so sure. Men like Russell Nathan have a way of recreating themselves...like Britney Spears or Madonna." Don smiled. "There's famous and there's infamous."

The rest of the team stared at Don.

"Okay...the train analogy comes to mind. You're sitting at the crossing. Train is rushing by in front of you. Bet you can't remember a single one of the cars in the middle. Just the engine and the caboose."

Karen blinked. "Clear as mud, Don."

"All I'm saying...very good and very bad stand out in a crowd. Don't count Russell the Naked Dancer out just yet."

Joel chuckled. "Maybe we should sign him up to help our side."

Don considered. "He does have a lot of connections." He shook his head. "Nope. Too risky. At least, we couldn't have his upfront support."

Ronnie Taylor clicked the play button on the YouTube segment. Russell Nathan gyrated. "Old hot pants Russ."

Don watched the clip again. "Look at it this way—Joel looks all the squeakier by comparison. So what if he drinks a little? Failed as a husband. Has a brother who's a convicted felon. Can't give a speech without tripping over his words. At least he didn't show up on computer monitors around the world, half-naked with bikini undies on his head. Joel, you look like a saint next to Russell Nathan."

"Glad he lowered the bar," Joel said.

"Joel, my boy...unless you do something worse than this, I think we can take on anyone. Even Eleana Silver," Don Farringdon said.

The others nodded.

Orr smiled. With a team like his, he might just pull it off. *Bring it on*, he thought. *Throw it all at me.*

Office of the Governor—Tallahassee, Florida

Aide Kemp Johnson looked up just in time to duck. A writing tablet flew past his left ear and skittered across the polished wood floor. If he didn't end up in the E.R. by the time the senatorial election was over, it would be a miracle.

"Did you see it? Did you see it, Kemp?" Governor Tad Myers asked.

His boss could turn a double cartwheel, and it wouldn't surprise him. The man was in need of serious medication. God help the country when, and if, he ever ran for President.

"Do you mean the YouTube segment, Governor?"

The Governor's manic laughter made the fine hairs on Kemp's neck bristle.

"I don't know how it all came down, but it did. Funniest damned thing I have ever seen. Russell Nathan whooping it up with jailbait. Got to love it! By tomorrow, it will be splashed across news reports around the world. God, you have to love technology. A few years back, this wouldn't have gone much past the state lines."

"It probably would have made the newspapers, Sir. He was arrested. Hard to hide that."

"Printed words, Kemp. Printed words. This picture is worth a thousand front page headlines. And it has already circulated the globe by this time."

Kemp Johnson knew; the same technology that could make a man could also break a man. Heaven forbid if Tad Myers ever pitched one of his little fits where anyone could record it.

Tad Myers held a fist in the air. "We have it clinched. Eleana Silver is in. Orr might have a few minutes of fame, but by this time in six months, people will barely remember his name."

The Silvers' Georgetown Townhouse

"You have the most beautiful butt." Ramiro stroked Eleana's naked bottom with the tip of one finger.

"It sticks out too far."

He kissed the small of her back. "No. It is perfect, *mi amor*. I don't like such women with no cushions."

Eleana stretched and yawned. "I need to get up."

"It is Sunday. A day of rest."

She turned over and regarded her lover. "I don't know if I should rest until after the election. I have so much to learn."

Ramiro nibbled on her earlobe. "I will teach you all you need to know."

Eleana gave him a gentle shove. "Seriously. I am like a fish trying to breathe on land. It's all so confusing. All the rules. A certain way to speak. A certain way to dress. To act."

"With your beauty, I don't know why you worry."

"I never thought I would like politics." She sat up and hugged her knees to her chest. "All the power. More than I ever imagined. So much more than Vizcaya."

"You don't have to stay here."

"I don't. I know. But I think I might."

He studied her. His compatriots in Cuba would be thrilled if Eleana Silver stayed in place. With Brad Silver out of the way, and Ramiro in a position to yield subtle influence and report back with inside information beneficial to the dictator, his standing in the Party would be greatly enhanced. The better his standing in the party, the better the chances of an overthrow of the corrupt regime. He thought of Dorothy Claxton. The wealthy socialite's continued support would help. A free Cuba would benefit the purses of many people.

The trick was to lead without Eleana realizing she had taken the bit.

"You are a smart woman. No one gives you credit." He brushed a strand of hair from her eyes. "You are so much more than the world sees."

"I think they are just starting to realize," she said. "Last week, I made some remarks when I questioned the Chairman of the Central Intelligence Agency. News pundits stood up and took note. Some of my comments ended up on the front page of the *Washington Post* and the *New York Times.*" She smiled. "How did that one reporter put it? 'Her thoughtfulness is hidden by her Spanish beauty. Florida has sent up a real player.' "

She laughed. "Funny, isn't it? Not that long ago, they were panning me." Eleana paused and looked at the Senate Committee binder on the bedside table—it read in gold leaf on the cover, *Senator Eleana Silver*. Her parents would have been so proud. Would Brad have been as proud? As a junior United States senator from Florida, she was a member of the most exclusive club in the world.

"Did you know...the room where we met is called the Church Committee Room, named after the late Idaho Senator Frank Church? He was a liberal and was probably most responsible for the deterioration in the country's intelligence gathering capability. There we were, deliberating improvements to our intelligence operations in a committee room named after the guy who almost destroyed the whole thing. Washington is so difficult to understand. So many contradictions. Everyone just shrugs them off as *just inside the beltway.* Like that's supposed to make it all crystal clear."

Ramiro thought about the confusing maze within Castro's regime. "Governments are often that way."

Eleana waved her hand through the air. "Why should I resign, Ramiro? I'm going to be elected. Cox and Belan assure me of that, especially now. I'm up against a has-been politician with a drinking problem. How could I possibly lose?"

"You have it—how do you say—in the sack?"

She laughed and caressed his cheek. "The *bag,* darling. I have it in the bag."

She rose and slipped into a silk robe. "Besides, that was a deal submitted by a man. A man who had his own agenda—not mine. I know I originally agreed to resign after the election when Governor Myers first appointed me to fill Brad's position. That was in a time of confusion. It was then. This is now. Who might Tad Myers select to replace me? Hmm?"

Ramiro shook his head. When Eleana Silver talked, he had found it best to just listen. The more she talked; the more he learned.

"...probably a flunky who wouldn't think with the independence I have already demonstrated. Not even close."

She wrapped her long hair into a soft bun and secured it with a hairpin. "I am the wife of a former, duly-elected senator from Florida, and the current sitting senator. I have no intention of resigning. Dorothy Claxton is right—as she always is—I am destined to sit with the mighty, not on the sidelines. If Hillary Clinton can do it, so can I."

Washington, D.C.

Eleana stood at the threshold to her Chief of Staff's office. "Gwen, will you be a dear and pick up my cleaning from the cleaners this afternoon? I need it by three p.m."

Gwen glanced up from the computer screen. "No, Senator. That is during working hours. Though it is a minor request, I am uncomfortable violating Senate rules."

Mark Cox and Mike Belan passed by on their way to the office conference room and hesitated by the open door.

Mark Cox stepped beside Eleana. "Excuse me, ladies, but I couldn't help but overhear. Senator, you may not know that federal employees cannot run personal errands on government time, even for U.S. senators."

Eleana glanced from Gwen to Cox. "I don't really see the problem, Mark. This is not a big deal. I have a caucus to attend. I need clean clothes to conduct my duties." She flashed one of her most alluring smiles, though the tone of her voice echoed irritation."No one will notice."

Gwen watched the exchange.

A few seconds passed before Belan said, "I'm sure you and I use the same cleaners, Senator Silver. I have to go, anyway. I can pick them up."

Eleana's dark eyes regarded the lobbyist. Damn, she was a fine specimen of the female species. What he wouldn't give...

"Thank you, Mike. It's a shame my staff cannot serve their senator as needed."

Mark Cox glanced toward Gwen. "Miss Reynolds, may I speak with you in the conference room?"

Gwen tapped a computer key to save her work. She brushed past Eleana and Belan with a slight nod.

In the empty conference room, Cox motioned her to one of the cushioned chairs. He sat down opposite the Chief of Staff. "Gwen, you did the right thing there with the senator. As it was in the mark-up the other day, Eleana is not familiar with Senate rules and regulations. She has been pampered all of her life. She expects anyone within her orbit to serve at her beck and call."

"I understand, Mr. Cox. That is not why I got a law degree. That is not why I worked so hard for her late husband—to position him as one of the country's foremost voices on intelligence matters of concern to the United States of America."

Cox rested his chin on his tented fingers. "We just need to get through this time and past the election. I really need your help to keep things on track."

"Maybe I'm not a good fit for Eleana. I gave Brad my word before he died..." Tears gathered in her eyes and spilled onto her cheeks. She brushed them quickly aside.

"Gwen, I am so sorry..."

"Let me finish." She took a shaky breath. "I promised Brad I would continue to carry out my responsibilities in this office with integrity. Chasing after dry-cleaning like a lap dog—on federal time—is against the rules, and the antithesis of integrity. I will honor my promise to Brad Silver, whether he is here...or not."

"Why don't you take a little time away from today's agenda? A cooling-off period. Take a couple hours of personal leave. Treat yourself to a massage? Do a little shopping? What do you say, Gwen?" said Mark.

"Don't insult me, Mr. Cox. I don't need a time out. How juvenile. I can—and shall—maintain a professional demeanor toward the senator. I will not budge on this one."

"God. I respect you, Gwen."

Gwen Reynolds stood. She stared down at Mark Cox for a moment before she said, "I wish I could say the same. I'm finding it difficult to believe all of this, even from you. Putting someone into a powerful position—someone whose main agendas are bringing Communist Cuba to its knees and...I don't know...buying a new pair of shoes?"

Mark Cox took a deep breath. Stood to face her. "It is not for me to say."

She shook her head. Her words, barely audible and devoid of inflection: "Coming from a man who has always been two steps ahead of every political circle-jerk in this town, that scares me more than anything else."

CHAPTER EIGHTEEN

Tallahassee, Florida

The late-afternoon thunderstorms pummeled the state capital with sheets of water and lightning bolts that sent even the most lion-hearted dashing for cover. Drivers intent on gaining a few extra minutes on their couches failed to slow down to accommodate the saturated roads. Wreckers circled like vultures awaiting fresh road-kill. Still, most of the locals—those who actually voted—managed to make it to the polls. They wore patriotic-themed "I Voted" stickers like military badges of honor. Downtown, television vans turned the narrow streets into an R.V. park.

The polls closed at seven p.m. in most of the state of Florida, but an hour earlier in the western panhandle due to the change from Eastern to Central time zones. After all the screw-ups with the 2000 election, the Florida Division of Elections took a little extra time to process the primary results. The last thing any of the officials wanted was to invite the inevitable barrage of lawsuits.

The Division had released partial votes from around the state after they had been reviewed and approved by the sixty-seven county election officials. Though Nathan had withdrawn from the race weeks earlier, the votes teetered back and forth between Joel Orr and Russell Nathan. The short notice had not provided sufficient time to erase Nathan's name off the ballot—especially the absentee ballots. The primary garnered national attention—not so much for its political importance, but for the potential for yet another Sunshine State whacked-out election. Everyone speculated.

If things went south for the Senate seat, what would happen during the next presidential contest? Emails flew. Text messages crisscrossed. Idle chit-chat over drinks turned from the late summer heat and humidity to politics.

People discussed. Lobbyists fidgeted. Lawyers salivated. Few things affected the Capital City as thoroughly, unless the annual Florida State vs. University of Florida football game happened to be on home turf.

The cameras rolled as the Florida Secretary of State approached the battery of microphones and glaring television lights.

"Ladies and gentlemen, we are able to now project that Joel Orr is the Democratic nominee for the United States Senate, by virtue of receiving 52% of the votes cast today by the Democrats."

One of the reporters—from the local CBS affiliate—mumbled in the front row, "Great. The guy wins an election against someone who isn't even running. Gotta love this state."

The adjacent reporter nodded. "Yeah, but at least the guy won. Can you imagine what would have happened if he would've lost?"

A third reporter—a non-local woman from Atlanta with a thick southern drawl—commented, "I really think Florida is going to give California a run for the money when it comes to the *land of fruits and nuts* title. You people can't run an election without some kind of weirdness to save your natural-born lives."

Orr for Senate Headquarters—Miami, Florida

Don Farringdon leaned in close to the small television, watching the Secretary of State's announcement. A clutch of campaign workers cheered behind him. He felt a little sorry for them. This kind of news deserved a flat-screen high-definition monitor. The television was a battered black and white, a left-over from someone's football tailgating days. Beggars couldn't be choosers, his mother used to say.

"Whew, we ducked a bullet," he mumbled. "Ronnie, Karen, let's join Joel in his office right away."

The team assembled in Joel Orr's office. His television—a small color model, not much larger than the other. At least it wasn't like watching old TV-Land reruns.

Don Farringdon slapped his hand on the table. "All right guys...I see this as a good news, bad news. The good news is we won. The bad news is it was only by two points. We have to shape this as a total downtrodden has-been *pol* who has come back and beaten a former Governor."

Ronnie Taylor laughed. "Don, Nathan wasn't even a candidate."

Farringdon smirked. "I understand. But this is the hand we've been dealt. We have a chance to spin this as an unexpected victory, flawed or not. It is not Joel's fault his opponent fell from grace."

Joel agreed. "Good point. If we can get the press to spin this our way, we can get the attention of the lobbyists and their deep-pocket clients. We need dough and lots of it to beat this lady." He gestured to the front page of the *Washington Post*. Eleana Silver—all smiles and glamour—posed with the Secretary of State. All chummy. Like they had been friends all of their lives. Probably been shoe shopping together. Swapped recipes. Joel stopped the line of thought. A bit too sexist. He admired women in positions of power, yet old male habits were hard to overcome.

"All right. Let's get a war room set up and start churning out press releases, e-mails, broadcast faxes, phone banks, the works," Don said.

Taylor sat down and tapped computer keys. "I'll update the website and drop by the political forums for a few posts."

Karen said, "I'll work on a piece for my blog."

Don Farringdon held up his hands to form a frame as if he was a world-famous film director staging a scene. "Joel Orr defeats a former Governor. Now, head to head for a seat representing the great state of Florida in the United States Senate!" He added, "Just don't get into the two-point margin of victory issue."

In the other room, shouts reverberated. "Orr! Orr! Orr!"

Joel smiled and said to Karen, "Bug, the death of your old man is greatly exaggerated."

Karen leaned down and kissed her father on the cheek. "Daddy, I love you. And I am *so* very proud of you."

Don Farringdon clapped his hands. "Love the sentiment, folks. Hate to break it up. Take a picture of it and post it online. We've got work to do."

Karen wadded up a campaign flyer—one that had been used as a coffee cup coaster—and pitched it toward Farringdon. It missed him by a couple of inches and banged Ronnie Taylor on the head before ricocheting into the wastebasket.

Joel laughed. "Good arm, Bug."

Destin Beach, Florida

Russell Nathan passed the time dreaming up creative analogies to match his current situation. He saw himself as the last rat aboard the sinking Titanic. The other rats had loaded up the only lifeboats with everything they could tote off. Unlike the infamous ocean liner disaster, even the rats in steerage managed to wrangle a safe spot. And the band did not play bravely while the last lights went out.

Other times, his situation reminded him of the small-town carnivals of his North Florida youth. The morning after the glamorous frenzy of greasy food and sideshows, poor little abandoned Russell stood in a litter-pocked field, wondering. Where had the Ferris wheel gone? The fortune-teller lady's booth? The bearded fat lady? The mounds of buttered popcorn and sticky cotton candy? In the middle of the night, the happy troupe had packed up and slipped off.

Either way, he had been screwed. Rode hard and put up wet. Road kill drying in the summer sun. Prized bass out of water.

The beach house—always a place of solace, not to mention endless libation and debauchery—was now an empty shell. Hades held no vengeance equal to Sarah's scorn. Hot on the trail of the breaking news, his *precious rose* had arrived in the country with fury as her back-pack. Two days after his withdrawal from the Senate race, she and a rat-faced boy lawyer had appeared on his doorstep. Two moving vans—their giant maws open and hungry—blocked the driveway for the morning. When they left, the decorating scheme had gone all to Hell.

Sarah had been generous. She left him one bed and the porch chair where he sat, looking out to sea.

Russell sipped the last of a strong cup of coffee—thank God she had left the coffeemaker—as he struggled to piece together the total weirdness. Benton and his powerhouse had vacated the defunct campaign headquarters before the lights went out. Now, they didn't take, or return, his calls. Not that he cared. The term *political friend* was the biggest oxymoron in recorded history.

The real surprise: his newfound fame amongst the younger set.

"You're a hit, my man," J. R. King had said in a recent phone conversation. "Get online and Google yourself."

He did, and nearly lost what little brain he had left. Of the over-one-thousand listings, the top fifty led to recent websites starring the former Governor as the new-found king of sin and debauchery. His favorite—www.weluvnathan.com—featured a live chat room where members from across the globe could log on and discuss his antics in detail.

The legend grew, as legends will. By some accounts, the Destin Beach Get-Down had encompassed two blocks, with coveys of naked bronzed beauties having anonymous sex with anyone willing to strip. Nathan signed online every couple of hours just to see what new pieces of expanded truth would emerge: The beach had been strewn with spent kegs. Someone blew up a fishing pier. It had taken two

"As much as I would love to, Mark Cox assures me that it would not be wise. We must keep up the unified front during the rest of the campaign. Though, I don't see why. Everyone knows I shall win."

"Yes."

Eleana shifted so that she could see Ramiro's face. "I'm scared."

He kissed her earlobe and neck. "What do you fear? I will vanquish these fears."

"Cox told me just yesterday. Brad's accident? Probably not an accident. There are strong leads tying it to Castro's supporters."

Ramiro hesitated. "I could see where that might be possible. He was not one of the dictator's favorites."

"Don't you see, Ramiro? I could be next. If I continue to work toward his regime's downfall, they will come for me. And you and I know...no safe place exists when you are targeted."

"Then you must think like him and play his game."

Eleana's expression darkened. "Become like him? Never!"

"You could not be like him, Eleana." He hugged her close. "But you could make him believe you are on his side."

She frowned.

"I know I am just your lowly servant..."

Eleana traced her fingertips across his lips. "You are much, much more, and you know that."

"How is the expression? Keep your friends close and your enemies closer?"

"Yes."

He continued. "Once you get into your full power, and the time is right, you shall become his advocate."

She drew back. "What? Me, support that butcher?"

He held up a hand. "Hear me out. I have often thought of this. But me...I have no position to act. If you can convince the proper parties to relax the trade restrictions against him, the United States could be in a position to infiltrate from within."

"They could do that now."

He nodded. "Yes. But, this coming in through the back door...it would be unexpected."

"It would make him rich, Ramiro. Why would...?"

He held a finger to her lips. "Think beyond the obvious, *mi amor*. The money will eventually filter down to the people. Your people. Plus—as the relations improve, you and I will be able to travel to our native land and see our families. As the ambassador of good will between the countries, you would be welcomed."

For a moment, Eleana felt a wash of nostalgia—such a sense of Cuba, she could almost taste the blend of tropical flavors on her tongue.

She smiled. "Do you really think we could do this?"

"We can...and will."

Homestead, Florida

Sid Dillard sat on the curb and drank the last sip of warm root beer. He talked to himself. No one seemed to care, or notice.

"Little shit kid. How was I supposed to know she was the owner's niece?"

Being a nice guy didn't pay. It had landed him on the street once again. Fired from a convenience store. How low could he possibly go?

"Not like those damned hotdogs were worth what they wanted me to charge. Hell, they turn to rubber after a few hours. Just rolling and rolling around in their own grease. I have to throw them out at the end of the shift, anyway."

She had come into the store in the late evening. A little, dirty ragamuffin young girl. No parents. No money. Just filthy and obviously hungry. Probably one of the kids who lived in an alley or beneath some overpass. He felt sorry for her. He, who knew what it was like to have an empty stomach. Just one hotdog. Loaded with everything. And a small drink. What harm would it do? The store would not go under if he fed one starving kid.

Only, the kid was a *shopper*. Used by her uncle to test the loyalty and honesty of his hires.

Less than an hour after she gobbled the hotdog and left, the big boss had come striding in. Five minutes later, Sid Dillard was unemployed and out on the street. His last meager paycheck—barely enough to last three or four days—had been docked to cover the cost of the cola and flaccid hotdog.

Sid sighed and picked up a copy of the *Fort Myers News Press*. Not a local paper, yet one that had caught his attention. A certain reporter, Louise Hampton, seemed to have a thing for Senator Eleana Silver.

Possibly, the back-up insurance his plan required.

Miami Vizcaya on Biscayne Bay—Miami, Florida

Dorothy Claxton kissed Eleana's cheeks and motioned to the chair opposite hers.

"It is so good to see you, my dear. This place is positively dreary without you."

Eleana motioned to the server. "Decaf, please."

Dorothy tilted her head. "Decaf? Since when?"

Eleana shrugged. "Oh, you know…I can be so edgy sometimes. I thought it best to cut back. I'm so glad you could meet me for brunch. I am ravenous."

"It's comforting that you have regained an appetite. I was so worried. Washington must agree with you."

The server delivered fresh-brewed coffee and a small porcelain pitcher of cream. Eleana poured a generous amount of cream and added a small sprinkle of sugar. She took a sip and smiled. "I can always count on this café for good coffee."

"I can't imagine they don't have good coffee in Washington."

"Nothing is as good up there, Dorothy. Absolutely nothing."

The older woman admired her young friend's outfit. "Very bright colors, my dear. Is that dress new?"

Eleana nodded. "It's Trina Turk. Isn't it cheerful? That's another thing about Washington. So conservative. Everywhere I look—gray, black, tan. The whole city is drained of color. Not like Miami."

"There is nowhere like Miami. I should know. I have been everywhere." Dorothy Claxton motioned for the server. "Menus, please."

"She's not one of the regulars," Dorothy said after the server scurried away. "I never have to actually ask..."

Eleana leaned forward. "Tell me. Tell me. I want to hear everything that has gone on here. I feel so cut off."

Dorothy waved one hand. "In time, Eleana. In time. First, you tell me—how is my favorite senator?"

Eleana sighed. "Just bumbling along. It's all so new and confusing. They have certain silly little ways of doing everything. The way to dress. The way to speak. The way to smile. It gets tiring. Such a game. I don't know how Brad did it. Yet, he seemed to live for the job."

"You will survive, Eleana. And triumph. You have maneuvered the shoals of Miami elite society for years. Certainly, Washington has met its match in you."

Eleana reached over and gave her mentor's hand a gentle squeeze. For the first time, she noticed how thin and frail Dorothy had become. Her mentor had always seemed so substantial. Ageless. Strong. Eleana fought back a wave of concern.

"I have called in favors on your behalf, dear," Dorothy said. "There are many owed to me. You won't have any problem soundly defeating the likes of Joel Orr. Then, you will be in a position to help everyone and everything you hold dear and important. Vizcaya. Miami." She smiled. "Me."

Eleana laughed. "Oh, Dorothy. You are such fun. What could I possibly do for you? You have it all."

The old woman took a sip of coffee. The menus arrived.

"I'll think of something." The old woman smiled. "Don't you know, Eleana? One can never have too much of anything. The more one has, the more one needs. And the world is out there, anxious to provide. That's why you must succeed in Washington. And you will succeed. I am counting on it."

After the two women ordered, Dorothy said, "I've never known you to covet so much food."

"It's just being back here. I can't seem to get enough of everything."

Dorothy Claxton tilted her head to one side, studying Eleana. "You are not fooling me, little girl. I know your secret. It is written all across that lovely face of yours."

Eleana felt a flush of heat rise to her cheeks. "I don't know what you mean, Dottie."

"Don't you worry. I won't breathe a word. It will be our strict little confidence. At least until after November."

CHAPTER NINETEEN

Tampa, Florida

Joel Orr stood in the back of a pick-up truck with Don Farringdon and Ronnie Taylor outside the fairgrounds in Tampa, watching the milling throng of mostly agricultural types. The men carried plastic cups of cheap beer. Most dragged on cigarettes. The women wore hair taller and more colorful than the cotton candy hawked by one of the vendors. Herds of children hopped up on funnel cakes and soda pop dashed between the adults. Joel shook his head. No one could call this group high-falutin'.

Evening at a southern fair: Generalized bedlam blended with liberal helpings of grease, sugar, and alcohol. Taking advantage of the ready-made crowd had seemed like a good idea. Now, Joel and his crew wondered if it was a mistake.

Competing with the crowd noise, a country and blue-grass band—The Dixiecrats—belted out a tune known by the locals as the official redneck national anthem: *Take this job and shove it...*

The band took a break. Joel jumped up on the stage and yelled into a megaphone.

"Evenin', y'all! I'm Joel Orr, and I'm running for the Senate."

Even with the aid of the megaphone, he strained to be heard over the horde. Sweat drew circles beneath his armpits and around his collar.

"We have to get out of Iraq. Keep jobs in America. Lower gasoline prices. And keep foreigners off our shores."

Not a perfect fit for his philosophy, but it sure was closer to his than that of the pristine Republicans of Eleana Silver's. For a few minutes, Joel pounded on the same themes from as many different angles as he could imagine.

"Now, I have talked enough," Joel yelled. "Let me hear from you—you people who have come from Auburndale, Bartow, Brandon, and all of God's country in Imperial Polk, and Hillsborough counties."

A lanky white man in overalls called out from the rear of the gathering, "We all work for a living. What do you do?"

Don Farringdon shook his head. "I told him not to open it up to questions." He glanced around the group to spot the handful of Orr campaign workers. Surely, one or two would have the timing to interrupt with one of the planned inquiries.

Joel peered into the semi-darkness, unsure where to direct the answer. "I work in a law firm. I am an assistant there."

"You mean you're involved in them crazy kind of law suits, like them idiots who sued about the burning coffee in McDonald's?"

"I hope that guy's not one of Mark Cox's minions," Don remarked. "If he is…where in the hell did he dig him up?"

"I don't like where this is going," Ronnie Taylor said.

"Well yes. We have been involved in some class action lawsuits," responded Joel.

"We want one of us up there in Washington. Someone that works with his hands and back. Paid a full day's wage for a full day's work," responded the questioner.

Several in the crowd mumbled agreement. One man whooped a boozy rebel yell.

Another voice: "Damn right! What gives here, Orr?"

Joel held up one hand. "Just a minute, please. Just a minute. I understand what you're getting at. I really do. It is only when you need help that you understand the true meaning of legal redress in the courts. I help protect that."

Don frowned. "Remind me to talk to Joel about using any kind of legal language. Keep it simple. Too much of that, and they'll think he's talking down to them."

Another male voice asked, "What does the one running up against you do?"

Finally. One our way, Joel thought.

"I can tell you she sure doesn't work with her hands and back. I don't know if she has ever worked."

"Ain't she a widow?" A loud female voice called out. "We sure liked her husband—that Brad feller."

Farringdon and Taylor surveyed the restless crowd. Many wore frowns. Not good, picking on a woman who had lost her husband. It wouldn't matter to this group if she was an ax murderer; she was to be pitied for her loss.

"Shit. We get back up off the mat, and they knock us down again." Don said. "Keep trying, Joel. You're losing them."

"Well, she is a nice lady, I am told..." was all Joel could muster.

"Hey, I heard you kilt your own wife," A loud voice called.

"You can't fault a feller for that!" A male voice answered.

A ripple of mostly-male laughter and back-slapping fanned out across the group.

Joel stood motionless for a few seconds before he recovered enough to speak. "No. No. My wife...my ex-wife...was ill...I..."

The crowd started to move toward the exit gate. Farringdon yelled over to the leader of the bluegrass band who gathered their instruments to regain the stage "Hey, Jimmy! Y'all play Lee Greenwood's *God Bless the USA*."

Don jumped onto the stage and grabbed the megaphone. "There's more free beer and chicken wings up here, folks!"

Joel sat on the tailgate of the truck and took a deep swig of cold bottled water. "Feels like someone let the air out of our inner tube."

Ronnie Taylor took a quick count of the line-up at the kegs: twenty-one. The chicken wings weren't flying off the table, either.

"Yep, and we are starting to run out of pumps. We'd better get an infusion of cash. Fast."

Joel sat on the toilet—one of many in a row of graffiti-pocked stalls. The men's bathroom at the Tampa fair-grounds: high living. Other than one inebriated local at the urinal who talked to himself as he watered the wall and floor, the place was quiet. Joel didn't need the facility—he sat, fully clothed, on a double layer of bath tissue—just the time to reflect while Don Farringdon and Ronnie Taylor loaded the signs and campaign literature into the rented van.

The drunken carnie finally left. Joel's cell phone rang. So much for time alone.

He frowned at the blocked caller I.D. notification and answered.

"Joel Orr?" A male voice asked.

"Yes."

Who the hell had given out his private cell number? The campaign volunteers knew better.

"This is President Buddy Benton."

Joel huffed. "Of course it is."

"Is this a bad time?"

Joel shook his head. "You people never give up, do you? I can't even answer my home phone, now this…Here's what I think of you." He stood up, held the phone receiver over the toilet and gave the flush handle a shove.

When he held the phone to his ear again, Joel expected to meet with dead air. Instead, the man spoke. "That was entertaining. Downright funny, as a matter of fact. Now, can we talk seriously?"

"Hold on a minute, will ya?" Joel washed his hands and walked outside. The night was still a balmy eighty-plus degrees. "What do you want, and who are you, really?"

"I'm Buddy Benton. I told you. C'mon, Orr."

Joel spotted a bench and sat down. "Prove it."

"All right. Hell. Let me think."

Joel waited. For a crank, the guy had staying power.

"I got it. I talked to you and your wife once a few years ago, back when I was in office. That's when you were in the state senate, and the wife and I came into Tallahassee. We visited the Governor and went to the FSU/ University of Florida game. I like college ball better than the pros— especially those big rivalries. We sat in the Governor's skybox. You and I got to talking—don't ask me what we talked about—but I do recall you as a big scotch drinker."

"President Benton?"

"That's what I told you, yes. I like it I can still use the title. No matter that I'm not living at 1600 Pennsylvania Avenue. Got to love that."

"How…how did you get my number?"

"I have connections, Joel."

"Of course."

"Now that we've gotten all of that behind us…We need to speak about your campaign."

Joel watched a family pass by on their way to the exit gate. The woman herded two whiny children, yet managed to continuously nag the man in a loud voice. He carried a sleeping toddler over one shoulder and clutched a handbag and two stuffed animals with the opposite hand. When he glanced Joel's way, his eyes conveyed dog-whipped desperation. Everyone had his own version of Hades.

Joel's attention snapped back. "My campaign…?"

"I'm prepared to fall in with your team, Joel. Do you know what that means?"

Without waiting for an answer, Buddy Benton continued. "Contributions. Big players with deep pockets. Just what you need. Just what you must have, Joel."

Joel felt the implications land on his shoulders. Ten-ton bricks of implications. A shit-pot load of implications.

"I'm not so certain…In light of the problems with Russell Nathan…."

Joel heard a heavy release of breath on the other end.

"An unfortunate turn of events."

"Your connections to Nathan…" Joel stretched to find a polite way to put it. "No offense, Sir. I'm not so sure my campaign could handle it. I have enough problems on my own."

"We could find a way to work it to both of our advantages. The party…"

Joel listened for a few minutes. "I do appreciate your call, President Benton. I really do."

Buddy Benton's voice carried an edge of irritation. "Think long and hard before you turn us away, Orr. You winning or losing could depend on it. This isn't some Podunk local contest. You don't have any idea who you are up against. You'll need my people's support if you do manage to pull one off against Eleana Silver."

The Moorings Club—Vero Beach, Florida

East of Orlando in idyllic Vero Beach, The Moorings Club development occupied over five hundred acres of transformed mangrove lowlands on the Indian River. The original clubhouse had been devastated in the fall of 2004 by two hurricanes—Frances and Jeanne—but had since been rebuilt to mirror the unique qualities of the site, infused with the beauty and elegance of the West Indies. An eighteen-hole par sixty-four, Pete Dye-designed golf course showcased the spectacular view. The tennis complex featured Fast Dry courts, six equipped with lighting for night play. A sixty-by-thirty heated swimming pool nestled between copses of tropical palm trees. Boaters enjoyed the ten boat docks, dredged channels, and an active Yacht Club.

The Moorings' spacious clubhouse provided the perfect spot for Eleana Silver to address the Indian River Republican Women's Club. As Mark Cox had planned, her campaign trail would weave through the central part of the state, eventually ending up in the panhandle.

Ramiro pulled the Mercedes limousine into the circular drive in front of the clubhouse. Behind him, Eleana, Mike Belan, and Mark Cox sat. For most of the trip, the trio had ridden in strained silence. Ramiro acted the part of the ultimate professional chauffeur, avoiding any overt hint of familiarity with the senator.

Eleana sighed. "Is this a friendly crowd, Mr. Cox?"

"Yes, Senator. Although you are beginning to hit your stride on these campaign stops, we didn't want to take any chances...at least not yet."

Eleana felt more confident. Her beauty—and showing some occasional cleavage—had proved enough to get her through most events. But this meeting was expected to have media coverage, so it was more serious. The Moorings would draw major financial backers. The exclusive club members weren't in the habit of bankrolling losers.

"Do you think Louise Hampton is going to be here, Mark?" asked Mike Belan.

"Probably. She is really starting to show up at our events. I suspect she might be a plant for Orr, but there is nothing we can do about it."

The Club President greeted Eleana at the entrance. After mingling among the two-hundred and fifty or so attendees, the senator took a reserved seat at the head table.

President Terry Hanover stood behind a small podium. "Good afternoon, and welcome to the Moorings. It is my pleasure to introduce one of the shining new lights in the United States Senate." She glanced toward the table where Eleana sat. "The senator is our friend. She is one of us...she believes in our values, our country, capitalism, the death penalty, our constitutional, inalienable rights to pursue life, liberty and freedom...and the American way."

A round of polite applause sounded.

Eleana wondered if the group might not have always felt that way, when she and the other proud Cubans had escaped across the Gulf Stream believing in the very same principles. Hoping for a better life. Longing for freedom. Hoping for sanctuary. They had not always met with a warm welcome. Had they known her then, would they have counted her among their closest friends? She doubted it.

"Ladies, I am especially happy to be here at the Moorings Club with you. You know, I have been active for many years with Vizcaya in Coconut Grove, and many of our members have reciprocals with you here."

A reciprocal member of one of the organizations could enjoy the benefits of the affiliated organization. Eleana looked out into the audience of white, middle-aged, well-dressed ladies. Her Cuban heritage aside, she was at home in the Moorings as she was in Miami at Vizcaya. Money and social standing provided the key to most locks.

Eleana took a deep breath to squelch a slight wave of nausea. She concentrated so that she wouldn't lose her train of thought. Good thing most of her campaign stops were after lunch. The mornings were not good.

She pointed to the Pete Dye golf course outside the Club. "That golf course reflects American ingenuity. It was built on land spoiled from dredging of this mangrove-laden property back in the '70s."

"Where in the hell is she going with this?" Cox mumbled to Belan. "That isn't what I wrote."

Mike nodded toward Eleana. "Stay with her. She is beginning to really handle improvising. We might have a pro on our hands, given a little time."

Eleana raised her voice to convey strong conviction. "It is that ingenuity that is the cornerstone of our freedom. Our capitalism. My opponent seems to feel the only freedom we need is for criminals and deadbeats to have access to our hard-earned taxes."

One of the front-row ladies clapped and called out, "Eleana, we love you. America, right or wrong!"

Others took up the battle cry until the entire gathering stood and applauded.

For the half-hour time reserved for her presentation, Eleana Silver managed to keep the crowd solidly engrossed.

She raised and lowered her voice for emphasis. A few times—as she spoke of infant mortality and women's health issues—she seemed to hold back tears. The women responded with matching emotion.

Belan shook his head and clapped with the group. "Gaawwd, these ladies are really out there. Why are we even pitching them? They are pumped."

At the side table reserved for members of the press, Cox noticed Louise Hampton of the *Fort Myers News Press*. "Damn it, she is bird-dogging us. This is trouble waiting to happen."

Eleana hit the peak attack part of her message. "I ask my opponent: What do you bring to these great Floridians as qualifications?" She spread her arms wide to encompass the privileged members of the Club. "It is my understanding that you, Joel Orr, have been a Para-legal, helping people who don't want to help themselves. If these people need a job, the want ads in the *Vero Beach Press Journal* are more than available to anyone willing to take the time to look. Why should they take advantage of the system? Why should they drag the rest of us down? We must take a stand against certain factions in our country who do not even try to support themselves."

The crowd noise was deafening.

Cox smiled. "Wow...a home run. I just hope Louise doesn't twist it in her morning piece." He glanced to the table where Louise Hampton sat, scribbling feverishly on a legal pad.

"I am Senator Eleana Silver. I ask for your vote in November. Thank you!"

President Terry Hanover stood and hugged Eleana as the crowd continued to applaud. "Ladies, the United States senator from Florida. Vero's dear and devoted friend, Eleana Silver."

Eleana beamed a practiced white smile toward the audience and stepped from the dais. The noise from the room continued. They loved her.

Outside of the clubhouse, Louise Hampton used a cell phone to submit her report.

Careful to maintain the charismatic smile before and after her words, Eleana leaned over to Cox and whispered, "Where did that little bitch go? I just spotted her a minute ago."

Tampa, Florida

Don Farringdon slowed the van, took one look at the non-descript building, and turned into the dirt parking lot. The High-Balls Lounge and Package Store was exactly the kind of place where he might find a down-and-out politician in the middle of the night in central Florida. It met the three requirements: within walking distance of the Hotel Six, not remotely on the media's radar, a harbor filled with cheap liquor.

Ronnie Taylor slept soundly—more like dead—back at the hotel. One room for the three men. Just ducky. Ronnie had agreed to the money-saving arrangements after Don assured him that sleeping in the same bed with another male would not make him gay.

When Don discovered Joel missing, he had thought about waking Taylor, but didn't. A sleeping nerd was such a sweet thing to behold. That and Don Farringdon had a feeling he'd locate Joel in the kind of joint his numbers guy could never appreciate.

The night front desk attendant had informed Don; only two bars were close-by. One—a hard-core biker bar known for at least a bloody assault each month. The other—a basic, no-frills redneck affair with two pool tables and a couple of regular hookers.

Don cut the engine. Why did all Southern country bars look the same? One-room concrete block shacks with tin roofs, painted in some god-awful dark shade of shit-brown, prison gray, or swamp-algae green. The windows—when there were any—were either boarded over or painted black.

The meager outside lighting came from neon beer signs and one bare bulb fixture that cast a dim circle around the only entrance.

For times like this, Don thanked his gene pool for his linebacker build. His friends knew he was a marshmallow-middle softie, but anyone meeting him for the first time might think he could stomp Mother Mary to a pulp. Especially when he put the dare-to-cross-me expression on his face.

Don stepped inside. A few cast disinterested glances his way. A juke box played old country and western standards above the sharp snick of balls off chalk-dusted pool cues. A thick haze of cigarette smoke burned his eyes. Cheap cologne wafted from several directions. For a moment, Don felt nostalgic for his college days.

In one corner, he spotted his candidate. Bingo.

He passed by the bar long enough to gather a mug of beer on tap. What was it they had called it in college—*Old Mill-Water*?

Don ambled over to the table where Joel Orr held court with two clearly intoxicated middle-aged farm boys.

One laughed and clapped Joel on the shoulder. "You all right, son."

High praise from a low source. Exactly the kind of strategy needed to win against Senator Eleana Silver. Don shook his head.

"Mind if I join you?" He slid a wooden chair opposite Joel and sat down without waiting for a reply.

"Now, fellas...this here is a good guy." Joel toasted Don with his glass. "Best P.R. man a man could get. Good as gold."

The men nodded. One stuck out a calloused hand. "Bubba Clark. Pleased." He shook Don's hand. "This other 'un is Mike Malone, but he goes by Big 'Un."

Don nodded to each man. "Bubba. Big 'Un."

Joel kicked back the last inch of his scotch and waved toward the bartender. "This one's on me."

The larger man—Big 'Un—stood. "My turn."

Bubba whistled. "He ain't much in the brains department, but he shore does make a fine waitress."

Don glanced around the room. Ten people not counting the barkeeper. He would place a bet; if he counted all of them, he might just come up with enough for one full set of teeth.

"Did I miss curfew?" Joel asked. He laughed. "I thought about leaving a note, but I didn't want to turn on a light."

The four drank like companionable old war buddies for a few minutes before Bubba and Big 'Un decided to play a game of pool.

"You okay, Joel?" Don asked after the tablemates left.

Orr twirled his glass around, watching the low light play across the amber liquid. "What was I thinking, Don?"

"About coming here? Drinking?"

"Nah…" Joel motioned to the room with one hand. "This feels like home. Even the woman behind the bar reminds me a little of Brenda Gayle." He squinted. "Only, she has fewer teeth and her hair color is all wrong."

Don glanced at the simple pine bar. Other than the fact she was female, the woman looked nothing like the Ironclad Alibi's owner. Brenda Gayle was a homecoming queen by comparison.

"How many of those have you had, bud?"

Joel shrugged. "Two or ten. Who's counting?"

Don sipped the cheap beer. It tasted like watered-down cow piss. "So, you tell me. What *were* you thinking?"

Joel's shoulders drooped. "I can't do this, Don. Everywhere I go, I hear the same damned things. *I killed my wife. I'm a no-account loser. I got a convict for a brother.* I'll let Karen down. I'll let you and Taylor down." He raked a hand through his sweat-spiked hair. "Hell. We're practically out of money. Got a lot of good-intentioned people giving up their time. To what end?"

"Because you give them something to believe in, Joel."

"Right." Joel sat for a moment before he said, "I didn't tell you. Benton called."

"Buddy Benton? As in the former President?"

Joel nodded. "The one. The only."

"When? Today? We've been together, practically joined at the hip."

"You and Taylor were packing up." Joel sighed. "He wanted to talk money. Big, fat, juicy campaign fund money."

"And you said…?"

"Call me stupid. You'd be right. I turned him down." Joel closed his eyes briefly. "Chance to get some real money into this excuse for a campaign. And— I. Turned. Him. Down."

Farringdon said, "Good decision, my man."

Joel regarded his public relations man. "You got a money tree stuffed up your butt?"

Don laughed. "If I did, I'd never flush again." He grinned. "Life is a long series of trade-offs. But that one— you're better off without."

"We could've had the support of the big-ball Democrats, Don. No matter how I told him, my answer put a lid on anything coming our way from them. Ever."

Don tipped the mug and finished off his beer. One more. Then, back to the motel.

"Joel, you remember a case about ten years back…in the panhandle. Little town called Chattahoochee? Young gay man was kidnapped and assaulted by a couple of teens?"

Joel stretched to recall. "Withers? No, Witherspoon. Yeah. That was during my time at the State Attorney's Office. All over the national media. Pretty brutal hate crime. Man damn near died. And one of the kids who did it committed suicide."

"One thing stuck with me all of these years. Something one of the local women said. You know how conservative most small southern towns can be. This one lady said something like *we don't take much to queers. But, he is **our** queer.*"

Joel studied him. "Okay. I'll bite. What is the point of this little history lesson?"

"No matter if you took Benton up on his offer or not; you're still his man."

Joel flinched. "Terrible thought."

"Not actually. Think about it, Joel. The big Dixiecrats have to throw support your way. They have no choice. The balance in Congress depends on as many Democrats winning as possible. No seat is dispensable."

Joel's boozy grin was lopsided. "I ain't much, but I'm all they got?"

Don Farringdon slapped Joel Orr on the back. "You've broken the code, my man."

Later, after he finally managed to steer a still-fully-clothed Joel Orr into the double bed beside the one where Ronnie Taylor slept, Don stood outside on the concrete balcony and dialed a number on his cell phone. He waited until the voicemail beep sounded.

"Karen? Don. No emergency. Just, when you get this message—call me. He's not going to tell you, but your daddy needs you right now."

CHAPTER TWENTY

Office of the Governor—Tallahassee, Florida

Aide Kemp Johnson stood back. The gubernatorial entity he playfully called *Hurricane-Emergency ADHD hamster* whirled around the executive office in a high rolling boil. Only an untrained idiot would get in his way.

Tad Myers paused long enough to fire a question toward his top aide. "Remind me again. Why did I want to be governor of Florida? I could be in some land-locked haven, far away from the Gulf of Mexico."

Kemp hesitated. How to answer? Honestly? With the senatorial election looming, his boss had become increasingly difficult to read. Every day was like a hellish game of *Truth or Dare*. If Kemp never heard the name *Orr* again, he would die a happy man. He had even asked his wife not to buy his favorite comfort food—Oreo cookies—because he couldn't bear to hear the first syllable. He switched to his second favorite, Fig Newtons, though the soft bar cookie didn't hold up well when dunked in two-percent reduced-fat milk. Life was full of compromises.

Kemp decided on truth. "Two reasons, Governor. One—you were born here and this is your home. Two—hurricanes give you an opportunity to show how well you mobilize resources during an emergency."

Tad Myers pulled on his chin, considering. "True. True. If it had been me in the White House after Katrina, there wouldn't have been the debacle in New Orleans. We damn sure know how to handle a hurricane in this state."

Kemp nodded. With enough practice, anyone could improve. Too bad it didn't pertain to the voting procedures. If there was a God, the next election would go off without the usual Sunshine State glitches. The thought that it might not was enough to make Kemp Johnson consider packing up the family and leaving in the middle of the night. For somewhere far, far away.

Governor Myers stopped pacing long enough to focus on the latest Weather Channel update. Other than a few scattered thunderstorms in the western panhandle, the state was calm. When the experts turned their attention to the extended forecast, they planted eighty percent of the peninsula into the conical computer storm-path projections. Tropical Storm Farina—now drenching Haiti—would follow a route into the Gulf of Mexico where she would gather strength over the warm waters. By mid-week, Farina would be upgraded to at least a category one hurricane. Depending on the tides at the time the storm made landfall, the storm surge waters could reap more damage than the over seventy-five miles-per-hour winds.

"We've dodged the bullet for the past couple of years. Have you seen the projections for this season?" the Governor asked.

Kemp blinked. *Did he really ask me that? I'm beginning to hum the music they play in the background on the Weather Channel.*

"Yes, Sir. Should be an active season."

Tad Myers' mind-set shifted. He pulled the internal file labeled *insurance companies* from his brain.

"We've had insurers bailing on us left and right, with a couple of major ones threatening to pull out of Florida. Rates have gone through the roof. If it gets crazy this year, we'll have a crisis of unbelievable proportions on our hands."

"I wouldn't want to own coastal property right now."

The Governor flinched. "I knew there was something else. Get the management company on the phone. I have to make sure they've rolled the storm shutters over the windows and doors at the beach house. My wife just had the living room refurnished. If we get any water damage, she'll be beside herself."

"Don't they usually do that as a matter of course?" Kemp asked.

Tad Myers shook his head. "Never trust fate to take care of the details, Kemp. One thing I've learned—and one that will serve me well when I make it to Washington—never, ever take your fingers off of the pulse. You can delegate, but not relegate."

Kemp Johnson nodded. As he flipped through his Palm Pilot to locate the number for Sun Coast Management Company, he had a thought, one that made his heart flutter for a couple of beats.

A hurricane. A major federal election. God help him if they happened at the same time.

Leesburg, Florida

In the shade of a Spanish moss-draped live oak, Don Farringdon looked over Ronnie Taylor's shoulder. The laptop sat on the top of an ornate metal picnic table, queued up to a popular political forum.

"I don't care if the damned Internet is the most useful tool since iron ax heads," Don said, "It's really beginning to seem more and more like a big fat pain in my ass."

Ronnie tapped a few keys. "It is a good thing. But it can bite you, too."

The fuzzy picture showed Don Farringdon supporting Joel Orr in the classic drunken-buddy hold.

Don scowled. "Shit! I didn't see a soul last night when we came in. Who took this?"

Ronnie shrugged. "Anyone with a camera phone could've snapped it. The resolution isn't very high, so I don't think it was a regular digital camera. Probably just some amateur who happened to be in the right spot."

"I'd place even odds that it was the night desk attendant. Who else would it be? He knew who Joel was, and I asked him where the closest bar was located." Don pounded himself on the forehead with the heel of one hand. "Stupid. Stupid. Stupid."

"Don't beat yourself up. It might not even make it past this forum, with any luck. At least it wasn't a video."

Don grimaced. "Oh, that would've been rich. Joel Orr and Russell Nathan—reigning stars of YouTube."

"One thing we can hope," Ronnie commented, "is that the folks in this group aren't the computer types. It's a garden club bunch, so maybe we'll dodge any questions about this latest issue."

Don held up his hand. "Correction, my friend—this is the Florida Garden Clubs Association. Don't dare underestimate them, or the fact Leesburg seems like a sleepy little town in the middle of the state. Plus, they invited Joel here to speak, not the other way around. That fact is significant."

Joel Orr walked up. "Nice little city. I have never been here. Have you, Don?"

"No, but I've heard some wild stories about this town."

Ronnie glanced up from the laptop. "Like what?"

Don looked around the park-like setting. Most of the trees were decades-old live oaks decorated with wisps of moss. A few cars moved past. Birdcall sounded. Idyllic. "Well, this is considered to be the Bible Belt times three or four, especially as it relates to education."

Karen stepped up with two carry-out bags. "I found a little bakery. Fresh hot cross buns and iced coffee."

"You are a God-send, Karen." Don dug into one of the bags.

Joel smiled. "Really, Bug. You sure it's okay for you to come on the campaign trail with your old dad?"

Karen handed out napkins. "Sure. Look, I never take time off. I have five weeks of leave built up. I can't be out for two weeks in a row—bank rules—but I can join you for a few days here and there. Besides, it's a break for me.

Something different. People can be so difficult when it comes to their money."

"Or, lack of it…in our case." Ronnie took a sip of iced coffee. "Hey, this isn't half bad."

"So, what's going on?" Karen asked. She took a bite of a hot sugary roll, leaned over Ronnie's shoulder and glanced at the forum picture, then at her father. "Um…what's up with this?"

Joel sat down. "I might as well fess up. I drank last night, Bug."

Karen nodded. "I see."

A few flecks of sugar glaze decorated his lips. "I never said I was perfect. I'm trying. I really am."

A few seconds passed. Don and Ronnie exchanged worried glances between bites of the rolls.

"Look," Karen finally said. "I can't control what you do, any more than you can control what I do. You have made promises to a lot of people, Daddy."

Joel held up his hands. "I realize that. I slipped. No excuses. I will do my best to not let it happen again."

Karen studied her father for a moment before turning to Don Farringdon. "So—other than the picture—what were you all talking about while I was out rounding up your sugar and caffeine fix?"

Don felt the tension ease a little. He took a long swill of iced coffee, then answered, "I was just telling your father and Ronnie about Leesburg. How it's the hot-seat of the Bible Belt in this part of the state."

"Here?" She looked around as if she expected to see the Crusaders marching through town.

Don said, "To start with, there are over a hundred churches in the area, and there are only 16,000 people living here—you do the math. But it is not just numbers. The local school board led the assault on the court-mandated separation of church and state. Made the national news."

"So, Daddy," Karen said. "Be careful. Less is more on this one."

"Got it," responded Joel. "I'm not touching religious issues today, so we should be okay. The presentation centers on my environmental platform— whether the government, even at the federal level, should have a say-so in permitting when it can be demonstrated that there is inadequate *carrying capacity* for new development."

"I enlisted assistance from multiple environmental organizations to help draft Joel's remarks," Don added.

"I don't see where that could conceivably be skewed to envelop religion," Karen said.

"Just stay on message, Joel." Farringdon added. "This is not your normal shtick."

Joel wiped the sugar from his lips and stood. "Nothing about this campaign has been normal, Don. Why should today be an exception? We'd best get on with it."

Joel Orr approached the podium. His head pounded with the remaining vestiges of a hangover. Beneath the cinnamon sweetness of the hot cross bun, he could still taste a sour edge—the flavor of the proverbial *morning after the night before*. Only, it was nearing midday. One of the joys of aging: he didn't bounce back as quickly from a dance with demon alcohol.

For a half-hour, he recounted the highlights of his environmental platform. Nothing inspired. Just a hint past dull. The crowd seemed receptive, but not overly so.

A rush of relief settled over him as he opened the floor for questions. A group of gardeners. How ruthless could they possibly be?

A heavy-set lady wearing a flaming-red sun bonnet stood and asked, "Mr. Orr, are you a Christian?"

Joel opened his mouth, but nothing came out. He had worked on the presentation for the better part of a week. He knew the issues of interest to these retirees, from health care to social security and a peaceful and undisturbed environment. What in the world did someone's religion have to do with anything?

Don leaned over toward Karen and mouthed the word: "Shit."

Joel cleared his throat. "Aw...umm, I consider myself to be a God-fearing person...and..."

The red-hat lady interrupted, "Mr. Orr, I asked you if you were a Christian. That requires a simple yes or no."

Ronnie Taylor whispered to Don Farringdon. "You got any ideas, you best work fast."

Joel reached for the glass of water that sat on the podium, looking in the direction of his team for a signal.

The red-hat lady barreled forward, honing in on the scent of a fresh kill. "Mr. Orr, I guess you are like all the rest of the politicians. You talk about government this and government that." She rotated to address her contemporaries as much as to Joel. "Here in Leesburg, we believe in the Almighty and goodness knows, now is the time for men of God to step forward to lead."

Don Farringdon was close enough to notice how the woman trembled as she spoke. "If she falls out on the floor and starts speaking in tongues, I am *so* out of here," he mumbled to Taylor.

A slow steady applause sounded from around the gathering and grew into a standing ovation for the lady's question and evangelistic fervor.

Joel paused for what seemed like an eternity, but actually was less than a minute. Nothing Joel could say—including lying that he was a practicing Christian—would win the crowd over.

"Shit squared," Farringdon said in a low voice.

Karen stood and walked to the podium. Joel stepped to the side, a shocked look on his face.

"Ladies and gentleman, I am Karen Hernandez. Joel Orr's daughter. My Dad is just getting over a debilitating case of the stomach flu, and he's not himself today. Although he will not admit it, he is really not able to complete his presentation today."

"The flu?" Ronnie Taylor whispered to Don Farringdon.

Don watched Karen. The corners of his lips curled up. "Shut up, Ronnie. Brilliant. She's just freaking brilliant."

Karen's gaze panned the room. "So if you will excuse my father, I would like to try to answer your question about my Dad's religion. I obviously have known him longer than anyone here."

Joel walked from the stage and took the vacant seat next to Don Farringdon.

Don leaned over and said to Joel, "It wasn't your fault. Sometimes these things happen, like run-away missiles and tsunamis."

Karen paused to collect her thoughts. Intrigued by the turn of events, the audience took their seats. Even the red-hat woman directed her full attention to the front of the room. Karen adjusted the microphone.

"Daddy has always lived by the principles found in the Bible. He taught me right from wrong. To treat others as I would have them treat me. To stand up for what I believe in. When he was young, he attended Sunday school and church, up until he went to college. He got involved with people he probably should not have..."

A tear slipped down one of Karen's cheeks and she wiped it aside, an action not lost on the audience.

"He got back on track when he went to law school, but it did not include going back to church. After he lost the last state senate election, my dad sort of lost direction. His marriage failed. My mother..."

Karen struggled to enunciate her words.

"We lost my mother to the horror of a very aggressive form of breast cancer. Those were very difficult times for Daddy...and ..." Karen wiped the tears now freely flowing down her cheeks. "...for all of us."

Many in the audience looked down. Clearly, some wished the red-hat lady had not even asked the question, though almost all of them held memberships in area protestant churches.

Karen paused. Inhaled and exhaled slowly.

"A few months ago, I almost lost my Dad, but God allowed him to live. He is working hard each and every day to change his life. Ladies and gentlemen, my father is far from perfect. How many of you are? I'm not. My Mom always reminded me when I tried to become judgmental, *Judge not lest ye be judged.* And, *He that is without sin among you, let him first cast a stone.*"

Farringdon nodded. "Quoting the Bible. Good move. These folks love their *King James.*"

Ronnie Taylor lifted one eyebrow. "Oh, like you weren't raised with it, too. Quit acting all urban. You're as southern as the rest of these people."

"Daddy is of fault," Karen continued. "I don't deny that. He doesn't deny that. He is a good man. And he is repentant. With your prayers and God's forgiveness, Joel Orr, my father, can come back and be a good senator for all of us."

A few people clapped. More joined. Soon, the noise from the audience was deafening. Joel looked up at Karen, his eyes shining with tears. Karen looked back at her father and offered a shaky smile.

"I wonder if we have the right candidate," Taylor quipped.

Karen turned and walked away from the podium while the ovation continued.

Joel met his daughter halfway and hugged her. "I will never forget this, Bug. Never."

Later, when the four returned to the van, Farringdon said, "what you did was nothing short of genius, Karen."

Ronnie Taylor nodded. "I can spin this flu angle on the forums. Nip the rumors about that picture."

Joel stared out the van's front window. His daughter had lied for him. The initial glow of pride had evaporated and he wasn't sure exactly how to feel.

Karen said, "What I did, Don, was the worst case of enabling ever. Any therapist would have a field day with it. We all know it wasn't the flu."

The three men in the van fell silent. Joel and Don in the front seat, Ronnie Taylor sharing the van's rear bench seat beside Karen.

"I lied today, Daddy. Flat out." Karen ran her fingers through her hair.

Joel turned around in the seat to face his daughter. "Why'd you do it? Why not just sit back and let me muck my way out of it?"

"Because that woman was clearly ready to skewer you for her own weird holier-than-thou pleasure. I hate that kind of crap. Because everyone deserves a chance. Everyone screws up. You drank last night. For whatever reason—I really don't care. But if you want me to stick around, it has to stop. You have made choices, Daddy. You have people pulling for you. People walking the streets singing your praises. People volunteering their time to cold-call and stuff envelopes. You have to keep up your end of this, or it is all for nothing—a big fat waste of time."

Don Farringdon wanted to intervene. Say something. Anything. This very moment could prove the turning point in the election. Joel had baggage. Serious baggage. Whether or not the red-hat lady had been planted in the audience by design or not, Joel's flaws were right on top and ripe for the picking. With Karen's help, Joel might continue to grow in time for the rapidly approaching November election.

"I've made more promises in my life than I care to count." Joel's voice sounded fatally weary, the voice of a man much older. "I haven't done such a bang-up job of keeping them."

"No time like the present. You always told me that when I was a little girl—anytime I tried to worm out of anything."

Joel smiled and nodded.

Karen sighed. "Do you want this, Daddy? Do you really want it?"

Joel turned back toward the front. "Yes, Bug. I do."

CHAPTER TWENTY-ONE

Office of Senator Eleana Silver—Washington, D.C.

On a Friday afternoon in the National Capitol, offices were no different from the rest of the country; few folks working, and most on their way to the coast or some favorite retreat for the weekend. It was doubly unusual for Eleana Silver to be in her Senate office on Friday afternoon, with Miami only a private jet ride away and Ramiro anxious for any piece of her time.

"Where is the report on sugar imports from South America?" Eleana asked her Chief of Staff.

Gwen answered, "I left it in your reading file last night, Senator."

Mark Cox glanced up from his laptop computer. "The issue of South American sugar is starting to resonate with the Chairman of the Agriculture Committee."

"You know, the more I look at the availability of Cuban sugar, the more I wonder about our embargo policy with Castro. We should push to ease our restrictions," Eleana said.

Mark Cox stared. "Senator, that is blasphemy, even if it is a little true."

Gwen Reynolds, clearly stunned, said, "It flies in the face of everything your husband ever did in this office."

Eleana's voice held a terse edge. "Gwen, in case you missed it, there is another Senator Silver in this office today...and for the foreseeable future, I might add."

The long silence seemed to hang in the air. "Who wants coffee? I'm getting some..." Cox asked.

Neither woman spoke for a few seconds.

"No, thank you," Gwen said in a barely audible voice.

Mark Cox settled down with a fresh cup of coffee. The temperature in the room seemed to have dropped several degrees.

Eleana switched gears. "I think it's time we redecorated this office. I'm tired of the conservative colors. Florida is a place of tropical excitement." She motioned toward the door leading to the reception room. "Like that space travel mural. That will be the first thing to go. I want one showing the dramatic Miami skyline. And the carpet. This dreary monotone should be switched. I'll have my decorator come in."

"Do you think that advisable, Senator?" Mark Cox frowned. "Florida is more than just its southernmost end. This office has always been a reflection of the state in its entirety."

"No one thinks of North Florida when they call our grand state to mind. They think of high-end shopping and beaches crawling with beautiful people. Not rednecks and backwater swamps."

"The next duly-elected senator will be the one to make that call," Gwen stated.

"That will be me. I don't see why I have to live even one more day in Brad's shadow."

"Excuse me, please." Gwen stood and walked from the room.

Eleana glared at her retreating Chief of Staff. "Really, Mr. Cox. She is beginning to wear on me as much as this down-trodden, dreary office."

Later, Mark Cox entered Eleana's office. "Senator, may I talk to you for a minute?" He seated himself opposite her desk. "I don't know if there was anything to your comment earlier today about Castro and our sugar imports, but you more than anyone, know that we support the embargo of everything from Cuba, particularly sugar...right?"

"Mark, I understand the drill. I have heard it my entire life—from my family, from my husband, and from all you lemmings in this office. I just think we have to be honest. Maybe there is something to a quiet and subtle rapprochement with Castro."

"My God, Eleana, this is the first I have heard of this. If you think John Kerry was a flip-flopper in '04, wait until word gets out about the junior senator from Florida, one born in Cuba no less."

Eleana brushed a stray strand of glossy dark hair from her eyes. "Oh Mark, I didn't say I would change sides. I just think it is something to think about."

"Eleana, please. If you have even the most remote thought about switching positions on Castro—any at all—keep it to yourself and do nothing until after we have won this damned election."

Eleana laughed. "What's the matter, Mr. Campaign Manager? You can't handle an independent-thinking senator?"

"Jesus, Eleana..."

She brushed his remarks aside with one sweep of her manicured hand. "By the way, I am really up to my limit with Gwen. I know she worshipped Brad, but it's quite obvious she doesn't respect me. I really think we need to make a change there."

"Eleana, you're not going to do this now, are you?"

"My life would be happier without having to see her every day."

"I think it's not a good idea to do it now, but if you have to, it must be done with absolute care. Nobody knows more about the operations in this office—before and after you—than Gwen."

"If I let her go, can we still trust her?"

"Gwen Reynolds is the most trustworthy individual I have ever known. For her to breach confidence...well, I don't think it would happen." Mark Cox's features darkened. "I am really kind of idle now, with nothing to do but reelect a new senator whose only qualification is her relationship with the deceased Senator Silver, and at a time when the balance of power in Congress is hanging on the wire. But what the hell? I would be delighted to handle a touchy personnel issue for you."

"You can drop the sarcasm, Mark. People come and go. I know she has been here for a while. Everyone is dispensable. Even my favorite pair of *Jimmy Choo* pumps will grow tiresome one day."

"Eleana, I wish you would take this a bit more seriously. First, you are considering a flip-flop on the biggest issue in this campaign—Fidel Castro—and now you want to jettison the most important member of your staff."

Eleana drew her painted lips into a pout. "That's why you are here, Mark. If it was easy, I wouldn't need you."

Mark Cox stood. "Promise me you won't make waves on Castro for the time being, and give me some time to work on Gwen."

"Fine, Mark. Just don't screw it up. Or, I might have to take care of her myself."

Pensacola Beach, Florida

Don Farringdon seldom took time for introspection, especially during an election year. As he stood on Pensacola Beach, his road-weary mind flipped to the summer of 1978. Five guys on spring break. Just barely of legal drinking age—eighteen back then—with a second-hand van full of cheap gas and cheap beer. Now, he couldn't recall the first names of all of the boys who had driven from Miami to the panhandle on the promise of loose women and sex on the beach. The same could have been accomplished in Miami, but the allure of exotic redneck country girls with big bosoms proved too great a draw.

The beach remained the same: miles of sugary white fine sand, different from the darker hard-packed coastline of the Atlantic shore. At low tide, cars could traverse the

Atlantic beaches within a few feet of the surf. Any moron stupid enough to steer anything heavier than a bubble-tired bicycle on the Gulf Coast beaches wouldn't get far before the tires burrowed to the axles.

Don turned away from the water. For as far as he could see, lines of stilted beach houses and surf shops crowded both sides of the coastal highway. In some people's eyes, progress. The night he and his compatriots had stormed the same strip of coastline—coolers full, joints rolled, women primed—the only structures had been the water tower, an open-air pavilion, and a couple of convenience stores.

Don searched his memory for the young, wild, dark-haired girl's name. Susan? Sheila? Something with an *s*. She was related somehow to one of his gang, a north-Florida farm gal with nothing on her mind but having a good time. The perfect spring fling. Other than the wanton sex that had left sand in every crevice of his body, the only detail Don could remember—she was a dental hygiene student at the local junior college. At some point in the animal-like mating ritual, she had lectured him on the importance of flossing. Every now and then when he had his teeth cleaned, he thought of her. Good thing his current dental hygienist couldn't read his mind.

Ah, the good old days. When the worst thing that could come of unprotected sex—for a guy—was something a good round of antibiotics would cure.

Remembering relaxed his brain. For a moment, he didn't worry about poll numbers, lack of campaign funds, or the press.

The long-ago night had started at a small bayside club on Scenic Highway—the first bar they had come to once they came into town, Shotgun Kelly's. Full of college-aged people drinking and dancing. From there, the four south Florida imports met a lively gang of Navy guys and the women in their orbit. The party continued until someone suggested moving the whole shebang across the bridge to the beach.

The sand glowed with a species of phosphorescent plankton. Every footprint shimmered for a few seconds before fading. They frolicked in the smooth surf and marveled at the way the water shimmered every time someone splashed.

Later, when he and the dark-haired girl canoodled on a thin blanket between dunes, their bodies shone with flickers of light, as if fairy dust had been sprinkled on naked skin.

Magic.

When had the magic left his life?

He knew the answer: when his fascination for politics became an obsession. He was as much of a junkie as Ronnie Taylor. The numbers guy had one failed marriage to his credit, and Don had a series of wrecked relationships. Women didn't cotton to the late hours spent pouring over the minute details of a campaign. Nor did they take kindly to missed dates, neglected birthdays, or calls not returned.

The only female Don had ever successfully cohabitated with was his mother. When she died at age eighty-two, he pressed onward in the small family house.

The surf broke in mild-mannered ripples at his feet. Hard to fathom: a tropical storm hovered only a few hours to the east, one of the not-quite-hurricane weather systems imported from the warm Caribbean waters. This one—Fatima—had entered the state near Key West, inched up the state, and continued to meander like a drunken frat boy on his way to puke behind the hedges. T.S. Fatima had soaked south and central Florida with fourteen inches of rain before wobbling into the Gulf of Mexico to refuel with enough moisture to share with the panhandle. The weather nerds called it *a rainmaker event*. No kidding.

Back at the hotel, Ronnie Taylor huddled in front of the television, glued to the Weather Channel. An emergency-band radio sat on the bedside stand, ready for National Weather Service announcements. Accustomed to hurricane readiness preparations, the campaign team had laid in bottled water, flashlights, a battery-powered lantern, a full ice chest, and non-perishable food.

The whole watery shebang would pass by the weekend, and they could leave Escambia County for a scheduled campaign stop in Tallahassee.

"Dip-shits," Don said aloud, thinking of the northern transplants who actually anticipated a tropical system with the glee of children awaiting Christmas morning.

They hadn't had the pleasure of sitting half-naked in darkness, sweating bullets in the humid air, eating beanie weenies from a can. Or, straining a rotator cuff tendon yanking on the pull-cord of a gas-powered generator.

Floridians watched hourly updates on the Weather Channel. One particular meteorologist stood out: Jim Carella. People in hurricane alley—the storm-prone region of the south—watched for the weather guru like a dying man straining to see the Grim Reaper. If Jim Carella and his team showed up in your area, you were seriously screwed. Load up the pooch, pack your belongings, and head for high ground.

The cell phone vibrated in his pocket.

A gruff, impatient male voice stated, "I need to speak to Joel Orr."

"Mr. Orr is not available at the present. This is Don Far-ringdon. How may I help you?"

"J. R. King here. When is your guy going to be avail-able?"

Don checked his watch. "Not for a couple of hours."

"Look, Farringdon. If that guy you're helping can get it straight, I might be able to get him some money."

"You have my attention. I can relay anything you wish to Mr. Orr. I'm his campaign manager."

"You ever hear of St. Joe?" asked King.

"I am not Catholic, sir. I'm not familiar with the saints."

"Damn it. Not that kind of saint. You sure I can't just talk to Orr?"

"No, sir. He is meeting with a group of county commissioners at present."

"Up in the panhandle is a little town on the gulf that actually has a sea port—Port St. Joe. But nobody—next to me and my pals—almost nobody knows about that. St. Joe has its roots in a little mom-and-pop company called DuPont. Students of Florida history know of a further blockbuster connection to Ed Ball and the DuPont fortune."

Don held his hand over the receiver so the caller wouldn't hear his irritated sigh. Political campaigns brought out all kinds of nut-jobs. Was this guy one?

The caller continued, "Florida is a peninsula. Everyone thinks of Port Everglades in Ft. Lauderdale, the Miami Seaport, Jacksonville, and Tampa. Few people know there are actually fourteen approved sea ports in the state."

"Yeah..."

"Do I have to remind you that to move commerce between the state of Florida and the Caribbean, it would help to have a port?"

"I'm following you."

"My partners and I have a sizable interest in that dinky little port in your panhandle, and well...let's just say that we would just as soon nobody know about it...until the third week in November."

"After the election?"

The man chuckled. "Now you're cooking with gas."

"Look, Mr. King..."

"Call me J.R."

"Okay, J.R. I don't know what the federal government can do about that little port, wherever the hell it is, but if the question is does Senator Orr believe in clean, economic development; the answer is yes."

"Now we're getting somewhere, son. You see; by our controlling that port and having the federal government in our corner, we could have a direct shot at Cuba, if that thing opens up."

Don paused. Whoever this guy was, Don doubted he was a crank. "So you would want the senator, if he gets elected, to help you connect your port to the potential opportunities in Cuba. Right?"

"You broke the code, son. I might add, we would be willing to put some real money behind that little project, if you know what I mean."

The possibility of real funding made Don's mouth water. He couldn't remember the last time they had a shot at TV ads. "I understand."

"Just let your new friend J. R. King and some of his friends help you out."

Don said quietly, almost unheard by King, "Let the deal-making commence."

"Huh? What did you say?"

"Nothing. Thank you, J.R. I will talk to Joel about this. For the present, let's just leave it that he will support economic development in the panhandle, OK?"

"Sure...but I was kind of thinking we might want to make sure there is no misunderstanding about this project—you know, maybe make a reference on the checks, my friend..."

"What are we talking about?"

J.R. said, "When I start collecting the checks for you, my folks will want to make sure there is no misunderstanding what kind of *good government*, shall we say, they are supporting. Just so you know who we are, I will have them write *Friends of St. Joe* on their sizable contribution checks."

Don shook his head. Subtlety wasn't the guy's strong suit. As soon as he could, he would make sure to go online and Google J. R. King. If the man had the kind of cash reserves and moneyed friends he claimed, his name would be all over the Internet.

"Now, son. Just picture that nice new color ad running on ABC, CBS, NBC and FOX television stations. Like it says in the Bible, *for every season, there is a reason*...or something like that."

Funny, how people would pull out biblical references to support just about any kind of agenda. The connection ended without as much as a goodbye from J. R. King.

Don slipped the cell phone into his pocket. "Yeah, God bless you, too."

Good news, bad news.

Good because their near-bankrupt campaign would have an infusion of money. Bad news because the money had strings attached.

"Strings, nothing. This sounds like chains going clang, clang, clang."

CHAPTER TWENTY-TWO

Homestead, Florida

Sid Dillard moved back into the van as soon as the storm shelters closed. He had lived in south Florida all of his life and seen numerous hurricanes. Fatima had been a dramatic failure in the big scheme of things, just inconvenient and messy. Still, the tropical system's menace had provided indoor accommodations for two nights. With another system sporting sixty-mile-an-hour winds brewing in the Caribbean—already officially named Gus—he might just get a few more nights of lodging courtesy of the Miami-Dade emergency shelter system.

Sid sat in the van and polished off the last of a super-duper fries order—cold, limp, and greasy. Another dead-end job—this time in the wonderful world of fast food—helped pay for the small amount of gas. He ate well: left-over burgers and fries, and even a salad or two past their prime. Not such bad fringe benefits.

In a small notebook, he scribbled details of the ongoing surveillance. What had initially been a lucky set of photos now morphed into a pot of gold so immense, Sid still pinched himself to believe his good fortune.

Eleana Silver and her Harley-riding paramour were as predictable as the tides that licked Virginia Key Beach. Sid rode through the Silvers' high-end neighborhood every Friday evening. When Eleana was in town from the gig in Washington, the estate teemed with activity. Sid didn't skulk at the curb like a spurned lover. Instead, he waited until the time immediately before sunset to cruise to the empty lot adjacent to the bay. On either Friday or Saturday evening—and sometimes both—the Harley would be parked with the senator and her Latino sprawled on a blanket by the water. So predictable.

One picture said a thousand words. He had two SD memory cards filled. With what he had so far, he could provide a documentary staring the senator. More pictures equaled more money. Sid considered his choices. Perhaps, he would send bits and pieces, a little at a time. Let the senator pay in installments.

A steady stream of cash.

Sid liked the idea.

With his first meager paycheck, Sid purchased a pocket-sized sound amplifier from a sporting goods store. Hunters used it in the deep woods to listen for game. Oldsters used it to hear conversations in crowded buffet restaurants. Nosey old ladies used it to eavesdrop on next-door neighbors.

Sid Dillard added the listening device to his spy kit—along with a cheap pair of binoculars. He lusted for a pair of night-vision lenses. A future in espionage awaited. With his blackmail earnings, he would be able to quit his job. Maybe he would goof off for a while. Take a little vacation. He had earned it. Then, he would go to college. Earn a degree in law enforcement. Then, on to the FBI academy. Sid Dillard: spy extraordinaire.

Of course, he would have to forgo the talk-show gig. Low profile. If he wanted to branch out into international affairs, he couldn't afford the exposure.

Sid licked the clotted salt and grease from his fingers and slipped the digital camera strap over his head. The binoculars fit into his shorts pocket. The listening device, he slipped into his shirt pocket. The night was balmy with a good breeze off Biscayne Bay. Good. No need for mosquito repellant. He hunkered down and followed a now-familiar path to the perfect vantage point. Eleana and Ramiro stood at the edge of the shore, holding hands.

"What? No hook-up tonight?" Sid muttered.

The last couple of trips, the two had become almost boring. Just a lot of hugging, hand-holding, and kissing—like an old married couple. Sid plugged in the earbuds and tuned in to their conversation.

Eleana: "I can't wait until the end of October. At that point, the election will be soon be behind me, and I can finally relax."

Ramiro: "Just a few more weeks, *mi amor*."

Sid gagged. This guy was so sappy, it made his teeth hurt.

He picked up the camera and aimed as Eleana turned to face Ramiro.

Eleana: "Don't let me forget. Tickets for The Halloween Sundowner at Vizcaya are on sale. I need to buy ours."

Ramiro: "Ours?"

Eleana: "I wouldn't be there without you."

Ramiro: "A bit bold, Eleana. And on the eve of the election. Do you think it wise?"

Eleana: "It's a costume ball. No one will know who you are. Even if they do…You are just the faithful hired man who is escorting the still-grieving widow. Everyone knows how involved I am with Vizcaya. No one would raise an eyebrow about my presence there."

Sid heard Ramiro's silken laughter.

Ramiro: "And what would you have me become for you?"

The couple drew close. Kissed.

Eleana: "I don't know. I will think on it. Maybe, you can be my brave knight. Or, a rakish pirate captain, anxious to ravish his captive."

Sid fought the urge to snatch out the ear buds. Did all spies have to put up with this? "Hang tough," he coached himself. "The job can't be all glitter and glamour."

Ramiro: "As long as you remember—you should not drink, *mi amor*."

Eleana: "I'll ask for the alcohol-free wine. Our baby is much too important."

Sid Dillard sucked in a lungful of air and almost choked.

Destin Beach, Florida

Russell Nathan ran his fingertips across the 14K gold pendant of a Phoenix—a gift from the owner of We Love Nathan Motors. Fitting, the symbolism of a mythical dying bird who arises from the ashes to become once more, beautiful and whole.

Life was far from marvelous since the now-infamous party, but not bad. Plenty of money had greased palms of the irate parents and local law enforcement. He was doing his civic repayment by financing a couple of little league ball parks around the county.

Sarah and her piranha attorney had raked her now ex-husband's bones nearly clean. She got the mausoleum of a house in the country near Pensacola. He got the shell of the beach house. No matter. With what he was raking in at the car dealership, he could hire some hot-shot designer to come in and refurbish the place. The French Cottage Countryside Chic meets Redneck Riviera décor had grown tiresome anyway. He didn't miss any of the damned fish wall-hangings and silk palm trees. If he saw another hibiscus-pocked tropical print—unless it was across some young woman's behind—he would lose what was left of his mind.

Nor did he miss politics. For years, every time he as much as farted, someone was standing by to record it for a playback later on. He was tired of kissing ugly, drooling babies, sucking up to greedy deep-pocketed developers, and smiling. Especially all the smiling.

Russell didn't have as many liquid resources. Sarah had taken her half, plus some. Still, he had plenty. With one call, funds would appear. Magic.

"Ah, the beauty of offshore accounts," Russell mumbled. "My dear, dear Sarah. Neither you nor your rat-boy lawyer could sniff out my little nest egg."

There was a way around just about any obstacle. He just had to search for the pig-trail off the main highway.

He didn't have any desire to travel abroad. Plane trips hurt his back. He didn't require high-end tailored suits in order to sit on the deck and admire the surf. He had seven expensive watches and no need to check on the time. He didn't plan on old-age care as many of his contemporaries. Their long-term care insurance. Their names on the waiting lists of retirement communities. Russell planned on going out in style when he deemed it the right time—high on pills and booze, and flat on his back with his toes curled in post-coital ecstasy.

Babes had come out of the bushes after the party scandal. Now, he checked a valid driver's license for the birth date before he so much as held hands. Plenty of good booze and unfettered female companionship. What more could a man ask for? When he stopped to think on his life, he was pretty content.

Russell looked down at the hand-written personal check—a generous five figures—before slipping it into the envelope addressed to the Joel Orr Campaign Headquarters. On a pink post-it note, he wrote: *Good luck, Joel. Go get the Bitch.*

Washington, D.C.

Mark Cox watched Senator Eleana Silver walk into the office, perfectly turned out in a navy blue designer suit, pumps, and attaché. In the few weeks she had been in Washington, her public relations man noticed less South Beach attire, but clothes couldn't mask her attitude.

As he did every morning, he tried to judge her mood. Elated? Angry? Tearful?

Why couldn't Brad Silver's pinch hitter have been a man? Not that he had anything against females. Women made life easier, more colorful, and certainly more interesting. Second only to his profession, he loved his wife and two daughters, though the occasions were rare when he saw any of them—awake and in the same room—for more than an hour at a time.

Eleana Silver's mood swings of late made his wife's hot flashes and periodic crying jags seem like a Disney ride in comparison. Given the choice, he'd take PMS from all three of his life-mates over a week of Eleana Silver's wild fluctuations.

Could she be bipolar? Maybe latent suppressed grief over her husband's tragic death? Mark Cox exhaled. Not grief. No. He'd seen more prolonged sadness from his cat when the family dog died. Unless Eleana fell to pieces the moment she left the Senate building, he had seen little emotion related to her deceased husband. Cox wondered if she missed Brad Silver at all.

He did.

With a man at the helm, Mark Cox wouldn't have to worry and second guess every nuance of conversation and mood. More and more, he felt like a glorified lady's maid. Maybe he should show up in one of those little black dress outfits with a white ruffle apron and feather duster. He'd have to shave his legs. Wear pumps. The mental image made him smile.

"What's up with the shit-eating grin, Cox?" Mike Belan asked.

"Nothing, Belan."

Like the twenty-something, college-graduate son who had blown off gainful employment to move home with the parents, Mike Belan had returned. A permanent fixture of the room. Low profile. But still there.

Could life be more hellish? Cox couldn't imagine. Only the dream of spearheading a presidential campaign and a move to the White House as Tad Myers' top advisor kept him going. That, and the thought of Eleana's promised replacement after the election. Even one of the South Florida Hispanic congressmen Tad Myers avoided would be welcome.

A few more weeks.

Cox glanced from Senator Silver to Gwen Reynolds. At least the two women seemed to have signed an uneasy truce. The set of the Chief of Staff's shoulders and jaw told a different story. Clearly, Gwen Reynolds held little respect for Brad Silver's merry widow. Cox had to give Gwen credit. She stretched to find common ground and keep the atmosphere tolerable for the whole dysfunctional senatorial family.

"How was your weekend, Senator?" Gwen asked.

Eleana checked a nick in her manicure and frowned. "Always good when I'm home in Miami."

Mark Cox: "Did you see any damage from the storm?"

Eleana shrugged. "It was just a little rain. Everyone acts as if it was such a big deal."

"There has been extensive flooding in North Florida," Gwen stated.

The senator brushed the comment aside. "Not my concern. The Governor worries about such."

Gwen's lips drew into a tight line. Eleana might as well have uttered the famous line from another arrogant aristocrat, Marie Antoinette: *Let them eat cake.*

Mike Belan walked across the room and helped himself to a cup of coffee and a warm Danish. "Might make you a few points with the media if you at least act a little concerned. You *are* a Florida senator."

Cox held his breath. Had the room's temperature dropped a few degrees?

Eleana tilted her head and tapped one of her chandelier earrings with the tip of a fingernail. "Good point." She looked to Cox. "Figure out who I should call, and I will."

Mark Cox nodded.

Eleana's features brightened. "Enough of all that. Too gloomy. I had the most interesting conversation while I was lunching at Vizcaya. The President of Florida International University has asked me to become a visiting distinguished service professor. I'll be obligated for a couple of sessions tied in with their Latin American Studies program."

"For free?" Mike Belan asked.

"Certainly not. The pay is nominal. Only about fifty thousand."

Gwen Reynolds visibly bristled. "Senator, that is ill-advised. Especially now, before the election. Of late, there have been several legislators who have come under scrutiny for what is seen as legislative legerdemain, or at least the appearance of it. It is difficult for people to grasp—when higher education is in deep financial distress. Professors are out of jobs."

"The pay is a pittance," Eleana snapped. "At least half will come from private donations. I don't see the problem."

"More, the perception, Senator." Gwen added, "The inference is that a cozy arrangement with someone in a position of power and influence could be worth much more than the cost of the salary. Your husband turned down such an arrangement for that very reason. I…"

"Enough!" Eleana stood so abruptly, the wheeled leather chair banged against the wall behind her. "I have had enough of you. This is my office. Not Brad's. And I will make decisions about my future."

Mark Cox moved forward to step between the two women. Eleana held up a hand to stop him.

"If you value your position, Mr. Cox…" Eleana turned her attention back to Gwen Reynolds. "I want you out of here. Now."

"Eleana," Mike Belan said in a soft voice. "Let's not be hasty."

Eleana's dark eyes flashed in the lobbyist's direction. "Stay out of this. It's not your concern."

"I…" Gwen started.

"You are fired. I want you and your belongings out of my office as soon as possible. I'll call security to escort you out." The senator smoothed a wrinkle in her skirt and avoided eye contact with her Chief of Staff.

Gwen's voice echoed the strain of control. "That won't be necessary."

"Gwen, why don't I walk you to your office?" Mark Cox asked. He guided her by one arm.

In a plastic bin, Gwen pitched a handful of mementoes: framed pictures of herself with Brad Silver, the President, and various political dignitaries, a tortoise-shell pen set, and a few personal toiletries. She cast her handbag and blazer on top.

Mark Cox stood at the door. "Gwen, give me a few days to smooth things over. She'll settle down. You can visit your father. Give yourself a break from all of this. Eleana is high-strung. It's the stress of the campaign."

Gwen paused at the threshold. "Don't give me the party line, Mark. I'm not buying. When I walk away from this office, I won't be coming back. Send my last check in the mail."

She stepped beside him and shifted the box to one hip as she unclipped her security clearance I.D. "I'll leave this with you."

Mark Cox watched as the Chief of Staff stepped from her office.

She brushed past, then turned back to face him. "I feel sorry for you, Mark. I expected more from you. Belan..." She huffed. "Belan will never change his stripes. He will ride the coattails of whomever provides the best and longest thrill. But, you? I'm just glad that Brad isn't here to see what a sham his office has become."

Mike Belan caught up with her in the building's lobby. "Gwen. Wait up."

She slowed her pace. "Best to leave me alone, Mr. Belan."

The lobbyist tagged along beside her until they stood outside. "Don't be so hasty to beat it out of here. Eleana has that whole Latino passion thing going on. It will blow over."

She shifted the bin to the opposite side. "I can't work here anymore. I don't care if she wakes up tomorrow and magically morphs into Glinda the Good Witch. Makes no difference to me."

"So, take a few days off. Chill out. We can make it past all of this transition period. Besides, you won't have to put up with her forever."

"Just another four years. No thanks."

Mike Belan offered a Cheshire-cat smile. "Oh, I don't think it will be that long. Not long at all."

Gwen studied his features for a clue. A blush of understanding hit her. She felt a little faint. Cox's uncharacteristic coddling. The way no one seemed overly concerned about any of Eleana Silver's actions. The mismatched pieces slid together and snapped into place.

"Are you saying what I think? That this is all some screwed-up manipulative master plan? Whose? Yours? Cox's?"

"I can neither confirm nor deny…"

Gwen shook her head slowly. "Oh, Mike."

"Sweet Gwen." Mike Belan reached over and brushed her cheek with one finger. "You still hold onto the whole patriotic, wave-ole-glory clap-trap. Don't worry your pretty little head. Your hands will stay clean. You will sleep the sleep of an innocent. Just stay. Do your job in that wonderful, efficient way of yours. Let us worry about the details. No one will ever question your integrity."

"No one but me."

She spun around and walked away.

Mike Belan caught up and matched her stride. "What are you going to do?"

She stopped. Closed her eyes. Took a deep breath and released it.

"Not that it should matter to you, Mr. Belan. I don't really know. Right now, I'm going home. Probably drink wine until I can't focus. The way I feel, I could get on a plane and leave this city and never look back."

"I really can't talk you into staying, then. The party…"

"Screw the party. I am sick to death of hearing about what's good for the Goddamned party!"

His eyebrows shot up. "Gwen Reynolds just took the Lord's name in vain. The world is truly turned on its end."

Gwen said nothing for a moment.

"Go inside, Mr. Belan. Your senator needs you."

The lobbyist tipped his head. "Can't blame a guy for trying." He reached over and rested a hand on her arm. "Good luck, Gwen."

As Mike Belan entered the Senate building, his cell phone rang. Belan checked the caller I.D. and grimaced. The Queen of Miami summoned. Could this day get any better?

"Morning, Mrs. Claxton."

"Mr. Belan."

He glanced at his watch. A quarter until ten. Still, a bit early for the octogenarian to initiate idle conversation. Little to do with her age; Mike Belan doubted Dorothy Claxton frequently interrupted her beauty sleep for a sunrise.

"What may I do for you, Mrs. Dorothy?"

"How is my girl? I'm quite concerned, Mr. Belan."

"It has been a bit rocky. She's coming along. Nothing we can't handle."

"An abundance of stress wouldn't be good for her...now."

Mike Belan pushed the button for the third floor. "Stress oils D.C., Mrs. Claxton. I don't know how we can insulate her totally."

He heard the elderly woman's irritated sigh.

"Are you at least seeing to her security, then? No matter what the media and my sources say, I still believe that bunch of lunatics on Cuba had a hand in bringing down Brad's plane. Too coincidental."

"You and everyone short of the moon think the same. No hard proof. If it was a set-up, they did a nice job of whisking over the tracks."

"They could come after her, Mr. Belan. What are you doing about it?"

Why the hell did everyone think he could take care of everything? Eradicate Castro. Keep the peace in the Middle East. End poverty. Find a cure for cancer.

Because I'm damned good, he thought.

"I have people in position—very close to her—so don't worry."

"I don't have to remind you, Mr. Belan. There are many, many important people who have much at stake here. We simply must stay in a prime position."

"Yes, Mrs. Dorothy."

Miami's leading lady hung up without so much as a kiss-my-ass.

Gwen's legs felt heavy. And weak. She found a near-by bench and folded. For a few minutes, she simply watched the area. Men in suits. Women in crisp professional dress. All moving with grave purpose. A slight cooling breeze ruffled her hair—the first hint of the gradual loosening of summer's grip. Soon, the leaves would change to colors so intense they would wound the eyes. People would smile more freely. Less angry horns would blast. Then, the holidays: Halloween. Thanksgiving. Hanukkah. Kwanzaa. Christmas.

Washington, D.C.

Tears formed in the corners of her eyes. She took a deep breath and willed the emotion away.

In her purse, the cell phone vibrated. Gwen checked the caller ID screen: a familiar Miami number. Wasn't it just like her father? Always, when she was undergoing some dramatic event, he would contact her, as if he instinctively knew when she needed to hear his voice.

"Hi, Daddy." She forced her voice to sound as upbeat as possible.

Silence. A barely audible sigh on the other end.

Then, a female voice.

"Gwen? This is Julia."

"Oh. Hey, Julia. What's up? Is everything okay?"

Gwen heard the older woman take a shaky breath.

"I don't know how to tell you. Not over the phone like this…"

Gwen felt the burn in her stomach.

"Oh, honey. It's your father. Your father has passed."

CHAPTER TWENTY-THREE

Miami, Florida

Gwen pushed through a group of rowdy sun-burned tourists at Miami International Airport and aimed toward the baggage claim area. To anyone watching, she would appear the epitome of a refined female professional: tailored pantsuit, low pumps, make-up and hair understated, carrying a tan leather laptop case.

What took over when emotion threatened to shut her down? She wondered. From the time she was a little girl, any kind of trauma sent her into what her father called *military mode*: Squared shoulders. Chin up. Dry eyes. Neutral facial expression.

"Look at my Little General." Her father's favorite quip.

Hell might break open and lick flames. Terrorists might drop bombs and maim thousands. People might perish. Your mother might go to heaven before you had a chance to know her. A beloved senator might step on a plane never to return. Your father might sit down to read the paper and die.

Amidst chaos, at least one woman had to keep her head. Make decisions. Stay calm. Maintain order. Later, after the dust settled and others started to smile again, Gwen would take the time to dissolve.

Somewhere deep inside, Gwen Reynolds wept.

Office of the Governor—Tallahassee, Florida

Governor Tad Myers took the third lap around his office, his cell phone plastered to one ear. Top aide Kemp

Johnson stood in the middle of the room and swiveled to watch the circular race. Yet another favorite persona: *NASCAR ADHD hamster.* Kemp amused himself by imagining his boss in one of the fire-retardant suits with all kinds of sponsor endorsement logos plastered across the back, front, and sleeves. What would the race car's murals look like? Pink flamingoes. Mickey and Minnie Mouse. The space shuttle. Palm trees. An alligator with an open maw painted across the hood.

Kemp would be the track spotter. Only, instead of instructing his driver *Go low! Go high!* to avoid accident snarls, he would yell out absurdities like *Watch the chair! Hey, swerve to miss the sharp corner of the desk! The bird-of-paradise plant!*

Kemp bit his lower lip to avoid grinning. Any job could be enjoyable as long as he used his imagination. Tad Myers gave him a lot to work with.

"What in hell were you thinking, Cox?" The Governor's voice rose in pitch. "You know how this will look?"

On many levels, Kemp felt sorry for the Governor. Tracking hurricanes. Keeping up with the buffoons in Washington. Balancing the media, the budget, the requisite social engagements.

"Can't you just grovel and get her back? Wave money in her face. Any change up there right now could be damaging if the other side finds out and magnifies it. It will appear as some kind of weakness. Some kind of internal struggle. Which it is."

Kemp watched his boss narrowly miss a collision with an armchair.

"No, you don't publicize the fact she's gone. If you try to put some spin on this, it will appear that you're covering up something. Which you are. I'll send someone from my office up there, just to get us by until after the election. The next senator will wish to pick his own staff. We just need someone capable for the interim."

Governor Myers flipped his cell phone off without saying goodbye.

"Who do we have, Kemp?"

"Sir?"

"That bunch in Washington have allowed Gwen Reynolds to leave. Who do we have who can pinch hit for a couple of months?"

Miami, Florida

Karen added the last few lines to her blog, used the spell-check, and hit the post icon. When she first started the online commentary, the idea of putting her thoughts down on anything—much less anything political—seemed awkward. Who would want to read her opinion? She still marveled when people she didn't know posted comments. The more Joel Orr made the headlines, the more they searched out information on the Internet. What had started as a weekly, one-paragraph quip, had morphed into a daily column of several hundred words. Refreshing for her, working with words instead of figures.

The front room of Orr for Senate Headquarters buzzed with activity. The late rush of campaign funds proved a needed transfusion. Fresh volunteers mixed with the loyal regulars. People talked on cell phones and sifted through mounds of mail. In a few short weeks, the room transformed from calm to calamitous. Everyone talked at once. Laughter and camaraderie flowed around the cramped office.

Karen rarely saw her condo, except to sleep. As soon as she left the bank, she headed to what the staffers now fondly referred to as *The Orr Hood*. Karen loved the place. The energy. The sense of family. The endless supply of sweet rolls and coffee. Most of all, working so closely to her father.

"Goin' down to Cup O' Joe. You want me to bring you one of those mocha thingys back?" Don Farringdon asked.

Karen hesitated a moment. "Oh, what the heck. Sure. But have Jennifer make it with artificial sweetener. And no whipped cream. I've gained eight pounds since I started hanging out at this place."

"Guess you don't want one of those apple-stuffed pies, either, then." Don leaned over her laptop. "Good blog, Karen. You should consider a career in P.R."

"Right." She picked up her purse.

"This one's on me. You bought last night." He called over his shoulder.

Karen watched her father's campaign manager stop around the room, taking food and drink orders and mingling with the volunteers. She wondered what politicos like Don and Ronnie did when they weren't in the midst of an election. She couldn't imagine either one as the homey, PTA-Dad type. Both men were divorced. As far as she knew, neither played golf or had any hobbies. Like remora fish attached to a shark, they existed to ride the currents with a favored politician. Where he swam, they tagged along. Happy to be part of the parade.

Daddy has to win, she thought. *If not, who will get custody of the boys?*

If—and it was a huge *if*—Joel Orr made it to Washington, he could find places for Don Farringdon and Ronnie Taylor in his office. Get them off the streets of Miami and into Respectable National Politics. Karen smiled at the oxymoron.

She hit the button to put the laptop into hibernation mode and dragged a tote filled with three days' worth of the *Miami Herald* onto the table. Where most people in her age group preferred the online version of the news, Karen didn't. She looked at a computer monitor all day. Reading the headlines on the Internet was the last thing she wanted to do when she finally settled down in the evening.

Karen talked back to the paper. Ruffled it in disgust. Snapped the pages when something angered her. Folded it down like origami to home in on a particular article. The tactile experience, satisfying.

After culling through the sales papers, she sorted the sections into more manageable piles. Sports on top. Then national news, local news, the funnies, and finally the social pages. Miami was a huge metropolis, but each area held a sense of community. Reading the obits helped her to stay abreast of regular bank customers who had passed away. She couldn't be a small-town banker, but she could still offer condolences.

One name caught her attention: Albert Reynolds. She scanned the column to the list of surviving family members.

"Oh, no."

Karen checked her watch. If she left now, she could make it to the viewing.

Miami Springs, Florida

Karen listened carefully to the GPS instructions. She wasn't one to acquire the latest techno-gizmo. Didn't have a cell phone with all the Internet bells, games, and whistles. Barely knew how to program her VCR. And had debated for months about signing up for digital cable. The same prove-it-to-me philosophy that made her a savvy investor and bank manager caused her to question the expanding gadget-based economy. What would it do for her? Did she really need it? Would the next one come along within days, months, and replace the current version for less money and aggravation? Was the owner's operation manual thicker than the Miami-Dade phone book?

The Global Positioning System device got high marks. It took her places she wanted to go. She no longer had to fight to refold a map or memorize directions. As long as she had a street address, the amazing instrument could guide her there. No matter that she had lived in metro Miami for the better part of her life, she still occasionally got twisted around. All that, a thing of the past.

The only aspect she took issue with—the GPS lady's voice. Crisp, clean American English. Informative. Polite.

Until Karen took a wrong turn. Then, the woman switched to a faintly condescending attitude. With one word—*recalculating*—the voice's inflection said it all: *You are obviously an incompetent idiot. Don't dare make another move or even attempt to think on your own. I'll have to redirect you. Oh, why didn't I go into health care like my mother told me to?*

Karen thought they should make a Deep South version of the guiding voice. A sweet, almost-sappy female with the nicest of manners. Then, when Karen turned opposite of the instrument's careful directions, the woman's voice might say, *Oh, well bless your heart. You've made a little mistake. You just hold tight for a moment and I'll get you some new directions, sugar.*

Sometimes, Karen took a wrong turn just to piss off the GPS lady. Surely, if she kept trying, the woman would heave a tremendous sigh or just shut the unit down.

"In three hundred feet, turn left," the voice stated. "Arriving at destination."

Karen pulled into the cramped parking lot of White Brothers Funeral Home and took the last available parking place beside a shiny black hearse. Today, she had made the GPS lady proud. Not one incorrect turn. It had been tempting.

An older neighborhood west of the airport, Miami Springs was sandwiched between the affluent and pricey Doral to the west and Miami Lakes on the north. The packed 836 Expressway stretched on toward downtown Miami—a twenty to thirty-minute drive even during moderate traffic times. Originally the area contained all single family homes and apartments, but like all of Miami, now had its fair share of condos. Most of the construction consisted of homes typical of the area: concrete, stucco, and some wood siding. Once known as the residence of pilots and stewardesses, Miami Springs held a mix of about a third white, a third African-American, and a third Hispanic.

The area's claim to fame— Miami Springs Villas— boasted the thickest prime rib in the south of Florida. Karen couldn't recall the last time she had bitten into one of the juicy rare cuts, but made a mental note to coax her father out for dinner soon.

The scent she associated with funeral homes accosted her nose as soon as she stepped into the cool foyer; she was sure it was from some kind of lily. She closed her eyes for a moment. Always, the odor brought the loss of her mother to mind.

"Buck up. This isn't about you," she coached herself.

She followed the sound of soft background organ music down a carpeted hallway. Wall sconces threw diffused light in round pools. Where were all the people who belonged to the cars outside? The place was like a morgue, creepy in a Halloween-ish kind of way. Karen smiled and mentally chided herself. *Brilliant thinking. It is a morgue.*

"Good evening," a deep voice said.

"Shit!" Karen jumped and twirled around to face a tall thin black man. "Oh, I'm sorry. You scared me."

"My apologies, Madam."

The guy was way too *Adams' Family*. With lighter skin, he could pass for Lurch.

"Um…I'm here for the Reynolds' viewing?"

His arm levitated and he pointed farther down the long dim hallway. "The Eternal Rest Room. Third door on the left."

Karen looked in the direction. *Eternal rest room? Did it have urinals?* When she turned to thank the man, he had vanished. A cold shiver crept up her spine and the fine hairs on the nape of her neck stood erect.

"Get a grip, Karen."

Due to good sound-proofing or some kind of invisible morgue force field, Karen heard nothing until she opened a walnut-paneled door leading into the room labeled: Eternal Rest Room—Chapel Three. The chapel teemed with people, mostly black, with a few Hispanics. Disjointed muted conversations echoed around the room.

She allowed her eyes to adjust to the rose-colored lighting, then searched for her friend. Gwen Reynolds stood beside the flower-draped coffin, surrounded by a group of people. Great. No way could she avoid seeing Albert Reynolds.

Dead people. Karen swallowed hard.

It was a fact of life, death. No one could live forever, nor should they. The only person she had seen in a casket had been her mother. All painted up to look as if her cheeks still held the blush of life. Laid out in her favorite dress. Diamond stud earrings and a gold cross necklace. Her wedding rings—though she wasn't married to Joel Orr anymore at that point. Karen remembered watching her mother's chest, waiting for it to rise and fall. When it didn't—naturally—Karen had felt her throat constrict. She had dashed outside to gasp for air.

Karen walked slowly down the middle aisle past groups of mourners. Noticed boxes of tissues placed strategically at the end of each cushioned pew. She stopped. Took a moment to calm her breathing and study her friend. Though still poised and beautiful, Gwen Reynolds radiated exhaustion. Karen knew the feeling.

As soon as Gwen spotted her, she nodded to the clutch of ladies and pushed past to envelope Karen in a warm, tight hug.

"I'm so glad to see you."

"Gwen. I am so very sorry. I came as soon as I knew."

"I thought several times about calling you. I did. It's just…"

Karen rested one hand on Gwen's shoulder. "Don't. You don't need to explain."

"This has been so…hard."

Karen expected Gwen's rush of tears. None came. "What happened?"

Gwen glanced back toward the casket, as if she expected her father to provide a reasonable answer.

"Stroke. A massive one. He was reading a book. Julia—that's his friend—was warming up something for their lunch. She came in to get him, and he was just..."

Karen hugged her again. For a moment, they stood in silence.

"Where are you staying, Gwen? You can come to my house."

Gwen offered a faint smile. "You're so sweet to offer. I'm at Julia's. She lives a couple of blocks from my father's house. I just couldn't stay there alone without him."

Karen nodded. "I know how you are about your job, Gwen. I hope you're not worried. I know it's a bad time for you to be away from Washington right now."

"That is not an issue."

Karen said, "Good. People just have to understand. Family comes first."

Gwen looked toward the door where a fresh crop of mourners entered. "Washington is the last thing on my mind."

CHAPTER TWENTY-FOUR

Office of the Governor—Tallahassee, Florida

Aide Kemp Johnson thought, *It would easy, so easy, to end up in a padded room somewhere...the institution only forty-five miles from here, over in Chattahoochee, might have some vacancies. I should check. That would be so nice, right about now. Quiet. Nothing around to harm me. No sharp utensils. Maybe some good antipsychotic medications.*

Some days, just watching his boss made him feel more than a little unbalanced. The Governor could slide from present to past tense and from one persona to the next as easily as some people changed underwear.

"I'm thinking about September eleventh. Such a horrible, horrible day for America. My speech for the remembrance service—was it sensitive enough?" Governor Myers focused his intense blue-eyed gaze on his top aide. "It was touching, don't you think, Kemp?"

Kemp rummaged through memory for the date a few weeks in the past. Even if he didn't recall the exact wordage, he could answer truthfully. Tad Myers excelled in public speaking, especially when he needed to squeeze emotion from the audience.

"Ah...yes, Governor. Most."

Tad Myers' eyes glistened. It almost appeared the man might burst into tears.

"I love Tallahassee's 9-11 Memorial with the area the Master Gardeners planted. So peaceful. A wonderful tribute to all the fine Americans lost on that fateful day."

"Your speech was well-received," Kemp offered.

"It was, wasn't it?"

Kemp waited. When the Governor showed inklings of true emotion—other than his usual frenetic programming—Kemp felt a little off-guard. Best to stay silent and watch how it played out.

Tad Myers stared from the window. "All those innocent lives…lost."

The Governor spun around. Compassionate, normal, cuddly-pet Hamster fell to the wayside. ADHD Hamster entered. Kemp could tell by the gleam in the man's eyes.

"Did Cox return my call from this morning?"

Kemp shook his head. "No, Governor."

"Get him on the phone."

A few minutes passed before Kemp received Mark Cox's return call. At the Governor's request, the conversation echoed through the room over the speakerphone.

"Mr. Cox. Good of you to call. Mr. Johnson and I were just talking about you."

Mark Cox: "Oh?"

Kemp's eyebrows rose. Interesting. Since when did Tad Myers act as if the two of them were buddy-buddy gab pals? Had to give it to Cox. At least he didn't ask *Who?*

"He's listening in, so don't give away any national secrets." Governor Myers chuckled. "I hoped to hear from you this morning."

Mark Cox: "I had personal business. My cell was turned off."

"Not good, Mr. Cox. You should always make yourself available," the Governor said.

Mark Cox: "Governor, you may always contact my office number. In an emergency, my staff knows where to find me, Sir. My dental hygienist doesn't take kindly to trilling ring tones. I don't like the idea of having a new piercing because she jumped, either."

"I suppose." The Governor paused before asking, "What did you do on September Eleventh?"

Mark Cox: "I attended a memorial service at the Pentagon."

"Ah. Yes. Suppose it was deeply moving. I haven't visited the memorial park as yet. I plan to. I understand it is starkly beautiful and serene. All those benches with names on them."

About now, Kemp Johnson mused, the public relations man is wondering why the Governor of Florida called—to play a game of twenty questions?

Mark Cox: "Yes. It is a fitting tribute."

Tad Myers made a move to circle the office, then opted to pace back and forth in front of the desk. Experience had taught him; words spoken as he rounded the back corners defied the speakerphone's capacity and necessitated reiteration. Governor Myers detested repetition above all else.

"Reason I called—so soon after the most grave of anniversaries—is to give you a heads-up. I contacted the League of Women Voters. Expect a call from them. They have agreed to host a debate between our candidate and Joel Orr."

Kemp heard what sounded like strangulation on Mark Cox's end.

Mark Cox: "Sir?"

"A debate, Mr. Cox. A debate! The numbers have slipped more towards Orr. It's too close to the election to sit on our haunches. We can't afford to lose any more points to the man."

Mark Cox: "I am monitoring the polls, Governor. And…"

"Listen, Cox. I want that debate. You get your lady ready. It's happening. A done deal."

Mark Cox: "Sir, I am not certain Senator Silver…"

Tad Myers stopped in place and stared at the speaker device. "I don't have to remind you how much rides on this election."

Mark Cox: "No."

"Then, we are in agreement. I'll have the League President call you to finalize the date and time. Orr will just have to make do with what we dish out."

Mark Cox: "Yes, Governor."

"Mr. Cox. You have a good evening."

Mark Cox: "And you, sir."

Kemp Johnson waited a moment to make sure Senator Silver's advisor had disconnected before asking, "Do you want to speak with the League President now, Governor?"

Tad Myers regarded his top aide. "Kemp. I don't think today is the time to do that, do you? So close on the heels of the anniversary of our national tragedy. It is a time of mourning for our country. You shouldn't even be thinking about the election at a time like this."

Kemp blinked. The white padded room looked better by the second.

Washington, D.C.

Lobbyist Mike Belan's cell phone sang out in the special little musical ditty he had chosen for Mark Cox: *When the Saints Go Marching In.* He smiled, imagining Mark Cox— stoic, conservative, sphinctered Mark—in a fancy, bright red, gold-trimmed band outfit high-stepping down Mainstreet, USA, blowing on a slide trombone. The image never failed to make his day.

"Afternoon, Mr. Cox. How'd your meeting with the Jacksonville insurance execs go?" Belan asked. He motioned to a server for a coffee refill and kicked back with his Bluetooth earpiece snug in one ear.

"Good. Good. They'll be making a considerable contribution to the campaign." Mark Cox said.

Belan heard the P.R. man curse. "What the hell are you doing?"

"Trying to get across this city to catch a flight out. And I thought D.C. drivers were insane. I don't think any of these morons..."

Belan heard Cox curse again. "Careful, bud. Those morons are potential voters."

"Right," Cox answered."I know you didn't call me just to discuss north Florida drivers."

"I've been thinking...about the upcoming debate with Orr. We only have a couple of weeks left."

Mike Belan huffed. "Thank your best buddy Tad Myers for that. Personally, I would have avoided putting her into any debate—not unless it was about shoes or clothing, or the latest hot handbag. She's getting a little better, but she isn't Brad Silver."

"Do you think Eleana is taking this seriously?"

Belan winked at the young blonde female server who delivered his sandwich. "Yeah, I think so. But I don't know if she can handle a punch from Orr."

"You're right. We have to get someone to really test her. I'll call the Chairman of the Party and see if he has suggestions."

Belan took a bite of a Reuben sandwich and replied as he chewed. "Senator Larson might be a good person to do a dry run with her. He loved Brad and was really up on international issues. I think he'll be willing to do us a favor."

"Good thought. I just don't want him to hit her softly. She's still living in that Vizcaya fairyland. Orr is a smart guy and I really worry about Farringdon. That bulldog will have Joel go straight for the jugular."

Mike took a swig of coffee and wiped the Thousand Island dressing from his lips. "Let me talk to some of my lobbyist friends to see if we can dig up anything new on Orr. The press has pretty much pressure-washed his underwear, but there may be more stuff there."

Cox said, "That's the ticket. We may not win on the issues or debating prowess, but we should be able to gut it out with him. And if you can find a little new dirt...well..."

Belan belched. "Oops, my bad. You know, Mark. We really must drill down on this debate...in terms of preparation."

"I should be back in D.C. by late this evening. We'll meet first thing in the morning."

"I want to review a checklist I always used to rate Brad prior to all his debates, and see where we are with Eleana."

"Is that the one where you can grade how we look going into the debate?" Cox asked.

Mike Belan glanced over the charges on his ticket and threw a couple of bills down on the table. He would pay dearly for wolfing down lunch. He was no different than his cohorts. Half of the city ate antacids like after-dinner mints.

"Exactly, just like on a test in school. Above a certain grade and we look good. Below it, and we are toast."

"We'll talk." Cox didn't bother to say goodbye before he ended the call.

Mike Belan wiped his mouth once more and nodded to the server as he stood to leave.

"Love you, too, Marky," he quipped to the dead connection. "Have a safe trip home and don't eat too many of those complimentary airline peanuts. You know they upset your little tummy."

Mike Belan knew of what he spoke. From Brad's earliest debates in college through all his campaigns, Belan had kept a checklist for review prior to each debate. With Eleana, he knew it was even more important.

The debate was not going to be pleasant, but he was glad Cox had brought it up. Convincing Eleana Silver of the weight the debate carried would take careful planning. Nothing less than empirical data would convince the Ice Princess about how much work she had to put in for the preparation.

Mike Belan found a bench next to the Capitol steps and took out a pen and notepad. Technological gadgets were wonderful. He used everything he could get his hands on. But nothing beat a plain pad of white paper to jog his thoughts into line—a kickback to his college days. Later, he could sit down and finalize them on the laptop.

The first subject: Issue Preparation.

Eleana was reasonably prepared on most domestic issues and a scattering of international issues, especially dealing with South America. When it came to Europe and the Far East, the sitting senator was clueless. Unfortunately, that is where the nuclear weapons resided.

"Preparation: Grade C."

The second subject: Issue Presentation.

Eleana's beauty and personality would be an advantage. From his experience in previous campaigns, Mike knew many techniques that collectively could have a real impact on the outcome. Brad Silver had been excellent with his eye contact and phased delivery, pausing to set up a crescendo to deliver major points. Could he teach Eleana this? No matter how he tried, Eleana just would not be as good as Brad. Belan's thoughts moved to the TelePrompTer. Eleana had never used one. It could be an important aid in her presentation, or it could be a disastrous complication.

"So many factors. Okay. Presentation: Grade B."

Third Subject: Debate Interaction.

This concerned Mike Belan the most. The one area Orr could get a glove on her. As a trained trial lawyer, Joel Orr was skilled at picking at specifics in her presentation. If properly prepared, he might land a punch out of nowhere. Training couldn't fully prepare her for that. If he agreed to help, Senator Larson could play the role without making her feel insecure. He and Mark Cox had to maintain an air of confidence. As Belan so often told Brad before his toughest debates, "Senator, just don't let them see you sweat."

"Interaction: Grade Incomplete. God, she's really vulnerable there."

Subject number four: Press Questioning.

Eleana was beginning to make strides in handling the press corps, especially those she most often worked with in Washington. He was not certain how the debate press would be selected, but that could determine how well she managed their questions. Almost without exception, Eleana seemed to be most at ease with the male reporters. No surprise there.

One reporter came to mind: Louise Hampton from Fort Myers. Mike made a note to schmooze with her in advance of the debate, see if she might be a problem if selected. Since the last fifteen minutes of the debate would be allocated for press questions, Mike felt hopeful and prayed for no surprises.

"Questioning: C+."

Final subject five: Intangibles.

Belan thought of the introduction of Alaska Governor Sarah Palin to America during the 2008 presidential election. In addition to her surprise inclusion, the woman had the kind of intangible—elusive, ethereal—quality that could capture people's imagination. Eleana might very well have that quality. Still, in Mike's mind, Eleana was untested in an unscripted setting like a debate.

"Sorry, Madame Silver. In the Intangibles area, I have to give you another Incomplete."

Mike was now hopeful, but concerned. He called Cox back on his cell phone.

"What, Belan? I only have a few minutes until I board."

"No prob. We can talk more at length tomorrow morning. I've looked over my notes, and I'm really worried. I think we need to get hold of Senator Larson right away. Eleana needs to really bone up on European and Far East affairs. I think she can probably get by on domestic issues, with the exception of abortion, and maybe Central and South America. I would shudder to think of how she might handle questions about the nuclear weapons associated with Iran and North Korea."

"What makes you think Orr is going to ace those, either?"

"I really don't think our problem is necessarily Orr, but the damn press. I'm going to make it a point to get with the reporter from Ft. Myers. She concerns me. Her columns haven't exactly been favorable towards Eleana."

"Okay, what else?"

"We can coach her up on presentation, though we need to really rehearse that against some real surprises. I'm kind of hoping her beauty gets us through that…"

Mark Cox hesitated for a moment."All right. We need to block out the next week for nothing but debate preparation. I'll call Eleana now and make sure she is on board."

"Mark, let's not spook her. She's been pretty prickly lately. The new Chief of Staff your friend in Tallahassee sent up is not making her particularly happy. It doesn't take much to make her fly off the handle. As long as we figure a way to impress the importance on her. I don't think she realizes what it is going to be like when she goes out there in front of thousands of constituents—the cameras, the hot lights. I don't know how we train her for that."

"We don't. We just hope she has enough of the intangible quality to pull it off."

Orr for Senate Headquarters—Miami, Florida

Don Farringdon sipped a Diet Coke as he paced and talked. The free hand, he used to gesture. "Okay, let's hit it again, Joel. The Federal Reserve must loosen money policy to counter this recessionary pressure."

Joel Orr pushed back in his chair and loosened the top two buttons on his sweat-ringed shirt. "Don, we have spent the last hour and a half on domestic policies and issues. I know they're important. But we haven't even talked about Europe and the Soviets."

"Senator, those issues are yesterday's news. Since the fall of the Soviets, all the focus has been on the East—Iraq, Iran, maybe even North Korea."

"I understand, but from information I have gathered over the years, I still think we are overlooking a critical threat to our country's safety—nuclear weapons."

Farringdon sighed. "They didn't find weapons of mass destruction—the now-infamous WMD's—in Saddam Hussein's Iraq. Most think the public is off that issue."

Joel stood and stretched to alleviate the cramp in his shoulders—the same knot he had lived with for weeks. "Don, you and I both know; there are still enough warheads in Russia to blow the world up many times over. I don't think Eleana Silver knows anything about Europe and the continuing Russian threat."

"Don't kid yourself. Mark Cox is no fool. He'll have her prepared. Unless..." The public relations man pulled on his chin, considering. "...she is so blinded by her misplaced loyalty to Cuba and all things Hispanic." He shrugged. "What the hell. What do we have to lose? Let's spend some time really drilling down on the nuclear threat issue. Maybe they will have their collective heads so far up their backsides on domestic issues; they will overlook the Russian nukes."

Joel nodded. He dug into a white take-out bag and pulled out the remaining crumbs from the morning's ration of sweet rolls. "Even if they prepare Eleana to talk about international issues, I'll bet all she discusses are Central and South America."

"Those were the priorities for Brad before his death, and she may not have heard him discuss anything else."

"Yeah, and if I am not mistaken, I think Karen told me once that Brad had asked Gwen to brief one reporter in particular on the nuclear threats...I don't remember who that was."

Don snapped his fingers. "I do. That perky reporter from Ft. Myers—Louise Hampton. She seems to have taken an interest in our race. I've seen her at several of our campaign stops."

"See? I think it *is* a hot issue, and I think it's one we should emphasize," said Joel.

Don Farringdon smiled. "That's why they pay you the big bucks, boss."

"And don't you forget it." Joel walked toward the door. "Right now, I'm taking some of my big bucks and heading down to see what Jennifer has left in the case. If we're going to be here half the night talking about nuclear warheads, I need a sugar fix."

CHAPTER TWENTY-FIVE

Miami Springs, Florida

Gwen Reynolds parked the rental car in the driveway of her father's house—a one-story stucco ranch with a red tile roof. From the road, the yard looked immaculate. Lush tropical foliage lined the property beneath copses of trees—one of Miami Springs' claims to fame as the *City of Trees*. Albert Reynolds had always been fussy about his yard. Unlike the plumber with the perpetual clogged sink, her landscape expert father had taken great pride in the exterior presentation of his home.

Her father's words echoed in memory, as if the landscaper had spoken into her ear: "Can't take care of everyone else's yard and ignore my own. How would that make me look?"

Since the stroke, Albert's pride and joy had suffered a little. The grass lining the driveway wasn't edged to military perfection. Several shrubs had sprouted fingers of straggly greenery. A few brown patches—evidence of some kind of fungus—interrupted the lush emerald green grass. Three of Albert's former employees—now owners of the profitable business—had taken turns mowing the lawn so the property didn't look totally neglected.

Gwen sighed and squared her shoulders. Might as well get to task. No one would do it for her.

When she walked into the small tiled foyer, she caught the faint scent of her father's aftershave. Her throat constricted.

She took a deep breath. "You will *not* cry. Too much work here. No time for all of that."

Gwen walked through the house, opening closet doors and bureau drawers. Everywhere: evidence of Albert Reynolds' careful organization. The towels and sheets, perfectly folded and aligned. Rows of underwear and T-shirts—none dingy—lay in the master bedroom chest of drawers. Very few dust-collecting knick-knacks. She moved on to the opposite end of the house. The kitchen counters held only the basic necessities: coffeemaker, microwave, paper towel stand. When she opened the refrigerator, she was surprised to notice no rotting vegetables, fruit, or leftovers. Julia. Of course, she would have thought to do that.

The doorbell sounded. Gwen walked to the foyer and peered through the peep hole. She smiled and opened the door.

"Karen! What are you doing here?"

Her friend held up two fast food bags. "I brought coffee and doughnuts."

Gwen stepped aside and allowed Karen to step past. "How'd you know...?"

"I'd like to say I was just in the neighborhood and decided to pop in, but..." Karen shrugged. "Truth be told, I spoke with Julia last evening."

Gwen led the way back to a small round table in the kitchen. "You know Julia?"

"Not well. We spoke at your father's visitation. I gave her my number in case she, or you, needed anything. I figured you wouldn't call, being you..." Karen handed over a steaming cup of freshly-brewed coffee and dug in one of the bags for creamer and sugar. "She told me you'd be over here today. What you were up against. Figured I might be able to help."

Gwen sat down. "I don't even know where to start."

Karen put an iced doughnut on a napkin and slid it in front of Gwen. "Ah, but you have an expert in your midst. I've been through this. With my mom's house. I know how hard it is. Sometimes it takes an *objective other* to muddle through."

"Objective other," Gwen said.

"Yep. That would be me. I have a boat-load of broken-down boxes in my car and plenty of tape. Markers to label everything. Bubble wrap for the breakables. Garbage bags for the discard pile."

"This is big, Karen. You sure you're up for it?"

"Not like a have a full social calendar. And I'm driving them nuts down at campaign central. I think Don Farringdon and my dad are ready for a break from the well-meaning daughter. Besides, even if I did have plans, I would cancel them. You need help, or you'll never get back to business as usual in Washington."

Gwen glanced down. "You haven't heard, then."

"What?"

"I am no longer Eleana Silver's Chief of Staff."

Karen stopped in mid-chew. "Get out! You quit?"

"I was asked to leave. Of course, the official party line is that I vacated my position for personal reasons."

"Whoa. What happened...or, can you say?"

"At risk of sounding all wounded and bitchy, let's just say Senator Silver and I had irreconcilable differences."

"What will you do now?" Karen asked.

"Take time to get this house ready for the market. The estate sale people will come in as soon as I—and Julia— have had a chance to go through personal belongings for anything we might want to keep." Gwen sipped her coffee. "After that? Assess my options."

"You could always work for our team," Karen said. "I know my dad would welcome someone of your expertise."

Gwen smiled. "The media would love that, wouldn't they?"

Karen waved a hand through the air. "I know you would never do it. My dad's a Democrat. You've worked for the opposition for too long. Why would you?"

"Anymore, I don't seem to discern too much difference between the two parties. I know...fundamental issues. You stay in Washington long enough, and you begin to see it for what it truly is. One big game. One big power game."

"You sound pretty jaded."

"No. Not really. Just realistic."

Karen wiped the sugar from her lips. "I've never been in the middle of it like you have, so I don't have your perspective. Still, I like what I see when I watch my dad. Working beside him these past months, hearing him talk about the real problems facing Floridians, getting a true grasp of what kind of man he is..." Karen paused. "Even if he loses this election, it will have been one of the best things to happen to me, and to him."

"He seems to be committed."

"Very."

Gwen felt the ache of sadness. "He reminds me of Brad Silver."

Karen allowed a moment to pass before asking, "Something I have always wondered, Gwen. And you can tell me if I am way out of line. I swear your answer will be in strictest confidence. You and Brad...did you ever...?"

Gwen hesitated. "I loved Brad Silver. I like to think he felt the same. But I respected his marriage to Eleana. In another place and time. In another life where we weren't under the media microscope. If he was a free man."

She took a deep breath and exhaled. "No. Brad Silver and I never crossed the line."

Senator Silver's Office—Washington, D.C.

Senator Eleana Silver sat behind her desk, a queen holding court with Mark Cox and Mike Belan as attendants. The interoffice buzzer sounded.

"Senator Silver," the assistant said, "Senator Larson is here."

"Send him in."

"Oh, Wilfred, what a pleasant surprise," said Eleana as Senator Larson of Mississippi entered the inner office.

"Senator Silver, remember?" Mark Cox said. "Once a senator, always a senator."

"Oh. Right. Sorry, Wilfred. Senator Larson. That whole title thing just evades me..." Eleana waved a hand dismiss-ively.

"Oh, that's all right, Eleana. No need to stand on formal-ity when we're not in the public eye. I got a message you wanted me to stop by."

Mark Cox said, "Senator, that was a message from me. Thank you very much for taking time out of your busy day. Senator Silver has a big debate with her opponent down in Clearwater, and we were wondering if you might be able to give her some tips."

The eighty-four-year-old, thirty-year veteran of the Sen-ate tipped his head. "I would be glad to help, but I am not as spry as I used to be."

"Wilfred...I mean, Senator Larson, thank you." Eleana shot a questioning glance toward Cox and Belan. "I didn't know my people were that concerned about my opponent, but I do appreciate your help."

"Our concern is not so much her opponent, as it is *her*," Belan mumbled under his breath.

"Have a seat, Senator." Cox motioned toward one of the upholstered side chairs. "I speak for Eleana, with her permission." He glanced toward Senator Silver. "She is most interested in any advice you offer regarding protocol. The proper way of proceeding. What are some of the courtesies of the Senate, which you might suggest for Eleana's use in her debate?"

Belan nodded approval to Cox. Both knew the answers. Eleana would listen to Senator Larson where she would brush off any suggestions the two of them made.

The elderly senator said, "Eleana, it is important that the tradition of the Senate and its decorum be maintained and respected, especially from a sitting senator. It is important that you show respect for the title of the person, even if you don't respect the person holding the title."

"Why? That would be untruthful. Don't I wish to be perceived as trustworthy?" Eleana leaned forward.

"Because it is an institution. All of us elected or appointed into it, recognize that it is the most exclusive organization in this country. There are only a hundred of us, out of the hundreds of millions of people in this country."

The aged senator continued, "This applies also to people who are serving, or who have served, in their state legislative groups. For example: you need to refer to your opponent as Senator Joel Orr, as he has held the seat in the Florida Senate."

She tapped a manicured nail on her chin. "I really didn't think of it in that sense..."

Cox interjected, "Senator Silver, the press recognizes a light-weight right away. They refer to neophytes as *hayseeds, falling off the next truck into town.*"

"That might be a little strong, young fella," Senator Larson said. "But it is true nonetheless. If you are a member of the U.S. Senate, you must conduct yourself with dignity and aplomb. If you fail to do thus, Senator, it will show. Begging your pardon, I do think you have some brushing up to do."

"It has always struck me as making a whole lot out of nothing," said Eleana.

"My dear, a lot of blood has been spilt for our freedoms. The framers of the Constitution envisioned three equal and independent branches of government. The least we can do, as members of one of the branches, is ably represent the legislative branch. Generally speaking, the House proposes legislation, and we dispose of legislation. Just remember that. A somber and grave responsibility."

Eleana's dark eyes sparkled. "Wow. That sends a tingle down my spine."

Mike Belan fought to control the snide remark aching to leave his lips.

The elder statesman continued, "I will make arrangements for the Secretary of the Senate to meet with you and review the do's and don'ts of senatorial conduct. I know you mean no harm, my dear. But tradition is everything in the Congress, and to the highest order in the Senate."

"So...say we are out there..." She waved a hand toward the window. "I just call you Senator Larson? Is that it?"

"In conversation, yes." Cox inserted. "If you are introducing him in a group, you should say, The Distinguished Senior Senator from the Great State of Mississippi."

Senator Larson nodded and smiled. "It's a bit cumbersome at times, but one must pay homage to a fellow senator's years of service."

Eleana sighed. "I think I have some more work to do before the debate with Orr."

Mark Cox nodded. "Indeed. But the fact that you recognize the importance of your position as a United States senator will help position you in the debate."

"I agree with Mr. Cox." Senator Larson rose to leave. "Senator Silver, I know Brad would be very proud of you. I think you will do fine."

Mark Cox asked, "Senator Larson...one more favor. Might you make time to meet with us this next week? It would help Senator Silver very much to have someone with your legal expertise. Someone to fire questions at her. Help her understand how to pull from her knowledge and think through her answers."

The senior senator smiled. "I'll find time. Have your assistants call mine. I'm sure we can work things out."

After Senator Larson left, Belan helped himself to a cup of coffee. "Now, let's get into the issues, Senator Silver. That's a whole different area."

"Oh, why don't we take a break? I need to freshen up, just in case a reporter stops by."

Eleana grabbed her purse and left for the executive restroom.

Mike Belan smirked. "Cox, old boy...I have a feeling you and I are in for a long couple of weeks. Like trying to push a pig uphill."

Homestead, Florida

Sid Dillard felt just plain twitchy.

The closer he came to unfolding his plans, the more he questioned the whole manic scheme. Who was he kidding? The pie-in-the-sky dream of college and the FBI academy? Impossible. No way would the big players allow him to peacefully coexist after he played his hand and scammed the cash. He knew way too much.

So. What then? He'd have to relocate. Costa Rica, maybe. It was warm there. He could buy a nice little piece of paradise and settle down. Grow something. What did they grow in Central America? Bananas? Pineapples? He'd have to stop by the library and check it out on the Internet. Was his life so horrible that he would leave the United States for good? Did they even have football and fast food in Costa Rica? He would miss so many things. Just thinking about leaving south Florida made his throat constrict.

Living in the back of a van wasn't such a bad life. No responsibilities, save for showing up for one in a series of menial jobs. He had clothes on his back. A small amount of cash in his pocket.

"Get real. This is thousands of dollars we're talking about!" he said aloud. "You can go anywhere. Be anyone. Change your name. Have plastic surgery to change your face."

The final countdown neared. Copies of the memory card and printed pictures labeled with date and time stamps waited in a rented locker. The letter was typed and ready to mail. He just had to muster the courage.

Fate handed him yet another opportunity. On a sterling silver serving platter. One of the customary caterers for

Vizcaya needed extra pick-up staffing for the October Halloween Sundowner event.

"When things are meant to be," Sid said. "The way is made easy."

CHAPTER TWENTY-SIX

Miami Springs, Florida

"Oh my God. Is this *you*?" Karen held up a faded wallet-sized photograph.

Gwen added an armful of men's shirts to the towering mountain in a box labeled: Charity Donations. She leaned over and grinned.

"Yep. That's me. I call it my pick-a-ninny stage."

Karen's mouth fell open. "I can't believe you just said that."

"What?"

"Pick-a-ninny! Kind of southern racial slur-ish, don't you think?"

Gwen smirked. "First of all—I *am* black. I *am* southern. If *I* make the remark, it's not a racial slur, or didn't you get the memo on the relativity of political correctness?" She jabbed one finger into the air. "Second—I *do* look like a throwback to plantation days with that hair. Look at it. All those little plaited sections—has to be a good thirty or more—tied off with ribbons on the ends. Sticking out like some cartoon character that's just had the shock of a lifetime. The two missing teeth in the front just add to the glamour."

Karen sucked on her bottom lip to avoid laughing.

Gwen added, "My Auntie Emma did that hair thing to me—God rest her soul. That's what happens when you don't have a mama. All the other female relatives around you take it upon themselves to make you look right...or not."

Gwen studied the photo for a moment. "I used to hate it. She'd sit me down in front of her, and it would take forever.

Pulling the hair. Fussing at me when I wiggled. When it was done, my scalp was so tight, it felt as if my brain was trying to burst through."

Karen put the photo into a plastic bin with several scrapbooks and loose family pictures. "One day, I'll share some of my school portraits with you. My mom was into big curls. In one of my elementary school pictures, I look like I'm wearing a basketball on my head. She used to go hog-wild with the hairspray. You can take one look at that shot and figure you'd probably sprain your fingers if you tried to rearrange the bangs."

"Makes you kind of wonder…when we're in our dotage and looking over photo albums in some assisted living facility—will we look at ourselves at this age and ask, *what was I thinking wearing that outfit?*"

"Probably." Karen snapped the lid and added the storage box to a stack of others. "That's the last of the pictures. I think."

"We've really made good progress. Just the outbuilding to go. One of my father's friends is coming over later to pick out what he wants, then I'm packing the rest for charity. Except the shovel."

"Shovel?"

"I know it sounds weird. And I don't have much use for one. But my dad had this one small shovel—more of an overgrown garden spade, actually—that he loved. He used to let me dig holes for him, and we planted I don't know how many trees in honor of Arbor Day with it."

"If you go back to Washington, a shovel might come in handy. It does get pretty deep up there," Karen said.

"Good idea. I can take it to work with me. Make a statement."

"Sounds like you've decided to go back."

"Word of my departure from Senator Eleana Silver's office has spread." Gwen closed the closet door. "I've already had a couple of inquiry calls. Suppose I have the option to return. I don't know what I'm going to do." She gestured to the boxes. "Going through all of this makes me want to go back and pitch out everything in my condo. So much stuff! Plus, where will I ever find room for the things I want from here? The desk in the study is an antique. Been in my father's family for years."

"I'd offer to keep it for you, but I don't have any room either."

"Suppose I'll just rent a small storage space until I decide. Besides, if I end up taking it to D.C., I'll have to ship it or rent a truck and drive it up there." Gwen rolled her eyes. "Ugh."

"Oh, you'll end up back there, Gwen. Politics is in your blood."

"Too bad it's not something they make an antibiotic for."

"And one to clear up one's complexion, and make one immune to falling for the wrong guy…"

"You are such a nut case, Karen Orr Hernandez," Gwen said. "I don't know what I would do without you. We've done in a weekend what would have taken me God knows how long. And you make me laugh. What can I ever do to repay you?"

"Vote for my dad."

Gwen shook her head and smiled. "You're the one who missed her calling. You should go into campaign management. You're really getting into this whole thing."

"I never have liked politics. Knew just enough to vote. Barely," Karen said. "He has good ideas. Really. This election has turned him around. I can see it in the way he walks and talks. He believes in something again. It's wonderful to watch. You should read my blog sometimes, Gwen. I have blurbs from some of his speeches online. They come from the heart—not just some scripted parody. He's a good guy. A little misdirected in the past. Well, a lot misdirected."

Karen smiled. "I am so proud of him. I just hope he has what it takes to go head to head with Eleana Silver in the debate that's coming up. I'm sure she has a whole team working on her behalf."

Gwen's thoughts ran to the probable scenario in Washington. "Oh, don't doubt that."

Karen stood and stretched. "You hungry? I could go for a nice fat burger. Something really greasy."

"With cheddar cheese fries. I know just the place. Before his health declined, my father and I went there every time I came to visit."

Destin Beach, Florida

Russell Nathan had never considered himself a writer.

Last of the red-hot lovers. Passable ballroom dancer. Grill master. Amazing bullshit public speaker. Professional baby-kissing politician. But, writer? Nope.

Twice a week, he sat down with the laptop computer and added to his new blog: *What Would Nathan Do?* Other than the many online forums and chat rooms, the web log provided hours of entertainment. He could write anything he wanted—an endless stream of consciousness.

At first, he limited the snippets to comments on the aftereffects of the ill-fated beach party. Used the blog to announce his new business affiliation with *We Love Nathan Motors.* He moved on to grouse about the unfairness of divorce. The outdated notion of monogamy. The use of imagination in sexual positions.

Comments on his blog were sparse at first. As the weeks passed, more readers added their opinions. One guy from Texas offered to move him to the Lone Star state and help him run for office. A housewife from Nebraska wanted to fly down and spend the weekend. Some religious fanatic from Tennessee gave him a list of reasons he was going straight to Hell. Nathan lived to turn on the computer and see what America had to say. Every day when he logged on, the number of hits to his online commentary grew.

He returned to pontificating about his first love: politics.

The former Governor of Florida looked out across the emerald waters of the Redneck Riviera.

"What can I title this one?" he asked aloud.

No one heard him. The only living thing in attendance: a curious seagull that sat on the deck railing, eyeing the crust of his sandwich.

"I got it!"

The startled bird squawked and flew away.

The view from the bottom: Why a former political star supports Joel Orr. And why you should, too, he typed.

For the next few minutes, Russell Nathan waxed poetic. By the end of the piece, Senate candidate Joel Orr sounded like the kind of man anyone would want to take home to meet the parents, lead the fleet to victory, and plant the first American flag on Mars.

The blog—along with the HONK FOR ORR sticker attached to the bumper of every vehicle purchased through the dealership—ought to help.

Miami, Florida

The brass bell hanging from the door handle of the Cup O' Joe trilled. Joel Orr glanced up. A tall black woman entered, glanced around the narrow room, and walked toward his table.

"Miss Reynolds!" Joel stood and pulled a chair away from the bistro table.

"Senator Orr." She sat down in the proffered seat.

"Please, do call me Joel. I told you, the last time we spoke. We can dispense with the title. It's been a number of years since my days in the Florida Senate—though, I know the title follows me for life."

Gwen removed her sunglasses and snapped them into a leather case. "Old habits, Joel."

"This is a pleasant surprise. You were just in the neighborhood and decided to stop by for the finest cinnamon rolls in Miami, I assume?"

Gwen smiled. "I'm not a huge fan of sweets, unless chocolate is involved."

"In that case, you should try one of Jennifer's killer brownies."

Gwen glanced toward the bakery case. "Normally, I would. I'm catching a flight in a couple of hours. I try to avoid sugar and caffeine before I fly. Both make me a little jittery."

Joel nodded. "My condolences on the loss of your father. Karen told me she has been helping you with some of his affairs."

"Thank you, Joel." Gwen felt the sting of tears forming in her eyes and forced them to stop. Typical. The dust was settling. A lot of the work had been done. The breakdown loomed. Just, not now. "Karen has been a tremendous support."

"May I buy you a cup of coffee?" he asked.

"Yes. Please. Decaf."

He returned with a pottery mug of fresh-brewed Colombian coffee and a small pitcher of cream. "One of the many things I like about Jennifer's little place—other than the best baked goods in the city. She believes in real mugs for her sit-down customers. Coffee just tastes better when it's not in Styrofoam."

"True." Gwen smiled. "I stopped by the headquarters. They said I would find you here."

Joel glanced around. "My new home away from home. Funny, my favorite haunt used to be a bar. I still go there, from time to time. Not to drink. Just to visit. Something about these small local places…"

"Senator Brad Silver felt the same way. No matter where he traveled, he sought out the little mom and pop restaurants. He would ask the locals for recommendations."

"Best food, and a good way to meet real people. Especially important for someone representing the public."

"He didn't necessarily look upon it as a political ploy."

Joel said, "I'm sure he didn't. Brad never struck me as a suck-up. I admired that about him. I didn't always agree with his views, but I have to give him points for having even a smattering of integrity after years in Washington."

Gwen sipped her coffee.

"So, you found me. What may I do for you, Gwen?"

"I wanted to wish you luck, Joel. The upcoming debate."

Joel sighed. "Ah, yes. I dream about it. Nightmares, if the truth be told." He paused. "Any suggestions from the former Chief of Staff would be welcomed."

"I'm returning to Washington this afternoon," Gwen said.

"I see. Eleana Silver came to her senses and begged for your return."

She shook her head. "No. I wouldn't accept if she did. Like you, Joel, I have to reinvent myself. I'm not certain how just yet." She offered a slight smile. "I'll have to make it up as I go along."

"Returning to the scene of the crime—if you'll excuse the cliché—offers one the chance to see through the muck. At least, that's what it's done for me. Clarity. I've found it. Hopefully you will, too."

"Thank you." She hesitated for a moment before adding, "I'm not ignoring your earlier question, Joel. If I gained the reputation of one who uses knowledge for retribution—"

"—your career in national politics would suffer," he completed.

"Funny, isn't it? I guarantee; there are people up there right now who would pay dearly for any information. Some—affiliated with your party, I might add—have already contacted me."

"*My* party. Not *my* people," Joel said. "It's a wonder anyone can see the sky in Washington for all the circling vultures."

She laughed. "I can see where your daughter gets her sense of humor."

"You kidding me? Karen leaves her old man in the dust."

Gwen studied him for a moment. "I can offer a little counsel—without the appearance of impropriety."

Joel leaned forward.

"If it was me facing Senator Silver, I would focus on learning everything I could on Central American affairs. By nature of her upbringing, she has an edge in that respect."

Gwen continued, "I would especially study anything related to foreign affairs—China, Russia, India, Pakistan, the Middle East. Particularly, nuclear non-proliferation treaty issues."

"All good points."

"As a matter of fact, Joel, one reporter that has been following your campaign asked for and was given a detailed briefing by our staff. Brad Silver asked us to do that after a speech he made on the floor."

"Who was the reporter?"

"The woman from the Ft. Myers paper. She's been covering your campaign, and especially tailing Eleana Silver."

"Louise Hampton?"

Gwen nodded. "Yes."

She hesitated, considering her words carefully before she spoke. "When a person is so intensely focused on one area, it is possible to miss extremely important issues beyond that scope."

Joel Orr smiled. "Gwen, I appreciate your candor. I will take your comments in the light in which they are offered— as a concerned citizen."

Gwen dabbed her lips with a paper napkin.

"Will you be back for the debate?" Joel asked.

She grinned. "I wouldn't miss it for the world, Joel. Karen is saving me a front and center seat."

"Good. I'll be happy for one more familiar face in the audience."

"Besides, Joel. I'm just another registered Florida voter who is trying to decide how to vote."

CHAPTER TWENTY-SEVEN

Senator Silver's Office—Washington, D.C.

As in the Army, rank brought privileges. In the U.S. Senate, seniority brought privileges, too. The spacious conference room of Senator Eleana Silver—its largesse, courtesy of her deceased husband's ranking—was lined with rich, dark paneling and provided a spectacular view of the Capitol, with room to seat over fifty. At one end of a rectangular conference table sat the venerable Senator Wilfred Larson from Mississippi. At the other end sat the student—the junior senator from Florida—and her two minions Mark Cox and Mike Belan. The first in a series of dry runs had begun.

Senator Larson turned his attention to Eleana. "Senator, let's start with the logistics. Are you familiar with a Tele-PrompTer?"

Mark Cox said, "Senator Larson, Senator Silver has not really made a formal speech at this point. We have that next on our rehearsal list."

The elder statesman nodded. "Good. Might seem a small detail, but very important. I have found the TelePrompTer can be of great help. But it also can be a challenge, if you are not used to it."

"In what way?" Eleana asked.

"Your staff will gauge the speed of the text moving over the TelePrompTer. That is fine as long as you are keeping up with it. I have had instances were I paused to clear my throat and lost my place. I remember one speech in Tupelo where I decided to insert a personal message, and the whole thing got off track."

"Ouch," Mike Belan said. "I guess the lesson there, is no improvising, no matter what."

The elder senator nodded. "Exactly. Do you understand what we mean, Eleana?"

"Sort of." She flipped one hand through the air. "I am sure it will all work out."

"Why do I have a bad feeling about this?" Belan whispered to Cox.

Senator Larson checked his handwritten list. "Let's move to one of the most critical elements of a debate—the visual part, when your opponent is speaking."

"Huh? If I'm not speaking, what difference does it matter what I'm doing?" asked Eleana.

The old gentleman offered an indulgent smile. "My dear, we all want to learn from the lessons of history. You might not remember when Bush 41 was debating Clinton in '92. When Clinton was speaking, Bush looked down at his watch. The press jumped all over that because the TV guys panned in on Bush for what seemed an eternity. The headline the next day was *Bored Bush Indifferent to Clinton*. Bush never got over it. A good lesson for you, Senator."

"Boy, you are a pro, Senator Larson. That never occurred to me. How about you, Eleana?" asked Belan. A career lobbyist, Mike Belan had heard it all—including Senator Larson's advice. Still, he hoped to make Eleana Silver take the counsel to heart.

"Of course I remember that whole thing," Eleana commented.

Belan and Cox exchanged puzzled glances. Neither could imagine Eleana Silver watching—much less recalling—a political debate. Not unless the said event had happened on the grounds of Vizcaya. Which it had not.

Senator Larson continued, "Practice, Senator Silver. Practice. Over and over. Learn to master an expression of polite attention while your opponent has the floor. No matter if you think he is the biggest fool this side of the Mason/Dixon line, you must respect his right to speak."

"I have to act like I care," Eleana said.

"Deeply. Public speaking—especially debating—is one part knowledge and two parts acting ability. That is where your natural charisma comes in." He glanced to Cox and Belan and asked, "Now, do we know who the panelists are for the final questions?"

Cox responded, "No, Senator. It is our understanding that they are to be randomly selected by the League of Woman Voters—to reflect balance among the media, areas of the state, and of course, gender and race."

The elder considered. "That might present some problems. Best to have a heads-up as to whom you'll be facing. The fewer the surprises, the better. I remind you; that part of the debate is critical—make or break. The press questioning period is the last impression the television, radio, and live audiences will take away from the debate. If you can't gain the list of panelists ahead of time, I really don't have a suggestion there, other than try to be on your toes."

"Yes, Senator." Cox glanced at Eleana. "We realize the importance, right Eleana?"

"Oh, yeah."

Eleana Silver studied her cuticles. Other than the high-potency prenatal vitamins helping her nails to become steel-hard, the rush of hormones had played havoc on her skin. Maybe with her next manicure, she'd ask for the deep-heat conditioning mitts.

Mike Belan spoke: "Senator, we have briefed Eleana on the major domestic issues, and even the international issues such as those related to the Caribbean basin. Are there any others we might need to add?"

"Well, it's a big world out there." The elder senator replied with a sweep of his hands. "Obviously terrorism, Afghanistan and Iraq are on all people's minds. Still, I would not overlook some of the threats that do not seem imminent, but are still very much present..."

He tapped his chin. "Iran and North Korea remain un-predictable, and of course the uncertainty in Pakistan—all of them could be nuclear threats if we are not careful...and that says nothing about our old, but continuing threats throughout Europe and with the Soviets."

"We have scheduled a full briefing with the Department of State for Eleana this Thursday," Mark Cox said.

Eleana glanced up. "Mark, did you say Thursday? That day just won't work. I have to be in Miami for an important board meeting at Vizcaya. One of our largest fund-raising events is coming up at the end of October—the Halloween Sundowner Ball. I simply must be there. The State Depart-ment people will reschedule for me. I'm sure."

"Eleana, the State Department briefings are a big deal," Senator Larson said. "I would really encourage you to keep that appointment. I still participate in those, even though I am not up for reelection for another two years."

Eleana rolled her eyes. "We'll see..."

Mark Cox and Mike Belan sighed at the same moment.

Mike smirked and muttered, "I'm really going to plan a long vacation after the election. Somewhere far, far away."

Orr for Senate Headquarters—Miami, Florida

Joel Orr sat in his campaign office by himself on a Monday night in late September. Just over a week until the Great Silver-Orr Debate—or, as the team called it, *D-Day*. It was really a question of political survival. The ultimate test.

Joel picked at the dregs of a cinnamon twist.

"I've come so damned far. What is it, then?" He stood and paced the small room, talking aloud. "What is it with me and public speaking? I have this weird brain cramp or something. Pause. Hesitate. How will the press and the audience take it if I pull that crap?"

He stopped long enough to take a sip of lukewarm cof-fee. "Is it because I've become rusty? Am I scared of the press? Am I not prepared?"

The answers rushed into Joel's mind. Yes, he was scared spit-less of the press. Any hint of weakness and they would nail him to the nearest palm tree. Was he prepared? How could anyone ever be prepared? It could be compared to being ready for the comprehensive SAT exam at the end of high school. He hadn't fared well on that, either.

"It's like trying to be God." He threw up his hands. "Okay, Orr...you just cram anything and everything into that pointy little head of yours. I mean *everything*! About any country the U.S. could possibly have as an ally, an enemy, or trading partner. Be able to spout it back at a second's notice. Not only that—you must smile, look good, and don't break a sweat while you do it!"

He recalled some of the great debates from history. As a kid, he had studied the famous Lincoln-Douglas debate. He vaguely remembered the Nixon-Kennedy debates and reflected on how much the visual aspect of debating affected the outcome. He chuckled, thinking of the legendary response of Senator Lloyd Bentsen to Senator Dan Quayle in the 1988 Vice-Presidential debate, "Senator, I knew Jack Kennedy. He was my friend. Senator, you are *no* Jack Kennedy."

Joel wasn't hoping for a game-changer or a quip that would be quoted for years on end. A solid performance— enough to convince the lobbyists to begin sending money— would be sufficient.

A song from *My Fair Lady* rang through his mind and he sang one of the lines and danced a few steps. "Wouldn't that be love-er-lee?"

Joel snickered. Then, laughed until his stomach hurt; the kind of laughter the experts say expels stress and delays heart conditions. Good thing Farringdon and Taylor and the rest of the crew weren't around. They would think the shelf life had worn off on his medication.

Vizcaya Museum on Biscayne Bay—Miami, Florida

Dorothy Claxton leaned forward. "I'm worried about you, my dear."

Eleana took a sip of sparkling water and grimaced. The aftertaste—a combination of something metallic and slightly fishy—lingered. For the past two weeks, nothing had tasted correct. She forced herself to eat and drink—only for the baby.

"Why's that, Dottie?"

"You are pale. And thin. Way too thin for someone in your condition."

"I have a baby bump." Eleana's hand wandered to the slight protrusion beneath the gauzy blouse. "I feel like a whale."

"You don't look like one. You look as if you're under-nourished."

"It's hard to find time. Between meetings and brief-ings…all the grilling on this debate. It's exhausting. Walk this way. Talk this way. Smile this way. Dress this way."

"Then, traveling down here for a board meeting…really. You must take it easy. You must remember…though you are in good shape, a pregnancy at your age is considered high risk."

Eleana sighed. "Flying down for the meeting was just an excuse to come home to Miami. Had I not left, Mark Cox and Mike Belan would be still firing questions at me."

"Are you sure this is what you want, dear? With the ba-by on the way…you could be here, being pampered every day. No worries. No stress. And I could put some meat on those pretty bones of yours."

Eleana glanced down to avoid tears. "Parts of it, I really like, Dorothy. I feel so overwhelmed and out-classed at times. Still…"

"It all comes down to what is important to you, then. The child just adds another piece to the puzzle. What will you do once you are in office—and we all know you will win."

"Work. Attend the endless meetings."

"Where does the child figure in on this, Eleana?"

"You don't think I will be a good mother?"

Dorothy shook her head. "No, no, sweetie." She reached across the table and grasped Eleana's hand. "I have all the faith in you in that respect. All I suggest is that you take time to figure out what you hold most dear."

Eleana tilted her head and studied her friend. "I don't understand, Dottie. Just last month, you sat right here and told me to take Washington by storm."

The older woman signaled the server with a lifted hand. "We'd like menus, please." Then, back to Eleana, "I remind you; it's a woman's prerogative to change her mind. Plus, at my age, I don't hesitate to flip-flop, as you political types call it. My concern—first and foremost—is your welfare. Washington will be right there, whether you are our senator or not. In a few months, no one would mention your name. Your child, on the other hand, will hold in his or her heart all the times you spend together."

Eleana took a sip of the bitter-tasting water. "I can't just stop now."

"Perhaps, not. But it is still an option. No one is forcing you to do anything, forever." Dorothy smiled. "But, if you are certain this is what you want, I will throw my significant support your way. Now, as to this debate. You must listen carefully to your advisors, Eleana. Mark Cox, Mike Belan, that senator you mentioned…" She tapped her forehead.

"Senator Larson."

"Of course. His name just slipped my mind for a moment." Dorothy took a sip of coffee. "Listen to them, dear. Those men have played this game for many, many years. I have all the confidence in the world in your ability to heed their counsel and pull this whole thing off, in brilliant fashion. You have absolutely nothing to worry over. You will be fabulous! Just smile and show them your true self. They can't help but love you as I do."

"Will you be able to attend?"

"Oh, Eleana. How could you doubt? I'm coming, and I'm bringing a huge group of the Vizcayans in tow. We'll be the section who's wildly cheering you on." Dorothy Claxton pushed a plate of warm bread and butter across the table. "At least eat a bite of bread. We'll order a nice brunch."

"I really don't…"

"Humor an old lady, Eleana. I plan on being the god-mother of that child."

Destin Beach, Florida

Russell Nathan propped his laptop computer across his tanned belly. A bit wobbly. A tailored suit could cover all ills, but beach attire left his distended stomach shining like a vine-ripened North Florida watermelon.

He finally gave up the balancing act and moved to the bistro table.

"Later," he pledged, "I'll lose the flab. Right now, folks, Ole Russ's got bigger catfish to fry."

A Call to Arms! he typed. *Time to get off your lazy asses and fight for what's right!*

A bit strong? Russell considered and substituted the less-insulting word *behind*, a gentler Southern body-part term.

Russell cracked his knuckles and dug into the body of the opinion/editorial piece that would appear on his blog and then flash to the inboxes of over three hundred We-Luv-Nathan fans.

Are you sick and tired of the sad excuse for leadership you see running our fair state up in Washington? Think there's not a damned thing you can do about it? Do you long in your heart for an old-fashioned public demonstration of voter ire?

Then, JOIN ME! Join your buddy Russ in Clearwater, Florida. We're gonna show those clowns whose sniffin' at their heels. We're going to pump up Joel Orr! The big dog is fixin' to leave the porch.

Russell Nathan entered the important details—time, place and attitude—and hit the send button.

CHAPTER TWENTY-EIGHT

Clearwater, Florida

The former Governor of the Great State of Florida glanced across the growing crowd of Russell's Rabble Rousers. He grinned. Beyond his wildest expectations.

Russell Nathan judged the herd of sign-toting demonstrators to number at least five hundred: all shapes, sizes, and ages, and not only from the Sunshine State. Only a handful of the most select would actually go inside the hall, but the media would get the full Monty.

He shrugged off the touch of one fanatic, a middle-aged seamstress from the panhandle of Texas. What the hell was she was doing in the midst of Florida politics? Russell couldn't figure. Just another nutcase, maybe. The woman dogged his every step and kept brushing imaginary flakes of dandruff from his shoulders and straightening the collar of his custom-screened T-shirt. A damned nuisance.

No matter. In every crowd, there had to be a generous scattering of nut jobs. Nut jobs could yell and stomp as loud as the sane, and they made for better press coverage.

A supporter from Key West offered to streak butt-naked in front of the cameras with *Vote Orr* painted across his bare bottom. Russell considered, then kindly turned him down. No need to go so far over the top. The rowdy motorcade of cars filled with demonstrators had already raised the hackles of the local law enforcement.

He counted the news teams on the periphery of the gathering. Twenty, so far. Someone in the middle of the crowd started to chant. Others fell in.

"Orr. Orr. He's our man! He can do it with the Nathan Clan!"

Nothing like a pre-game pep rally to bring high color to the cheerleaders' cheeks and get a rise from the players. Russell made a mental note to use the clever analogy in his follow-up blog.

"What'd'ya think?" Don Farringdon asked Ronnie Taylor.

The Orr campaign numbers expert glanced around the crowded Ruth Eckerd Hall—a 73,000 square-foot facility at the Richard B. Baumgardner Center for the Performing Arts.

"At full capacity, it seats over twenty-one hundred. The actual number of seats is 2,184." Taylor nodded. "Not a bad seat in here. Near perfect acoustics. The architects designed this place with continental seating. No center aisles, so the audience is closer to the performance area with an ideal view from all seats." He looked to Farringdon. "In November of 1986, the State of Florida awarded the Barmgardner Center with The Governor's Design Award for excellence in facility development. This hall was nominated as one of the top five concert halls in the U.S."

Don Farringdon smirked. "Your facts are fascinating as usual, Ronnie. How the hell you hold all that in that little pinhead of yours still amazes me, even after all these years."

Ronnie Taylor ignored the gibe and continued. "My point being: if Joel isn't received well, it won't be the fault of this facility. Plus the location is great. Mid-State. Between Tampa Bay and the Florida Suncoast beaches. Convenient to all of the Tampa Bay communities. Perfect location in the cross-hairs of the acclaimed I-4 corridor: the key to any election in Florida."

"Thank you, Ronnie Taylor," Don said in his best TV-announcer voice. "You should work for the Clearwater City Tourist Bureau."

Don watched the mass of people. The Silver supporters wore red. The Orr supporters wore blue. The rest—a mix of undecided voters and the omnipresent members of the press—mixed in. Counting in the abundance of flag-themed banners and streamers, the result looked like a bizarre patriotic pep rally.

"The reds appear to outnumber the blues," Ronnie said. "But not by much."

Joel Orr walked up and glanced around the standing blind screen on the left side of the stage. "Looks like we drew them in, boys."

"You've picked up points in the pre-debate polls," Taylor commented. "A tight race creates a lot of buzz. All the online forums are hot."

"The dried-up old man versus the hot young Latino woman," Joel said. He dabbed his temples with a handkerchief. "If I don't pass out from all this grease paint, I might be able to make a passable impression. Is this really necessary?"

Don Farringdon nodded. "Yep. This one's being televised, Joel. Without makeup, beneath all these lights, you'd look pale and sickly. Better that you have the glow of sun-kissed health."

"Right." Joel tugged at his tie. "At least I know Eleana will be wearing stage makeup, too. I did draw the line at hairspray. They'll just have to get over it."

Joel wore the debate standard-issue attire: dark suit, blue button-down oxford shirt, and bold red power tie.

"You won't believe who I spotted a few minutes ago," Farringdon said. He motioned to a massive clump of people in bright blue T-shirts. "Check it out."

Joel chuckled. "Well, I'll be damned. It's Russell Nathan. Looks like he brought along half of Okaloosa and Walton counties." He squinted. "What do their T-shirts read?"

Ronnie Taylor answered, "I saw a couple of them in line for the bathroom earlier. They read *What Would Nathan Do?* across the front and *Vote for Joel Orr, that's what!* across the back."

Joel spotted his daughter Karen seated at the end of the first row. Gwen Reynolds sat beside her. A handful of his top volunteers took up the other coveted spaces. Two vacant seats awaited Farringdon and Taylor to their left side. He glanced at the opposite end of the same row. A line of nicely-dressed women took up the majority of the row—the entourage from Vizcaya—with two vacant seats reserved at the end for Eleana Silver's top advisors, Mark Cox and Mike Belan. Beyond the closest rows, the rest faded into a blur of faces—all ages, races, and both genders. For the first time since the start of the senatorial election, all of the players were in attendance.

To the left of the backstage area, the Silver team hovered around Eleana.

"Here's the format, Senator Silver," Mark Cox said. "Each candidate will have five minutes to make opening remarks. Then both will be given a chance to rebut those opening remarks. From there, we go into direct questions of each other for thirty minutes. Since it is anticipated that both of you will dredge up campaign speeches, the League of Women Voters has scheduled the final thirty minutes for questions from three members of the press, unknown to the public up until their introduction."

Mike Belan stopped pacing and jiggled in place. "We still don't have a clue as to the panelists or the subjects they'll cover?"

"No. But neither will Joel Orr."

In a few minutes, the President of the League of Women Voters called for order. The last stragglers wandered in and took seats. The television crews cued in on the banner-decorated stage as she offered her opening remarks.

As determined earlier by a coin toss, Senator Silver was selected to speak first. She entered the stage and approached the podium, dressed in a navy blue Exclusively Misook tailored business outfit that looked like it came directly from Wall Street. Her lustrous dark hair was swept up in a loose chignon, exposing a long graceful neck. An American flag pin decorated one lapel. The only other jewelry was her wedding ring and a thin gold necklace. Her shoes—Jimmy Choo classic leather heels. The audience provided the senator a standing applause, even those dressed in blue.

Gwen Reynolds leaned over to Karen and commented, "She's going for the understated look. All designer. But not over-the-top."

"By tomorrow, it will be all over the news and Internet. Women everywhere will rush to buy whatever she's wearing. Remember Sarah Palin and that one style of glasses? They were a hot item for awhile."

"Thank you, thank you." Eleana said repeatedly. "Thank you, thank you very much."

"Damn, enough is enough. They can cut the applause any time now. They're eating into our time," Mark Cox whispered to Mike Belan sitting to his side on the front row.

Eleana finally motioned for the audience to sit down. "Ladies and gentlemen..."

The audience quieted and regained their seats. Mark Cox crossed his fingers. Eleana's presentation would be iffy, but with his little insertion, it ought to stir their emotions.

Eleana looked out across the audience, careful to pause for a few seconds at each section. Her first words—planned deliberately by Mark Cox to get the crowd back to their feet and generate momentum for the speech—rang out:

"God! Bless! America!"

The noise in the auditorium was deafening.

"Partner, you are the best. That was brilliant," Belan said to Cox.

Eleana looked out at Cox and Belan in the audience and gave them the symbolic *fist bump*, made famous by Michelle Obama in the '08 Presidential campaign.

Mark Cox flinched. "Wish she hadn't done that."

Belan clapped "Why? It's only a glorified High-Five."

"It caused a stir then. No need to have her associated with any kind of controversy."

Mike Belan stared at the Public Relations man. "Oh, for the love of Pete. Relax."

Joel Orr watched from his seat on the side of the auditorium as Eleana Silver dug an ever-deepening hole for his presentation. Don Farringdon and Ronnie Taylor also sat in the front row, looking dejected. Ronnie scribbled notes on a small pad and mumbled to his side-kick, "Cox probably has her dressed in red, white and blue underwear."

Eleana Silver spent the next five minutes painting an impassioned patriotic portrait of her love of the State of Florida and the United States. She worked in a tear-jerk story of her birth and youth in Cuba and the grueling boat trip that brought her and her mother safely from the grasp of Communist Castro's Cuba. Not even a soul-less terrorist could deny the tug of emotion.

Generous applause peppered her rehearsed remarks. Eleana flashed her best front-page-model's smile before she left the podium.

"Have to admit—she's a knockout," Don Farringdon said.

Joel Orr took a quick sip of water and straightened his tie. He walked to the podium as the audience in blue stood and applauded. Russell Nathan's covey whooped and shouted encouragement. The red-dressed members of the audience politely applauded, but did not stand. Compared to Eleana's reception, the response to Joel Orr felt limp and lukewarm.

Dread slipped into Don Farringdon's midsection. His stomach churned. Would the weak audience response spook Joel?

"Thank you ladies and gentlemen, and thank you League of Women Voters for inviting me."

"Damn it, Joel," Don said. "Pause a little between words and get closer to the microphone."

Joel started into his presentation. He stopped. Put his notes aside.

"I have decided to skip my introductory remarks and move directly to a discussion of the issues. You can read about my background in the material provided by the League. The issues today are more important than we, the candidates."

"What the hell is he doing, Don?" Ronnie Taylor asked.

"Damned if I know."

Joel repeated the statement, enunciating each word slowly, "The issues are more important than the candidates."

The Hall fell silent for a moment. Some of the audience dressed in blue started to clap, then more.

Orr just looked out into the audience and said nothing.

"Oh, crap. He's not freezing up, is he?" Taylor asked.

Don Farringdon held up one hand. "Shh. Watch."

The tactic worked. The audience slowly rose and applauded.

Don Farringdon grinned as he clapped. "Wow...what a stroke. Hang on. This is going to be the whole enchilada tonight."

Orr began by discussing the sensitive subject of immigration. He moved on to include key statements on the struggling economy, planned development of Florida's resources balanced with the ecology, and the care of the aging senior population. His speech carried none of the usual pie-in-the-sky partisan promises, just statements of existing problems and possible solutions.

Mark Cox leaned over to Mike Belan. "This guy is breaking all the rules tonight."

"Yeah, but it might work, unless Eleana can slam him."

Mark Cox closed his eyes for a second. Brad Silver could have matched punches with the guy, no matter what tricks he pulled. The same talent—not in Eleana Silver's DNA.

The question and answer portion took a predictable course. Both candidates served rote queries and volleyed scripted answers. No slam-dunks. No smoke and mirrors. No surprises. The teams had prepared them well.

The moderator announced a fifteen-minute break. Three guest panelists waited in the wings, ready for their invitation to the brawl. Other than a few members of the LWV, no one knew their identities.

Eleana retreated to a room off the platform to fix her hair and freshen up. Joel elected to take his seat on the side of the platform, a good viewpoint to catch the first view of the panelists coming out of the chute.

In a small room backstage, Ramiro waited. As soon as the stylists finished, Eleana shooed them out and locked the door.

Eleana curled into Ramiro's arms. "I'm so glad you're here with me."

Ramiro kissed her lips, then both cheeks. "I would not be anywhere else, *mi amor.*"

She closed her eyes. "How I wish this was over."

"Only a few more minutes. You are doing wonderfully. *Usted es tan hermoso.* You are so beautiful. Who wouldn't love you?"

She wobbled. "I need to sit down."

He led her to a small loveseat. "Are you feeling unwell?"

"A little dizzy. I think it's all those bright lights. It is so stuffy out there. It feels as if I can't breathe."

Ramiro located a hand towel and rolled ice from a small cooler inside. "Here. Place this behind your neck." He grasped her hand. "Promise me, Eleana. After this, you will rest."

She laid her head back on the chilled towel and closed her eyes. "I will."

"We can take a drive. Find some small inn. Somewhere away from D.C. and politics and reporters."

"They will find us, Ramiro. I'm lucky to step outside without someone pointing a camera in my face."

"Then we'll lock ourselves away from the world. The mansion in Coral Gables. The condo. It doesn't matter where. I can have the staff stock up the refrigerator with all of your favorites. Turn off the phones. Just you and me."

"That sounds like heaven." She smiled.

A loud rap sounded at the door. "Five minutes, Senator."

Eleana opened her eyes. "Here I go. Wish me luck."

He touched her cheek, then pressed one hand gently on her rounded stomach. *"Buena suerte."*

The teams—Cox and Belan, and Farringdon and Taylor—had remained seated to study the panelists and pull up any information from their files. All four knew: the panelists—if not completely objective—could be the make-or-break difference.

A ripple of chatter filtered through the audience when the moderator led three individuals onto the stage. The first man, a recognized television commentator from WJXT in Jacksonville—generally thought to be a conservative. The next panelist was a male African-American reporter of liberal persuasion from the *Fort Lauderdale Sun Sentinel.* The last one—a woman—was a print reporter from Ft. Myers. The moderator introduced each panelist with a brief biography.

Joel studied the seated panelists. When he heard the last name—Louise Hampton—Joel probed his memory. The male panelists, he vaguely recognized. He had heard the name Louise Hampton, somewhere. Where was it?

It came to Orr. Louise Hampton—the reporter who had dogged Eleana's campaign stops, and whose columns often questioned the senator's actions in Washington. The same one Gwen Reynolds had mentioned in casual conversation. The reference to nuclear proliferation treaties—especially those dealing with Russia—followed closely by Louise Hampton's name. No coincidence.

Joel froze. He glanced toward Gwen Reynolds, then back to the reporter. The disparate pieces fit. Without the appearance of impropriety, Eleana Silver's former Chief of Staff had provided the bejeweled sword, the one he would use to slay the dragon. Louise would ask questions about the treaty issues. He knew them, and he knew the answers. Did Eleana?

Joel racked his memory for any details and how they might lead to talking points. Were the treaties with the Soviets verifiable? Were the terms realistic? Would the other allies support our position? Important issues and very complex, but they had not come up at all in the campaign.

Eleana walked back out on the stage, poised and polished. The audience in blue stood. The men whistled. She smiled.

Cox and Belan beamed. Barring any surprises, they were almost home with this election. Might as well call the interior design team and ready the office to look like a Jimmy Buffett bar scene. Eleana Silver would soon be able to settle in—at least, until enough time passed for Tad Myers to insert her replacement without raising too many eyebrows.

Karen leaned toward Gwen. "I know you won't tell me details, but isn't she the one you and Brad briefed?"

"Correct."

"Oh, c'mon. What harm would it do to share, now? No way can I get the information to Daddy in time."

"If your father is the smart man I suspect, he will draw his own conclusions," Gwen said. "I know one thing. If the issues come up, Eleana will be clueless. She defied any of my attempts to brief her before she asked me to leave. And with her mindset, I doubt Cox and the team had any luck with her, either."

The questions started. Most were softballs, and both candidates handled them well. With a few minutes remaining, the moderator directed the panelists to ask their final questions. No one left the auditorium. All sensed history unfolding: the first Hispanic woman to win a debate plus the coveted prize of a duly-elected seat in the United States Senate.

Louise Hampton cleared her throat. She looked first to Eleana Silver, then to Joel Orr. "The relationship of our country and the Soviets is less precarious than it was. Is a non-proliferation treaty necessary today, in your opinion?"

Mark Cox fidgeted. "Where the hell did that one come from?"

A frightened, vacant expression blanketed Eleana's face. Joel looked at his notes and fought the urge to smile. The audience—deathly silent.

"Senator Silver, your answer please," the moderator prompted.

A sheen of perspiration surfaced on Eleana's forehead. "Could you repeat that question, please."

"Very well. In reference to the relationship between our country and the Soviets. Is a non-proliferation treaty necessary?"

Eleana's eyes sought out Mark Cox and Mike Belan. The glare of the stage lights prevented her from seeing anything save their shadowed outlines.

The moderator said, "Senator, you have three minutes..."

Time passed. Don Farringdon and Ronnie Taylor sat forward in their seats. Karen and Gwen stared straight ahead.

Cox and Belan knew. It was over. Eleana had done well on domestic issues. She had even absorbed pertinent information on international issues, especially those of Central and South America. Yet, each time Gwen Reynolds had tried to brief her on issues related to Central and Eastern Europe, she had no time or interest.

Less than a minute remained when Eleana finally spoke. "That issue is no longer relevant today. And besides, that is an issue that I would delegate to my staff."

A sound rippled through the Hall—an audible collective intake of breath from the audience.

My fault, Mark Cox thought. *I made a note to check out Louise Hampton and never followed up on it.* He had forgotten. And now the Silver campaign would pay. A huge ration of shit was poised to rain down on his head.

Don whispered to Ronnie Taylor, "She might as well have said she was abducted by aliens who told her not to worry."

The moderator motioned toward Joel.

He adjusted the microphone.

"Ms. Hampton, thank you for that important and timely question. Unlike my opponent, I do feel the relationship with the Soviets remains very serious. We need only look at how they took over the democratically-elected adjoining country of Georgia..."

Cox and Belan slumped in their chairs as Joel continued.

"...and that is why verification of the nuclear non-proliferation treaty is so important. I would insist that the United Nations be petitioned to intercede. Furthermore..."

The moderator interrupted, "Senator Orr, we have ten seconds remaining."

"Thank you, but madam moderator, this issue is of critical importance to all of us, our children, our grandchildren..."

The moderator signaled the end of allotted time. Joel stepped away from the podium with a brief acknowledgement to the panelists and audience, then approached Eleana Silver.

In the customary gesture of all civilized debates, Joel offered his outstretched hand to his opponent. Eleana hesitated. Frowned down at the proffered hand. She turned and left the stage.

CHAPTER TWENTY-NINE

Clearwater, Florida

Mark Cox slipped into one of the rental limos and instructed the driver to follow the ambulance. Belan slid into the bench seat opposite of him. Cox's cell phone vibrated.

"Three guesses who that could be," Belan commented. "And the first two don't count."

Cox glanced at the caller I.D. "Shit." He pushed the button on the side of the I-Phone. "Governor Myers. Good afternoon."

Tad Myers: "What the hell is wrong with you people?"

Cox: "Governor, sir...I..."

Tad Myers: "I can't believe what I just watched on the CNN live feed. First, I see Russell Nathan in the middle of some kind of riot. You know those media idiots. This could be a one-hour Fox/O'Reilly special before it's done. Unbelievable. Then, I watch Eleana Silver trip all over herself! What have you been doing with that woman for the past two weeks? Carrying her Tiffany's bags?"

Cox: "No, Governor."

Tad Myers: "Brief her, I told you. Brief her until she knows more than the combined heads of the CIA and FBI."

Cox: "Yes, Governor. We did brief..."

Tad Myers: "Quite obvious—you did not! No worries about Russia? Are you kidding me? She might as well have declared Korea and Red China no threat, too, while she was at it. Hell, let's just get warm and fuzzy with every country that has nukes aimed in our direction."

Cox: "Governor..."

The door opened behind them. A tall dark-haired man entered with a nurse in tow, then closed the door in their wake.

"Good afternoon, Senator Silver." When he smiled, the tanned skin around his dark eyes crinkled. His hair—the blend of silver and black that made women crazy—curled in tousled clumps around his face. "I'm Dr. Charles Kight."

The physician looked from Eleana to Ramiro. "In keeping with confidentiality rules, I have to ask…"

Eleana waved the hand not connected with the IV. "You may speak in front of him. You have my permission. Plus, we have the necessary legal papers, if you need to copy them for your files."

"Very well." He consulted the notebook computer. "I have been called in by the emergency room physician to…"

"Oh my God," Eleana interrupted.

"No need to be upset, Senator. Obstetrics is my specialty. The attending physician thought it prudent."

"Is everything…is my baby…?"

"We visualized the fetal heartbeat with the ultrasound. Your vitals— blood pressure, temperature, pulse—are within normal limits. Blood tests will further rule out infection, though no signs point in that direction. Your baby appears to be fine. You, on the other hand, are quite dehydrated. Also, your blood sugar levels are dangerously low. When have you eaten last?"

"Some time yesterday. Mid-afternoon, I think. I haven't been hungry."

The doctor nodded. "Ah, but your unborn child is."

Ramiro shook his head. "I told her to eat."

"I'm certain you are under some degree of stress." The physician stood at the end of the gurney.

Eleana huffed. "A little."

"I think it best if we admit you for at least twenty-four hours. Get you hydrated. That alone will make you feel much better. I want to assure that you and your baby are fine. The first trimester is a crucial time, Senator Silver."

"Yes. I know."

"Since you haven't experienced any spotting or fluid leakage, I suspect your syncope—the fainting spell—to be a direct response to your lack of food and water. At this early stage, if you were indeed miscarrying, there wouldn't be a lot we could do to stop the process." He smiled. "I feel we shall have a positive outcome, but I recommend you stay with us for bit, just to make sure. Are you currently under a physician's care for your pregnancy?"

Eleana nodded. "Yes. I have two, actually. One in Miami. One in Virginia."

"Good. I suggest you check in with him, or her, within the next few days."

Ramiro asked, "Could you tell…was it a boy or girl?"

Eleana answered before the doctor had a chance. "It's not large enough yet. Not until eighteen to twenty weeks."

Dr. Kight entered information into the notebook computer. "Absolutely correct. At this point, the baby looks a little like a peanut. Someone has done her homework. Not surprising for a U.S. senator, I would think. We should have you moved to a room soon. In the meantime, please take the opportunity to rest."

After the physician left, Eleana turned to Ramiro. "You'd better go and get Cox and Belan. If you don't let me talk to them, they will drive you crazy."

"As soon as they move you to a private room."

Eleana considered. "Right."

Mark Cox entered the hospital room first, followed closely by Mike Belan.

Eleana—dressed in a standard-issue blue cotton gown—was propped on two well-fluffed pillows. Ramiro sat beside the bed in an upholstered recliner.

"Eleana." Cox set a vase of gift-shop flowers on the bedside table. "How are you feeling?"

"Better."

"Good. You really gave us quite a scare."

"I know we've been pushing you pretty hard, Senator. I feel responsible…"

Eleana held up a hand. "Stop."

Mike Belan weighed in. "Me, too. But you have to understand why we rode you so hard."

Cox looked toward Ramiro. "You can go now. We can take it from here. I'll call you when we need you."

"He's not going anywhere," Eleana stated. "I want him with me. I might as well go ahead and tell you both. You'll know soon enough. I'm pregnant. Brad is not the father."

Mike Belan was the first to speak. "Sweet Mother of God."

Mark Cox recovered enough to speak. "Mike. Ramiro. Would you please give me a few minutes alone with the senator?"

Ramiro looked to Eleana. She nodded. The two men left the room.

"This changes things, doesn't it?" Mark Cox asked.

Eleana's tanned shoulders rose and fell. "I don't know. Maybe. Maybe not. The doctors insist I rest."

Mark Cox crossed the room and stared from the third-floor window. "No chance this is Brad's child?"

"No."

"Okay." He took a deep breath. Blew it out slowly. Turned to face the senator. "I think it best not to share this with anyone, Eleana. Later…after you win…we can handle it."

"There're only a few weeks until the election, Mark. I won't be waddling around and eating pickles and ice cream, if that's what you are concerned about."

Mark Cox shook his head. "I have kids, Eleana. When it comes right down to it, they are all that matters."

"So…what do you suggest?"

"We lay low. Go with the stomach flu story. God knows, you aren't the first politician who passed out under campaign pressure. People understand."

His thoughts went to the crowd of reporters who clogged the emergency room waiting room and chain-smoked outside its double doors.

"Don't worry about anything. I'll issue the statement."

Later, as the rental limo carried Silver's team to the hotel, Mike Belan asked, "Stomach flu?"

"You have a better idea, Belan? What was I supposed to do? Oh, folks, don't worry about Senator Eleana Silver. She's pregnant with the driver's illegitimate baby?"

"What now? How do we keep this under wraps? Hell, what's to keep the hospital from leaking it to the press?"

"I took care of that with one call to the administrator. He fully understands their role. They don't want to be sued for privacy violations. Not a hospital of their outstanding reputation. Secondly, I mentioned how very pleased the senator was with the kind and accomplished care she had received thus far. How she planned to make a generous donation to their building fund."

"A little extra insurance never hurt." Mark Cox twirled his wedding band around on his finger, a habit he had developed to alleviate stress.

"I'd rather keep the pregnancy private until at least end of November. Then, we can play the poor, pregnant widow card. Everyone—even the most hardened politico—has a soft spot for a mother-to-be.

"I'll schedule a one-on-one limited, carefully-scripted interview with a select television news person. We can use this sudden onset of illness to explain why Eleana did not fully communicate the answer to Louise Hampton's question. It will all work to our favor, in the end."

Mike Belan whistled low. "You—my man—are the Sultan of Spin."

CHAPTER THIRTY

Orr for Senate Headquarters—Miami, Florida

Don Farringdon took a swig of Diet Coke. "Mark Cox is better than Karl Rove."

Ronnie Taylor toasted his friend with an uplifted can of Java Junkie, a super-caffeinated energy drink. "*That* is an understatement."

"Joel, you were superb...especially on the question on nukes and Russia," Farringdon commented.

"Yeah, how did you do that?"asked Taylor.

Joel smiled. "Let's just say... I recognized Louise Hampton and had a sense that she would ask."

Don's brows knit together. "How?"

"A little birdie told me."

Joel decided; his conversation with Gwen Reynolds and her subtle hints connecting Louise Hampton and Russian nukes were really no one else's business. Besides, she had not spelled out the answer, just a good allusion to the question. In a tight debate, that had made a major difference.

"Well, anyway, even with that jewel, that damned Cox came up with the fainting spell, or stomach flu...or whatever he called it..." said Farringdon.

"Has anyone heard how she is?" asked Orr.

"As if she really was sick," Ronnie Taylor added. "Of course, we have used the stomach flu card, too, if you recall."

"All right, guys, it is what it is." Joel took a deep breath. "The clock's ticking. We were counting on this debate to refill our finance coffers, and now it may not happen."

"Got to love ole Russ, though. No wonder that guy can sell cars. The TV crews were all over him." Farringdon grinned and shook his head. "I couldn't have scripted it better myself."

Ronnie said, "That little chant ditty has been running 'round in my head. Catchy...Orr, Orr. He's our man. He can do it with the Nathan Clan."

"It was a break, for sure," Farringdon said. "Nathan's little party will beat the debate itself for ratings on any of the news feeds."

Joel nodded. "We'll take whatever we can get. Momentum is momentum."

"Ronnie, where are we with the polls?" Farringdon asked.

"Up until the debate, we had closed it to single digits—something like seven points—but that doesn't include the post-debate polls."

Don frowned. "We should have closed it to even with the debate, then she faints and the press is all *pity, pity poor Eleana*."

"If I had known it would be such a positive thing, I would have keeled over as soon as I stepped behind the podium," Joel said. "Maybe we'll catch a break on the reviews of Louise Hampton and the others. Beyond that, I don't know how we shake loose any contributions to place ads down the home stretch."

"I may have met my match on this one." Farringdon raked his hands through his hair.

"Any aces up your sleeve, Don?" Ronnie Taylor chided. "We could use a little hocus-pocus about now."

Ignoring the remark, Farringdon said, "Ronnie, you live and breathe public records. What can we get on her? Finances, traffic citations, neighbors, anything?"

During every student election in his FAU college days, Ronnie Taylor had made it a point to research any and everything he could on his candidate's opponent. He would check attendance at all meetings, financial contributions, and talk in detail to friends and foes of the opponent. His opponents would typically not take the time or energy to dig into the details. Side-kick Don Farringdon gave Ronnie's research the credit for an upset campaign victory against an opponent named Jauber. "Jauber" became the code word for Ronnie Taylor to start digging and not stop until he had something that would stick.

Now, the public records laws would back him up, if he could find the right ones. Florida was renowned for its aggressive "government in the sunshine" laws. Under public records law, all information was available to the public but not always easy to obtain. Some agencies thwarted public inquiries by charging to provide the information. It was not uncommon for some regulators to flat-out deny access. Ronnie knew that, but he also knew the Florida Statute, Chapter 120, known as the "Administrative Procedures Act", which could overcome the denial. It just took time and tenacity. If the subject was numbers and data, Ronnie Taylor had plenty of both.

"I've checked." Ronnie held up his fingers, ticking points off one by one. "Eleana's votes in the Senate, her attendance both on the floor and in committees, her campaign contributions—who gave what, and who did not—endorsements, tastes, likes, dislikes. I even interviewed old neighbors from their days in the Kendall and Cutler Ridge areas. Eleana Silver lives for Vizcaya, and now the Senate. That is her life. Other than spending the equivalent of some third-world country's yearly budget on clothes and shoes, she's clean."

Don nodded. "Remember the counsel of the late former Governor Lawton Chiles, 'When you are checking someone out, start in the Dempsey dumpster'."

"Speaking of public records, guys. Don't forget to vote absentee. No telling where we'll be on Election Day. It all comes down to the vote."

"What you said might be more important than breathing, boss." Don nodded and shot a loaded look at Ronnie Taylor.

Back during college days, the numbers guy often became so buried in his calculations that the actual election day whizzed past him. Farringdon constantly reminded Taylor of the importance of voting, especially in presidential elections. Now, Don's nagging was a running joke between the two men.

Farringdon's tone dripped with patriotism. "After all, that is what our men and women fought and died for—to protect our rights. The Bill of Rights specifically provides for the right for our citizens to vote. There is no higher calling. If someone does not take the time to vote, what would they take the time for? It's fundamental. It's sacrosanct."

Ronnie rolled his eyes. "There he goes."

Ronnie Taylor hovered over his laptop in his customary round-shouldered posture.

Don Farringdon stood at the inner office's threshold. "C'mon, Ron. Take a break. You're starting to look like the Hunchback of Notre Dame."

The numbers guy glanced up. "Can't. Time is running out on us."

"And if you miss one forum post, it will make a difference?"

Ronnie Taylor talked aloud—as much for his own benefit as for Don Farringdon's. "During every campaign since the days we were at FAU, I have made this checklist to review my voting research. I always start with attendance records of the politician, then go to floor votes, followed by the committee and subcommittee votes. I've covered it all."

"You've already said all of that, Ron. I, above anyone, know you can *Jauber* with the best of them."

Taylor continued to talk, oblivious to Farringdon's statement. He pushed his glasses back onto the bridge of his nose. "Under public records law, all of the information is available. Sometimes, I hit a wall—resistance from the holder of the records. Reason—they're lazy. It takes time to pull the information from the archives: sometimes hard copies, sometimes on microfiche, and sometimes on CD's. There's a fee, authorized by law, but the cost generally doesn't prevent adequate data gathering on opponents in campaigns."

Don Farringdon felt his eyes glaze over. No use trying to stop Ronnie Taylor when he was on a roll. He'd pout like a wounded teenager.

"I look behind the actual votes for exceptions like pairing of votes," Ronnie continued. "If a member knew they were going to vote *no*, they could pair their vote with someone voting *yes* if both voters had the objective of mitigating each other's votes."

Ronnie stood and began a long, slow lap of the small office. He gestured as he talked.

"Even if a member were to miss a vote, they could submit their vote to be entered onto the public record. But most importantly, the vote would not affect the actual outcome."

"Fascinating," Don offered.

Don had watched his nerdy friend perform the same rabbit-from-the-hat magic numerous times. Ronnie's extraordinary talent, the ability to predict the outcome of an election based upon his experience with given variables: name recognition, endorsements, grass-roots support, and even the weather. Ronnie Taylor didn't miss on his numbers very often.

"Please, do go on." Don's tone held an edge of humor. He pulled out a chair and mirrored rapt attention as Ronnie Taylor continued his little class in Numbers 101.

"After the big debate, I reviewed my checklist for Senator Eleana Silver. Really—nothing to research because she has never held office."

Ronnie stopped pacing long enough to ask, "How in the world can this lady—albeit a very nice lady—possibly think she can serve in the United States Senate? She couldn't even answer a very elementary question on a nuclear ban treaty with the Russians without checking with her staff." He frowned. "Bet Ronald Reagan would never do that."

"Probably not."

Ronnie Taylor's mouth hung open. "Oh, my God!"

"What?"

Ronnie rushed to the desk and jabbed keys on the laptop. "It just hit me like a ton of bricks. Good ole Ronnie Reagan. The hero of the right."

Don Farringdon stared at his friend. Sometimes, conversations with Ronnie took on a surreal quality, as if he had walked into the middle of a movie, didn't know the characters or plot line, and was expected to follow along with the rest of the audience as if he had been in his seat since the opening previews.

"Okay. I give. You lost me."

Ronnie Taylor unplugged the laptop and stuffed it into a padded case. "Republicans and conservatives voted in overwhelming numbers everywhere when Reagan unseated former President Jimmy Carter in the 1980 presidential election. Don't you remember the landslide votes cast by the Cubans in Miami in that election? You know, she was born in Cuba, and was naturalized at eighteen. That may have been one of the first times Eleana voted in a national presidential election."

"I know there is a point in here, somewhere…"

The numbers guy continued the running commentary, unmindful of Don's confusion.

"Should I even bother to check that vote? A Cuban would never fail to vote for President Reagan, if given the chance. Especially one married to a United States senator." He chuckled. "Wouldn't that be a hoot? A Hispanic conservative Republican from a political family who doesn't even bother to vote...for Ronald Reagan at that."

Don made the quantum leap. "I gather you are going to check?"

"I pass the Courthouse on the way home. It may be a huge waste of time…but what else do I have to do?"

Don grinned. "Shower, for one thing. You are getting a bit rank."

Ronnie gathered the laptop case and a second bag stuffed with papers. "You don't smell like a rose, yourself," he threw over his shoulder on the way past.

Joel Orr walked into the office as Don stood to leave.

"What's Ronnie's hurry? He nearly knocked me down when I met him coming through the front door."

Don Farringdon shrugged. "I'm not really sure. He's bird-dogging something. I've seen him like this before. He gets this weird gleam in his eyes like a tired pack horse that has caught scent of the barn." Don yawned and stretched. "Doesn't sound like such a bad idea. I'm so tired; I can barely remember my name. You need me for anything?"

Joel shook his head. "Go. I won't be far behind you."

"If I can keep it between the ditches long enough to make it home, there's a recliner with my name on it."

Lake Worth, Florida

"No questions. Zero. That is a must," said Mark Cox to Mike Belan.

The men tailed behind a black Lincoln Navigator— Eleana and four of her Vizcaya friends—on the way from Clearwater to a campaign appearance in Lake Worth, just south of West Palm Beach.

"Actually, one exception. I spoke with a reporter from the paper in West Palm. He owes me a favor. He'll ask her about her comment on Russia."

Mike Belan glanced away from the road for a moment. "Think that's wise? Why give her an opportunity to foul that one up again?"

"She knows exactly what to say. It's the only way, really, to ease past the fall-out." The public relations guru parroted in a high-pitched female voice, "I was quite ill with some sort of stomach flu. Actually, my people suggested we cancel the debate. I wouldn't hear of it. Too many people had gone out of their way for me. Toward the end, I felt very light-headed and nauseated. I was afraid I might just get sick right there in front of everyone. So, when Ms. Hampton asked her question, I wanted to give the fastest answer to get me off the stage."

Mike Belan chuckled. "God, you sound just like her. Even the society drawl bit."

Cox continued, "My answer was just too short, you see. What I would've said—had I been completely myself—was that I knew perfectly well, the threat of nuclear arms, and that I hoped for the best with future relations with Russia and other countries with that particular capability. There are many complex issues that require a United States senator's attention, and I depend on my highly-qualified staff to alert me to such matters as they arise."

"You are good, my man." Belan cocked his head toward the rear of the vehicle in front of them. Compared to their rental van, the high-end SUV looked important and impressive. With fuel prices at an all-time high, only the best-off could afford the luxury. "Still amazes me. That clutch of society women—along for the ride, just to see what a campaign is like. Eleana almost makes this thing an extension of her Vizcaya activities, as opposed to a seat in the most exclusive body in the world."

"That's why we can't afford any more Louise Hampton surprises. Other than allowing that one important question—nothing but photo ops from this point forward. Besides, after this stop, she'll be going home to Miami for a couple of weeks. Got that flashy Halloween thing at the Museum. Has to go play dress-up."

Mike Belan nodded. "I just hope she rests up. I certainly don't want her ending up in the hospital again. Once, we can explain. Twice, and it will give our opponents more fuel."

"She seemed pretty distressed about the possibility of miscarriage." Mark sighed. "I still can't believe she's pregnant. Talk about lousy timing. We have to stay focused. We can deal with the other as soon as she's squarely seated in the Senate. For now, let's keep her far enough from the press so she won't be able to hear their voices."

"Kind of like Reagan used to do when he walked from the lawn to the White House?" asked Belan.

Cox laughed. "Yeah, except we don't have the helicopters to drown out the questions."

The gamble was greater than it seemed. Women had become increasingly involved in politics and aggressive campaigns. In recent races, both the Democrats and Republicans had selected women for their parties' vice-presidential nominees, and Hillary Clinton had hit a raw nerve in 2008 in her bid for president. Eleana was intelligent, but her interests just didn't rest with politics. Insulated by the Vizcayans, she never really had to get down in and among the people. She really didn't want to start now and it showed. Mark Cox and Mike Belan knew that almost as well as Eleana.

"K, V and G. Right, Mark?"

Both men knew; the initials stood for *Kids, Veterans, and Grandmothers*. Aim the campaign toward issues closest to the voters' hearts.

No mistakes. No chances. Finish out the race on autopilot.

Miami, Florida

Ronnie Taylor couldn't get the niggling thought purged from his head. The closer he drew to the Courthouse, the more excited he became. It was extremely unlikely that Eleana had not voted. Wasn't it? After all she was the wife of a senator, and she was a Cuban who obviously was extremely proud of being an American. She was a conservative. A true blue American. She must have voted. She couldn't be called for jury duty if she didn't vote.

He talked aloud as he tried not to push the accelerator to the floor.

"Not casting a vote in a critical election could be an issue by itself, but it would have to be framed to focus on how fundamental voting is to Americans. The whole democratic process."

Wait a minute, hadn't he read a rumor that Eleana had never served on a jury? Ronnie was nervous and sweating as he drove into the Courthouse parking lot on Flagler Street. Taylor entered the Miami-Dade County Courthouse. A bored receptionist sat behind the first desk he approached.

"Excuse me. Where might I locate the previous Miami-Dade voting records?"

"Ninth floor, second door on the right." The county employee answered with a quick glance before returning to the paperback in her hands.

Ronnie entered the ninth floor suite. Only a handful of people occupied the office, with no one waiting in line. He was directed to an area with files lined from the floor to the ceiling, encompassing the whole floor. He began to search.

"Silva. Silvable. Ah! Silver." He muttered. "Oh great. Must be thousands of them."

Almost an hour later, he found the correct area where the records reflected all of the Silvers who had voted in the 1980 election, the earth-changing election of Republican Ronald Reagan, arguably the most important conservative president, especially for Cuban Americans. The first names resembled *Eleana,* but they weren't the same...Eleanor, Eileen, Elsie. The letters blurred together. He was tired, and he began to lose the sense of urgency and conviction. The whole thing was a big, fat waste of time.

The listing ended. No Eleana Silver. He flipped the page to the next section, then back just to make sure. Still, no Eleana Silver.

"Unreal."

Ronnie rubbed his eyes and held the record book closer. He double-checked the outside binding. It read: Public Record Voting, Miami-Dade County, November 1980 Presidential General Election.

Ronnie's hands shook. He held a political time bomb in his hands. He continued to check, using the maiden name he located in the Senate Handbook—earlier records, from before Eleana married Brad Silver. No votes. Never. Zippo. Not one.

"This is it! The official, undisputable record. And a candidate for the United States Senate didn't even bother to vote for President, in the country where countless thousands died for her right to vote." He shivered. Eleana had been absent when conservatives needed her most.

Ronnie caught his breath. He checked his watch. Only thirty minutes until closing time.

He dashed to the file clerk, asked to make copies of the records, and had the clerk notarize all of them. He couldn't recall the nominal fee. He threw everything he had in his pocket on the clerk's desk—including a ball of lint and two breath mints—and ran out the door.

When Ronnie reached Don Farringdon's house, he rang the doorbell five times in succession.

"What the hell?" Don opened the door, stood aside, and allowed his friend to breeze past.

"I found it! I found it!" Ronnie Taylor spread his arms wide and fell backwards onto the couch.

"You found what? Grace? Religion? A new lease on life?" Don stared down at Ronnie Taylor. "One thing you didn't find…a bar of soap."

Taylor smirked. "I haven't been home yet. I came straight here from the Courthouse. You are not going to believe!"

"The suspense is killing me. Or, is it that I really should be killing you? Clearly, someone should be killed, since you woke me from a particularly good nap."

Ronnie sat up straight and jabbed a finger in his direction. "Eleana Silver did not take the time to vote for our country's president, and it was Ronald Reagan to boot."

"Get out! You have got to be kidding."

"I'm not. And I have the documentation to prove it. I checked all the way back, from the time before—when she was Eleana Martinez-Estevez. Before Brad. From the beginning, she obviously didn't take the time."

"How could you ever become a senator if you didn't vote? I mean; she was appointed, but now she's actually running." He considered for a moment. "Know what I'm thinking?"

Ronnie Taylor's thin lips morphed into a slow smile. "Same thing I'm thinking. If she didn't cast a vote for a pivotal presidential election, how many more elections did she miss? Or...has she *ever* bothered?"

"This could be the key, my friend. Follow me. If she is running for senate, and the most important thing an elected official does for his or her constituents is vote..."

"And she has shown a historic pattern of not doing so..."

Don stated the obvious. "If she was absent then, what guarantees she will be present now...and in the future?"

"I'll be sitting on the Courthouse steps first thing in the morning," Taylor stated. "I have a hunch, Don. And you know me and my hunches..."

"I do. You find the paper trail, Ron. Get your *Jauber* going, man. You find it, and I have a brilliant way we can use it. No way Eleana and the Silver goon-squad can worm around this."

Farringdon and Taylor—just like the old days at FAU—scheming, schlepping, cutting corners, but finding seams.

Don Farringdon recalled a favorite Dr. Seuss Christmas video from his childhood: *The Grinch Who Stole Christmas*. One scene in particular, where the Grinch first happened upon his brilliant, evil plan. The corners of his green lips had curled into spirals and his spiked topknot had flattened to either side.

He wished he could get his lips to curl. Like the legendary Seuss curmudgeon, Don Farringdon *got a wonderful, awful idea.*

CHAPTER THIRTY-ONE

Homestead, Florida

Sid Dillard glanced over the hand-printed letters for the fifth time. One, a thick manila envelope addressed to Mark Cox. The other, a plain white legal-size envelope to the person who he counted on to watch his back. Where it might have been better if both had been compiled on a word processor and printed out in crisp black Times New Roman, the careful block hand lettering added a certain artsy, mystery-novel flair. Most of the infamous characters in history had forgone typed blackmail letters. The Unabomber hadn't used a computer for his missives. Why should Sid Dillard? He imagined the hours that scores of hand-writing analysts in the FBI would spend poring over his hand-written letter.

The universe kept setting up the timing. Paving his way in rose-strewn splendor.

"Your slip-up at the debate was mail-order perfect, Senator Silver," he said. "You will be glad to pay for my little scrapbook of memento pictures. Sorry, Eleana. Nothing personal. You simply can't afford to have any more bad publicity right now."

Sid carefully attached the stamps—one for the regular envelope, several for the larger packet. Licked and sealed the closures. Who cared about his DNA-laced saliva on the glued flaps? By the time the federal authorities got around to processing them, he would be sipping margaritas in a beach cabana far from their clutches.

He walked to a blue standing mailbox and fed the letters to its metal maws. Fast, before he had a chance to second-guess.

Sid stood in front of the mailbox for a moment, mentally tabbing through the itinerary. Mark Cox would receive the letter in two to three days, tops. He would call the cell phone Sid had purchased—off the street—to arrange the exchange. After the Vizcaya Sundowner Ball—Sid's last chance to secure photos of Eleana and her costumed lover in action—they would meet. The monetary gain from weeks of careful surveillance would be his, and Eleana Silver could reap her Senate seat reward.

No harm. No foul.

Sid turned and walked back to the van.

Washington, D.C.

Mike Belan waited by the tidal basin. Across the Potomac, the Lincoln Memorial teemed with happy, oblivious tourists. He wished he was one of them.

Mark Cox walked up and took a seat on the bench beside him. "Nice day."

"It is."

"We've got a big problem." Cox handed over a 6 X 9 manila envelope. "This arrived on my desk this morning."

Belan slid a small stack of color photographs from the sleeve and flipped through them. "What the hell?"

"Check out the digital date stamp."

Belan glanced down, then back at Cox. "Isn't that the…?"

"Same date Brad Silver's plane went down in South America."

"Son of a bitch." Mike Belan unfolded the hand-printed letter. "Who sent these?"

"Don't know. It's just signed: *a concerned citizen.*"

"Nice round figure he's asking…assuming it's a he."

Cox nodded. He looked out across the tidal basin. Had he not just received a blackmail letter, he might have spent the afternoon lolling on the grass in some park. Right. How long had it been since he had *lolled* anywhere?

"Do we tell Eleana?" Mike asked.

"No. Best not to involve her."

"Think it's some of Orr's people behind this?" Belan asked.

Cox shook his head. "No. I don't. Joel Orr is a lot of things. Blackmailer is not one of them. I don't see him doing something like this…too much at stake. It could backfire and boot him out of the race in record time."

"True." Mike Belan considered. "Maybe Russell Nathan and some of his cronies set this up."

"He's too busy banging teenagers and selling used cars to take this kind of time. Plus, his ex-wife cleaned his clock, from what I heard. No way would he have the cash to hire a P.I."

"Buddy Benton?" Mike offered.

"This reeks too much of amateurish. My guess—just some opportunist slob who lucked up on a gold mine claim." Mark Cox gathered the letter and photos, sealed them in the envelope, and slipped it into his inside coat pocket. "Question remains…what do we do about it? We have to pay this person off. No other choice this late in the game."

Mike Belan's expression darkened. "I'll take care of it."

"Do I ask…?"

Belan shook his head. "You don't need to know, Cox. The fewer people involved, the better. Just give me the cell phone number."

From across the tidal basin, Mike Belan imagined the vague outline of the statue of Abraham Lincoln, a shadow behind the white columns. Good Old Honest Abe.

Belan stuck the slip of paper with Sid Dillard's contact number into his pocket. "It will be handled."

Orr for Senate Headquarters—Miami, Florida

Don Farringdon's cell phone vibrated. "Tell me what I want to hear."

Ronnie Taylor: "Code Jauber! Code Jauber! You sitting down?"

Don grinned. "Jauber me, baby. Jauber me."

Ronnie Taylor: "Not only did she not vote in 1980…Senator Eleana Silver didn't vote in the Presidential elections of 1984, 1988, 2000, and 2004. She only took the time to vote in two elections. She did not vote for President roughly 75% of the time she could have. Don, it wasn't once, it was a clear pattern."

"Even the whisker-close Bush-Gore race in 2000?"

Ronnie Taylor: "Bingo."

"Incredible."

Ronnie continued, "But here's the bomb. Eleana, from these records, could not have voted for Reagan *ever*. But she did vote in both Clinton elections. And, you're not even going to believe this: she missed one of Brad's elections! Talk about AWOL. She wasn't there when the conservatives, or her husband, really needed her. I have notarized copies to back this up in my hot little hand."

"Ronnie, do me a favor and call down to the Fort Myers paper and see if you can find that Louise Hampton lady's schedule through the election night. My guess, she'll be up in Tallahassee for the election night returns, but I would like to know if possible."

Ronnie Taylor: "Got it boss, I'm on it. But why?"

"Something I think might stir up the waters a little. And within our lack of budget."

Farringdon hung up. Especially with only days until the election, this could be a game-changer. Something novel to generate debates and media coverage. They had no money, and there were no more public appearances. It was literally the eerie, overcast calm before a Category Four hurricane.

A few minutes passed. His cell phone vibrated. "Speak to me."

Ronnie Taylor: "Confirmed. She'll be there. Most of the reporters covering the campaign will be, she told me, to capitalize on the national television feeds."

"I have a plan, Ron. But we need to avoid telling Orr. Just in case we run into trouble."

Ronnie Taylor: "We going to need bail money?"

Farringdon laughed. "Hopefully not. What I have planned is a gamble. What do we have to lose? This could be our last hope. Be optimistic and daring, my friend. Have I ever led you astray?"

A pause. Then, Ronnie Taylor's reply: "I could come up with a few examples."

"Hey, you don't have one scar on your permanent record. Besides, what else do you have to do? Get home, pack your duffle, and be ready for a little road trip to Tally-town. We'll beat Joel up there by a few hours, but he'll understand afterwards. I hope."

Ronnie Taylor: "Will do."

"And, Ron?"

Ronnie Taylor: "Yes?"

"Don't wear your Florida Gators shirt and the matching gosh-awful blue and orange camo-print pants. We don't want to draw any unnecessary attention. That outfit will piss off the FSU Seminole fans up there."

Ronnie Taylor: "You can suck the fun out of anything, Farringdon."

Miami, Florida

Eleana Silver looked out across Biscayne Bay. The evening breeze smelled of the ocean, the scent as essential to her well-being as breathing. She took a deep inhalation, then released it slowly.

"This is what I miss the most," she said.

Ramiro wrapped his arms around her from behind. "Then we shall find a place of our own close to Washington. A place where you may fill yourself with the sea."

She turned to face him. Her body warmed—with this man, on deeper levels than she had ever felt with Brad Silver. Eleana closed her eyes. Breathed in the other scent she loved more than the sea—the musk distinctive to her lover, the father of her child.

"It is too far from home. Here..." She turned to look out across the bay again. "Here, I know if I could just look hard enough, I would see Cuba. I can sense it out there. In Washington, all I sense is...the craving—men's cravings—for power. I try. I really try. There is so much to learn. I don't know if I can..."

Ramiro turned her face to his. "You remember, *mi amor*. As a senator, you hold that same power. The things you can do for Cuba...for your family." He kissed her lightly. "It will make the sacrifice worth it."

Eleana turned away. Faced the direction where she could sense Cuba.

"Will it, Ramiro?"

Jose Marti Park—Miami, Florida

A dark late-model sedan pulled into a deserted parking lot of Jose Marti Park and idled for a moment. The driver killed the headlights. Other than the gentle swoosh of the Miami River meeting the banks, the park was quiet. A few minutes passed before a motorcycle approached—a Harley—and parked in the shadows. The rider walked to the car, opened the passenger-side door, and got in.

"Were you followed?" The car's driver asked.

"No."

"Good."

Mike Belan turned to face the other man. "We have a problem."

The Latino did not answer.

"You really screwed the pooch this time."

"*¿Perdóneme?*"

"Don't pull that *no hablo Inglés* shit with me. You speak better English than half this state."

The Hispanic man glowered. "I don't know what you are talking about."

"That's better. You live in this *got-damned* country, speak the language!" Belan pitched a manila envelope toward the man. "Take one look at these and you'll know perfectly well what I am talking about."

The man pulled several glossy photos from the sleeve. "Where...?"

"From a half-wit idiot who lives in the back of a van," Mike Belan huffed. "Not even a real P.I., for God's sake."

"Blackmail?"

"Very good. Maybe you didn't use all of your limited gene pool on muscle and looks after all." Mike snatched the envelope. "Now, it's your problem, *amigo.*"

"You know where this person is?" he asked.

"Like I said...he's a moron. Lower than rank amateur. He provided a cell phone number. When we called to set up his little drop-off, all we had to do was triangulate the signal from the phone's internal GPS—idiot didn't know enough to switch it off—and one of my men down here located him in a matter of minutes. He lives in the back of a van and, up until last week, flipped burgers."

Mike Belan shook his head. "Have to give it to him, though. Once he honed in on you and the Ice Princess in your little trysting place, he hung on like a pit bull on a rare roast."

"You want me to find him?"

"Bingo. Only, you won't have to look far. Seems our little budding Sherlock Holmes has gotten himself hired on with one of the caterers for the dress-up ball this weekend. My guess—he wants to add a few last-minute photos to his scrapbook."

"Vizcaya?"

"None other." Mike handed over a digital photograph. "Wormy little guy. You won't have any problem with him."

"I will be occupied..."

Mike snapped, "You make it work out! You owe me this. You and your blundering Castro-lovers killed my best friend."

The lobbyist leaned over. His tone—low and menacing. "When I put you into the Silver household, you were only supposed to observe. You took that a little over the top, don't you think?"

"Eleana. She is a beautiful woman," he said.

Mike Belan nodded. "A bit high-maintenance for my blood."

"I am in a position to help guide her."

"That what you call it in the tropics? I can't help you can't keep it in your pants. We have a mutual interest in the outcome of this election. Different motives... but if you jeopardize this election, you better hop the next boat back to Cuba," Mike Belan said. "There won't be a safe place for you in this country."

Ramiro opened the door to leave. Mike Belan grabbed his arm.

"By the time the last glass of champagne is served at the Vizcaya Halloween party, I expect Sid Dillard to be one of the ghosts."

CHAPTER THIRTY-TWO

Vizcaya Museum on Biscayne Bay—Miami, Florida

Sid Dillard had spent most of his life feeling invisible: Ugly baby. Not a cute child. Stringy-haired adolescent. Less than attractive adult. The best thing about not standing out and never achieving anything: no one gave him a second glance.

This is how serial killers do it, he thought.

He wove through the costumed revelers.

Blend in. Look like a normal Joe. Work a menial, minimum-wage, service job.

He could be Jack the Ripper and no one would be able to pick him from a police lineup.

Sid offered a silver tray of canapés to three women dressed as two-bit hookers. They brushed him aside as easily as someone would an annoying housefly.

Silly me, he thought. These women never actually eat.

Too bad. An array of catered food stretched out under the Halloween-themed canopy.

His gaze roamed across the crowd. People at parties fascinated him. For the first few minutes, they acted as shy as virgin brides. Then, emboldened by the free-flowing liquor, wine, and champagne, and the fact most wore masks, the singles clumped together and the couples drifted apart. All, in search of titillation.

Batman walked by, his middle-aged paunch straining the top of black tights. His partner—resplendent as Wonder Woman—trailed in his wake. Sid watched as she stopped a server and grabbed two flutes of champagne. She slugged one back, returned the empty glass to the tray, and started on the second. Sid smiled. He'd lay even odds there'd be no superhero action in their bedroom tonight.

Around him, the cream of Vizcaya mingled with the commoners, the event being open to the few fortunate public who could afford the price of tickets. Sid's gaze roamed between the canopied food area, the linen-decked tables, and the entrance to the decorated gardens. He congratulated himself on the stroke of genius that allowed him entrance.

Sid patted the slim-line digital camera in his uniform pocket, the result of another trip to the pawn shop. The camera was a trade-off—not as many settings or as precise as the larger digital, but perfect for the occasion. With all the cameras flashing shots of drunken partiers, who would notice one or two more?

Sid stopped dead. Even behind the costumed garb, Eleana Silver stood out. The most beautiful and stately woman in the crowd. Eleana—the rogue sea-captain's woman. Sid searched for her lover. Ramiro—masked, a swarthy swash-buckling pirate—stood behind her.

The hair on Sid's neck prickled when the dark eyes of the pirate rested on him. Sid shivered involuntarily.

God, he'd be glad when this whole affair was behind him. Everything and everyone made him paranoid.

Orr for Senate Headquarters—Miami, Florida

A bowl of cheap candy sat on the front desk, just in case some trick-or-treaters happened by. Instead, half the volunteers had dug into it. Everyone seemed a little edgy, a sugar high combined with growing anticipation of the next few days. One of the volunteers had added a few seasonal decorations to the office. Fake spider webs laced the doorway to the private office. A carved pumpkin scowled from atop the copier. An oversized cut-out of Eleana Silver stood in a corner, resplendent in a witch's hat and cape. Her perfect smile had been altered to include two blacked-out front teeth.

"What do you mean no? That's bullshit!" Don Farringdon bellowed to the lobbyist for the National Cable Television Association. He gripped one of the campaign's prepaid cell phones so firmly, his knuckles turned white.

The annoyed man on the other end replied, "Like I said, we have not really had something like this come up, and...well, the FCC would probably yank our licenses if we did something like that."

"Look," Don said, trying to control the pitch of his voice. "I realize The Federal Communications Commission regulates content on the cable stations. All I want is approval for Joel Orr to make a couple of Public Service Announcements for charity. Specifically, on behalf of the American Cancer Society and the United Way, two of the outstanding charities in the country."

The PSA's had been produced by campaign supporters at no cost—the perfect price tag for the underdog candidate with dry coffers.

Don continued, "Senator Orr appears in the PSA's as an expression of support for the charities, with no mention of his campaign. He's demonstrated his life-long commitment to both over the years. You and I know; there have been instances of candidates paying for advertising for their businesses, while campaigning, and the FCC opposed that activity."

"Yes, I..."

Don interrupted. "This is different. He is helping the two greatest charities anywhere, and he has been involved with them all his life."

If he could pull this off, it was a stroke of genius. Given the current balance in the dwindling account, the Orr Campaign could not pay to produce and air commercials. Farringdon pulled out every stop.

"This is a hassle we don't need," said the lobbyist. "If you go forward with the PSA's, the FCC would be forced to go into court to block the ads."

Don smiled. Perfect. How totally un-American would that seem—to block ads for the American Cancer Society and the United Way in an election year?

Don tried his most convincing tone. "Now look, we have already cut the PSA's. I promise you; there is not a mention of the campaign anywhere. And surely you can agree, there has never been a greater need."

The lobbyist took a deep breath and exhaled. "All right. I'll take it to the top...but the same rules will apply to any other folks, as well. If your opposition does the same, we will allow it, too."

Farringdon said, "Of course. We wouldn't have it any other way."

No problem there, Don thought. Cox had already bought all of his air time through the election and could not even fit in PSA's if he wanted to.

Plus, Don Farringdon had yet another trick up his sleeve. Florida election laws provided that with five days to go in an election, new charges in a campaign could not be filed since there would not be enough time to answer them properly.

Farringdon added, "By the way, we're making plans to run the PSA's on the 1st and 2nd of November."

"Whatever," said the lobbyist.

"I thank you for your help, sir. Have yourself a nice Halloween."

Don snapped the cell phone closed. He felt as if he had just smuggled a truck load of illegal moonshine past a revenuer.

A series of public service advertisements for Joel Orr on behalf of the American Cancer Society and the United Way. At no cost to the campaign. In the final five days of the campaign without an opportunity for Eleana Silver's minions to respond.

Don Farringdon clapped his buddy on the shoulder. "Ronnie, is this a great country, or what?"

Vizcaya Museum on Biscayne Bay—Miami, Florida

Dorothy Claxton—dressed as Glinda the Good Witch from *The Wizard of Oz*—grasped Eleana Silver's hands and leaned over to deliver air-kisses to each of the younger woman's cheeks.

"My dear. Don't you look marvelous in your pirate costume? And this fits you." Dorothy leaned back to take in the outfit. "With your long tanned legs and that wonderful black hair. You look as if you stepped off a movie set."

Eleana beamed. "It does make me feel daring. After being with that stuffy group in Washington…"

"I don't know, dear. If you showed up in Congress in this outfit, you would be the personification of what most of them really are."

The women laughed.

"Where did you have your costume made?" Eleana asked.

Dorothy patted the sparkly pink gown. "A designer in Ft. Lauderdale. I told her to rent the movie and make me look exactly like Glinda." She waved the glittered wand. "The original Good Witch is a few years my junior. Perhaps with my wrinkles, I should have opted for the Wicked Witch of the West."

"You don't have the personality for that, Dottie."

Dorothy glanced around. "Now, where did your handsome pirate get off to?"

Eleana leaned over and whispered. "I thought it best to keep a low profile tonight. Just in case any of the press took notice. He's waiting for me in the gardens."

"Ah…" The matron smiled. "You must take a stroll, then. You'll be amazed at how the decorating staff has transformed the area. Positively spooky. Oh, and Eleana? Your special non-alcoholic champagne is chilled and waiting." She motioned toward one of the three refreshment tables. "Just ask…the one on the far end."

Eleana hugged her friend. "You are always looking out for me."

"I always shall, my dear. Now, go to your handsome consort before the ghouls get him."

When Sid Dillard noticed the caped pirate abscond, then Eleana, he left the serving tray on a side table and melted into the shadows in her wake. The Gardens had been transformed into the resemblance of a long-neglected graveyard. Eerie green and purple lighting illuminated fake headstones and statuary. Hidden fans poured dry-ice fog through the shrubs. Sid took a deep breath to steady his nerves and took the digital camera from his pocket.

From his vantage point behind a clump of low palmettos, Sid took careful aim on the costumed couple: a pirate and his brigand queen in a passionate embrace.

The last thing Sid Dillard felt was a hand clamped across his nose and mouth. A pungent scent. Then, darkness.

CHAPTER THIRTY-THREE

Tallahassee, Florida

The day before election day, Louise Hampton drove west on Apalachee Parkway in front of the Old Capitol, heading to the Florida Press Center on College Avenue. When she had business in the capital city, she always stayed at the Marriott Courtyard on the Parkway: clean, affordable, and near the Press Center.

"There it is—the Prick of Florida," she said.

The first time she had seen the new high-rise Capitol building in person several years back, Louise had failed to notice the obvious phallic nature. The ramrod-straight building stood twenty-two stories, centered behind the Old Capitol, with two low domes located on either side.

A college friend from Michigan who had ridden up with her for a conference stated the obvious, "Your capitol building looks like…well…a prick."

From that point forward, Louise Hampton grinned every time she saw the tall spire at the crest of Apalachee Parkway.

It was about 5:15 a.m.—still dark—and Louise knew she was in for a long day. She noticed a crowd of about a dozen people in front of the steps of the Old Capitol. She checked her watch.

"What in the world are they doing out so early?" she wondered aloud.

Protestors and campaign workers would often line the section of Monroe Street, but not before the sun came up. In the shadows of the streetlights, she couldn't make out what they were doing. They held no signs, but there appeared to be a platform and something on it.

Louise pulled over in front of the adjacent Leon County Courthouse Building and parked in the loading zone. The sign read: No parking. Violators will be towed.

"This is the election season, guys, give it a rest."

She walked briskly across Monroe to the sidewalk in front of the Old Capitol. As she approached the gathering, she noticed a platform with a large oak chair in the middle. The American and Florida flags were posted appropriately behind the chair. A large sign on the left read, "THE UNITED STATES BILL OF RIGHTS". Below it, the rights were listed in numerical order. "THE RIGHT TO VOTE" stood out, printed in large red letters. Red, white, and blue ribbons surrounding the platform added a feeling of patriotic solemnity.

She glanced around. Even in the illumination from one streetlight, the sign was dramatic. No way could anyone miss the display from the road. Louise felt a tingle.

On the other side, a similar-sized sign stood. It read:

PUBLIC RECORDS OF FLORIDA

Below the title, the dates in sequence read:

2004 Presidential Election: Senator Eleana Silver did not vote.

2000 Presidential Election: Senator Eleana Silver did not vote.

1988 Presidential Election: Senator Eleana Silver did not vote.

1984 Presidential Election: Senator Eleana Silver did not vote.

1980 Presidential Election: Senator Eleana Silver did not vote.

At the bottom of the sign in large letters:

SENATOR SILVER DID NOT VOTE FOR PRESIDENT ALMOST 75% OF THE TIME.

The simple vacant oak chair had a sign in front of it which read:

THE EMPTY CHAIR AWARD: ELEANA SILVER

Louise gasped. What did it mean? Where did it come from?

She walked up to one of the people staring at the display and asked, "What is this? Do you know what's going on?"

"No, Ma'am," a young man dressed in FSU colors said. "We just came by to get set up with our campaign signs and saw it. We're waving at commuters this morning...during the rush hour traffic, you know... It is pretty interesting isn't it? Kind of makes you wonder. If she didn't take the time to vote for President, what's she going to be like in the Senate?"

"I can see why she got the empty chair award," another said.

"Can they do this?" asked Louise, motioning to the display.

The young man in the FSU T-shirt answered, "I know whoever put it there had a permit, because the Capitol police require all of us with signs and displays to have one. I guess you would say that this is all about the ultimate freedom of speech—demonstrating the right to vote."

In her years of covering election shenanigans, Louise Hampton had not seen such a simple, yet effective, display.

"My God, it's brilliant." She glanced around."And there is no one here to explain it. You just have to let your mind run."

The student agreed. "Wonder what Senator Silver has to say about it?"

"I don't know, but I am sure the hell going to find out."

Louise stepped away a few feet, grabbed her phone, and called the Associated Press desk.

"Get over to the front steps of the Old Capitol right away. We have got to get this on the early morning news."

Across the lawn, Don Farringdon and Ronnie Taylor lurked in the shadows.

"I knew she'd see it," Don said. "There's no way she could get to the Press Center without passing in front of the Old Capitol. I had no idea she'd be up before the crack of dawn, but okay."

"I kind of feel like we just launched the missiles under Defcon 1, and the enemy doesn't even know it," said Taylor.

"Now let's tell Joel and hope he doesn't make us take it down."

Don Farringdon dialed Orr's cell phone number. Still in Miami at Campaign Headquarters, the group prepared to head out for a twelve-hour drive from one end of the state to the other. Joel answered on the second ring.

"My man. What's up?"

Don gave a quick rundown of the early morning's events. "So...that's what we did. You want us to rip it down?"

Don Farringdon heard Joel Orr's deep laugh.

"Take it down? Hell no. It's brilliant! How do you get more American than reporting on voting? Especially dead-on since this is the eve of Election Day. I wish I would've thought of it."

"Glad you're okay with it, Joel. Maybe this along with the PSA ads, will give us a little edge."

"At this late point," Joel said. "I'll take any kind of edge."

Don glanced at the horizon. "The sun is just coming up. Ronnie and I are going to cruise around and create a little more buzz."

"You guys are the best. I'll keep in touch. We're lining up the wagons now. If I can get this group all headed north, we should be in Tallahassee by sundown. Nobody wants to miss a single minute of tomorrow. By the way, Karen said she heard the tropical system that had been putting around the Keys might be headed into south and central Florida late today or tomorrow. Check on that, will you?"

"You bet, boss. That could actually work to our favor, especially if our church get-out-the-vote effort works well. It's like a phantom campaign," Farringdon said.

Ronnie Taylor added, "You realize, historically, the Republicans don't turn out to vote when the weather is bad."

Don snapped his cell phone closed. "You've only told me that about a thousand times, Taylor. I hope you're right."

Office of the Governor—Tallahassee, Florida

"What the hell?" Governor Tad Myers asked. "One of the staffers in the Old Capitol just called me. The press is crawling all over the lawn! What the hell is going on?"

Besides top aide Kemp Johnson, two additional staff members stood in the Governor's office on the ground floor of the Florida Capitol. Crack of dawn. Eve of Election Day.

Kemp Johnson—always the courageous one—answered, "Governor, I just saw it myself. It's an empty chair. There's no one in it. There's no one around it. It's roped off...but it's surrounded by camera people."

The Governor took a lap.

"The signs are the part everyone is interested in," Kemp continued. "Seems they claim Eleana Silver failed to vote in the majority of the past presidential elections—75%, to be exact."

Tad Myers stopped, mid-stride. "Well, has anybody checked? Did she actually miss those votes? Three-quarters of them?"

Kemp Johnson stepped back to allow room for the ADHD hamster to complete a lap. He signaled the other two staffers to join him in the safety zone. "Yes, Sir. That's the first thing I did when I heard about it. Their numbers guy

Ronnie Taylor has documentation posted on their website. I'll have someone double-check the public records, but I doubt they'd pull this kind of stunt without the facts to back it up. Too risky."

"If the dates are right, that means she skipped two Reagan elections. And the only times she did vote were when Clinton was on the ballot. Gawd!"

Kemp decided to keep quiet. Best, when the hamster was thinking aloud.

Governor Myers frowned. "What does Eleana have to say?"

Kemp Johnson knew the answer. He cringed.

"Governor, I tried to call Mr. Cox this morning. It went straight to voicemail. It has been my experience, though, that they might not want to wake her up. She can be cranky this early in the morning—from what Mr. Cox has told me in the past. They're still over in Jacksonville. They plan to head over first thing in the morning."

"Cranky? Cranky!" The Governor whipped around and started to circle the office counterclockwise. "I appointed her to this seat! I am betting my whole political career, which I might remind you lemmings, includes the presidency. And she can't be awakened because she might be *cranky*?"

The Governor pitched his morning copy of the *Tallahassee Democrat* at the window. It bounced and fell in scattered clumps at the staff's feet. Kemp wondered how long the other two would stand their ground before they broke and ran.

"Governor, that's not the only unsettling news." Kemp kept his voice even and mild-tempered. "That small tropical disturbance that has been brewing off the Keys. It's not anywhere near storm level, but it has turned and is heading into the south and central part of the state. Should make landfall by morning of Election Day."

Governor Myers narrowed his eyes. "I have told you before, Kemp. Unless the winds are above fifty miles an hour, there is no need to sound the alarm."

Kemp Johnson glanced at the two staffers. Both green. Neither one with the experience to handle the Unhooked ADHD Hamster. "Yes, Governor. I understand that, Sir. I am referring more to the heavy rain it will dump on the state. Normally that would help the incumbent, but in this case she really does not have a core base of support."

"Neither does Joel Orr."

"Governor, he has Don Farringdon. No one gets out the black church vote like Farringdon...and it doesn't matter what the weather is..."

"All right, all that bad news together." Tad Myers spun around and circled clockwise. "We'll have to just ride it out. What about the polls?"

Kemp Johnson caught a hint of the Governor's cologne as he breezed past.

"The current polls show them dead even, Sir. I will keep you abreast of developments when the exit polls come out tomorrow."

Tad Myers stopped and stared at his top aide. "What's your feel for it, Kemp?"

"Close, Sir...very close."

Orr for Senate Headquarters—Miami, Florida

Joel motioned toward the gathering of volunteers. The buzz of conversation quieted.

"We'll be pulling out of here shortly, folks. It's a long drive. As you all know, we've had to use every dang dime for the campaign, so...," Joel shrugged and smiled. "None of us will be catching a quick flight to Tallahassee. Nor will we be holding up at the Hilton."

The room rippled with titters of laughter and exchanged nods.

Joel glanced around the familiar faces. "I wish all of you could come along. We've been through a lot of ups and downs together. We all have our jobs to do on November 4th. All across this great state, people—dedicated people like you—will be using their time and precious gasoline to offer rides to constituents who might not otherwise find a way to the polls. For this—all of the phone calls, the door-to-door visits, hours spent stuffing envelopes, and the support in so many ways I can't count them all—I thank you."

Joel paused while the Orr supporters applauded and cheered. Karen hugged her father.

The Reverend Louis Jones of the Grace Abyssinian Church stepped forward. "We are proud to be here, even at this early hour." He swept his outstretched arms through the air. "I'd like to offer up a prayer for Brother Orr."

Joel stepped beside his daughter and took her hand. The five volunteers who were also making the trip linked hands until the group formed a circle.

"Let us pray." The preacher's deep resonant voice spread over the bowed heads. "Dear Heavenly Father. We ask for your protection for Brother Orr and the team as they journey forth. The path to truth unfolds from your hands. Lead us all in the way we must go, with uplifted hearts. Keep us all in your careful care. All of your children, regardless of race, creed, or the manner they choose to honor you. Amen."

Amens echoed across the room.

Joel looked up into the hopeful eyes of the people who had been his helpmates, day and night, hour upon hour, for the past few months. Emotion welled inside him. In the cramped, low-rent room, Joel had felt a sense of united purpose. In a few days—no matter the election's outcome—the place would stand empty. He took a moment to remember.

The Reverend stepped over and shook Joel's hand, then Karen's and each of the volunteer away-team. The others cheered and clapped.

"Thank you." Joel called out over the hub of voices. "Now. Let's go kick some Silver butt!"

The travelers filed from the campaign headquarters, heading for the crescendo of the Senate race.

The theme chant rose around and behind them.

"Vote Orr! Vote Orr! Vote Orr!"

Destin Beach, Florida

The used cars, trucks, and SUV's from the front lot of We Love Nathan Motors had been shifted to the side and back lots around the low block building. In their place, row upon row of empty chairs: all colors, sizes, and shapes.

Russell Nathan stood with his hands propped on his hips, a wide smile plastered across his face. The morning news—usually a sad waste of his time—had provided inspiration. Who would have thought one empty chair in the lawn in front of the Old Capitol could make such an impact?

If one chair equaled press time, sixty-seven chairs might start a revolution.

Russell panned the video camera across the rows of mismatched chairs. The last frame, he focused on a tricked-out used Hummer with a block-printed banner across its side panels.

ELEANA SILVER'S
EMPTY CHAIR GRAVEYARD—
ONE CHAIR FOR EVERY
COUNTY IN FLORIDA.

One final chair—a toilet—sat alone. Russell paused long enough for the hundreds of potential Internet viewers to read its printed sign:

DON'T LET YOUR VOTE END UP IN THIS SEAT
VOTE for JOEL ORR

"This is going to look great on YouTube," the former Governor said. "Bite me, Senator Silver."

CHAPTER THIRTY-FOUR

Jacksonville, Florida

Mark Cox and Mike Belan opted for lunch at the 4th Down Sports Bar and Grille in Baymeadows, a popular suburb in South Jacksonville.

"Hope our candidate and Lover Boy at least come up for air long enough to eat," Mike Belan commented.

"I had a call from someone in the Governor's office early this morning. Wanted to speak to her. I put them off. She can see them when we get over there tomorrow. The calmer we keep her, the better," Cox said.

Mike Belan pushed aside a tray piled high with spicy-hot chicken wing bones, took a sip of beer, and bellowed a resonant belch.

"Nice," Mark Cox said.

"More room outside than in, my dear mama used to say."

Cox smirked. "You actually had a mother? I always thought you were raised by a kindly clan of apes." He signaled the server for another scotch. "Those two. God, what are we going to do with them back in Washington? We still have to handle the pregnancy issue, too. At least Ramiro keeps her happy and on track. I told him to order room service later, make sure she doesn't go all wonky on us tomorrow in Tallahassee."

Mike nodded. "Good plan, staying over here until election morning. It's only a couple-hour drive, plus the press doesn't have a clue where we are."

"Keeping them at bay until she's declared a winner is in all of our best interests. Well Mike, that's about all we can do."

"You're right, pal. Just like with Brad—God rest his soul—Eleana has no idea what all we did on her behalf, but we sure didn't leave anything on the field," responded Mike Belan.

Cox lowered his voice, "That other little issue...?"

Mike offered a smile, one that made the hairs on Mark Cox's neck bristle.

"Been taken care of."

Belan noticed Cox glancing periodically at the closest of the fifty-one television monitors in the packed grille. It was just past noon and almost all the stations were carrying the national sports feed from ESPN. A couple of the flat-screens were tuned to local/state news.

"Did the Republican National Committee get on the vote set for tomorrow?" Belan asked.

Cox nodded. "I talked to the Washington RNC people just before we got here, and Florida is set. We have pre-recorded voice mails that will go into our targeted lists, especially the young Republicans and the Women's Clubs."

"Great. In Brad's races, that made a big difference. I just hope they thought to use an Anglo voice so there would be no confusion."

Cox didn't hear Belan. He stared at one of the few sets airing the news.

"What? Hey turn that up!" Cox called to one of the bartenders.

The program announcer said, "Ladies and gentlemen, Good Evening. I am Marty Standers. We bring you a breaking story from Tallahassee. Let's cut to our reporter on the scene in front of the Old Capitol...go ahead Angie."

"This is Angie Macleod and I am standing in front of the Old Capitol in Tallahassee. You are probably wondering what that is behind me on the platform. It's a chair. As you can see—an empty chair. There is no one here, but the boards next to the chair say it all." The reporter motioned to the block-printed signs. "Apparently, someone in support of the Orr Campaign has alleged that Senator Eleana Silver did not vote in the last presidential election...excuse me, it appears they are saying she did not vote 75% of the time!"

Belan's mouth hung open. "What?"

The reporter continued, "That's right, Marty. If this information is correct, on the eve of her own election, this display may be suggesting that the senator didn't vote in over half of the presidential elections. Marty, it has to raise a patriotism question, plus well, even whether she is going to take the time to vote on the critical issues."

"Angie, is there no one there to explain this? Is it just those signs and the empty chair?" asked the news anchor.

"Yes, Marty. It is a clear suggestion that the senator has proven that she has not voted in the past, and it can't help but raise the question of when and what she will vote for in the future. We have tried to reach the senator and her staff for an explanation, but we are told they are traveling to Tallahassee for tomorrow's election."

"Angie, what about the sign under the chair?"

"The Empty Chair Award," the reporter read, "Eleana Silver."

"You have *got* to be kidding," Mike Belan said. He looked to Mark Cox. "This can't be...is it true?"

Mark Cox's face paled. "I don't know. It never occurred to me to ask. I just assumed all people involved in politics vote."

"Eleana hasn't been involved in politics. She has been intrigued with it," Belan said. "Bit of a difference."

The two men turned their attention back to the monitor.

"Well Angie, continue trying to reach the senator and her campaign," the announcer said. "In the meantime, we have no alternative but to believe that her opponent has provided solid proof. Hardly a testimony, when that's exactly what she is asking her constituents to give her—the right to vote on their behalf."

Mike Belan winced. "Ouch."

Cox downed his scotch in one gulp. "We better hope that's the only station to pick this story up. I don't know how we can respond to it. If they got the documentation from the public record, we have no excuse. How can we ask the public to vote for us, when there is the implied threat that we won't be there to vote for them? We can kiss the Hispanic block goodbye. There is nothing as important to a Cuban American as the flag...and the right to vote."

"Typical Farringdon," Belan said. "He kept us occupied with the gaffe on nukes and Russia, and he nailed us on something like this. Much more damaging in the public's eyes. Plus, we have no way to respond, with the election tomorrow. Got to hand it to him. He's good. Too bad he's not working for our side."

Tallahassee, Florida

Ronnie Taylor stared at the laptop screen. "Don! C'mere! You gotta see this!"

Don Farringdon walked through the threshold of the adjoining room at the Marriott Courtyard. "What's up?"

"Our old nemesis Russell Nathan, that's what." He pointed to the screen. "He posted this video on YouTube. Pretty clever stuff. Then, he put in this plea for people around the state to drag out chairs and make signs, too."

Don watched as Ronnie clicked on frame after frame of empty chairs, all with signs that read: EMPTY CHAIR AWARD. ELEANA SILVER.

Ronnie clicked to one of the political forums. "It's all the buzz. They're popping up all across the state."

"Well, I'll be damned." Don chuckled. "Remind me to send ole Russ a bottle of Crown Royal Reserve."

CHAPTER THIRTY-FIVE

Myers Park—Tallahassee, Florida

Along the jogging trails in Myers Park one block off Apalachee Parkway, the early morning mists curled around Live Oaks draped with Spanish moss. Joel Orr had always liked the northern part of his state, especially the terrain around the capital city. The city of Tallahassee—situated midway between Jacksonville on the east and Pensacola on the west—sprawled across seven hills, much different from the flatlands in the lower part of Florida. In the nature-themed city park, the earthen trails wove up and down small hillocks between tall stands of hickory, sweetgum, oak, and pine. Palmetto bushes grew in the lower areas around a winding stream.

Joel Orr liked to run when he felt tension, especially since he had abandoned the all too frequent drinks. Plus, he hoped the exercise somehow mitigated his sugar intake.

His daughter Karen fell in beside him and they held a steady, easy pace.

"What do you think, Bug...do you feel lucky?" Joel managed between breaths.

"I feel good, Daddy, but I really think that chair thing is kind of hokey."

Joel sidestepped to avoid a gnarled root across the path. "It may be, but since the Internet, the established media has fallen on hard times. That Rupert Murdoch has changed everything."

"Speak plain English, Daddy. I've learned a lot about this whole political game, but I'm far from an expert."

Joel slowed his pace to allow his breathing to catch up. "Whew. Maybe we should walk a little, Bug. Your old man has a ways to go before he's in decent shape again."

They walked side by side.

"Rupert Murdoch. Global media mogul. A wealthy conservative magnate from Australia. Without all the boring details, let's just say he bought the *New York Post* and went on to change the whole industry. Substantive investigative, unbiased reporting quickly became a thing of the past. He introduced the idea of fast, quick clips. The distorting and twisting of the media was accelerated by the Internet—a sign of our times, really. No one takes the time, or has the time, to dig deeply into issues and people. Instead, news is blasted at us in jarring spurts. Sensationalized. Marginalized. Mostly biased."

Karen nodded. "The video game generation—one with an attention span of a flea."

"Nice analogy." Joel smiled. "That is why something like an empty chair can communicate so effectively. It's simple, direct, and most importantly, correct when the facts are checked out. Give Ronnie and Don the credit on this one."

"How could Eleana Silver have possibly missed those votes? That's so fundamental. Especially with a senator for a husband. And, can you believe, Brad was *on* the ballot for one of those elections? Unreal."

"She's not a bad person, Karen. So many of us take voting for granted...and it really is a strategy if you are involved in politics."

"I'll bet she'll never miss again," Karen said.

A gray fox squirrel eyed the pair from a safe distance. Humans in the park carried no weapons—in theory. The animal inhabitants of the park rarely bothered to hide.

"I remember one election down in the Keys that was decided by one vote," Joel said. "A County Commissioner named Curt Blair beat a well-entrenched incumbent by one stinkin' vote."

"I bet Brad Silver would have remembered that, Dad."

Joel nodded. "Ironically, he's the one who told me about it, Bug."

The Marriott Courtyard—Tallahassee, Florida

"You know, this is fun," said Ronnie Taylor.

"What is?" Don glanced up from the morning paper. Scattered empty bags and crumbles of sugar dotted the crumpled sheets. Joel would be ecstatic when he returned from the park. Ronnie had located a jam-up bakery on Thomasville Road and stocked up on fresh baked goods.

"Well, here we are, with no money left, running against an incumbent senator supported by both the Governor of this state and the President of the United States. And we are whopping them good...with what...a damn empty chair! Partner, you are the best, bar none," said Taylor. "You ought to read the buzz on the forums. People are going nuts."

Don licked the dried sugar from his fingers and took a sip of coffee. "You won't guess who called while you were taking that marathon shower. Brenda Gayle from the Ironclad Alibi. She actually sat an empty chair out by the road and she's hosting a huge Election Day party. She said people are coming in droves."

Ronnie smiled. "Good for her business. I always did like that woman."

"Plus, Jennifer at the Cup O' Joe called. She's named a special double cinnamon bun after Joel. Calling it *Joel's Hot Buns*, or something like that. She put an empty chair in front of her place, too."

Ronnie Taylor laughed.

"It was all contingent on Louise Hampton driving by the front of the Old Capitol on the way to the Press Center," Don said. "Had she not done that, I don't know if any of the other press would have bit on it. They are pretty lazy, even on Election Day."

"Speaking of E-Day, what is word on the weather, Ronnie?"

"Storms from I-4 corridor south. Most of central and south Florida will be socked in until late tomorrow."

Don threw his head back and whooped. "Yahoo! Let it rain, baby, let it rain!"

"As long as the reverends across the state have their part covered, this should shave off four to five points in the end." Ronnie Taylor frowned. "Shit. One of the volunteers just flipped me an email. Seems our friend Mark Cox took out three pages in the statewide section of the *Miami Herald* for today's edition."

"Son of a bitch. I should have known Cox would hoard part of Eleana's war chest until the very end when we couldn't counter...even if we had any money left."

Ronnie shook his head. "Cox will probably duplicate the tactic in *USA Today* and the major Florida dailies, English and Spanish."

Don Farringdon crossed his fingers and rolled his eyes heavenward. "We better hope those R's see the morning ads in the papers."

"Why?"

"They'll see them, look outside at the horrible weather, and think...why go to the trouble of sloshing out to the polls when we have the Democrats beaten already."

Ronnie pointed his finger. "The logic is twisted, but statistics prove..."

"I know. They prove Republicans don't show up in bad weather." Don smirked. "Do you have an *off* button somewhere?"

Ronnie Taylor pushed his glasses back on his nose. "You'd miss me if I wasn't here."

"Probably. Anyway, we need to have the folks down at campaign headquarters check in with the churches. Make sure they have plenty of chicken boxes. Get 'em anything they need."

"A chauffeured ride to the polls and a bite to eat along the way. It has been magic for the Democrats time after time."

"It is not illegal, or really improper," Don said. "Anyone can do it, as long as it's reported as a legitimate campaign expenditure. I can't help it if the Republicans don't bother with the tactic. They wouldn't waste their time—what with plenty of cash to buy advertising to mitigate black turnout."

Ronnie Taylor shook his head. "Cox uses the last of his funds to buy full-page ads, and we use ours on fried chicken."

"It will make a good story to tell your grandkids one day, my man."

The Governor's Plaza—Tallahassee, Florida

The Governor's Plaza, a distinctive boutique hotel in downtown Tallahassee, claimed the city's most well-appointed and well-positioned address in the shadow of the new Capitol. Its historic style was reminiscent of the days of the Old Capitol Building with a graceful, southern décor, gleaming antiques, and a friendly, highly competent staff. The Plaza provided the perfect vantage for the crest of the Silver campaign, within easy walking distance of FSU, the Supreme Court, the Challenger Learning Center, and Leon County Civic Center.

Eleana, Ramiro, Cox, Belan, and the core campaign staff holed up in the Spessard Holland Suite—the most requested accommodation, named after Florida's 28th Governor. A spacious two-room suite, the Holland offered separate living and sleeping spaces and a large bath featuring a whirlpool tub. The living room sofa opened to a sleeper bed, though no one but Eleana and Ramiro planned to share the suite past midnight. The rest of the staff would overnight in three smaller rooms.

The two flat-screen televisions were on, one tuned to CNN and the other to the Weather Channel. The color-the-weather radar view showed over two-thirds of the state beneath bright green and red storm bands.

Mike Belan stood court over his favorite part of the luxurious suite: the wet bar.

"Fix you up, Cox? Might as well pre-medicate for the big victory bash tonight."

Mark Cox shook his head and listened intently to the conference call between the campaign teams in Jacksonville, Orlando, and Ft. Lauderdale. "What are you getting on the exit polls, guys?"

Larry, the staffer from Jacksonville, reported, "Looks great, boss. I don't think we've gotten more than a dozen that have said they pulled the lever for Orr."

He was lying. Cox could hear the doubt in his voice. "C'mon, Larry. What have you really got?"

Cox read all he needed to know into the silence at the other end.

No doubt, the head of Jacksonville operations was concerned about his job and knew that most voters wouldn't tell the truth when they exited the polls. The reality was: neither they nor the pollsters had any real idea. Cox sought something non-existent, a cushy comfort zone.

"No, really Mark, it feels good," the senior staffer assured.

Eleana sat on the edge of the king-size bed in the adjoining room, flipping through the latest issue of *Washington Elite*, a glossy magazine with a feature and picture layout of the Hispanic senator from Florida.

"Ramiro, do you think these pictures make me look fat?"

Ramiro stood at the bedroom's threshold, listening to the political jargon in one room and his lover in the other. "Not at all, *mi amor*."

Mike Belan rolled his eyes and took a long swill of scotch.

Mark Cox heard nothing but the voices on the conference call.

"Carmen, what have you got from the I-4 corridor?" Cox asked his Orlando staffer.

"Mark, this storm has gotten worse," she said. "I just hope our ads are strong enough to get these R's to the polls."

Cox's lips drew into a thin line. "Philip, what have you got in South Florida?"

"It's pouring down here in Lauderdale. You can barely see two feet in front of you. Who ordered the damned hurricane?"

Normally, inclement weather worked to the incumbent's favor, a fact both Cox and Belan knew. They had, at a minimum, a base that would vote no matter what. In this case, since Eleana was appointed and had never been elected, she lacked a core constituency.

"We better hope they get off their butts," Mark Cox stated. "I know Don Farringdon. His get-out-the-vote campaigns among the black churches are legend. Nothing deters them from getting to the polls. They give them rides and usually feed them, to boot. Shit, first the damn empty chair fiasco, now a monsoon in half of the state."

Eleana Silver stood next to Ramiro and yawned. "When do we go to the party? I'm getting hungry."

Mike Belan picked up the phone and punched the number for room service. "I'll order a couple of appetizer platters."

"Got to keep the Princess happy," he mumbled.

CHAPTER THIRTY-SIX

6:00 p.m.—The Silver Campaign—Tallahassee, Florida

In the lower level ballroom of the Leon County Civic Center, The Silver Campaign election night party was well underway. The cavernous room held five hundred. A jovial, well-dressed crowd of over four hundred already plowed through the long tables piled with imported caviar, fresh Gulf of Mexico oysters and shrimp, assorted canapés, and decadent desserts. The open bar bustled.

"You knew *she* would throw a party to end all parties," said one reveler, adorned in red, white, and blue from top to bottom.

"Who cares if we win, just party on," said another.

Situated around the room, twenty-four television screens echoed the first returns coming in from North Florida.

6:00 p.m.—The Orr Campaign—Tallahassee, Florida

Joel, Karen, Farringdon, Taylor, and the core campaign team huddled at Joel's spartan suite in the Marriott Courtyard. All eyes were on the television set, watching the predictions for the election. The polls were slated to close in an hour at 7:00 p.m. EST.

Ronnie Taylor—who had been on the phone with campaign workers all over the state—yelled to the noisy group, "Shit, we are going to need Noah's Ark down there..."

Karen grabbed the remote and switched to the Weather Channel. "Man, Central and South Florida are getting slammed."

Joel turned to his campaign director. "Don, what do you hear from the Reverend?"

Don gave the thumbs-up. "All is fine...plenty of food and vans...just keep 'em coming."

Farringdon stared at the weather radar. The image looked as if an angry kindergartener had cut loose with a red crayon across the lower part of the state. The get-out-the-vote campaign had made the difference before. His antagonists often claimed his people took any person with a valid registration and a pulse. But he had never run it in a storm of this magnitude. It took real conviction to stick it out, and Don was glad that he had paid so much attention to the needs of the African-American churches over the years.

"Only appropriate," Ronnie Taylor commented when they parked at the Fairgrounds a few minutes later. "The Republicans celebrate in the Civic Center with unlimited food and drinks, and here we are in the livestock pavilions with a cash bar."

The Orr Campaign Party congealed at the Leon County Fairgrounds, just south of the Capitol on Monroe Street. The local black churches had come through. The women brought covered dishes—piles of fried chicken, pot roast, greens, peas, sliced tomatoes, cornbread, and deviled eggs. One table displayed homemade desserts. A beverage table held an assortment of sweet tea, water, and lemonade for the supporters not able or willing to purchase cheap beer.

Don Farringdon smiled. "Yeah, but you gotta admit; we got heart, Ronnie."

Joel leered in the direction of the dessert table. "And we got Red Velvet Cake. And looks like chocolate and coconut. And if my eyes aren't deceiving me...some kind of meringue-topped pie. Hope it's lemon. I love lemon."

The disc jockey spun one of Joel's personal favorites, *Johnny Be Good.*

"What the hell does that have to do with an election?" asked one of the campaign workers, a thirty-year member of the AFL-CIO.

One of his fellow supporters handed him a beer. "Who cares, man...just let it hang out."

"How many do you suppose will turn out?" Karen asked.

"Who knows?" Don answered. "All we can do is have a good time. This might be our final hoorah."

Gwen Reynolds wove through the crowd and approached them. She hugged Karen and shook Joel's hand.

"What? You decided to slum with the underdogs tonight?" Joel asked.

Gwen shrugged. "You are not as stuffy as that *other* crowd. Besides, I have always had a taste for..." She glanced to the beer table. "...Pabst Blue Ribbon."

Karen laughed. "Somehow, I find that suspect. But we're glad you're here."

"Oh, I wouldn't miss this night in the capital for anything. I would have been here earlier, but all the flights were booked solid. Plus, we had an hour delay coming out of Miami International."

Four rented television sets blared election predictions from across the nation. No one paid attention until the announcer mentioned Florida. Then, they cheered, no matter what the television personality had to say.

"You gotta love this," Karen said. "Kind of makes you want to hoot and holler."

7:45 p.m.—The Silver Campaign—Tallahassee, Florida

The television announcer's voice could be heard above the rabble. "We are showing Orr taking a surprising lead 58% to 42% over Senator Silver."

Boos echoed through the building.

"Can you bring me some shrimp, please? And two more bottles of Dos Equis?" one of the many campaign workers asked a uniformed server. "I'm going to need 'em tonight."

The band played louder, but the results continued to show Orr's lead inching upward.

7:45 p.m.—The Orr Campaign—Tallahassee, Florida

Joel held Karen's hand as the ABC affiliate reported the first returns from Jacksonville, "58% for Orr, and 42% for Silver...a surprise there, but very unlikely to hold for very long."

Joel said, "It's going to be a long night, Bug."

Karen squeezed her father's hand. "It's okay, Daddy. I'm a big girl. I can stay out way past midnight if I want."

Ronnie sat in an aluminum folding chair, checking the e-mails and blogs. In most cases, they proved more current than the television networks. Though, perhaps not as accurate.

Don Farringdon flipped his cell phone closed. "I'm getting some ugly weather reports from Orlando south."

"If my flight up here was any indication," Gwen added, "the weather has only deteriorated. The turbulence was awful. Once we got past Gainesville, it improved."

"Let me run my numbers. I should have something for us in a few minutes," said Taylor. "Nothing solid will probably come in until around 9:00 p.m. eastern time, unless it turns into a cliff-hanger."

8:07 p.m.—The Silver Campaign—Tallahassee, Florida

In the Spessard Holland suite, Mark Cox asked for everyone's attention.

"Look folks, this is still early. The first returns are from up here in the North. When the South Florida votes start coming in, it will change our way. Let's wait a little longer..."

Ramiro frowned. The scant appetizers had not appeased Eleana. She picked at the fruit and pitched a small spear of broccoli across the room. With luck, the lavish Lobster Thermadore he had just ordered from room service would tide her over.

Mike Belan blinked to clear his vision. The straight scotch helped to smooth the jagged points of his worry. "How late do these things go, Mark? Eleana is getting more peevish by the second."

Cox shot an aggravated look toward Belan "I have to get back on the phones. *You* do the baby-sitting."

8:15 p.m.—the Orr Campaign—Tallahassee, Florida

The noise level at the Fairgrounds elevated. The crowd had swelled to over three hundred supporters. The disc jockey played on—*Your Cheating Heart.*

"I'd even take polka over that," Karen said.

"Can that guy give it a rest?" asked one of the supporters.

Another answered: "It's better than nothing...besides, the VFW is closed on Election Day."

The latest returns showed Orr's lead holding, but barely. A large block of votes from The Villages in Central Florida had just come in, and they were notorious for the Republican base.

One of the television sets went on the blink. A fast-thinking campaign worker got out a portable radio and tuned it to CNN radio.

"Damn, this is like the old days, listening to old Frank Pepper on the radio," Joel overheard one older supporter remark.

"Frank Pepper, statesman Claude Pepper's brother," Joel explained, "was a fixture in Tallahassee radio and television circles during the '60s and '70s."

"Let the good times roll baby!" yelled a middle-aged supporter.

In one corner of the gathering, a small group of young black dancers set up an impromptu dance floor. Rap music filled the air, competing with the country drawl from the disc jockey's tunes.

Joel led the way to the latest entertainment. The Orr campaign foursome and Gwen Reynolds clapped as the agile dancers spun, dipped, and dived for an appreciative crowd.

"No matter how this turns out, Daddy, I will always remember this night...and the past few weeks."

"Not to jinx it, Bug. If I win this thing, will you come with me? I'm sure we can find something more interesting than banking for you up in Washington."

Karen smiled. "No, Daddy. This is your gig. I've decided to go back to college. Get my business and finance degree. I've been stuck in a rut for too long, just waiting...If you can do it, so can I."

"You know I'll help you any way I can," he said.

"I know, Daddy. I know." Karen glanced toward Gwen Reynolds. "That's the woman you should be asking to go with you."

Joel nodded. "Good point. How 'bout it, Gwen? I could use a savvy Chief of Staff."

"I might consider it...if..." She smiled. "I had not already accepted a position."

Karen grabbed her friend's hand. "Where? Where?"

"I start next Monday for the distinguished senior senator from Mississippi, Senator Larson."

Joel nodded and smiled. "It will be good to see a friendly face in Washington." He glanced to the television monitor where the numbers kept rolling in. "First, I have to get there."

10:30 p.m.

Joel Orr fidgeted.

The returns showed him holding a steady, but precarious lead of about two points. Much of Central and South Florida had reported. All of North Florida had been counted. Farringdon's eyes were bleary and bloodshot. Karen leaned her head on her father's shoulder. Gwen sipped warm beer from a plastic cup and winced. Once the food and beer ran out, the crowd had moved on. Only a handful of loyal local campaign workers remained.

Ronnie Taylor looked up from the laptop. "I'm showing our lead will hold, but so much depends on Don's get-out-the-vote campaign. If they all come through, we should make it, but not by much."

All the pre-paid phones were in use. Taylor's personal cell phone rang as soon as he hung up with campaign workers in Sebring. In spite of the storm, things were going well there.

"Who the heck is this?" Ronnie stared at the caller ID.

Two weeks prior, Taylor had fielded a call from the Elections Division requesting a number to call in an emergency. Ronnie didn't know if he should provide Farringdon's number. He was pretty sure he shouldn't give Orr's. Who knew exactly where they would be on election night? Possibly, nowhere near a land line.

"Who is it, Ronnie?" Farringdon asked.

Taylor put his finger to his ear and raised his hand, requesting silence. The group continued talking.

"I can't hear you. Could you speak up?" Ronnie shouted.

"Shhh everyone...let Ronnie take this call," Farringdon said.

"Yeah...he is here...just a minute." Ronnie Taylor handed the phone over. "Joel, it's for you. It might be a joke; I don't know..."

"Yes, this is Joel Orr."

Joel covered the phone and whispered to the group, "...says it is the President..."

"Uh, yes, I can hear you...ah, thank you. Sir...I'm sorry I can't hear you, Sir." Joel rolled his eyes and whispered to the group, "...says he's on Air Force One."

"Well thank you, Sir. Do you know something I don't know, because none of the networks down here have called anything..."

The expression on Joel Orr's face morphed from bemused to shocked.

"It really *is* The President," he mouthed.

Joel listened intently for about a minute, and inserted, "Mr. President, I thank you for your courtesy. I have always said I am an American first and a Democrat second...I pledge to help you any way I can...I...," Joel stammered. Tears pooled in the corners of his eyes, then rolled down his cheeks.

Karen took the phone, "Mr. President, this is Karen, his daughter. Daddy is a little overwhelmed. Yes, Mr. President. Thank you so much for your call. God bless you, too, and the American people. Good night, Mr. President, Sir."

"Thank you, Bug," Joel managed to say. "We won it." His voice came out in a barely-audible squeak.

Gwen Reynolds reached over and shook Joel's hand. "Congratulations, Senator Orr."

Amidst the raucous round of back-slapping, high-fives, and hugs, Ronnie Taylor stood up—his can of Java Jolt in hand—and called out a famous quote from the 1972 Robert Redford Movie, *The Candidate*: "Now what do we do?"

Joel clapped a hand on Don Farringdon and Ronnie Taylor's shoulders.

"We're goin' to Washington, boys!"

11:30 p.m.—the Silver Campaign—Tallahassee, Florida

Over three-hundred die-hard campaign supporters partied in the Civic Center. Most were visibly drunk.

"Well, hell," a suited man said to another. Both, with ties askew and eyes streaked with red. "That's the sum of it, I suppose."

The announcers called the election for Joel Orr by four points. Most of the South Florida votes had come in, and all the I-4 corridor votes—Daytona, Orlando, Tampa, St. Petersburg—were in.

"There is no statistical way that the outcome could change," the first suited man said, stumbling over the word *statistical* three times before it slurred out. "It's time for our gal to concede."

Mike Belan peered into the semi-dark bedroom. "How can we get her down there? She's sound asleep. And that damned Latino is snoring beside her."

"Let's just go down there ourselves and tell them," said Cox.

Mike Belan nodded. "Are you sure there aren't enough absentees to swing it, Mark?"

"I counted them 75% to our favor. Even with that, we will still come up short. Look, she probably isn't going to run again ever, but she is still a sitting United States senator. I think we owe it to Brad to make sure the campaign goes out with class...with or without her."

Mike Belan scrabbled in his pocket for the rental car's keys. "Let's go..."

Mark Cox grabbed his arm. "No way you're driving, not even less than a mile to the Civic Center. Me, either. We do this, we're showing up in style. I'll have the Plaza limo take us down. Last thing we need is to end up in some Leon County jail with DUI charges."

Mark Cox stood before the dregs of the ruined campaign—a hundred and fifty tired and mostly drunk workers. He could only imagine the scene repeating itself all across the state.

"Ladies and gentlemen, on behalf of Senator Silver, I want to thank you from the bottom of our heart for your efforts, support, and love."

One supporter leaned on the beverage table and called out, "Hey are there any more Swedish meat balls?"

A titter of laughter flowed across the room, the only joviality any had heard in the past two hours.

The Public Relations man continued, "The senator is not feeling well, but she specifically asked me to thank you..."

Mark Belan stood next to Mark Cox. For once, Belan looked more rumpled than his political cohort.

"Give it up, Cox," he said in a voice too low for the microphone to carry. "Let's put this damn thing out of its misery."

Office of the Governor—Tallahassee, Florida

Aide Kemp Johnson could not recall a time when he had been more exhausted. Election day—now night—had proved to be one of the longest of his career. He felt sorry for himself—tired, hungry, punchy.

But he felt more sympathy for the Hamster.

Governor Tad Myers sat at his desk, one of the few times Kemp Johnson had ever seen the man actually sit anywhere. All Kemp could see was the top of the Governor's silver-streaked, lowered head held between spread fingers.

"It's a nightmare. It's a nightmare."

Kemp, too weary to grope for a soothing answer, shook his head.

Tad Myers sighed. "Get him on the phone. Get Orr on the damned phone. I have to make nice."

The Ironclad Alibi Bar—Miami, Florida

Brenda Gayle put her fingers in her mouth and let out a piercing whistle.

"Listen up!"

The crowded bar calmed. The patrons focused attention on the flat screen monitor hanging over the bar.

The local news station commentator broke in with the announcement.

"And, in the race for national Senate seat for the State of Florida, Democrat Joel Orr is declared the winner by a two-percent margin."

"That's my boy." Brenda Gayle smiled, then yelled, "drinks on the house!"

Destin Beach, Florida

Former Florida Governor Russell Nathan stood ankle deep in the surf, naked. The Gulf of Mexico's offshore winds, stoked by the tropical system miles to the south, kicked up generous waves that licked his knees. An almost full moon shone on the white-caps. The water glittered with reflected light.

Russell grabbed himself and wagged his weenie back and forth at the heavens.

"Take that!" he yelled. "Take that, universe!"

Luckily, no one shared the patch of beach with the exposed ex-governor-turned-used-car salesman. Good thing. Russell Nathan didn't want any more visits from the local police, and nothing to spoil the glow of victory.

Life was good. The underdog had won. Joel Orr had killed the giant and tripped down the beanstalk with his bag of loot.

If that was possible, anything was.

He sloshed in the surf, rocking to keep his balance.

"You watch out, Joel Orr! You just watch out, buddy boy. In four years, Big Daddy's comin' at cha!"

Russell pumped his fists in the air.

"Russell Nathan is ba-a-a-a-a-ck!"

CHAPTER THIRTY-SEVEN

The Silvers' Mansion—Miami, Florida

Eleana Silver sat by the pool. The moon above, perfect and round. It was the kind of balmy night for which Miami was famous: Palm fronds painted with silver tips of light. Deep shadows cast on tropical foliage. Gentle breezes bringing the scent of the ocean.

Ramiro walked from the shadows and stood beside the chaise lounge.

"Eleana. We must talk."

She sighed. "Not tonight, Ramiro. I'm so tired of talking. It's all I've done for the past months. Talk. Talk. Talk. In the morning…"

"No. *Mi amor*." He sat down on the end of the lounge. "Now."

The tone of his voice caught her attention.

"There are things I must say to you."

She leaned forward and caressed his face with the tips of her fingers. "You look so serious."

"I must leave tonight, Eleana. I want you to come with me."

"Leave?"

"For Cuba."

She sat in stunned silence.

"There is much to tell you. Much you will not understand until later," he said. "Do you love me, Eleana?"

"Yes. Of course."

"Then, I must ask you to also trust me."

"I do. But…Cuba?"

He paused for a moment. "I am not who I seem. My family is very influential. I am returning to Cuba and I wish for you to come with me."

"Not until you tell me more. The truth."

"I can give you great details later, Eleana. For now, it is important that we leave as soon as possible."

She shook her head. "You really can't expect me to leave Miami and go to a place where the murderer of my family reigns freely. And why would *you* want to go there?"

The breeze ruffled the banana tree beside the cabana. Eleana and her lover sat in silence for a few moments before Ramiro answered.

"My family is among the high-ranking members of the Cuban government. But not in its support. *Guarde a sus amigos cerca. Guarde a sus enemigos más cerca.* Keep your friends close. Keep your enemies closer. Remember...I told you that."

Eleana stiffened.

"For years, we have been working to overthrow the regime."

"You are...what? Some kind of spy?"

He shook his head. "More, someone sent as protection."

"Protection?"

"Many people will benefit from a free Cuba, Eleana. Many people will not."

The implications shook her. She took his face in her hands. "Tell me. Did you...Did you have any part in killing my husband?"

Ramiro shook his head. "I did not, Eleana. I was sent to watch over the senator."

"Then, who? You know!"

"The pilot was one of our people. Dependable. Loyal to the cause. Entrusted with the life of Brad Silver. Still, we do not know how—or, if—someone within Castro's regime sabotaged the aircraft. No one has stepped up to claim credit. It may have been a sad, yet timely, accident."

"It sounds like some kind of intricate conspiracy. Who else is involved? Mark Cox?"

"No. Mr. Cox has no knowledge of our group, or our plans."

"Mike Belan?"

Ramiro chuffed. "Men like Mike Belan work only for themselves. But, yes, he has his hand in our operations, as do many involved with the sugar industry. As I said, the trade between Cuba and the U.S. stands to benefit a lot of people."

"My uncle…?"

Ramiro nodded. "He has long been involved. Also, your friend from Vizcaya."

Eleana's mouth hung open. "D…Dorothy? Dorothy Claxton?"

"And many wealthy Floridians. Some from the northern part of the state, and the nation," Ramiro said. "This goes very deep, Eleana."

"This is all too much." She took a shaky breath. "I can't believe you, throwing this all at me! And asking me to return with you? How could I possibly live in the shadow of that murderer? Even, to be in the same room with him?"

"I have watched you. If you can learn to hold your own in Washington, you can survive in Cuba. As long as you know your actions go toward creating the New Cuba, you can do it. You are an amazing woman, Eleana. I want to take you home with me. To be my wife. To have our baby on the home soil of our ancestors. And to be with your family."

"You…you know of my family?"

"Your eldest brother is one of the key members of the movement. A good man. An honest man."

Eleana stood, walked a few paces away, and spun back around. Her eyes glinted in the low light. "You know my brother! When were you planning to tell me, Ramiro? Or, is that even your name?"

He stood and faced her. "Does my name really matter? I am your love and the father of your child. I planned to tell you everything as soon as you were safely ensconced in the

Senate. Then, we would have been able to work together to bring the corrupt regime to an end."

"I...I don't know what to say to you..."

Ramiro rested his hands on her shoulders. "If you love me, Eleana, you must trust me. I leave tonight."

She motioned to the house. "Just...leave?"

"Pack a few things. I can have everything here brought over later—every pair of shoes, every piece of furniture if you wish. My family's home in Cuba is as grand...much more so. You will have only the best."

"I have to think."

"Don't take too long, *mi amor*. Your uncle's yacht is waiting."

Ramiro leaned over and kissed her. He walked away.

Eleana stood in the moonlight and felt Miami curl around her. Her hand went instinctively to the roundness of her stomach.

What would she miss, really? What held her here? In the light of Ramiro's confession, everything took on a sinister hue. Her friendship with Dorothy Claxton. The people surrounding her. How many led a double life? The betrayal caused a toxic miasma of anger and sadness.

She looked around the well-appointed inner courtyard.

Nothing felt the same.

Eleana Silver walked to her bedroom and threw two large Louis Vuitton suitcases onto the bed.

Fort Myers, Florida

Louise Hampton settled into the daily grind at the *Fort Myers News Press*. Back to the usual local political mini-dramas, murders, and civic concerns of an ever-growing city.

For someone who lived for political intrigue, the after-math of the national senatorial election dimmed like the week following Christmas when the torn wrappings and shreds of ribbons waited with the curbside trash. Louise scanned the A.P. reports for any hint of excitement in South Florida.

One brief blurb caught her attention: *Alligator Alley Claims Motorist.*

Louise shook her head. No doubt, just another hapless drunk on the way home from some Halloween party, one who had the misfortune to veer off the road beside one of the most notorious canals in south Florida. She skimmed the short piece.

"City workers find submerged van. Body identified as Sidney Dillard of Homestead, Florida. Police suspect foul play," she read.

"Wait a minute…"

Louise rummaged in her bottom desk drawer for the fat pile of mail she had received a few days prior to the election. She flipped through the stack. Election season seemed to bring out the fanatics—the same as any emotion-stirring event. At first, she had dismissed the letter as just another crank. One of her college professors once told her, "be ever vigilant. You never know the source of your next big story— perhaps, the one that will send your career over the top". If she overturned enough rocks, eventually one would reveal the coiled snake.

The reporter's hackles stood straight up when she reread the block-printed letter.

THE TRUTH SHALL SET YOU FREE. IF YOU WANT TO KNOW THE TRUTH ABOUT ELEANA SILVER, FOLLOW THIS:

Below, in the same careful handwriting, were directions to the location of a rented locker in Homestead with a tape-attached key.

The signature: CONCERNED CITIZEN, SID DIL-LARD

"Has to be the same guy. How many Sid Dillard's could there possibly be?"

Louise checked her contact roster and dialed the number for the corresponding Metro police district.

"This is Louise Hampton—*Fort Myers News Press.* Would you please transfer me to your investigative unit? I may have a lead on the Sid Dillard case—the van found in Alligator Alley."

Senator Silver's Office—Washington, D.C.

Mark Cox sat in his office. Alone.

"House of cards," he said aloud.

He could almost feel the wisp of tumbling face cards— the King, the Queen, and now, the Joker. The Joker always got the last laugh.

The senatorial office had a sepulchral feel. Since the election, the staff slipped between the rooms as if one small noise might bring the whole place tumbling to the ground. Ashleigh and Twyla—the two administrative assistants—still offered strained smiles and good-morning's, but the mirth didn't make it to their eyes. To his credit, Governor Tad Myers interim plug-in for Chief of Staff still came to work.

Everyone waited.

For the change of the senatorial guards. For Eleana Silver to return to her position until the holiday session break. For their inevitable pink slips.

Mark Cox—for the first time—thought about retiring. Spending time with his wife. Actually talking to his daughters. Doing a little fishing. Sleeping. Sleeping would be nice.

Staying in this office wasn't an option. Don Farringdon would claim the spot as was his right. Remaining in the capital was possible. With his reputation, the Sultan of Spin could go most anywhere. Amidst such a vast nest of venomous King Cobras, an experienced snake charmer could always find a place to park his mat and basket.

But did he want to?

Cox tried the Miami phone number of Eleana Silver, as he had each morning for the past few days. Most calls went immediately to voice mail. On one occasion, a Hispanic housekeeper had answered his queries with "Missy Silver not home". The rest of the frustrating conversation, a combination of broken English and *"no comprendo"*.

He tried her cell number. Voicemail.

"Looks like I'll have to make a little visit to south Florida."

A trip to drag the sitting senator back to Washington to fulfill her obligation until Joel Orr took the seat. To get Tad Myers and the President off his back. Everyone wanted to know where Eleana Silver was. Hell, so did he.

A female voice: "Excuse me, Mr. Cox."

He glanced up to see Twyla standing at the threshold. Two men stood behind her.

Without introductions, Mark Cox knew. The men were Feds. Dark suits. Dark expressions. The aura of undisputed authority, one of *you're guilty until we decide you're innocent*. No doubt, somewhere a dark Crown Victoria with tinted windows waited.

"Thank you, Twyla." He nodded and smiled.

She glanced from the men to Mark Cox. "Do you need anything, Sir?"

A cloak of invisibility? A magic wand? Someone on the mother ship to beam me up? Mark thought.

"No, Twyla. Thank you."

As soon as she walked away, the two men stepped forward. As if on cue, they flashed I.D. badges.

The older of the two spoke, "Mr. Cox. We need to ask you a few questions."

He felt his heart rate accelerate. Forced his breath to remain even. From past experience, he knew; the Feds generally had the answers or most of them. The questions were intended to ensnare.

"How may I help you gentlemen?"

"Have you been in contact with Eleana Silver?"

"I have not spoken with the senator since the night of the election. She left the Governor's Plaza before I awakened the next morning."

"And Mike Belan?"

"Nor do I have any idea of Mr. Belan's whereabouts." Mark swung his arms wide. "Look around. Other than the regular staffers, I am the only one here."

The senior agent's eyes narrowed to slits. Mark could envision the well-oiled cogs spinning.

"We have reason to believe Senator Silver has left the country for Cuba."

Mark's eyebrows shot upward before he could will them to a neutral position.

"Guess that would explain why she's not returning my calls."

"What do you know about a man named Sid Dillard?" the agent asked.

Mark felt his face flush. Here it was. The puff of wind that would bring down the last teetering cardboard walls.

"You might ask Mike Belan that question."

The agent replied, "Mike Belan and his family left the country yesterday."

Mark Cox closed his eyes and pressed his lips together. After a couple of beats, he spoke.

"Of course he did."

"We need you to come with us, Mr. Cox."

CHAPTER THIRTY-EIGHT

Miami, Florida

Second chances happened to other people. Didn't they?

Characters in novels and date-movie chick-flicks, where the poor, misdirected slob of a guy realized what an absolute disaster he'd made of his life, turned it around, and won the girl.

Joel Orr slowed. The wee-morning-hour patrons of his favorite tavern, The Ironclad Alibi, would be parked at the run-down wooden bar swilling cheap liquor and trash-talking Brenda Gayle. She would half-listen—as she had countless times with him—with a slightly bored expression, nodding at the right spots.

For a moment, he considered turning into the cracked gravel parking lot. Just one quick scotch, neat. Then, home to sleep. Tomorrow, he would pack for his new life in Washington—as the duly-appointed sitting senator until the official inauguration the first week in January.

Before he changed his mind, he pushed the accelerator hard.

The universe seldom doled out second chances. Joel Orr had his. He wasn't going to blow it this time around.

THE END